MW01243310

Thank you for buying an authorized edition of this book and for complying with copyright laws by not reproducing, scanning or distributing any part of it in any form without permission. By doing so you are supporting writers, so they may continue to create books for readers.

This is a work of fiction. Names, characters, places and incidents either are the product of the author's imagination or are used fictitiously, and any resemblance to actual persons, living or dead, business establishments, event, or locales is purely coincidental.

This book is brought to you by the letters M and F, and by the number 3.

Cover design by Krista Wallace and Brian Rathbone, with extra expertise from Brayden Fengler and Jonathan Lyster. The snake photo is by Peter Andersen.

978-1-7780895-1-0

Also by Krista Wallace

In paperback, ebook and audiobook

Gatekeeper's Key
Gatekeeper's Deception I - Deceiver

In audiobook

To Serve and Protect
The Inner Light

For my daughters Maggie and Heather, whom I love, admire, and continue to learn from.

Gatekeeper's Deception II - Deceived

Please note that this is Part Two of *Gatekeeper's Deception*. Be sure to read Part One first, or you won't know what's going on here.

~Krista

Twenty

On Proving Herself

K yer rode northeast, Kayme's tower vaguely in her mind. For a long time, she didn't pay attention to where she was headed. Her focus had been stolen by Derry's accusations, and they replayed over and over in her head.

As your captain, it is my duty . . . The satisfaction of your own desires has preceded the needs of our company . . . You only ever give us part of the story . . . your flagrant neglect of our mission . . . some doltish boy entirely beneath you . . . just as bloody obdurate as ever . . . Have you nothing to say?

"That bastard," she told Trig.

Wind whistled in her ears. She drew her hood up, but it just blew off again. She left it.

You once told me I could be counted on to do what is right. That was true: she had told him so, but she never dreamed he would use it against her.

You insult us, Dunvehran, Kien, and especially Alon Maer with your flagrant neglect of our mission. Blood churned through her body so that she had to remind herself to breathe. Sharp, chilly air sucked into her lungs when she did.

A good league after taking off, she came to a sparsely wooded area. There was no path to speak of, so she dismounted to lead Trig through the stands of pines and balsams. Layer upon layer of needles cushioned her footfalls. The ground was springy beneath her boots, which crunched with the occasional pinecone. The cold, clear light of Frog moon peeked down between the branches, its pure white shafts ghostly and unnatural. Kyer inhaled deeply of the aromatic trees, and only after several such breaths did she realize she had been stomping through the woods. Fury still coursed through her.

"Hold a while, Trig." She dropped the reins to the ground with a soft plop. She drew her sword—*steal a sword from a dead body*—and stepped away from her horse into a more or less open space. Swinging her weapon a hard left and right, she parried an unseen enemy's slashes. Up and overhead, then it crashed down into the spongy ground, and up again, horizontally, to block. An imaginary enemy screamed in agony as she cut him to ribbons. She hacked its head off. Kyer dismembered several orcs in this manner, and with a long, deep exhale, she flopped to the needle-strewn earth, only now remembering that she'd left her bedroll back at the camp. *At least the ground isn't so wet now.* Lying on her back she glared up at the shadows of tree tops.

Her body was shattered with fatigue, and though it still vibrated with anger, her mind had cleared a bit. She had never felt such rage. Certainly not aimed at someone who was supposed to be her friend. Friends were supposed to give each other the benefit of the doubt, weren't they? Somewhere along the way, Derry had stopped doing so. He had started reading into her actions, looking for things to find fault with. *If you trust somebody completely, that doesn't happen.* So what was his problem?

Two months ago, Derry would have known there was some reason she was late for breakfast, some important thing that she couldn't share. He would not have questioned it. She truly had not expected him to believe that she'd slept with—what had he called Tod? *Some doltish boy entirely beneath you.* And honestly, she didn't ever say that's what she had done. She simply didn't deny that she had. Necessary repression of the full truth.

But could she really blame Derry for his anger at her lateness? *You gave no other explanation,* he said. That was true. Should she at least have explained that she could not tell him and asked him to trust her?

That was the trouble. She didn't like to have to ask. Kyer pursed her lips in a stubborn pout.

Alon Maer is on her deathbed, waiting for us to save her life, and where are you? Off physically indulging yourself . . . Well, yes, she couldn't deny that she'd had her own pleasure in mind, but by the gods, she was doing it for a reason. She wouldn't have gone at all if it hadn't been for the runes. But she hadn't explained why she was walking out on them. Sure, she'd told herself she couldn't tell them or they'd not let her go, but how much of it was just a tiny bit of enjoyment at needling Derry?

The stars, peering out from the clouds that wisped across them, blinked down at her through the open-armed pines. She *had* been obdurate; there was no denying it. But did he have to be such a prig? She snorted.

And he'd accused her of neglecting Alon. She couldn't believe his nerve. *I was the first one to volunteer for this mission, and she's never left my mind.*

A sharp pain prodded her in the back of the head, and she sat up. *That's not true.*

Kyer felt like sinking into the chill-hardened ground, glad no one was there to witness the flush that passed across her face. She *had* denied Alon, in those brief moments of weakness after her encounter with Fredric. She had chosen to follow Fredric. Her own personal mission had taken precedence. Even when they'd found her, it took her quite some time to decide whether she was happy about it or not. She recalled her jumbled mixture of relief at being discovered and longing to be left on her own.

Derry couldn't possibly know that. Could he? And she'd made up for it. Hadn't she? She'd tried to. She pulled her knees up to her chest and dropped her forehead on them.

Even if Derry didn't know, Kyer did. How could she blame him for thinking she had deserted the mission when that's exactly what she had done? Her eyes stung.

So long she had worked to prove herself as a swordfighter, as a vital addition to the group. She thought she had achieved acceptance, finally. And now it had come to this. How many others in the party shared Derry's opinion? Kyer wished she'd spoken to Valrayker before she'd come away. *You already have a reputation for disobeying direct orders.* The dark elf would have dismissed her, and then none of this would have happened.

An unfamiliar sensation gnawed at her. It stabbed at her heart, forming an ache in her chest and throat, something she didn't remember feeling for years.

The woman whom Kyer called mother, Della, was highly regarded for her knitting. She raised the sheep, sheared them, cleaned and carded the wool. She dyed the soft, lanolin-smelling fibres all sorts of rich colours and spun it into beautiful yarn. After all the preparation, Della either sold the wool or neighbours chose their yarn and she would knit it for them. Kyer remembered being thirteen. Della had knitted her a sweater from a deep red soft wool. It was a yarn that had just won Della first prize at the fair for its quality and fine texture. Kyer wore the sweater to school, not trying to impress, which was not her way, but because she loved it. And wearing it, she felt proud to display Della's superb product and just a bit smug. Her sweater could be compared to those worn by her classmates without coming up short. There was no way anyone could make a sneering comment this time.

Sheska Bolen proved Kyer wrong. The pretty and popular blonde girl took one look at the sweater and sniffed. "Too bad. Even in that sweater, you still just look like a big mistake. Why don't you go back to your cornfield?"

Kyer had had enough experience with Sheska to not really be surprised. Her pride had been ripped away and trampled on, and her throat and chest ached. Kyer hadn't thought of that event for years, but the similarity to her current situation had reawakened those emotions. Her satisfaction at procuring the runes had turned to dust.

Derry's unjust words had quashed the triumph she ought to have felt as she placed the pouch in his hand. His *just* words pierced her with their truth and reason. He'd called her negligent. He'd all but called her a whore. She was terribly angry at Derry for saying those things. Still, there was something else.

Hurt? Dreadful hurt. An unusual emotion for Kyer. Why could she not just let it go, as she had in the past? Sheska Bolen had tried to hurt Kyer countless times, and Kyer couldn't be bothered to spare any emotion for her. Probably because she could so easily take revenge on Sheska. Two days after the incident, she'd sneaked into Sheska's yard and shredded all her dresses hanging on the clothesline with her knife. But Kyer hated Sheska; it was easy to take revenge on her. This was different. This time there would be no such purging of feeling.

She had begun to see Derry's point of view, to understand why he'd thought those things about her. No, she couldn't bring herself to hate Derry.

Moreover, she didn't *want* to hate Derry. Her final words to him echoed in her head, and she knew she'd hurt him as much as he'd hurt her. Possibly more.

He was right about one more point. Something that hadn't occurred to her until he'd said it. *Why don't you trust me?* She'd accused him of the same thing more than once in these past few weeks. When—*how* had it broken down? Derry had been, not all that long ago, the one person in whom she had complete faith. Somehow her trust of him had eroded. As had his of her. Was one the result of the other? Which had come first?

Kyer cupped her chin in her hands and wondered what to do now.

She couldn't stay here. She couldn't, and didn't want to, go back to a group of people who were preoccupied with watching her every move, waiting for every little mistake. She could give up. Go home.

Not a chance.

Kyer straightened. Memory carried her back to Gilvray's cabin, sitting at his desk, carefully cutting the rune pattern into her pouch. Etching it into her mind at the same time. The pattern stood out in her memory, vivid as if it were in the palm of her hand.

You're a fool, Kyer, if you let this go. It was time she took her share of the blame for the terrible misunderstanding that had arisen between her and her friend. It was not too late to make it up. Swinging up onto Trig's back, she nudged him west. The Indyn Caves lay somewhere in that direction.

Plus, her fatigue-crazed mind had come up with an interesting thought about red lights.

At some point Derry fell asleep, for when he awoke, the sun was peering over the mountains in the east. He was in his bed and felt the lumpy, hardened ground beneath it. His body felt like lead, as if he hadn't slept at all. He must have relived his argument with Kyer all night. The morning light brought new perspective to his troubles. She hadn't answered any of his charges, and she'd admitted to where she had gone last night. *Something has seriously botched up your judgement, Derry.* Well, not anymore.

If she were innocent, she'd have defended herself. Weeks ago he had thought that whatever her motivation for coming on the mission, it might not be strong enough to keep her here. Either the danger would wear her down or she'd realize the offer from Kayme was too good to pass up. He was right on that score, but it was more than that: she had left because she truly did not care.

Murmurs told him he was not the first one awake. Reluctantly he pushed up on one elbow to see Jesqellan putting the teakettle on the fire and Janak and Phennil standing over Kyer's bed. Derry's heart flipped in the brief second it took him to assess the situation. No, Kyer had not returned in the night.

Jesqellan noticed the captain was awake. "I gather things did not go at all favourably."

Phennil and Janak looked expectantly at him. Skimnoddle came trotting up with a few more sticks of wood, just enough to get them through breakfast.

"Where is my lady?" the halfling bellowed indignantly. "Did she not return from her tryst?" He dumped the wood and drew his little dagger. "I shall storm the encampment! Major Gilvray, prepare to face thy—"

"She left, damn it." Derry had no patience for Skimnoddle's posturing. He flung aside his blankets and, shoving his feet into his boots, rose, glaring round at the group. "She came back last night. I said everything I intended to say. We argued. She left." Anger, discouragement. Betrayal. He lowered his voice. "I honestly do not know if she's coming back."

He began to roll up his bed.

"Not coming back?" said Phennil, hurt in his eyes. "I knew it. I knew you shouldn't have said anything."

"It was my duty to speak out." He had nothing to apologize for.

"And she wasn't happy about it. Wonder of wonders."

"Enough, Phennil," Derry ordered.

The old Phennil would have held his tongue. But this Phennil owed his life to Kyer. This Phennil had stood up to his father. "I don't know what's going on here, but you and Jesqellan have been picking on her for days."

Jesqellan tossed a stick into the fire as he rose.

His courage mounting, Phennil continued. "It's true. You two have been sulking constantly, mostly when it comes to Kyer. You can't imagine that the rest of us don't notice. Kyer too. She's damn perceptive, you know it; you're a fool if you think she isn't completely aware of what you two have been thinking about her. At least, she may not know exactly what you're thinking, but she sure as hell knows you've decided *something* about her. Begging your pardon, Derry, you have not been exhibiting good leadership lately. We're used to better from you."

"What?" Derry gawked. Twice in less than twelve hours was hard to take.

"You're not Kyer's watchdog; you're the leader of this whole group, and this whole group is suffering. Morale has plummeted and I don't think you've even noticed. Until we got here, we had yet to fail at any part of this mission, and yet everyone's moods are lower than tree roots. I don't understand that. We've been successful and still you're just . . . mouldy, which tells me that all this is not related to our mission."

The truth of his words pierced Derry's heart. They bore an odd resemblance to some things he remembered Kyer saying. He started to speak.

"You're right." Jesqellan stepped forward. "I believe it is time to share with you the news I learned in Seaview. This may shed light on Kyer's actions and why she is no longer with us this morning."

Jesqellan launched into the conversation he'd had with Fredric in Seaview. They listened, open mouthed or tight jawed depending on their individual faith in the mage's tale, as he described Fredric's deeply rooted devotion to Kien, his entrapment in a terrible situation, his continued desperate attempts to thwart the plans of those who would see Alon Maer dead.

"I have to tell you that I believe him to be sincere. It is difficult for me to accept, as I'm sure it is for you. I have thought about it at length, and I can only ask that you consider my training and track record for dealing with people. It is my duty to understand them."

"What about understanding Kyer?" Phennil muttered.

"And so in this case, I assure you of my faith in Fredric Heyland, despite his troubling situation. I intend to help him restore Kien's faith and trust as well."

"All right, this is a lively tale." Phennil folded his arms. "What does it have to do with Kyer?"

14

"Janak." Jesqellan appealed to his friend. "We've known each other a long time. Would I conjure up a story from nothing? Have you ever known me to deal in fancy, in fiction?"

The dwarf paused to give the question due thought. He shook his furry head. "No. If I may say it, you've never had much of imagination about you."

"Thank you. I ask because this may be hard for you all to take. There is no way to express it easily. Fredric has it on excellent authority that . . ." He lowered his eyes. "Lady Alon Maer has been cursed. The curse was administered in a *Malison* that takes the form of a jewel: a necklace in the shape of a serpent. She was told the necklace was a gift from Kien, but she was deceived. The gift was delivered by a young maid who worked at Bartheylen Castle only for a short time. There is reason to believe that maid . . . was our Kyer Halidan. In disguise. Working at the time for Ronav Malachite."

"Outrageous." Skimnoddle's forced cry came out more as a plea.

Phennil's face looked stricken.

Janak's head shook again. "Demon's balls." Jesqellan shot a glare at him.

"I have been sensing magic on her since we left Shael; it has grown stronger. You all have noticed as well as I how aloof and distant she has been of late. It may pain us all to think on it, but we surmise that after she met with Fredric, she *deliberately* followed him, with the intention of killing him. She did not want us to find her. Do you remember how she reacted?"

Phennil could not maintain eye contact with Jesqellan.

Skimnoddle and Janak looked uncertain. Jesqellan went on, fuelled by lack of opposition. "She has not been truthful; she has withheld information —all the things that Derry confronted her with last night."

"And as soon as I confronted her, she bolted," Derry said.

"This is utter rubbish!" Phennil waved his arm. "I refuse to believe any of it."

"How many of you," Jesqellan challenged each of them in turn, "are aware that the serpent is a symbol of undying love?" Their eyes showed recognition of the phrase Kyer had spoken only two nights ago. Jesqellan looked triumphant. "You see?"

"That is why you jumped up when she said that?" Janak asked.

Jesqellan held his arms out in a gesture of acknowledgement.

Janak sighed. "My friend, I have never known you to speak without being absolutely convinced of the validity of your arguments. I hate to speak out against the girl, though you may laugh to hear it. If Jesqellan believes this to be true, then, much as I hate to, I must accept that his view has merit. I have to think about it."

Skimnoddle lowered his head.

The old Phennil might have acquiesced. This Phennil did not. "You can't possibly all sit here and accept this. You can't take her comment about the snake as *proof* that she did such a horrible thing." He turned to Derry. "You talked about her self-indulgence in sleeping with Tod and being late for breakfast and all that. Don't you remember that Tod came into the inn delivering a letter as we sat there?" Derry's face blanked with thought, but Phennil didn't wait. "She wasn't with him. I don't know who she was with, but she was gathering *information*. I believe her when she said Gilvray was lying. Like Kayme said, everything has a price, and the information about the runes cost her. If you weren't so busy making shit up about her, you might notice that she left her bastard sword in Seaview."

He sat down on the dewy grass and scowled, wondering what his fate would be for such an outburst.

Jesqellan looked expectantly at Derry; his eyes demanded the captain's support. Derry was at a loss. He had not noticed that Kyer's sword was missing. Now that Phennil had brought it to his attention, he thought back: the irksome elf might come across as a scatterbrain, but this time he was right. Kyer had bought the information about the runes at a high price and was not willing to lose faith in her purchase at Gilvray's cheap denial of their existence. *Hence her defensiveness when I told her this trip was a waste of time.*

"Tea's ready," Skimnoddle ventured.

They helped themselves to what was left of the food they'd obtained from the army. "I don't like to let you think I don't believe you, Jesqellan," Janak remarked. "But I have to say I take it hard. I watched her kill Ronav Malachite. I just—" He blinked heavily. "I don't know."

Derry just shook his head.

"As Fredric pointed out," the mage poured his tea, "Ronav did not ever do her serious harm physically."

Phennil gawked. "I recall her being three breaths short of death that night."

Jesqellan glared at him. "From which she recovered. We do not know what their agreement was; perhaps he betrayed her in some way."

Skimnoddle looked crestfallen. "The evidence is so strong."

"Oh, out of sight, out of mind, eh?" Scorn edged Phennil's tone. "Funny how quickly you stop defending your 'beloved' when she's not here." *Maybe now she'll know that there are others more worthy of her.* "I say it's dead easy for us to sit here and pick apart her every action and conveniently adapt them to a new interpretation. That doesn't make it true."

Derry raised a hand. "Obviously we will remain open to evidence from either side. But we still have a mission to perform. The question is what do we do now? Have we enough information about the ingredients to continue on our own?"

"The alternative is to admit defeat and return empty handed to Bartheylen Castle," Jesqellan said. "I say we carry on. We must be able to access the caves somehow."

Less than an hour later, they were headed northwest across the rolling plains under scattered clouds and a thin sunshine. Kyer's bedroll was tucked in next to Phennil's. The elf felt a sort of triumph. He may not have changed anyone's mind—not yet—but he had pointed out a key piece of information that no one else had noticed. *It turns out that when you demand to be heard, they listen.* He grinned for the first time in days.

The grin, however, was short lived. The pounding of horses off to the north tugged his gaze in that direction. With Jesqellan on foot, they could be intersected in a matter of moments.

At about a furlong distant, the pale sun briefly caught a sheen on the red hair of the man in front.

Damn! The elf hesitated in reaching for his bow. *I don't even know anymore if Fredric is friend or foe.*

Trig had had a good long rest between the time they'd arrived at the Indyn Hills encampment to the time Kyer flew off late last night. He'd been still while she'd battled with her conscience and a few more times since she'd arrived at her decision. He'd found water to drink in a few hollows that were not drained of the other day's rainfall, and of course there was grass to eat. So Kyer did not feel abusive of him by pushing him toward the blue hills that grew ever taller as she neared them.

It was a full day's hard ride from the encampment to the Indyn Hills, and she'd started her day in the middle of the night. She also didn't have a party of companions to slow her down. Still, it was well after midday that she gained higher ground and finally stopped to put some thought into the potential location of, not only the caves, but the path leading to them. She sat on the stubbled grass to take in some water and food, and waited. Kayme's dream hadn't yet failed to connect her with the information she needed. Would he know the answer to this query?

Breathing calmly, she closed her eyes and pictured the mountain in front of her. Trig, sensing her concentration, nuzzled her arm. Unconsciously stroking his neck, she felt his warmth seep into her hand, up her arm, through her shoulder. It softened her neck and made its way into the recesses of her memory.

Ah, there it was.

On Trig's back again, she chirruped to him, nudging him southward. After about twenty minutes' riding, she stopped. Like the tunnel into the trees that had led her to her sword she sensed its presence before she saw it. She retraced a few of Trig's steps. All but concealed by brambles, the path would have been impossible to find if she hadn't been looking for it. So Gilvray's men didn't come here often, then. Nor did anyone else. Drawing her weapon as she dismounted, she took a page out of Phennil's book and spoke to the bushes. "If you please, may I pass?" They quivered and allowed her to use the blade on the most tangled of gnarled branches, but it didn't take much. An overgrown path presented itself before her, beckoning her to follow.

Without hesitation, Kyer stepped onto it and led Trig upward to the right, switching back to the left after about fifty paces. Back and forth the path carried her up the mountainside, like the swinging of a great pendulum. Horse and woman picked their way through the underbrush, surrounded by trees, underscored by birds and small animals. She didn't care to identify the sights and sounds. She was bent on success. On making amends. On proving herself. Again.

And oddly enough, it was not Alon Maer's face that came to her mind.

If this was the new Fredric Heyland—in recovery from deep sorrow and regret whilst leading his band of cutthroats—Derry was not impressed. To Derry, the former captain of the Shael Guard wore the same air of condescension and superiority as ever. *Though now he's in a role he's much more suited for.* Still, Valrayker's captain raised a hand to stay Phennil's bow.

Fredric misinterpreted this as a greeting and hailed in return. Phennil lowered his bow, but the arrow remained nocked.

The party of ten riders slowed to a halt a few paces away, and Fredric dismounted, joined on the ground by one other: a dark-haired woman. *His second in command?* One young rogue exchanged a look of recognition with Phennil, and Derry guessed he was the one who had convinced Kyer to accompany him. Fredric drew on a friendly yet businesslike expression, as though he were reuniting with colleagues from days gone by.

"It is good to see you again, Captain Moraunt." Fredric gave a short bow. "Even though it is under such circumstances as these."

Derry pushed up on his stirrups, stretching his legs a little, but did not dismount. He took his seat again. "What circumstances do you mean? Yours seem to have changed rather dramatically since last we met."

Fredric had the grace to flush. The top corner of his lip smiled. "I refer, of course, to the illuminating news of a—" he glanced around, "—certain acquaintance of both of ours, who is noticeably not in attendance today."

Derry congratulated himself that he did not mimic the blush of his old nemesis. He did not owe Fredric an explanation, so he did not offer one. "I was hoping you might 'illuminate' us further, Mr. Heyland."

Fredric's eyes narrowed in annoyance, and Derry pondered its source: was it that he'd used the man's name? Or was it more because he'd pointed out the difference in their stations? "Around here, I am called Hunter. Chief Hunter, as a matter of fact."

Derry acknowledged this with a polite bow and didn't congratulate the other man on his promotion from mere vagrant.

"Now, did Jesqellan here not inform you of what I had to share?"

"Yes, he did, but I would like more detail." Derry folded his hands on the pommel of his saddle. Hearing the story from Jesqellan was one thing, but he still felt a need to defend Kyer when it was Fredric Heyland throwing out accusations. "I am open to hearing what you have to say, and if Kyer truly is guilty of this thing of which she is accused, I certainly will wish to see justice done. But to this point, I have heard only circumstantial evidence and conjecture. From whom did you obtain this story?"

Derry watched Fredric struggle with his frustration, but eventually common sense won over. If the former captain were trying to reinstate himself into Kien's favour, after all, it obviously would not do to lose his temper with Kien's best friend's captain. He sighed. "I understand your scepticism. Certainly. And I recognize it is a heavy charge to place on one who is . . . a friend. Would that I could reveal my source to you, but sadly, I cannot. Suffice it to say he is one of the most powerful men in Rydris and makes it his business to know the details of the continent's activities."

Derry remarked to himself that there were an awful lot of "most powerful men in Rydris," but he held his tongue.

"My source told me of Kyer's coincidental first meeting a few months ago with Lord Valrayker. No one seems to know where she had been before that, though the story I was told said she was at Bartheylen Castle, not far from what she claims to be her hometown. She was working for Ronav Malachite, which was why she went to him later, to report, though between them they put on a good show of her pursuit and capture. You will recall that she was not seriously harmed while in his company—"

Derry couldn't hold back a sarcastic laugh. "You have a strange definition of 'not seriously harmed.' She was barely mobile."

Fredric brushed him off with a wave. "She recovered. Obviously he did something that threatened her position because, as you know, she eventually killed him in Nennia. One cannot always tell what will set women off, particularly one so . . . intense as Kyer can be." He scratched the growth of beard under his chin and shrugged.

"She showed an uncanny awareness about the serpent and its symbolism," Jesqellan put in helpfully. "She brought it up herself and certainly appeared to wish she could retract her words."

"Is that so?" Fredric said. "Unwittingly revealing her connection. Captain Moraunt, I can only add that I have the story on faultless authority, and beyond that, I shall have to ask you to trust me."

"And why exactly should we do that?" Phennil said. "Because you're a trustworthy individual? I can tell by your choice of friends."

Fredric nearly lost his cool. "These are all honest people," he fumed. "Ill treatment and bad experiences have made them disillusioned by the way our leaders run the continent. They only want the same as each of us: to make a living, to survive, to be treated with some modicum of respect." A few nods from his men. And woman. The man who'd made eyes at Phennil sat a little straighter in the saddle. Fredric pushed his hair off his face. "Do you have any idea what this is like? Being in the same position as people like them? I was banished from my post, and from my home. To be told I can never return! I made some mistakes, but haven't we all?

"Derry, you've served Valrayker for a long time; you know what it's like to devote your life, your loyalty, your love to the service of that one man. I was ripped away from Kien. He is—was—my lord, and he tossed me aside like he . . . like a cloak when the weather is hot! After over twenty years of loyal service. And all for a few indiscretions. Mistakes, I tell you!" Fredric's fingers clenched into tight fists. "Derry, think on it. How would you feel in my position?"

Derry wanted to say that he would never get himself into such a position, but he couldn't find his voice. Fredric's words had merit, Derry couldn't help admitting. Besides, Phennil's words had sunk in. What would Val have to say about the way his captain had neglected, even ignored, the steadily declining morale of his company? If Val ever saw fit to punish his captain, Derry knew exactly how he'd feel. He thrust those thoughts aside and recalled his rage of last night at Kyer's reprehensible behaviour. Now, on the other hand, if Kyer had given Alon the curse, then Val would undoubtedly commend his captain for his good use of instincts . . .

"Captain Moraunt." Fredric's eyes were pools of sincerity. "Derry. I want to help on this mission to save the Lady Alon Maer's life. I would do anything—*anything*—to regain my lord's favour."

Derry peered down at him from under furrowed brows.

"Anything?" Phennil said. "Like condemn an innocent woman?"

Fredric wheeled to face the elf. "Anything, like bring truth and justice upon someone who I know is a dear friend to those around me. Don't forget that she and I—" He lowered his eyes, his head swaying from side to side. "Believe it or not, Kyer was special to me too."

Derry lifted his gaze to Phennil, whose eyes burned blue fire with outrage and challenge. The captain glanced around at each member of his company, but none of the others could look at him. Janak sat on his pony, turning his discouragement skyward. Skimnoddle's frown and limp shoulders gave him an air of sheepish sadness, and Jesqellan was nodding dejectedly at Fredric. There would be no help from any of them.

Finally the captain dismounted and faced Hunter. "All right." His voice was tight and hoarse. "I'm prepared to hear you out."

Skimnoddle listened to every word the two leaders said. Kyer's position was precarious at best, and he did not want to believe it. He needed time to sort through all the bits and pieces of information. Both sides made compelling arguments. He understood that Chief Hunter was really Fredric Heyland, recently banished ex-captain of the guard to Lord Bartheylen. He had made some excellent points. The comment about the symbol of the serpent was indeed puzzling.

The chief had certainly come across as emotional and sincere during his speech, but the halfling was curious about his last words: *Kyer was special to me too.* Skimnoddle, not having been a part of the group at the time, had been told the summarized version of what had happened between Kyer and Sir Fredric: how they'd slept together; how Fredric had bragged about his association with her to his men; how Kyer, true to form, did not let him get away with it. And how all Fredric's other indiscretions had been revealed, resulting in his demotion and banishment.

Skimnoddle didn't understand how Fredric could refer to Kyer as "special" yet be guilty of boasting of their intimacy. *If I ever had the honour of her company, I would never defame it that way.*

But what did Skimnoddle know? He dismissed it and kept his eyes averted while vowing to eat a bushel of potatoes if only Misty and Juggler would not recognize him as the halfling who had played dice with them.

Twenty-One
Determination Won

S weating in spite of the sunshine's pallor filtering through the trees, panting as if she'd been running for two hours, rather than walking for one, she wondered if the path would ever end. *Why is this place called the Indyn Hills when it ought to be the Indyn Giant bloody Cliffs?* For ages they had climbed. They were on a southward part of the switchback when Trig whinnied in discomfort, and Kyer finally woke up to recognize that she was pushing herself and her animal through thorny tendrils of plants that lined the path. "Sorry, boy." She gently pushed her sword against the spiky arms to create more room. The path did not open.

In fact, the path came to an abrupt end in front of her. Too focussed, she had been, on her destination, to notice that the bush was growing. Each touch against its branches inspired several feet of new life. "Whoa!" Kyer cried, stopping and leaning backward into Trig to persuade him to reverse. Spiny arms criss-crossed rapidly in front of her, a deep creaking sound emanating from the plant that made Kyer's skin crawl. "What are you doing? I'm sorry!" Then she felt foolish for apologizing to a plant. *Well, Phennil would approve.* Despair tugged at her chest as she watched the prickly limbs form a canopy over her head. Just as panic swelled, the growth slowed and finally halted.

Kyer looked helplessly about her for some other path. Had she missed a fork somewhere? The shadows were already lengthening along the downhill side of the trail. In just over an hour or so, the sun would descend behind the mountain she had climbed, laying a blanket of darkness over her mission. Leaving her alone.

Kyer sat down in the dappled light, her blood chugging through her veins. *What do I do?* Where was Kayme now? The great wizard was supposed to tell her how to get everything they needed. She stared up at the plant that completely barred her way. "Am I to understand I'm close to the cave entrance? Is that why you're doing this?" Trig replied by nuzzling her neck, and she absent-mindedly held up her hand for him to sniff. He *hooshed* air onto her palm, reminding her that he still cared, even though she was a lying, negligent deserter who now would end up with nothing to show for her efforts but some holes in her skin where thorns had pierced.

Then a thought struck her. Gilvray had said he had seen the cave doors. Obviously he could get by. There must be a way. *Alon, Kien, Valrayker, help me out here. Give me some ideas.* The blade had annoyed the bush. What would soothe it to submission?

A shiver went through her, and Kyer assumed it was a breeze. Except that she did not feel the air move. Then she felt the plant shiver again in the dim light. She jumped to her feet, spinning wildly about, waiting for the plant to begin its crazy spurt again. Kyer didn't so much *hear* the bush speak as she *felt* it send words into her mind.

Why do you come?

Kyer was startled, not by its words, but by the language it chose.

The plant spoke to her in Dark Elvish. How did this . . . creature know that she was familiar with that forbidden tongue? *Hold on,* she corrected herself. *How does a plant speak Dark Elvish?*

How do you? the plant said. Kyer was certain the "voice" held a hint of amusement.

I was taught it, Kyer said to the plant, standing straighter to maintain dignity.

Very well, the plant said, *I return to my initial query.*

Was this some sort of trick?

Uh, I come to—Oh, by the gods' breath, how would this thing react to her saying she intended to enter the caves? Kyer doubted that lying was an option. She settled on the truth. *I'm on a mission from Lord Kien Bartheylen.* Her chin lifted a touch. *For Lord Valrayker. I wish to enter the Indyn Caves to find a type of dust. It's the ingredient in a—a medicine. For a friend. She may die without it.*

The plant's Dark Elvish words flowed into her head like a song. *And how do you propose to enter?*

I have the key, Kyer answered. *I can't believe I'm carrying on a conversation with a bush!* she said to herself, and the plant laughed. Laughed? This whole thing was preposterous.

Show me.

I can't, Kyer said automatically. *I have it memorized.*

A tremor shinnied through the bush that Kyer could only interpret as surprise.

Show me, it said again, *in your mind.*

Kyer nodded and pictured herself once again sitting at Major Gilvray's desk, the leather pouch clear in front of her eyes. The completed rune pattern etched into it was as vivid as if it truly sat before her.

The motion from the bush, the creature, felt more or less like a nod, and again Kyer sensed surprise.

That you can memorize this is—interesting to me. How is it that you speak the ancient dark tongue? the thorny plant asked.

Kyer's reflexes leapt to defence. *You spoke first. How did you know I speak it?*

To Kyer's surprise, the creature was not quick to answer. She sensed its hesitation. *If you do not know, then it is not the place of this treyurne to tell you,* it answered finally.

Know what? Kyer demanded, annoyed. "Tell me what?" All these people dropping hints at her, but nobody giving her the straight goods. Kayme, the Guardian, Fredric, and now a plant. It was bloody irritating.

As if the young warrior had not experienced enough amazement for one day, the treyurne withdrew. Its gnarled vines untwisted and recoiled, ungrowing almost as quickly as they had grown. The long, intertwined thorns criss-crossed in the reverse direction, essentially shrinking back into their source. The main plant was hidden from Kyer's view so it appeared that the treyurne was retreating into nothingness.

Her frustration gave way to wonder as the path widened in front of her. *Thank you,* she thought and led Trig along the final few paces of the trail and into an open space. The twenty-by-twenty-foot "veranda" was enclosed by trees on three sides, though Kyer's familiarity with the switchback trail told her there was a pretty nasty drop over the edge on the left side. Heart pounding, she took a deep breath and turned to the right.

Two rectangular pillars of stone stood about four feet in front of the doors, obelisks like sentries guarding a great edifice, with only enough space for one average person to walk between them. They obstructed the view of the doors from the clearing. Above the pillars, the mountain stretched up and both west and north. Kyer willed herself to take the few steps to navigate herself around one side of the pillars, and there, bold and daunting, timeless in the lack of overgrowth that framed them, were the great doors to the ancient Indyn Caves.

Kyer stared at the mass of designs that covered the doors from top to bottom and allowed her shoulders to sag in dismay.

Ten feet high, each four feet wide, and a mess of scrawled lettering. Though when Kyer studied the doors more closely, she could see that these were no scrawled letters but the result of likely many months of painstaking effort. Minute attention had been paid to the detail of the carved designs. A maze. Every inch of the stone was occupied. *And I'm supposed to find a section of three-inch diameter?* How was she ever going to find the tiny spot that matched the rune pattern in her memory? She could be here for days. And even if she found it, what was she to do? Stepping back, she realized the sun was sinking behind the mountain, and with the stone pillars before the door, Kyer and the doors were already in shadow. Soon she would be in darkness. She had a half hour at best.

And I'd far rather sleep indoors than out here. I think.

Then she remembered the gift Valrayker had given her upon their departure from Shael. Digging around in her saddlebag, her fingers closed around a key. With it in hand, she stood before the doors and stared at the key. There was no obvious keyhole, so where . . . ? She found a spot near the centre, a likely place for a keyhole to be situated. She touched the tip of the key to the spot and gave it a turn, as if it were a keyhole in any door. A small flash startled her, and the key fell to the dirt. It had had no effect on the door. Cursing the waste of one of the key's four uses, she stuck it in her pocket and glared at the door again. Time for Plan B.

She scanned the door's upper section. She was going to need a system. A methodical approach. Common sense told her that the pattern was more likely to be found near the middle than near the bottom. After all, grown men and women had to enter here regularly, so would they put the "keyhole" in a location that would prompt convoluted contortions for use? At any rate, it was a way to begin.

Starting on the left, just below her own eye level, Kyer examined the rune engravings in one-inch sections, one by one, searching for the same design as on the left-hand side of the stone disc. A set of concentric circles with a slightly curved zigzag attached just below on the right. She drew it forth from her memory, the stone cool in her left hand as she'd studied it. Her fingertips recalled the roughness of the grooves as she'd traced them before etching them into the soft leather. She felt again the weight of the penknife in her right hand but focussed her vision on the design she was re-creating. The memory had risen so close to the surface that Kyer could virtually feel the stone disc clutched in her hand, could see the painstaking detail of the runes carved in it, and she glanced down at it to watch both it and the door for a match. *Of course, I could have been holding the damn thing upside-down.* But she didn't think so.

Back and forth, left to right and right to left, heading higher by an inch with each passage. More than once she found one or even two or three of the connecting patterns, but then the surrounding ones strayed from the picture. Her eyes were beginning to ache.

She left her finger on the door, so she wouldn't lose her place, but stepped back to rest her eyes for a moment. When she returned her gaze to where her finger rested, she got confused. Surely that was an inverted Y a moment ago? Then ... *what?* She went back over the places she'd already looked. None of it was familiar. Hands shaking, she went back to where she'd started. Sure enough. The pattern had changed.

Bloody dark elves! No wonder they needed the key. It wasn't just that one had to remember a certain location on the door: The runes would be in a different configuration every time the door was approached. *Shit.* She'd have to start again.

Dimmer and dimmer was the light, and Kyer had to move in closer. *This is ridiculous. It's going to be blacker than under the Cold Fells in moments.* She stepped back. Drawing her dagger, she approached a tree. This time she did not need to be reminded what to do; she'd learned from the treyurne never to hack and slash at bushes ever again. *I need a torch. May I?* No response. She glanced anxiously around at the deepening shadows. Inhale. Exhale. *Okay, this is a dark elvish place, right?* There was no harm in trying, so she repeated the question in Dark Elvish.

This time she received a response. In the affirmative. She chose a straightish limb and bent it at the Y to break it, cutting it only when it would break no further. She trimmed it and wrapped the head of it in a rag doused in oil. She stuck it into the ground near the doors and applied flint and steel. *That should give me about an hour.*

Then she set to thinking like a dark elf.

"We will halt here," Derry said, "and begin the hike up the trail in the morning."

"What's wrong with going now?" the woman called Misty demanded.

Derry dismounted and didn't bother looking at her. "It's too dark and we don't know how far up that mountainside we have to go."

Misty spoke to Fredric this time. "I thought you were chief, Hunter. Why are we taking orders from this one?" Scorn tipped her words.

"Because you lot joined us, not the other way around," Derry said, asserting his authority. "And I give the orders for this mission, not . . . Hunter."

Misty eyed him through her lashes, glanced at her chief, and did not respond.

Was that resentment or shock on Fredric's face? Or both. Derry stared him down.

Not surprisingly, the two camps did not intermingle but separated themselves by about twenty paces.

The mood around the fire was gloomy.

Janak kept a wary eye over at the other camp. "What are they talking about over there, do you think?"

"Does Fredric know about the key?" asked Skimnoddle.

Derry shook his head and swallowed his bite. "Not unless one of you told him."

"What are we even doing here?" said Phennil despondently. "We have no idea what we're looking for."

"Well," Derry said with forced cheer, "we're going to do the best we can."

"I don't see how we'll get anywhere without the key."

"I am not prepared to give up at this point." Derry spoke more firmly.

"It seems futile without Kyer," Phennil insisted.

"Look, Phennil." Derry's patience was wearing thin. "We can't keep going on about Kyer. Kyer, in case you hadn't noticed, is not here. She had other things to do that were more pressing than saving Alon Maer's life, so she left. Again. And this time it's for good." His volume rose as the many hours and days of emotion and frustration flowed out of him like escaping chickens. "Kyer went off to play with Kayme, who's evidently a better friend to her than we are. At least, he has what she needs, and we don't, apparently —"

"I don't blame her." Phennil sat up straighter. "How well have we treated her lately? Talking about her behind her back, accusing her of negligence without even— *Did* you actually ask her what's been going on?"

A small pang of regret touched Derry's heart, but he dismissed it angrily. "She had plenty of time to explain herself." *I will not let him make this my fault.*

"Maybe there's something wrong that she's afraid to tell us."

"I am her friend and her captain. She can tell me anything; she knows that." He looked to Jesqellan for support. The mage opened and closed his mouth.

"Does she really?" Phennil demanded. "You haven't exactly been approachable lately. I suppose you came right out and told her what's been wrong with her behaviour."

"You have no idea how she evaded every point I made. I asked her questions; she was nothing but vague and mouthy."

"I'd get mouthy too if I were being—"

"You *have* been getting mouthy, Phennil." Derry didn't mean to voice that.

Phennil stood up. So did Jesqellan. The mage broke into the argument. "This is becoming too personal, gentlemen, and is not healthy if we intend to —"

"Oh, it's personal, all right." Phennil's glare rested on Derry, who remained stubbornly seated. "Did you give any thought at all to the things I said this morning, Derry? You too, Jesqellan. Don't think you're blameless in all this. You're the one who brought up the accusation about Kyer in the first place. You got it in at a good time too, when Derry'd already made up his mind that she was guilty of *something*. I can't stand it anymore." He cast his fury around the camp. "Every one of you is all set to believe what you want to believe. I'm the only one who sees that Kyer's being sent down the river. This mission doesn't have a hope in seven hells of success because we're a mess! And the one person who truly cared is gone."

That got Derry to his feet. "You miserable, filthy, putrid elf. How dare you?"

"I'm going," Phennil said. Derry's stomach lurched. "And don't try to shame me into staying because 'Valrayker might not be pleased with me.' My loyalty is to the Guarded Realm, not to him." Phennil turned his back and prepared his horse.

Derry couldn't believe his ears. The elf's hypocrisy was insupportable. "So now you think it's all right to cause *another* rift in the group? This is absolutely unacceptable."

Phennil scoffed. "Come on, you'd ditch me in a heartbeat, Derry, if you found another tracker." He nodded toward the other camp. "Maybe Fredric can loan you his."

"Phennil, no." Skimnoddle stood by the fire, wringing his hands.

Derry was breathless with wrath. His thoughts were a confused tangle. He settled on one thing Phennil had said and grabbed Leoht's bridle. "How can you accuse me of not caring about Alon?"

Phennil picked up his pack and slid it into position on Leoht's back. Only then did he face the captain. His blue eyes had turned black. "Kyer was in it for the right reason. Not for glory. Not for a reward. Not even to get in anyone's good graces." Phennil looked pointedly at Derry. He put his foot in the stirrup and threw his other leg over Leoht's back. Derry's body was rigid as granite. Phennil stared down at him. "Kyer *reveres* Alon Maer. She just wanted to meet her. That's all. Meet her while she's still alive."

Something snapped in Derry's mind. "Bullshit," he blurted, and the word sounded foreign, even to himself. "Rubbish." He fished in his pocket, whirling around to face the others. "She ran off!" He yanked out the pouch he hadn't had the nerve to drop in the fire. "She took this stupid pouch off her belt and chucked it at me." Derry flung the pouch at Skimnoddle, imitating Kyer's move. "Does that tell you she cares?" He spread his arms wide in supplication. "Nothing she said gave me reason to believe she had any motivation but her own desire."

Skimnoddle fiddled with the pouch. Janak rubbed his forehead with his palm, as if undecided what to think.

Jesqellan sighed deeply, moving toward Phennil. "Please Phennil, can we not talk—"

Leoht *hooshed* and pranced. Phennil held him. "I'm not interested in talking to people who aren't listening."

Derry thought his brains might burst. "*You* are the one who is not—"

"Captain!" Skimnoddle cried sharply. The halfling's tone demanded attention. Leoht stood still. Skimnoddle's wide eyes looked ghostly in the firelight. The pouch was suspended by his nimble fingers as if it were of gossamer. "Captain, this is the answer to one of the questions you did not ask. Sir."

Derry stepped forward and snatched it from him. He hadn't noticed that the pouch had been inside-out, but he saw at once that Skimnoddle had turned it the right way around. At first he couldn't make out what the halfling meant, but the firelight picked up a marking that caught his eye. His breath stuck in his throat as he finally saw what was scratched neatly into the soft leather, with every possible attention to detail. In his mind he heard Kyer's voice: *Maybe I'll go steal the runes.*

"Oh look," Skimnoddle murmured. "She stole the runes."

Derry's legs liquified. He sank to his knees. With shaking hands, he tilted the pouch toward the firelight to scrutinize the rune pattern that had been painstakingly re-created there. "By the Goddess, what have I done?"

Phennil couldn't remain on horseback amid the frenzy of emotions. Excitement at the discovery, a babble of speculation around how she'd accomplished this outrageous feat, the validation of one man's loyalty, the shame of the others' lack of faith. In the midst of it all, Derry found himself suddenly face-to-face with Phennil. No words were exchanged. Derry could think of nothing that would sufficiently repair his actions. And the elf seemed to feel enough words had been spoken. Derry held out his hand. Phennil frowned, as if reluctant, but at last his eyes gleamed blue again. He shook Derry's hand.

Regret and dejection at the loss of Kyer were renewed tenfold, now that there was no question as to her movements of the night before. None felt it as keenly as Derry, who had spent the past night and day thinking such terrible thoughts about her. *What have I done?* he thought. *What have I done?*

Jesqellan found himself more confused than ever about Fredric's claims. He could not deny that Kyer had proven a certain dedication last night, but neither would he deny the soundness of Fredric's words. *It is beneficial that I am capable of clear thinking.* Someone had to remain objective.

———†———

"I want us to keep a decent watch throughout the night," Derry said quietly to his group when they were finally ready to bed down. "As much to keep an eye on them as for anything else."

He took the first watch himself.

Phennil was smarter than Derry'd given him credit for. How could he have been so thick? He was so caught up in his own indignation over Kyer's behaviour, so hurt—yes, he had to admit it—by many of her words, staggered that she'd taken control of the argument and crushed his triumph with her reason. *Something has seriously botched up your judgement, Derry. What kind of a knight lets that happen?*

Kyer was too right. He didn't know how it had begun, or when, but he had indeed lost perspective, lost his judgement of character. His mind was mired in perplexity. He, who had always known who he was, what he wanted. And above all, Derry Moraunt knew right from wrong. Didn't he?

My friend. The icy words came back to chill him.

Every little thing he'd said seemed to make so much sense at the time. Now, as his own and her remarks replayed in his head, it all felt wholly ridiculous. He had accused her of wantonness. He had accused her of neglecting their mission. Indeed some form of madness had come over him. He ought to have known there was some good reason for her being late, for her leaving them, for everything. He couldn't even remember why he hadn't trusted her. None of it made sense anymore.

Kyer had produced results where the rest of them had spent the evening arguing. She was worthy of his highest regard, not his contempt. Derry closed his eyes. He felt terribly ashamed and foolish. Probably the closest friend he had ever had, and in a fit of madness, he had destroyed everything. He could not bear the thought of being without her steady, loyal friendship, which he suddenly was aware he had come to rely on. And now she was gone, and he was enmeshed in a hunt for evidence that she'd cursed Alon Maer. She'd have been within her rights to kill him for his accusations. But instead she'd given him *a good long time to think about how utterly absurd you've been.*

Derry accepted his sentence and woke Phennil after a couple of hours.

The elf ambled around the camp, noting that the other group had relied on them to post a watch. Evidently that crowd feared nothing out in the Indyn Hills during wartime.

Phennil hadn't slept much during Derry's watch. Kyer's vindication was a powerful stimulant. His euphoria would keep him going for days. And now he was more determined than ever to carry on where Kyer had left off. The mission would be a success, and Phennil would let everyone know Kyer's part in it.

After a while, his legs grew tired, which did not strike him as odd. He sat down to rest for a few minutes. Not long after, he grew drowsy, so he rose to fight it off. It was because of the emotional day and lack of real sleep in the early watch. In spite of all his efforts, he became unaccountably weary and lay down on his bed. Just for a moment or two. *And they don't need a watch; there can't be anything to worry . . .*

Misty sat up. She repeated the cantrip and waved her hand enough times to ensure the deep sleep of both parties. Except Juggler. He was in on the plan.

Stealth was hardly necessary, but it came naturally to her. Quickly and silently she hunted through the belongings of each of Valrayker's group, including pouches that were on their sleeping bodies. Her deft fingers detached pouches and vials of lichen, slipping them into her own pockets. It pleased her that she did not find any of the tahleema. The only sample of the little white flower was in a bottle in her own possession. Without that ingredient, their antidote was likely useless anyway, but Misty did not take chances. She left no trace of her intrusion; until they checked their supplies, no one would know they'd been searched. They each carried samples of the ingredients, as she'd suspected. The halfling was the only one who disappointed her. Halflings were known for being clumsy and careless. Perhaps they didn't trust him to take good enough care of his share. By his baggage, he looked to be only the cook for the group anyhow, though she imagined he must have some other uses. *Probably as fodder to throw at wild animals.*

He slept facedown with his hood half obscuring his face. She thought he might be familiar but dismissed the thought. *Those stupid creatures all look the same.*

With her prizes securely tied in a sack, she returned to her bed. Chief Hunter thought he was going to be showered with glory upon his arrival at Bartheylen Castle? *Think again.* She hid the sack in the bottom of her bedroll, gave Juggler a loving pat on the cheek, and lay down. As an afterthought, she waved her hand toward the elf.

Phennil sat bolt upright. *I fell asleep, damn it!* Heart pounding, he looked frantically around. What had awakened him? A look up at the position of the moon told him he'd been unconscious for more than half an hour. He sighed. *That's not so bad.* At least he felt refreshed and would not have to keep fighting fatigue for the rest of his watch. He decided there was no need to admit his lapse to Derry.

If I were dark elven, Kyer thought in their language, *where would I put the keyhole?* She closed her eyes and tried to recall every word Brendow had ever told her about dark elvish ways. She imagined herself in his drawing room, chatting in Dark Elvish over tea and biscuits, discussing their artwork, their music, their trade goods, their philosophies.

"Dark elven children are taught from a very young age to be independent," Brendow said. "From the time they can walk, they are taught survival skills, including spells to protect themselves."

"Protect themselves from what?" Kyer asked. "What could a child have to protect themself from if their parents are around?"

"Ah, but that is the problem," her mentor replied. "What if they are not? There is always the possibility that the adult will be harmed in some way. The world seems a safe place to a child, but the reality is the opposite. A child must protect themself from their own fear. They learn to hunt and cook; they learn to keep warm and dry—"

"Isn't that everyone? That isn't limited to dark elves."

"No, that isn't. But dark elves were always considered more threatening to the other elven races. I do not know why. But they were often persecuted. No other elven race learns to hide from their enemies in quite the same way or learns to feel and to listen in quite the same way. Plus, the dark elves had their own method of communication. They used to say, *Thank the fates for dark elven traits.*"

Kyer looked at him with a doubtful grin. "Really, Brendow? In what way? I mean, I used to be able to hide from Della for ages, and she wouldn't find me until I was ready to be found. Aren't all children good at that?"

Brendow shrugged. "To a certain extent, that is true. But hiding out in the open is a different skill altogether. And as for listening . . ."

The conversations would extend into the dusk when Kyer would finally recall her duties at home and hasten away.

As she now hastened back to the doors of the Indyn Caves. Her left hand raised, she still felt as though the stone disc were solid, cool in her palm. She closed her eyes. Felt. Listened. Hiding out in the open.

Something touched her. Like a soft fingertip between her brows.

The hairs on the back of her neck rose like the spears in an enemy front line. A breeze flitted through the stone pillars behind her where she had not felt any air movement from the time she'd arrived. She shivered, fear climbing up her spine. She listened. And heard voices. A jumble of them, talking, chattering, singing, as if a party were going on somewhere. They faded out and in again, like waves on a windy sea. Kyer swallowed the fear back down. She had an urge to spin around and flee. Her skin crinkled as if a ghost had just brushed against her. All senses were heightened, but still she did not allow herself to run.

She listened.

And opened her eyes.

They were fixed on the left side of the door. At a place a little below where she had begun her search. Not taking her eyes from the three-inch spot, she stepped nearer to confirm it. Plain as the disc itself in broad daylight was the rune pattern on the door. It stood out so boldly from the rest of the etchings in the stone that Kyer was floored that she had not seen it before. She blinked slowly, testing herself. Yes, it was still there.

Thank the fates for dark elven traits.

Palms sweating, she fixed her gaze on the spot. She licked her lips in concentration. *Now for the red light.* It was just an idea, but it was all she had to answer that part of Soren's poem. No, it was a gut feeling, a sixth sense. The key that Gilvray had in his possession was inlaid with five coloured gems. She'd thought them merely decorative at the time. But some instinct told her they meant much more. At least . . . one of them did. One of them was red.

She'd left the key with Gilvray, but if her idea were correct—*oh, please let it be correct!*—she didn't need it. Without shifting her eyes, she wiped her palms on her trousers, and slowly drew her sword. She adjusted her footing, planting them firmly, as she held the weapon, pommel up, in front of her. The gem gleamed in anticipation, as if it had been waiting all its life for this moment. She reached behind her, feeling for heat to grab the torch without burning her hand. The spot on the door had not disappeared. Every fibre of muscle in her body was taut. Holding her breath, she clutched her sword by the hilt, point down. The red gem stood at attention, as breathlessly expectant as Kyer. Then Kyer adjusted the position of the torch behind it. The guttering light fixed on the massive ruby the way a compass needle clings to north.

A spray of tiny red lights exploded out from the gem like fireworks. Kyer gasped openly at the beauty of it. They danced on every surrounding surface as her hand held the sword and quivered ever so slightly. But she needed a pinpoint. Twisting and tilting the gem, she managed to capture a larger beam of red light through that side. It refracted on the outgoing side, and she focussed it on the still-unmistakable keyhole. *Please let this work!*

A sound, like a piercing high note held by a soprano, intensified inside her head.

Another breeze, stronger this time, *whooshed* through the entranceway, threatening to blow out the torch. Kyer's hair whipped across her face. But suddenly she noticed that the breeze was blowing the wrong way. The breeze was coming from inside. The doors were opening.

She pushed one with a foot and thrust the torch forward so the light would shine through the door to the inside.

Kyer gasped again, for it seemed as though brilliant light were emanating from inside those massive doors. The flickering torch reflected off countless flecks of colour and cast a rainbow down onto the awestruck woman in the doorway. With the caution and hesitation of a thief, she stepped into the foyer and held the torch high to look around. The air was as fresh as if she were by the sea. In spite of herself, she had not stopped listening, and though the voices had ebbed, she still fancied she could hear, or at least feel, that someone was aware of her entry. She also sensed their displeasure.

In size the foyer resembled Kien's meeting room at Shael Castle. A half-domed archway straight ahead proved to be the source of luminousness. The stone was inlaid with bright and shiny beads, gems, and bits of glass of all colours and at all angles, dazzling her with reflected light that sparkled in every direction. Tiny dots of colour scattered the floor like stars. The only thing that caused her to tear her eyes away was the sputtering torch as it gave one of its last spurts of light. Kyer wheeled around and thanked the last dark elves to vacate the place for leaving some extra torches by the door. With the dying breath of her own, she lit the one in the torch bracket.

She kissed the brilliant red gem on the pommel of her sword and placed it tenderly in its home then lifted the torch out of the bracket.

Below the archway, a set of half a dozen semicircular steps descended into shadowy unknown, and the torchlight could not penetrate the blackness. The light that glittered up here stopped at the edge of the steps, keeping itself separate from whatever lay below. Kyer held the torch up, and it pierced the darkness around her enough to reveal a set of heavy wooden doors over to the right side of the foyer from where she stood. A guard room? Moving closer, she tentatively pushed one open.

The homey and familiar smell snuck out instantly, distant with age and disuse. She opened the door fully, revealing a stable, large enough for several horses. She went back to the cave entrance and led Trig through the main doors and into the room. Though there was no food for him, and the water troughs had long since evaporated, she felt more comfortable leaving him in here than out in the open for however long she would be exploring within the caves. She relieved him of her saddlebags and left them by the entrance to the stable. Then she regarded the front doors.

Would they open to let her out as easily as they'd let her in? Her fear of allowing someone else easy access to the caves outweighed her trepidation that the doors wouldn't reopen. She'd worked hard to find the rune pattern, and so could the next person.

With one hand on the carved-out stone handles on the back of each door, she swung them shut. A gust of wind carrying murmurs of ancient voices burst in through the last crack between them. The singing voice danced like spiders up her spine. The crack closed, the doors were shut.

Kyer was surrounded by the silence of unawakened dead.

Not dead, she insisted. *Gone.* They had left. The dark elves had not died. Had they left from here in the caves? Soren had said this place was the centre of their travel and communication. What did that mean, exactly?

Kyer felt the weight of an entire race on her shoulders. She knew without a doubt that she was the first human to ever set foot in this sacred, secret place. Waves of air shifted, leaving the pervading feeling that she was not welcome. Her back prickled like the treyurne's tendrils. Had they all indeed left? Maybe there were still dark elves lurking in the passages beyond this entrance. Maybe they had taken offense to her presence here. That would explain the voices she kept hearing.

Oh, Kyer, you're being an idiot.

She was in, and that put her much closer to finding the last ingredient, to saving Alon Maer's life. To convincing Derry that the goal mattered to her. She could not estimate the hour, but she realized she had not eaten since last night before going to see Gilvray. *No wonder my mind is messing with me.*

She set the torch in the bracket, sat, and pulled some food out. The voices seemed louder once the light had weakened. Faint, far-off sounds like the babbling of a group of people around a dinner table, unintelligible. Not even recognizable as words, just sound. And it did not come from a particular direction within the caverns; the voices floated in the air around her, or in her head. Weariness soon swept over her, but the feeling that something was aware of her, even observing her, could not be shaken. She strained into the darkness, listening. Still, she felt light-headed and needed rest. She lay down with a saddlebag for a pillow, wrapped in her cloak, more against the aloneness than any cold. The red jewel–pommelled sword next to her gave her comfort.

By now Derry would have found the rune pattern. Kyer hoped he had forgiven her. Uneasy sleep overtook her.

My slippered feet pad up the stairs from the foyer, along the straw mats in the brightly lit corridor. I can't walk properly in this shift. I resent the baskets of fresh and dried flowers and the evenly spaced candelabra on the walls; she has everything when others— But not for long. I glimpse the twilit sky through the window of the library as I pass its open door. Little wooden box in hand, I stop outside her door and straighten my apron. I can't wait to be rid of these clothes. I wipe the excitement off my face. Everything is about to change. I knock. Her clear voice answers and I enter. She sits reading in her wing-backed armchair, with her gorgeous hair and that blouse that makes her eyes glow. It won't be long now.

"For you, my lady," I say. "It just arrived." I hold out the box. I can't help but smile, but I at least keep it friendly.

"From whom?" she replies, receiving it from me.

"From his lordship, my lady." Eyes are steady. Heartbeat too. You'd think she'd have learned to be more cautious.

She opens it and touches the necklace. "It's beautiful." She turns to me. "Do you know what this is, Misha?"

Yes, I do. I made it. "No, m'lady."

"The serpent is a symbol of undying love," she tells me. She puts it on and

centres the circular snake on her chest. It is done.

"Please get my looking glass off that table, Misha. I want to see how it looks."

I fetch the glass and hold it up for her. "Do you like it?" she asks.

"Yes, m'lady," I assure her. "Is there anything else you need, m'lady?"

I take a quick glance at myself in the glass, and Alon doesn't see me grin smugly at myself before setting it down. The maid kerchief is too cute and doesn't suit me.

"Thank you, Misha, no. You may go."

She's done it. She has begun killing herself.

"Dear Kien."

Kyer leapt to her feet, sword in hand, eyes shifting furtively around the chamber. Her cry echoed far away into the depths of the intensely quiet halls. Her heart raced. Beads of sweat pooled in her hair and trickled down the side of her face. The torchlight flickered as brightly as before, but it made eerie shadows dance on the walls and ceiling. The dark elven ghosts murmured all around her.

She shook her head and bent her knees until they brought her bottom to the floor.

C'mon, Kyer. Pull yourself together.

That damn serpent! What did Jesqellan know about that serpent?

On the other hand, what did Kyer know about the serpent . . . and the rest of the dream? Besides that the person whose body she "occupied" was the one who wanted to kill Alon Maer.

First of all, she wasn't really a maid, that young lady. The dress Kyer had worn to have dinner with Kayme was the first dress she'd worn since she was about five. She managed all right in it, but that shift in the dream? How did maids manage stairs in those things? And the sleeves were too tight around her armpits. Her dream body was not accustomed to wearing such a garment, nor did she normally wear slippers like that. Kyer recalled having to make sure they were on her feet properly; they felt so loose compared to her boots. She had had to think about the protocol used to address the Lady Alon Maer. It had required some concentration. It was as if the dream woman were not only unused to being a maid at Bartheylen Castle, she was unused to being a maid at all.

And the strangest thing about the woman Kyer became in the dream was the confidence she felt with regards to the gift. She thought back. Regular heartbeat, no heightened breathing. Confidence that the gift would be well received. Anticipation. Not eager curiosity to learn what was in the box, but the sort of anticipation she felt when she gave Brendow the wind chimes for his name day when she was thirteen. And the more she thought about it, the more Kyer became aware of the difference. *I knew what was in the box.*

She put her mind to bringing back the image of what happened just before she'd woken up. That part was new. Something had startled her. What was it?

The mirror. I looked in it.

Pale face. Narrow. Dark curls peeking out from under the maid's kerchief. Coal-black eyes with a vague familiarity that Kyer could not place. A self-satisfied grin that Kyer wanted to slap off the horrible woman's face. No, not slap off. Slice off.

Whoever that dark little goddess was, she could conceivably already be the murderer of Kien's wife and child. Anguish twisted Kyer's gut. She screwed her fists in her eyes.

It was no use. She was awake now, and the sooner she did something about finding the last ingredient to the antidote, the sooner she could add it to her share of the lichen and get it to the afflicted woman. Skimnoddle had the tahleema—there was too little of it to share around—and she would just have to count on the others for the sap. Then, and only then, would the anguish dissipate.

She slung her cloak around her shoulders, sheathed her sword, and buckled the baldric across her chest. She emptied a cloth sack of the last few pieces of stale bread and shoved it inside her cuirass. Another lit torch in hand, her heart thudded and her scalp prickled. But determination won over, and with a brow furrowed in concentration, she descended the semicircular steps into the hall of the ancient dark elvish caves.

Twenty-Two

What Are We Doing Here?

Derry purposefully positioned himself at the head of the procession, with Phennil at the rear of his own party. The elf's hearing would pick up any murmurs from the group that followed, murmurs that could be clues of an imminent betrayal. The captain was not prepared to blindly trust the words of Fredric Heyland, and his benefit of the doubt extended only so far. Fredric and his band could accompany them, but Derry would not relinquish control of the operation.

They had awakened at sunrise. The first sign of positive interaction between the two otherwise disparate companies was the agreement to leave the horses below in case the condition of the narrow path was poor or its destination was unaccommodating to horses. The one called Harley had volunteered to stay behind. Derry thought quickly then nodded at Skimnoddle to remain with him. The halfling was the one most likely to be underestimated.

We are outnumbered more than two to one, Derry thought, *but Heyland can't risk harm to any of us*. He needed the ingredients as much as Derry did, and Derry was sure he didn't know about the key. Besides, if Fredric truly wished to recover Kien's favour he would be strongly advised to be an active participant in finding the ingredients. *And we could use the help, since we are one down* ... Derry's reasoning gave him cautious comfort as they started up the path that hugged the eastern side of the mountain.

After an hour, every member of the group was puffing protestation at the steady but slow incline. The air felt heavy and stale. Their pace had grown sluggish, and sweat ran down Derry's midriff under his plate armour. He ran a hand across his damp forehead, swiping the bangs aside.

Some time later, the path levelled off in the southern direction, and Derry was hopeful it was a sign that they were trudging along the last leg of the journey. The way was narrow and overgrown with thorny bushes. The going was unpleasant. Jesqellan's robes caught on the prickles, and he stopped to disentangle himself. Derry and Janak walked in front, wielding sword and axe to slash their way clear, when asking politely didn't work. Phennil didn't approve but it couldn't be helped. The rising sun's warmth filtered down and got trapped beneath the thick trees like an oven. Soon all the weary travellers were fountains of sweat and volcanoes of frustration. Derry and Janak were having considerable difficulty with their current barbed foe. The path seemed to be getting smaller in front of them instead of opening.

Jesqellan, free of the prickles, suddenly yelled, "Stop!" The weapons were stilled abruptly, mid-swing, but a creaking sound followed for several seconds. "Look at the bush, you fools!"

The thorn bush was growing. It twisted and coiled across the path. The spiky vines looked just as old as the original from which they stemmed. Derry watched in horror as the plant produced new and even more tangled growth. It continued to burgeon, two, three, four weathered-looking vines for every nick of blade it had endured.

"Will it ever stop!" Derry cried in despair.

Skimnoddle looked across the camp to Harley and gave him a little wave, acknowledging the awkwardness of them being left behind together, to watch each other. The last of the others had just been sucked into the path up the mountainside.

Skimnoddle wondered if Harley had been the one to search him, and likely his friends as well, last night. A good thief could prevent himself being thieved, and Skimnoddle was an excellent thief. Whoever had explored the party was an amateur, at least in the area of thievery. Unsuspecting hands had groped his person in the night, not quite stealthily enough to avoid the traps the halfling had set to alert himself to any intruder. All three had been tripped.

Fortunately, Skimnoddle was also a clever enough thief to have more unusual hiding places than the average person. He patted the hidden pockets where he'd put his share of the ingredients and gently tapped the little bottle of tahleema still concealed within his garments. He couldn't help a self-satisfied smile. If the intruder had been successful with the halfling's companions, he, at least, still had possession of the antidote.

Whoever it was, being an amateur, would have had to ensure the targets did not awaken, since he—or she—could not trust they could complete the task without disturbing the sleepers. A sleeping draught during the evening meal? No, no opportunity, nor had any of them had an uncanny desire to sleep at bedtime. No, the most likely answer was that someone in Fredric's party could perform a Sleep spell. And Skimnoddle knew at least one member who fit the bill. When he stole the bottle of tahleema, he saw the Mages' Guild symbol sewn onto the hem of Misty's tunic.

So were Misty and Juggler together on it? Undoubtedly. And were they working under Fredric's orders? Or someone else's? Skimnoddle shuddered to think it. Kyer? Kyer allegedly wanted the mission to fail, yet she was not present to have had anything to do with the search last night. Were Misty and Juggler carrying on with the plan in her absence? on her behalf?

Skimnoddle knew what he had to do. Until the culprits were sussed out, he wanted the ingredients in his own possession. They would be safest there. He must simply find them and steal them back.

"Harley, my good man," he called in his most heartily welcoming voice as he strode toward his neighbour. "It is apparent that we have a copious interval within which to ameliorate and fortify our association. Are you familiar with the game of Dice?"

The hall at the bottom of the steps echoed largely around her, and the feeble torchlight failed to penetrate its depth. The tiled floor reflected the light like a mirror, and Kyer moved as noiselessly as her battery of skills allowed her to. She was utterly alone, yet a gnawing fear in the back of her mind told her to avoid drawing attention—any kind of attention—to herself. Any sound, any misstep, might awaken something or someone who had been undisturbed since the residents had departed. She hugged the perimeter of the chamber, some nagging hesitation preventing her from venturing into the centre, where she'd be within bow range of some nameless enemy watching her from a high catwalk, ready to pierce her with unseen arrows. Whispers of the voices swirled nearby and were whisked away.

Her footfalls brushed against the marble floor. The wall to her left curved inward, indicating a circular room. She continued to follow it, though the ring of torchlight illuminated only blank stone.

Kyer jumped, a sharp intake of breath. What was that? Exhale. Only an empty torch bracket. *Come on, you're behaving like a child.* Sticking close to the wall for fifty paces had yielded her nothing. She put her back to the wall and focussed her vision on the depth of darkness ahead. She took a step forward. And another.

Why is it I keep finding myself underground in total darkness? She couldn't manage a wry grimace. *I only hope there isn't an earthquake.*

Were those whispers growing louder? No, just more of them at once. Fear thrilled up her back as she exposed it to the darkness behind her. There was no longer a wall to steady her. The light revealed a change in the flooring ahead. The plain marble slabs were now reddish in colour, and several triangular slabs laid together formed a larger triangle, its peak pointing ahead of Kyer. A sidestep showed another similar formation next to it, and beyond it, another. The triangles pointed into the centre of a circle on the floor.

I'm not going into that circle. No question about it.

She turned left, estimating that to be the direction exactly opposite from the archway by which she had entered. So consciously was she avoiding the inner circle, she did not see the white line of stone slabs. She only noticed that the floor suddenly felt different under her booted foot. Less polished. Chalky. At the same time as she saw a black patch ahead out of the corner of her eye, she heard the voices.

Fo'wul fo'wul fo'wul. Intruder. Intruder. Intruder. Overlapping one another, still in hushed tones, but for the first time intelligible. In Dark Elvish. Some voices slow and thoughtful, others sharp and decisive. Hostile? Quite possibly.

She hastened over to the dark patch, hoping it was a door. Nearing it, her suspicion was confirmed. An arched door. Closed with a simple latch. That inner voice she never listened to told her explicitly not to open the door. Her conscience said only that she had no dust for Alon Maer. If she left the caves now, she would never return. She had to get it right the first time.

Kyer wiped a sweaty palm on her trousers and flexed her fingers, eyes fixed on the latch. Better to do it fast and get it over. Don't even think about what's on the other side.

Quick as a bird darting out of a tree, she flicked the latch and threw open the door. A staircase led down. She shuddered. But before she could begin her descent, it occurred to her that the torch had grown brighter. A horrifying thought came to her. The skin on her back crinkling she slowly straightened and turned around.

The centre of the circle of triangles was frighteningly visible where before it had been cloaked in blackness. Red-yellow light swirled like smoke, lifting the veil off the entire chamber. The light revolved, growing taller, spiralling up toward the vastly high ceiling. Kyer's gaze involuntarily followed it upward until a different movement startled her back down to ground level. A billowy figure took shape within the smoky light. A cloaked figure, with arms folded, though as she watched, it spread its arms wide and stepped out of the light toward her. As it did so, the voices rose, too jumbled to make sense of, the murmurings more and more intense, harsh-sounding. Angry.

Kyer did not wait to see if the figure wanted a friendly chat. She hurled herself down the stairway, no plan in mind, no way of knowing where the stairs led, and no clue where to begin looking for the dust.

Kayme help me!

Fifteen steps, twenty, twenty-five and she'd reached the bottom. Torch held high, she raced along the corridor, puffing for air, blood pulsing in her brain. A door, a room, she needed something! Some place where dust might have accumulated. She risked a glance behind her and regretted it.

Outside of the swirling smoke, the figure appeared not as a solid being, but as a transparent heatwave rippling above a dirt road in high summer, such that if it were to stop moving, Kyer had the idea that it would be invisible. It neared the bottom of the steps just as Kyer reached a corner. She went right. From behind her came a throaty growl. Heart somewhere up near her collarbone, she pressed on.

An archway on the right. She thrust herself in and held up the torch. No time to determine what kind of room it was; all that mattered was that it was utterly devoid of dust. Whirling around, she flew out and carried on down the passage. She gasped as she looked back down the corridor to see the figure rounding the corner. She picked up her pace.

Doorway after doorway yielded nothing. Occasional tables and chairs, nothing to indicate the purpose of the rooms, nor was that on Kyer's mind. *Dust.* For a place that had been unused for so long, the Indyn Caves were dismayingly dust free. The ghostly figure floated closer and closer.

Door on the left. Closed. Her damp hand fumbled with the latch but finally opened it. Inside. She slammed the door, not caring that she might never open it again, thinking only of keeping out that thing.

Yes, yes, a voice in her head said earnestly. *Kayme?* The torch lent only feeble illumination but the sound of Kyer's own breathing echoed around what felt like a fairly large chamber. Several of some sort of apparatus huddled here and there. A few steps closer to the nearest of them revealed it to be a thing Kyer would never have guessed but recognized instantly to be what she was seeking. A potter's wheel. She swept a finger across the disc that had once held a dark elven potter's creation. But the surface was rough, like a grinding stone. Not a potter's wheel, then. She frowned, puzzled.

Her raised torch revealed at least half a dozen of the apparatuses, with possibly more farther into the darkness. The walls were lined with shelving, a few cracked and broken stones strewn among them. She picked up one of the stones and held it up to the light. *Not pottery. Gems!* These were not potters' wheels, they were machines for polishing gems. The grinding stone would turn with the pressing of the pedal beneath. And below the stone disk, in a sort of basin, lay a fine layer of dust.

The torch found a temporary home on a shelf, and in the bizarre shadows cast on the walls around, Kyer pulled out the small sack.

The latch rattled behind her.

Get out. A Dark Elvish voice.

"No!" she yelled, scraping the side of her hand across the disc to gather what little dust remained.

Startled silence beyond the door, but she hardly noticed. *This can't be all there is.*

The voice was deep and haunting, in spite of being soundless. *You understand the forbidden tongue?* it said in Dark Elvish.

Shit!

Kyer had always intended to ask Brendow what might happen to her if a dark elf discovered that she spoke the language. This was not the time to find out. She could be signing her own death warrant.

You understood the words spoken before. Rydrish this time. The words were a demand, not a question.

Sweat ran down her chest and her face. She did not respond to the voice. If her pulsing heart rose any higher, it would choke her. *All that matters is the dust.* She bent to see if more of the red powder could be found in the basin, and ran her finger along its smooth surface. Her luck was holding. Luck? *If I had luck, there would be no ghostly being awaiting me outside that door.* She scraped her cupped fingers around the perimeter of the tray, gathering the chalk-like stuff into a small heap. There was precious little of it, and she needed every bit. The spectral being was unlikely to give her time enough to attend every machine in the room.

"No," she answered finally, unable to quell the tremor in her voice.

What are you?

"Nothing."

What do you seek?

"What I've found."

The thing's chuckle sent another quiver through her arms, and she nearly dropped the tiny scoop of dust.

Her skin crinkled again as she realized she was no longer alone in the room. She wheeled around to see the shimmering figure take position by the door. Her guess was correct; it was visible only when it moved.

She'd run out of time. In a last-ditch effort to get every minute particle, she thrust her hand against the outside of the bag, turning a section of it inside out. Swiftly she swept out the tray with it, wiping away virtually all the fine particles of ground red gems that remained. She repeated the movement in the second wheel, and raced to a third. The figure approached.

I'm out of time. She hoped it was enough. With a twist, she turned the bag the right way around and shoved it inside the front of her leather breastplate.

Why do you do this?

"Because I need it. Let me out." Kyer snatched up the torch and waved it at the figure.

The figure raised its arms to block her. Kyer quick-stepped to the left, then danced to the right ducking under its arm to the door. Shaking hands had trouble with the latch, and the all-too-close proximity to the dark elven sentinel raised gooseflesh on her neck. She flung the door open and picked up her pace to tear back down the way she'd come but nearly ran headlong into another of the shimmering sentries. A shriek rising in her throat, she whirled around and pelted down the corridor in the other direction, flying past the doorway from which the first figure was only just emerging. A shudder rippled through her as she evaded its outstretched arm for a second time.

Another junction approached. Left, right, or straight ahead? Any instinct she may have had about the direction she should choose was drowned out by the voices and her fear. She chose right, if only to get out of sight of those figures. She didn't dare look around to see if they still pursued her. Getting out was her only thought. Whispering and murmuring had amplified to yelling and wailing, as though she were a convicted criminal enduring the taunts and jeers of onlookers before her execution. Covering her ears failed her; the noise pierced through.

This passage curved left and right and left again, until Kyer could not guess which direction she was headed. Her leather boots made muffled poundings on the stone floor. Hair straggled into her eyes, and she brushed it away. Her breath came in gusts as loud as storm winds in the corridor that was both alive with the sound of sourceless voices and deadly quiet with its long emptiness. How much longer would her torch last? *Stairs, I need stairs,* she begged. Another corridor opened up on her right. She slowed a touch to determine if she should take it. Almost near enough to peer down it.

The figure stepped out before she had time to skid to a halt. She careened to one side to avoid it, but it hadn't finished its movement to enter her path. She slammed into it. Icy chill like diving into a glacier-fed lake perforated through every pore, penetrated her bloodstream, and flowed with it. Each frigid heartbeat pulsed frostlike blood through her lungs, through her brain, through every limb, benumbing her. And the voices had stopped. Either that or she simply could not hear them any longer. Sudden, heavy stillness. *I must be dead.*

Then she was through it. Her stiff, icy body hit a blast of heat like stepping out of the shade into blazing sun. She landed on the floor, knees and elbows taking the impact, too numb and chilled through to move. The voices had returned, though they had hushed expectantly, awaiting something. The figure loomed over her. Soon it was joined by another. And another.

You are ours now.

"No," she managed to croak. "I . . . out . . . Alon . . ." The kindly face of Kien's wife appeared in Kyer's cold-deadened mind. The distant smile as she toyed with a blue-gold serpent on a chain around her neck. Fury glowed somewhere deep inside Kyer and sent warmth surging along her veins, eliminating the freeze in its path. With every iota of energy she could summon, Kyer hauled herself to her feet, picking up the fallen torch in stiff, grasping fingers. Without a backward glance, she stumbled into a run and carried on down the corridor. And reached another junction.

A quick peek revealed what she most desired: Stairs.

Assailed by a strange mixture of relief at the sight of them and dread at what might await her above, she forced herself onward. It was the only way out that she knew, if these steps would even take her back up to the echoey entrance chamber. Nothing could prevent her from fighting to the last to escape these haunted halls.

Hostile voices descended the stairs like mist. Behind her, the rippling forms of the guards, all three of them, approached, torturously slow.

This must be what Brendow meant by being stuck between the hammer and the anvil. There was only one choice. Out was up.

With full strength restored, she flew up the stairs two at a time and flung open the door. The brightness from the centre of the room made her squint. It was indeed the same chamber where the first sinister sentinel had appeared. The door by which she'd exited could just be seen on the far side over to her right. A figure materialized in it and she stopped. Her automatic reaction was to back down the stairs she had just climbed, but over her shoulder, she saw they were coming. Three there and a fourth in the other doorway. *Hellfire, how many more?* The disembodied voices were all around. Kyer's adrenaline surged and she ran forward, her goal the entrance archway on the other side of the chamber. She felt the blast of cold as the figures of the guards reached the top of the stairs behind her. She dared not pass through that billowing, spiralling light in the centre of the room and circuited around it to the left—the more direct path to the arch. Something knocked her aside, and she dropped her torch, which abruptly went out.

Blackness enveloped her. As if someone had pinched a candle flame, all light was extinguished. The angry voices hissed. Palms over her ears she screamed.

A hand pushed her from behind. She fell. Trembling knees did not allow her to rise. She curled into a ball with her arms covering her head.

Who are you?

"Nobody," she pleaded.

Dark elf? a guard challenged, though she couldn't tell if it was the same one.

"No."

What, then? A chilly finger poked the back of her neck.

"Human."

You know our language?

"No!" Kyer shook her head frantically.

How did you get into our caves?

"I have the key."

You lie. An ice-booted foot nudged her in the ribs, and she rolled to retreat from it.

"I do not."

Where is it?

"In my head."

Impossible.

"I'm in, aren't I?"

The voices stopped. Kyer's ragged breathing echoed throughout the chamber as if she were but one of a hundred terrified warriors.

You intrude on our sacred space.

"Then let me leave!"

You are a thief.

"I'm sorry," she pleaded. "It's only dust. I need to get out."

Kyer put one foot under herself and pushed up to standing, all the while trying to steady her breathing.

Hunlish verrun? Who sent you? Dark Elvish again. A trick.

She ignored the question. Her own voice came purposefully projected, as if to prove to herself that she could still speak. It quavered and she tried to quell it. "I need this to save a friend's life. I'm helping Dunvehran. You ought to know him, at least."

A thoughtful pause. The voices murmured again. Disapproval.

Dunvehran ought to know better.

"He doesn't know I'm here."

And he will not learn it.

The chamber blazed with sourceless firelight. Between the fingers that shaded her eyes, Kyer saw seven shimmering, ethereal figures surrounding her.

The voice hissed. *You will not leave this hall.*

The bush stopped growing, finally. Faces peered over shoulders to stare at the deeper, thicker, thornier, deadlier obstacle that now confronted them. Each vine was, at the narrowest point, thicker than Janak's thumb and even more callused. Derry rubbed his eyes.

"What the blazes do we do now?" demanded Janak of Jesqellan. The mage did not respond right away.

"I'm reluctant to try fire," he said, thinking aloud.

"No, it's not our objective to clear the entire forest of greenery," Derry agreed.

Jesqellan finally settled on a miniature lightning bolt, just to see the effect it would have on the plant.

"It is more like a zap. Hopefully a small spell will have only a small effect." He took aim. "Especially if it is not the effect we are looking for." He tossed it right at the centre of the wall of vines. The flash passed between the vines, and spread outward and onward throughout the thick growth. It wove in and around each tendril and was visible as it travelled from this end of the bush to several feet farther on, like lightning forking through the offshoots. It appeared to dissipate; either that, or this bush was so thick, they could not see through to its other side. Apart from the spectacular light display, the bolt had no effect on the plant.

Without warning, the plant hissed and spit a multitude of sparks at them, as if it had gathered up Jesqellan's zap and was vomiting it back at its source. Jesqellan and Derry were in front and took the brunt of it. They shrieked and stamped and patted themselves all over to extinguish them. Derry felt more than one spot on his face that stung, and there were several singe marks on his clothing. He sighed. There was no other way up the mountainside. No other path had opened to their view. Derry rested his hand on the back of his neck and pressed his cheek into the forearm. They were stuck.

"All right. Now what?" one of Fredric's men said with unchecked impatience.

"If the so-called captain can't manage to break through, let Hunter have a go," said another.

"Misty's turn," said Juggler, and the group fell silent.

"I think it's very simple—" Phennil began.

"Shut up, elf," Misty interrupted.

"Shut up?" Janak said to no one in particular, and Derry put a hand on his shoulder.

"It's clear that your mage can do nothing," Misty said with modest superiority. "So why not let a more advanced personage make an attempt?"

Derry's muscles tightened at her manner, but he could think of no reason to object, and also thought it prudent to allow it. "Why not, indeed?" He bowed and gave her the floor. He also gave a warning glance to Jesqellan, who looked to be stretching to full height in preparation to defend his honour.

The dark-curled woman wove around the others in the path. She strode by Derry, the top of her head reaching his nose, where Kyer came up only to his chin. This woman was willowy, where his comrade at arms was solid. Not ungraceful, no, Derry had always appreciated the lithesomeness and balance with which his friend executed each movement. The mage's skin looked to him as polished and untarnished as the bone hilt of a dagger owned by his father. Derry as a young boy had admired its sheen, so smooth under his fingertips. Misty's cheeks had an untouched quality that made her look wholesome. Yet somehow Derry did not believe it. It was superficial. Kyer's scars and physical imperfections gave her a striking, rugged beauty that could easily be overlooked at first glance but was unmistakable at the second.

Strange that I should compare the two. Right here, now. And his jaw clenched at the unbidden memory of his last conversation with Kyer. Would it be his last ever?

Derry shuddered back to the here and now as Misty made a gesture with one hand that remarkably resembled a harpist plucking her strings. The result surprised them all.

The plant did nothing.

Misty's forehead wrinkled in disbelief.

Jesqellan lifted his chin in a self-satisfied attitude, and Derry gave him another warning glare. *The last thing we need is to end up in full battle on this hellfire path.*

Misty raised her hand again. Her fingers at full extension, Derry saw the energy pulse through her to stiffen them as the spell shot out their tips. So fast, it was almost simultaneous, the plant fired back. Two tendrils whacked together, spikes inward, with Misty's forefinger between them. Derry jumped backwards in alarm, and Misty howled with pain and rage. She was too smart to try another spell on the plant, even in retaliation. Derry reached into his pack for his physicker's kit, but before he could finish the movement, she lashed out at him.

"You keep away from me with your pitiful little treatments," she snapped, and Derry held up his hands in surrender. He didn't mind not helping her.

She performed some healing spell on herself. The bleeding stopped and she flounced back to join her twin.

"If I might suggest we just wait a minute," Phennil started again.

"Do we have a choice? We can't exactly rush off anywhere," grunted Janak, back to his usual temperament.

Phennil made a *hoosh* sound at the dwarf, the closest the elf had ever come to imitating one of Janak's growls. "Will you please just listen for a second?" Phennil insisted. "This is obviously a most excellent barrier," he continued upon establishing that he wasn't going to be interrupted again. "for the purpose of keeping visitors out. These are *elvish* caves we are trying to reach. If this is an *elvish* bush—"

"What do you think we should do, offer it some *elvish* wine?" Misty said.

"Enough!" cried Derry impatiently. "What is your idea, Phennil?"

The elf bowed ceremoniously. "Considering we have tried every possible aggressive method, I thought perhaps we could attempt more diplomacy." And without waiting for a response from either company, he approached the bush amid all scoffs and rolling eyes. He spoke softly to it in Elvish. The others looked at each other doubtfully but were stunned to silence when the bush rustled its thorns as if in response. Derry could hear nothing but saw the subtle movement of the plant. It seemed to consider what the elf had said. He was as astonished as the rest when Phennil turned to him. "It's a treyurne. It wants . . . to speak to you."

Janak grimaced. "Did it say, 'Take me to your leader' or something?"

"No, it asked to speak to the one who possesses the runes," Phennil corrected. "I explained the urgency of our errand, and it is not unhappy to accept us. Kien and Valrayker are handy friends to have; at least their names are, since bandying them around is proving to be quite helpful. But it wants proof."

Derry hesitated. How was he supposed to prove their errand to a bush? Finally he accepted the necessity of attempting communication with it and stepped forward. Warmth crept up his neck, and he cleared his throat. But before he could utter a word, he felt a localized push in the side of his head, and words entered, as if they had somehow bored a passage through his skull like worms in an apple. He even understood its words.

You have the key?

Derry started to voice his response, but the plant had already heard it within his thoughts. It was most unnerving.

Show me.

Well, Derry said tentatively, getting the hang of the voiceless dialogue, *I don't have the stone. It has been copied . . .* He pulled the pouch out of its home. *Scratched, actually, into this leather pouch. Do I hold it up?*

The bush shivered again, and Derry felt it chuckle with a tingling inside his head. *Let me see it through your eyes.* Derry looked at the runes and felt the plant seeing them.

"What the hell's the holdup?" someone shouted.

"Shut it, Kep." Fredric's voice.

Who did this and where is the stone? If a plant could speak with a tone, it was one of curiosity or suspicion.

The stone is safe with the Realm Guard. It was copied by . . . a friend of mine, who knew it was needed.

Derry sensed that the treyurne was thinking, and he thought it not fair that it could read his thoughts but he could not read the plant's. He only felt it murmuring to itself.

Where is this friend of whom you speak?

I don't know, Derry admitted, casting his eyes down. *She left us.* He felt the pressure in his temple again, as if the treyurne were probing his thoughts. "Hey, cut that out." He rubbed the side of his head, for all the good it would do.

Very well, you may pass.

And with that, to the amazement of all, the treyurne began to withdraw. It coiled back its twisted limbs amongst the trees and bushes. Thorns, prickles, and barbs had evaporated, and no evidence whatsoever of a treyurne plant remained. Within moments, an opening appeared before them, the exit from the stuffy, arduous incline. Derry led his company through, followed closely by Fredric and his eight companions. Derry half-expected the vines to entangle them within the pathway. But they did not.

A plateau spread out on the mountainside, about fifteen paces from the entrance to the far side, and perhaps ten from the hill face to the drop-off on the left. Both sets of travellers filed onto it. Two flat, stone pillars had been erected on the right, in front of the doors, with the mountain extending above them and far to the north. Derry followed it with his eyes. The eastern sun gazed upon it between the trees without opening its curtain of thin cloud, casting soft-edged shadows across the hills. The captain stepped toward the pillars, the pulse in his throat beating the rhythm of his excitement. He looked at what lay behind the stones, and his eyes widened in dismay.

The chaotic zoo of runes that spattered the doors all but caused Derry's eyes to cross. He held up the leather pouch, and his heart sank to his knees at the futility of the search. *What are we doing here?* He wished again with his whole heart that Kyer had not left.

A commotion behind him tore him from the daunting task of finding the rune pattern. The group was quarrelling. He stepped back through the pillars to hear Phennil say, "What have you done with them? I knew you were in this for yourself!"

"Phennil, what's going on?" Derry demanded, grabbing the elf by the shoulder and urging him to step back from Fredric.

Phennil shoved off Derry's hand and pointed. "I was standing there, next to the treyurne, and it told me to check my pockets." He shook his head violently, as if trying to knock his wits together. "Damn it, I knew we shouldn't have trusted you, Fredric!"

"Whoa, whoa, what is this all about?" Derry grabbed Phennil by both shoulders this time.

"The ingredients for the antidote!" he cried. "My pouches are gone. The stuff has been stolen!"

"Mine are gone too," Janak announced.

Jesqellan looked shocked.

Derry dropped Kyer's pouch, his hands rushing to his own share of the ingredients. He wheeled around to face Fredric Heyland.

"You," he said. "What have you done with it?"

Fredric blanched. "Nothing! I give you my word—"

"You expect us to trust your word?" Phennil interjected.

"Why would I take it from you?" Fredric said emphatically. "It would make me a hero, but betraying my lord's best men wouldn't exactly make the good impression I'm looking for."

"You're accusing us of stealing from you?" someone said.

"Outrageous!" said someone else. Flashes of steel flew about the clearing.

Twenty-Three
A Cry, a Clang of Steel

Kyer's training instinctively kicked in. She bent her knees in a defensive stance and automatically analysed the movements of the ghostly beings.

One step from each apparition brought the circle closer.

You will not escape.

"Just try and stop me," she snarled. She was a caged animal, desperate, and she'd go down fighting. Her sword flashed as she drew it. Whirling around, Kyer pointed it at each of them. "Round and round it goes, where it stops . . ."

Looking wildly about her, she recognized a new emotion from them. They had no faces that she could see, but their attitudes and posture no longer suggested offense but confusion. One figure's head was turned as if looking at her sideways. Another had raised its hands.

Kyer sensed an advantage and readied for the attack.

No! Wait. A hand was held up in warning.

She arrested the movement but did not relax her stance.

That sword, the being said. *That sword should never be drawn against us.*

Kyer sensed the horror in the voice. She sneered at it. "Then back off and let me pass."

The figures swayed and twisted, as if looking around at each other.

Clearly this was highly irregular. They did not want to let her go, but her sword was causing them some imbalance.

Put it away. Again turbulence. More trepidation than threat.

"I will not. How much of a fool do you think I am?"

Kyer showed the tip to the figure directly in the path to the entrance. It did not cower but swayed uncertainly, and that was all Kyer required. She charged. The figure vanished before her. She darted through the opening and dashed toward the steps.

At the top, she risked a glance back to see them approaching again, but they dared not get too near while she held that weapon in both hands. She had no desire to make a leisurely departure and thanked whatever gods might pay attention that the torch in the foyer still provided light for her. She fetched Trig from inside the stable and flung saddle and bags across his poor back, all the while feeling that the beings were counting down. They would most certainly be on her heels if she took too long.

She passed a hand over the entrance, and a crack appeared between the two doors. She pulled on the handle. She flung the door wide and burst out into the morning sunshine, blinded by the sudden brightness. Sounds of a battle came from beyond the stone pillars, and a hand was clamped over her mouth.

Neither had coppers to spare, so they played for pebbles. Skimnoddle sat cross-legged opposite his opponent.

"Aha! My roll of 1300 points wins over your 700. I'll just take these two somewhat jagged stones into my keeping." He held the two pebbles between his forefingers and thumbs, waving them enticingly in front of his opponent's eyes. "Shall we each bet two this time? I have these nice roundish ones that can be yours, my good fellow, should your total score this roll be greater than my own!"

Harley grinned. "All right, hotshot. I'll see your two roundish ones and raise you another two with pointy bits." He lay on his side, propped up on one elbow.

The stakes now set out between them, the rolling began again.

"Now, you were saying that your chief is new." Skimnoddle picked up the discussion where they'd left off.

Harley glanced up at him with a glint in his eye. "I know your game, mister. You're trying to throw off my roll." He rolled three threes and picked up the other two dice to try adding to his three hundred points. "Yes, he's new. We picked him up only a couple of months ago or so. Ronav was killed so Hunter was made chief." He rolled a check, so picked up all five dice and rolled again.

"Did you hold a secret ballot to decide? How many men were willing to stand for the position?" The halfling's eyes were wide with eagerness.

"What are you talking about? Naw, he was appointed by the Spectre."

"The Spectre?"

"Yeah, I'm sure he has a real name, that's just what the men all call him because he appears and disappears so suddenly, y'know? And he's ghostly pale and all dressed in black. I'm gonna stop on 950; don't want to risk another roll. See if you can beat that." He scooped up the dice and laid them in front of Skimnoddle and marked his score on the dirt scoreboard.

Skimnoddle looked doubtful. "Fascinating. What if you do not approve of the chief he appoints? Will this . . . Spectre entertain any expressions of disapproval? Any suggestions for an alternate choice?" He shook the dice in both little hands.

"Entertain? Oh sure, he'll entertain the rest of the group by disembowelling the one who spoke out against him," Harley answered, shaking his head. "Not that I've ever seen it happen. No, you just don't question what he says. Trust me."

Skimnoddle tossed the dice for a first-roll total of a mere fifty. He picked up all but the five to reroll. "Accepted. So how is Chief Hunter faring compared to your previous commander?"

"Who, Ronav?" Harley snorted. "He's infinitely better than Ronav. Ol' Ronav was okay, but his ambitions were . . . umm, you could say he'd aimed a little higher than he could clearly see. I wasn't sure of Hunter at first, but he's come around. It must be frustrating to work for someone who keeps changing his mind, but Hunter and the Spectre seem to have come to an understanding. Were you gonna roll or what?"

"Ah, yes, of course." Skimnoddle let the dice loose. "You had me captivated with your story, good man." He counted, picked up three dice and rolled again.

"That friend of yours, the woman?" Harley dug his hand into his bag of nuts and raisins.

"Ah, the lovely Kyer." Skimnoddle sighed rapturously, a hand on his heart.

Harley nodded in agreement as he popped a few nuts in his mouth. "She's an interesting one, all right."

"Interesting?" The halfling stared at the other man as if he'd just said Kyer was ugly as a sea-hag. "She is my joy, my inspiration. The render of my heart." He lowered his eyes.

Harley's right eyebrow went up. "By the gods, man, are you gonna be all right?" He held the bag out for Skimnoddle. "I only meant she's a tough one to figure out."

"How so?" Skimnoddle helped himself.

"Umm, when I brought her up to talk to the chief, she seemed really sure of herself. Confident, yeah? Then Hunter said whatever it was he had to say, and she went all pale." He shook his head again, this time in disbelief. "It was odd, I tell you. Then Misty did her thing, and your friend flopped to the ground. A few days later, Hunter tells us he's just found out she's the one who gave Lady Alon this *Malison* thing. You've heard about that. What do you think of it?"

Skimnoddle picked up all five dice and shook again. "The evidence is damning, to be sure. I find myself believing it, yet I have no wish to."

"Aye, that's what I think too."

"Now what about this Misty woman," Skimnoddle ventured. "Have you any idea as to whether they are collaborators?"

Harley scoffed. "Misty and Juggler are; that's a fact. They think each other's thoughts for them."

"You misunderstand me," Skimnoddle said. "It occurs to me that perhaps Misty and her brother are working in conjunction with Kyer. What say you to that?"

Harley wrinkled his nose. "I doubt it. I really do. Those two work for nobody but themselves." He tossed a nut in the air and caught it in his mouth. "Even when they did errands for Ronav, they tied it up with their own business. I swear, this working for Hunter and the Spectre is really to cover some goal of their own. Look, are you bored of this game? I keep having to remind you to roll."

Skimnoddle bowed in his seated position. "I am most humbly sorry, my dear fellow." He let the dice go and rolled an automatic five thousand points.

Harley pushed himself up to sitting. "That's it!" he cried with mock disgust. "You can have the damn pebbles. The dice are probably loaded, anyway, aren't they? I'm off to the bushes for a visit with nature. Hey, in fact," and he grabbed his whole pile of stones as he rose to standing, "have 'em all, you lucky bastard. You'd probably take 'em while I'm gone, wouldn't you?"

Skimnoddle blustered out his defence as the agreeable fellow disappeared into the trees.

Though he could not believe his luck, Skimnoddle the thief did not hesitate an instant. While sitting in their camp, he had appraised the area with his expert eye, waiting patiently for the right opportunity. He had two or three ideas where Misty might have hidden her stash but leaned toward the most obvious one: hers was the only bedroll packed away onto her horse. In a flash, he had removed it and flown with it over to his own camp. Swift and nimble hands found the satisfying lump they sought, clapped gleefully, and retrieved the sack. He concealed it in yet another thief's hiding place, among his own belongings, and returned the bedroll to its original position.

When Harley got back, the halfling was seated cross-legged exactly where Harley had left him, juggling the dice. Harley's face lit up in amusement. Skimnoddle caught the dice expertly and, indicating the pile of stones in front of him, threw Harley an innocent beaming smile. As if a thought had just occurred to him, he cocked his head to one side.

"Does this mean I win?"

Harley nearly crumpled with laughter.

Janak's battle axe leapt into his hand and promptly sliced straight through his attacker's sword leaving him with a bladeless hilt. The man gaped and Janak let out a gleeful laugh at the effectiveness of his Oil of Unbreaking. As his opponent scrambled to toss the useless weapon and draw a dagger, Janak amputated his arm. The severed limb swooped into the face of a neighbour, whose shriek echoed through the stone pillars and around the clearing. Soon all manner of weapons arced and sliced in the morning sunlight. Phennil's bow at close range expeditiously devastated three of Fredric's men before the elf took a clout in the back with a mace, sending him sprawling.

Derry's sword at first lashed against Fredric. But the former captain of the Shael Guard shook his head. Something in his pleading eyes called to Derry, and the younger man found himself listening. He straightened his body out of the ready position, and Fredric Heyland's shoulders dropped as he breathed a sigh. The next thing they knew, they had taken up their weapons against a common enemy: Derry fought Kep and Fredric faced down his own man.

Hew's eyes glittered as he gripped his falchion. "I been waiting to take you down since you walked in the door."

Fredric stepped forward, sword in hand. "Come on, then."

Janak had not been challenged by a two-weaponed man in many an age. It was a struggle from the start. Juggler was a human whirligig with his two swords; Janak could barely see them with only one eye. The dwarf was all too aware of how easily he might be taken out. Using his battle axe like a quarterstaff, Janak blocked and parried the skilled swordsman's moves but had no opportunity to attempt an attack. At this rate, he would tire before he dealt a single blow. The dwarf's armour turned a direct hit to his chest, but he staggered backward. Reaching up with his axe, he fended off the slice from Juggler's right-hand blade. But the left one swiftly switched direction and caught the sturdy dwarf on the right upper arm. Liquid warmth oozed out and down to his elbow.

Kep deftly flicked his rapier and cut a slit in Derry's cheek. The captain answered with a grand sweep from his bastard sword that knocked his opponent out of line. But Kep employed a balletic hop and instantly recovered. Derry took the tip of Kep's rapier just above his left wrist. Crying out, Derry raised his weapon and flung himself at his foe, determined not to allow Fredric's band of rogues to bring about the failure of his mission.

Fredric's sword whipped from side to side, horizontally, overhead. Each connection with Hew's falchion sent jarring shivers up his arms. Hew hacked at him. Fredric never broke eye contact with the other man.

Jesqellan never broke eye contact with the other mage. Tall, willowy, beautiful in a deadly way. She had no visible energy cell and an overconfident gleam in her eye, Jesqellan's split-second assessment told him. Those could work in his favour. On the other hand, he had felt what she had tried to do to the plant at the gate. Elimination was not a spell for a dabbling mage; this one possessed high skill. *What else can she do if she can do that?* He clung to the fact that the spell had failed. That was either because she had not mastered it or merely that the plant was stronger. Sometimes the failure of a spell as strong as an Elimination could absorb and carry off some of the magic-user's source energy, dissolving it. He could not count on that having occurred. If ever Jesqellan needed to trust himself, this was the time.

His own energy cell, his staff, held close in front, he focussed, centred, and summoned his power from its source. Hand flung out, he cast. She smiled. *She had time to smile!* he moaned. A brush of her hand diverted his spell and sent it off into the trees. A nearby aspen shrivelled.

Jesqellan's blood drained from his face. *I'm doomed.*

The mountain plateau had never seen this much activity. The plantlife shuddered with distaste.

Within the throng of battle, nobody observed that beyond the stone pillars the door of the Indyn Caves was open.

Sword in one hand, Trig's bridle in the other, Kyer struggled against the hands that restrained her. A soothing voice in her ear murmured, "Shh, hush, it's all right," and the fragrance of lilacs and rosemary told her whose voice it was. She closed her eyes in relief and drooped into the Guardian's arms, breathing deeply. She felt instant calm, the weariness and fear of the past two days washing away as if by a cool mountain stream. "There, it's all right." He fully embraced her. "You've had an awful fright, I can tell, but it's over now. I'm here."

Trig, still in the doorway, prevented the rune-covered door from closing. "What's going on? Who's fighting?"

"All those silly, childish people you used to travel with." The calming voice encouraged her to let go, find tranquillity with him. "Listen to them, arguing, fighting, never solving anything. Such a waste of time." Kyer felt him shake his head. "You've been through so much. Haven't you had enough? Is everything you've been through worth all this? Did I not warn you that you were in danger?"

"What are you talking about?" She lifted her head unwillingly from its resting place on his chest. The ink-black eyes bathed her in compassion.

"They don't know you're here, you know. They think you deserted them. They've just as much deserted you."

"But—"

The white face was bright with eagerness. "Come away with me, and leave all this madness behind."

"Away? Where?"

"To my home, of course. Let us go away, we two. They don't need you here." She began to think he might be right. "Besides," he went on, boyish excitement in his tone, "there is someone at home who wants to meet you."

Kyer gave him a quizzical look.

"She's been waiting a long time to see you again. Don't you think you ought not to keep her waiting any longer?"

"Who? I don't know who you mean." She peered up at him.

"Oh, you must hazard a guess."

"I don't like riddles."

The guardian clasped the hand that had released Trig's bridle. "No riddles. No strings. You owe me nothing. I am your Guardian, and I am here to help you. Why don't you come and meet her?"

"Who?" Kyer demanded.

"Your mother."

Kyer looked at him, dazed. "Della?" she asked stupidly.

"No, dear heart, your real mother. Come and meet her."

Janak roared in rage and got in his first attack swipe of the melee. Juggler crossed his swords in front to block him, but that left his flanks open for Phennil.

The winded elf came around quickly and leapt to his feet. Whipping his sword from its sheath, he pounced to where he was needed and slashed eagerly at Juggler's unprotected ribcage. The assassin sensed his intrusion at the last second and swung downward with the saw-toothed blade in his left hand, nicking Phennil's blade and sustaining only a trifling cut under his arm. He adjusted his fighting style to suit two challengers. His two blades flickered like fluttering leaves.

Phennil and Janak would have to work efficiently together if there was to be any hope of defeating this crazed man. And neither of them could afford an injury; if one fell, the other would soon follow.

"I hear the south is pleasant this time of year," Phennil said as brightly as he could between puffs of breath. He could not risk attempting eye contact with Janak for fear of losing it with Juggler. He could only hope that the dwarf would pick up on his hint. *Crash. Clang.* Juggler's weapons spun and darted, giving the impression of a swarm of wasps. Janak was taking a long time to think about what Phennil had said. Should he word it differently, or just make his move?

"Of course, you and I are polar opposites," Janak said, just as Phennil was about to give up. "Particularly now."

Phennil took the returned hint and hopped on his nimble elven feet to get in behind Juggler, directly opposite, or south, of Janak. Juggler would have a more difficult time defending himself if they could stay as separate as possible. The assassin tried to shift outside their circle and found himself teetering on the brink of the drop-off. It shook his concentration, and Janak managed a solid blow with his battle axe to Juggler's elbow. The sound of a light clink indicated the presence of armour underneath the assassin's jerkin, and though Juggler's arm seemed to vibrate momentarily with the jolt, the blade turned. Juggler swung round, away from the precipice, and forced the two friends to chase after him to regain their polar opposite positions. A cry could be heard from behind Janak, and Phennil cringed as he wondered what had happened. He could not afford a glance over Janak's shoulder. His left wrist had just been struck, and he clutched it to his middle.

Jesqellan learned quickly that Misty did not like to fight her opponents. She liked to torment them. Her duelling was like a folk dance, wherein the partners took turns performing fancy steps, each more complicated than the last. As the music rose to a fever pitch, so did the footwork and dips and twirls become faster and more breathtaking. But all the while she smiled.

After she so effortlessly deflected Jesqellan's lightning bolt, he braced himself. He was not expecting to suddenly feel something or somethings crawling up his bare legs under his Moabi robes. Hopping and shaking his legs and the brown cloth, he saw two scorpions drop onto the ground and scuttle away. The crawling sensation continued to climb upward beneath his robes. Jesqellan quickly drew the Dispel Illusions rod Val had given him and cast its spell. The sensation ceased. Sheathing the rod to save its final use, Jesqellan felt more puzzled than anything and looked at her as if she were mad. In answer, he used a simple Slowing spell, but with a blink and a toss of her curly black head, it blew away.

Misty set Jesqellan's robes on fire, and for a moment he panicked. But quickly gathering his wits, he dismissed her Illusion and pummelled her with Flying Fists. The first one caught her on the side of the head, but with a hand up, the next came back to clobber Jesqellan in the chest. He threw up his own barrier, and the rest bounced away into the trees.

She's going to block everything I throw at her, Jesqellan reasoned. He was hot from the physicality of the duel, but the internal heat of anger was working its way to the surface. This was not a real duel. And it made him hate her.

Jesqellan, momentarily dismissing magic, raised his quarterstaff and dealt her a true blow to the side of the head. So engrossed was she in the amusement of spell-casting that she did not expect a tangible weapon. She staggered and nearly fell.

As her eyes met his, he read both horror and terrifying rage.

"Fool," she sneered. She raised her hand.

Jesqellan summoned everything he could from his energy-cell staff, but he was not quick enough to shield her blow. With the speed of an arrow, she fired at him. His body seized up, as if he were wrapped in cobwebs. Still able to hear and see, his body was frozen solid, balancing on his bare feet, in danger of tipping over should someone bump him. Not content with just that, Misty hit him with blow after blow of her own Flying Fists. To the head, to the chest, to the gut. He fell, his head hitting the ground with an unavoidable crack. She kept them coming, like hard kicks with her boot. She remained motionless, her hand extended toward him, only her finger adjusting the aim of each blow. Pain, sharp and intense, shot through him with each contact. Ribs cracked, an eye swelled, bruises purpled. He could do nothing. Not shield himself, not cry out.

He wished he could close his eyes. He was helpless and completely at her mercy.

Kyer felt warmth radiating from the Guardian's encouraging smile. Her *real* mother? The clangs and cries of the battle were as if heard from under water. Fear, lack of food, lack of sleep had all taken their toll. Her head whirled and bobbed, as if she'd been on board a ship for days on end. Her brain felt fuzzy like wool. She smiled into his eager eyes, which only wanted an affirmative response before he would whisk her away to the blissful silence of his home and she would meet her mother. The woman who had carried her and birthed her. Named her. *Left me in a cornfield.*

Why had she done that? The question had plagued Kyer since Della and Gareth had first told the story of her arrival into their lives. Yet Kyer had never given a moment's consideration to what might have become of her real mother after they had parted. Why would she be with him? The implications of her mother having left her in a cornfield to go be with this man passed across her thoughts like wisps of cloud.

"Would I be free to come and go?" She recalled Kayme's similar offer.

"Of course. If you really wanted to." He sounded as if he thought it strange that she would.

"But what about—?" She struggled to see what was going on behind the pillar that separated her and her guardian from the melee.

"They won't miss you," he assured her apologetically. "They've carried on without you." He dismissed her former companions with a wave. "Wouldn't you rather meet your true mother, learn everything about yourself? Come. Live the life you were meant to live."

I left Hreth to learn this. That was the point of it all. And unlike Kayme, there were no strings attached.

All else was forgotten.

Kyer gazed up into her Guardian's kind, gentle face. "Yes, I'll go with you."

Kep did not fight like a gentleman. Derry preferred to but was not captain to Valrayker for being a gentleman. He was able to adjust his style to match any adversary's. The look on Kep's face altered swiftly from smugness to determination. Derry's blade swung and his feet danced—that skill being useful for pleasure and for business. Derry's own determination was fierce. Kep fought to defend himself, and possibly his honour, if he had nothing to do with stealing the antidote. Derry, on the other hand, battled not for his own life, but for Alon's. *Parry, slash, stab.* He released all his emotions from the past few days, his unfair treatment of his friend, and her loss.

Kep's determination changed to concern. His breaths came hard, and sweat coated his palms and ran down his face. Derry felt warm but it did not impede his progress. Finally, with an upward sweep, he flung Kep's blade above shoulder height and thrust his bastard sword into the opening. Kep cried out as he went down.

No time to wipe his blade, Derry spun around to see where he could help. Janak and Phennil were on the far side of the clearing with Juggler. Behind him, Derry could still hear Fredric and Hew.

Dear Goddess! Jesqellan lay on the dirt ground near him, his black face swelling and puffing with invisible blows. His body lurched and shifted with each kick. And yet he was static. Frozen.

Misty was on her knees in front of him. Her hand was poised, pointing at Derry's friend, juddering with the spells that flew out of it.

Derry instinctively did the only sensible thing. Weapon hurtling down, he cut off her hand.

Misty screamed, the throaty, rasping sound like charcoal scraping rock touched nerves all around the clearing. She staggered to her feet, moving dangerously close to the drop-off, gaping at the stub of her arm as blood gushed from it like a hot spring. Raising her horrified expression, her mouth twisted in fury, she met Derry's gaze.

Misty had another hand.

She directed it at Derry, fingers stiff and outstretched, and sent a surge of power through the air. Derry dropped his sword to clutch at the unseen hand that constricted his throat. He tried to twist away. Choking, gasping, he reeled, eyes bulging, begging for release. He dropped to his knees and knew he was about to die.

The Guardian looked as if he'd just learned he was a father. An enormous smile of joy spilled across the tall man's countenance. He gripped Kyer's hand. Just ahead, on the far side of the second pillar, a shimmering archway formed in the air in front of them. The archway itself was oddly familiar. Through it, a gust of chill, wintry air billowed, making her shiver, yet it incongruously carried a glorious medley of fragrance. Beyond the doorway she caught a glimpse of her new home: A humble little castle, more a stately manor, of pale grey stone with towers topping two of its corners jutted up next to a small, lily-dotted lake. The castle was surrounded by a voluminous flower garden. Greenery and blooms of a million colours and varieties poured over the walls of the parapet. She now understood why her Guardian always seemed to carry a multiplicity of scents with him. Her hand in his, he drew her toward the archway. *I'm about to meet my mother.* Excitement billowed inside her.

"Wait." She stopped.

"Kyer?"

"I need Trig."

"Of course." Her guardian smiled down at her with fathomless fondness, and she was bathed in warmth.

Giving his hand a squeeze, begging his indulgence just this last time, she let it slip out of hers, the fingertips' lingering contact sending a shiver of connection through her hands and up her arms. She turned back to fetch the animal who had been her companion for so many years. Transferring her sword to her left hand, she picked up the reins. "I couldn't leave you, boy." She led him forward and turned back to her new companion, a smile just beginning to open on her lips. She stepped onto the threshold of the doorway.

Some vague thing, a movement, a cry, a clang of steel, drew her awareness into the clearing. Just as her foot was about to step through the archway, she stopped.

Something was wrong there.

A castle and breathtakingly beautiful gardens sparkling in dewy morning sunshine lay just on the other side of that doorway. Peace.

But what was that? A scream.

She took a step toward the sound.

"Kyer." The Guardian's voice held a note of a plea. "No."

Wait, she thought but didn't speak aloud. She stepped out from behind the pillar.

Two men fought just to the left. She caught a glimpse of more fighting far on the right. Bodies strewn around. But she barely saw them. Not ten paces in front of her, at the edge of the clearing, nearly facing her directly, stood a woman.

A tall woman with dark curls framing a familiar face. The woman who had put her hand on Kyer's forehead after Fredric had spoken *her* language. That woman with her hand outstretched as if in the act of—

Derry.

Sword in both hands now, Kyer rushed forward. That woman was killing Derry.

"No!" she screamed.

Kyer rammed her sword straight through the black-haired assassin. Shocked, the woman let go of Derry and stared in terror at the monster that had flung itself at her. That was the only reaction she had time for.

The jolt of the connection drove the dark-haired woman over the side of the precipice.

And Kyer, still grasping her sword, went with her.

The Guardian paused. A flash of disappointment crossed his features. As he watched Kyer plough through the other woman and topple over the edge, he even felt a tiny jolt of anxiety.

Wait, he told himself sternly. *Just wait and see.*

He drew an object out of his cloak. It was flat, about the length of a woman's forearm, and wrapped in black cloth. He considered it, and its many uses, and swiftly tucked it into one of Trig's saddlebags.

He passed through the archway and was gone.

Twenty-Four
Though at Enormous Cost

P hennil and Janak hardly knew what had happened. They saw a figure hurtle toward Misty, screaming, a blade in hand, and both bodies pitched over the edge. Their reflexes didn't allow them to stop fighting. Juggler cried out as if he'd been mortally wounded, glanced at both his opponents, and dropped his weapons to his sides. Janak and Phennil were both mid-swing and couldn't avoid it. Juggler took two killing blows from opposite directions. Elf and dwarf stood panting and staring at each other over the bloody corpse. Then they finally awoke to the scene on the other side of the clearing.

Jesqellan on the ground, immobile and groaning. Derry on his knees, one hand on his throat and the other preventing his face from hitting the dirt. Fredric bleeding from a chest wound but standing. All Fredric's men strewn about the clearing, dead.

"What *was* that?" Janak finally voiced between breaths.

A horse whinnied and Phennil recognized Trig.

"Kyer?" In shock and disbelief he ran to the precipice to look down. "Oh, godsblood, Kyer."

Janak looked over and saw the narrowing crack between the doors to the Indyn Caves. He ran toward them just as they closed with a soft *phoom* of escaping air.

"Was she *in there*?" He hooked his thumb back at the doors, staring in shock at his companions.

"Derry." Phennil whirled around to check on the captain. "Derry, are you all right? C'mon, we've got to help her. She's down there." The elf helped Derry to raise himself so they were face-to-face.

Derry gulped hard a few times. "Oh, gods," he breathed. "It was Kyer. I thought I—but then—" The captain pushed himself upright and followed Phennil's gaze over the drop. At once he pivoted and, hesitating only a moment to meet Fredric's eye, stumbled down the path.

Phennil paused and glared at Fredric. "I suppose *that* somehow proves Kyer gave Alon the curse?" He followed Derry.

Janak scowled at Fredric. "Let's get busy. Make yourself useful." The dwarf knelt at Jesqellan's side to assess his friend's condition.

Fredric pressed his hand on his chest, nearly breathless with pain. Blood oozed out from between his fingers. He wanted to dash to the edge of the drop and see for himself. He hoped Derry would get to her in time.

If Kyer died, all hope of vengeance was gone.

Misty was dead. She had probably died before the two women had hurtled over the edge of the precipice. About a twenty-five-foot drop, though it wasn't sheer. The hill was steep, not quite a cliff. Derry spared no more than a passing thought on the perfidious assassin. It was Kyer he had his eye on. She had flown overtop of the dead woman and lay in a crumpled heap a few feet below. The physicker-adept could not tell at first glance whether she had survived the fall. Heart in his throat, he forgot his own near-death experience and knelt at her side, placing his two fingers at the base of her neck. He took a deep breath and bowed his head in a sigh of relief. There was a pulse, faint, but steady.

"Captain." Phennil knelt beside Derry. "Is she—?" The elf could not complete the question.

"What news?" called a voice from above. Derry and Phennil looked up to see Janak's bushy head, his forehead creased in anxiety, peering down from where Kyer had toppled.

"She's alive," Derry answered without delay to spare their worry. "She's badly wounded. I haven't identified her injuries. "Phennil," he held his anxiety in check, "we'll need a sledge, or . . . or a travois, if you please."

"Sure thing." Phennil turned away and Derry could already hear his elven tongue asking his friends, the trees, for their assistance.

Derry fell willingly into his physicker persona; dealing with the ailments of friends was less complicated from the distance of fact-gathering. Emotions could be more easily masked.

This time, though, it was hard. With every scratch, bruise, and bump he found, he was given a clearer picture of what had happened as the earth drew Kyer toward its merciless solidity. And the more serious injuries revealed themselves. Hands on her hilt as it jutted out of Misty's side, she'd let go one hand before they'd hit, but not the other. Her left wrist was broken. *Good thing her muscles are so strong; that will help it heal faster.* She had been impaled by her own pommel as her body collided with the ground, doing serious damage to the muscle tissue in her right shoulder, just outside the protection of her breastplate. *Will she ever wield a sword with the same strength?* She'd been thrown overtop of Misty and continued her rolling tumble, being scratched and battered by underbrush, and eventually hitting her head on the bole of a larch. A knock like that could take months to recover from. Her left leg lay with an unnatural rotation below her knee; Derry wasn't sure whether the break had occurred in the initial impact or after she'd flown over the assassin's dead body. *She might walk with a limp for the rest of her life if I can't set it properly.*

In spite of Derry's every effort to disallow his emotional connection to his friend, he realized that the droplets of moisture that kept appearing beneath him as he worked had come from his eyes. Jaw set, shoulders stiff, eyes narrowed with concentration as he made mental notes of everything he found, it couldn't be helped. The last words he'd spoken to Kyer had been unkind. And he knew now that if those were the last words he ever spoke to her, his own life would change dramatically.

He loosened her breastplate and gently ran his fingers along her ribs, checking for fractures. Something sharp poked his forefinger, and he yanked his hand out. His finger had been pierced, and a tiny droplet of blood oozed out. He pressed it to stop the bleeding then gingerly lifted Kyer's armour to locate the cause. He soon came across an item that twigged his memory and sent a shiver up his spine. A perfectly formed white rose still lay concealed next to her heart, where she had promised Kayme to keep it. What kind of magic kept a rose fresh after so many weeks of being squashed inside her armour? It was firm and fresh as if it had just been plucked.

Derry sat among the undergrowth and sniffed the flower. It smelled as any other rose would. Yet it obviously was not. Why had Kayme wanted her to keep it? Was it affecting her in some way?

Why would Kayme want to harm Kyer? And why would he not have done it when he had the chance?

After brief reflection, Derry tucked the rose in his own pouch, though he trembled. When Jesqellan was feeling better, the captain would have the mage try to disclose its magic.

Jesqellan! Derry got back to work, remembering that the mage would require his assistance as soon as Misty's spell wore off. When he carried on with his assessment of Kyer's ribs, his hand fell upon another puzzling item. Cloth this time, crumpled. He carefully drew it out from where she had obviously shoved it in haste. A sack, such as one might use to carry a loaf and a small round of cheese for a quick lunch when working in the fields. He held it gingerly in both hands, as if afraid something might pop out at him. Not much weight to it. Holding it in one hand, he used the other to squeeze the bottom of it, trying to guess at its contents. It yielded easily to the pressure of his fingertips. Finally, the captain opened the top of the sack just a slit and peered in.

Derry was a man of less imagination than many, having trained virtually his entire life to know wrong from right, false from true, fanciful from factual. But a few of those facts seemed to fall into place like seeds from a skilled farmer's sowing hand. Kyer had not been there when they'd arrived. She suddenly appeared from the direction of the caves themselves. She had left him two nights ago, travelling alone; plenty of time to get here. She possessed a sack containing a small amount of the finest glittery powder. One might describe it as . . . dust.

Kyer had done it again.

Making her as comfortable as he could, he leaned down to her ear. "Hang on, Kyer. Please."

He started to race up the switchback trail but stopped short before reaching the bend in the path when he remembered that someone had stolen all their ingredients. *I'd better keep Kyer's success quiet for a while.*

He located Phennil and the two of them hastened to fashion a means of transporting their friend.

Major Gilvray sat at his desk, quill poised to write yet another stilted line in his letter. But his mind had wandered. Laying aside the quill, he leaned back in his chair and brushed his fingers on the flat pouch that held the stone. The key to the Indyn Caves. How he had always wondered about them! What was inside? What had the dark elves left behind? Marcus Flemming's voice reverberated in his thoughts from the night he showed him the key. *You should try it before the colonel gets back.* What a good idea.

Gilvray glanced at the portrait of his wife. He flushed guiltily. *I'm coming home soon, princess.* Why, oh why had he given in to temptation? Why did that damned girl have to show up just before his home leave? The night before last, she'd brushed her hair across his torso, scratched her fingernails down his back, squeezed him with her— He'd need more than two weeks to recover from her. *Shit.* He did not want to go home with that girl in his thoughts. She'd left an impression deeper than the runes carved into the stone. He got up and went outside, escaping the reproachful image of his pretty wife.

Acknowledging the sentry at his door, he stepped around the corner and leaned against the building, breathing deeply. He opened the pouch.

The stone felt cool in his fingertips. The complex etchings were even more pleasing to the eye in the light of day. The gems trimming the edge sparkled, and he held up the key to see the light shine through the coloured stones. *Did they leave behind any other treasures like this?* Jewels, pottery . . . magical items? Wouldn't his wife squeal with delight if he could present her with such a gift?

A gift like that would make up for his being away such a long time. And other things.

He stepped around the cabin. "Corporal."

"Sir?"

"Fetch Lieutenant Flemming and Major Chadha, and then you can help me pack."

"Pack, sir?"

"Yes, Corporal. I'll be going away for a few days."

With the heat of the afternoon, Skimnoddle and Harley moved out of the sun, under the mottled shade of the aspens at the base of the mountain. They figured the rest of the company had been gone several hours, although they stopped keeping track once they began playing music. Skimnoddle handed Harley his little drum and taught the man some basic rhythms to play. The halfling played his flute, and they shared old favourites. Harley had a good singing voice and a natural feel for the drum.

Mealtime rolled around and Harley traded some spicy sausage for one of Skimnoddle's sweet dried apples. Skimnoddle insisted on letting all of their food items sit in his little pot with the lid on for a few minutes, even though they weren't using a fire.

"Why?" Harley asked.

Skimnoddle squatted. Holding the lid on fast, he gave the pot a little shake and wiggled his eyebrows mysteriously at his companion.

"Is this some bizarre custom among your people?" Harley stretched his legs out to cross his ankles. "Or have you spent too much time in the sun?"

Finally Skimnoddle removed the lid and handed Harley his lunch. The man turned his bread over a few times, looking for irregularities. Finding none, he took a hesitant bite. The two returned to their shady spot beneath the aspens.

"The saucepan has a unique feature," Skimnoddle revealed at last. "I've never told the others of my party this, but it is a Healing pot. Mild, you understand, but after eating this, you will perhaps . . . find you have more energy than bread, meat, and fruit would normally give you. As if you'd slept for an hour or so, you might say. If you had any wounds, depending on their severity, you might find that any pain had eased somewhat or blood might clot more readily. For instance."

"That's pretty neat."

Skimnoddle glanced at him sharply then looked away. They fell into a discomfited silence for the first time since their friends had left.

"Uh . . ." Harley began after a moment. "So why haven't you told your friends about the pot?"

Skimnoddle tilted his head as though he'd forgotten Harley was there. "Hm? Oh, the pot. Yes." He shrugged. "Quite simply, it hasn't come up in conversation. I mean one doesn't open a chat with, 'by the way, my cooking pot is magic, you know,' now does one?"

"No, I suppose not."

"I'm sure there are many things about yourself you have not shared with your friends. Am I right?"

"Are you kidding?" Harley scoffed then softened. "I guess that's a difference right there between you and me. These people I work with?" He hitched a thumb in the direction of the path they'd taken. "They aren't my friends. I hang with them right now because Ronav was looking for people and I'd just lost everything. You don't say no when you're in a position like that and someone makes you an offer. I don't trust any of 'em. Apart from following orders, it's every one for themself. Any one of 'em would sell me down the river if it meant more of something for them." He tossed his apple core into the bushes. "Seems like just the opposite with your group."

Skimnoddle thought a moment. Then he nodded. "Yes, yes, it is."

"How'd a fellow like you link up with them?"

Skimnoddle's smile broadened and he looked at Harley with a shrug. "I had nothing. You don't say no when you're in a position like that and someone makes you an offer." The halfling leaned against his tree and contemplated the contrast in their situations. He had been a member of this party only since they returned from their last mission. He did not make friends easily. No one in the party was a confidant. Yet Skimnoddle knew without question that his companions would watch his back just as unfailingly as he'd watch theirs.

Instinct told him that the troubles the group had experienced on this journey, the suspicion and doubt, were not typical of the way they related to each other. Some strange mood had settled over them all, himself included. Janak and Phennil were both stout companions, and Kyer ... Funny how Harley had said his magic cooking pot was "pretty neat." That had sounded so much like something Kyer would say.

Oh, he wasn't really in love with her. He extolled her beauty and virtue because he delighted in the incongruity of complimenting a woman who did not wish to be complimented. His words always grated on her, and he loved the reaction. He had the feeling that she otherwise wouldn't notice him at all. He also praised her beauty because it was true.

"So, what happened to Kyer?" Harley asked. Skimnoddle was startled, thinking for a split-second that he might have spoken aloud.

"I guess the long and short of it is that she and Derry had an argument."

"Derry won, then?"

Skimnoddle paused, screwing his face up in thought. "No, I would have to say that Kyer won. We don't know where she went, but Derry thinks she might have gone back to see Kayme."

As if in response, they heard the sounds of footsteps tromping down the pathway above. The two companions stood, one several feet taller than the other, and looked each other in the eye. It was as if both understood it was time to go back to opposite camps, yet neither had a wish to.

Skimnoddle stuck out his hand. Harley clasped it. Then they started back to their own sides.

The sound of a horse's whinny from the direction of the trail caught their attention. They'd left the horses below. Whose was it? Skimnoddle's bow was in his hands, and Harley readied his broadsword. When Phennil emerged from the path, leading an animal that Skimnoddle instantly recognized as Kyer's horse, he cried out and tucked his weapon back into its sheath on his back. His little legs flew him over to where his beloved rattled along on a makeshift travois pulled by Derry, and followed by a stumbling, drastically shrunken collection of battle-broken warriors.

Harley was right behind him.

"Where did she—?" Skimnoddle began. "What happened?" Even he knew the gravity of the circumstances would not support his usual histrionics.

"Where is everyone else?" Harley put in, looking sharply to the one and only remaining member of his party.

Fredric's face was unreadable. "Dead."

Skimnoddle searched the faces of his companions and could only make out that something unthinkable had occurred.

Derry spoke no word but, with Janak's assistance, gently lowered the travois and settled Kyer to the ground near the firepit.

"Path was too narrow to connect it to the horse," Janak explained.

A bruised and battered Jesqellan hauled himself to Derry's horse and ruffled through his belongings to bring out the physicker's kit.

Phennil, relatively unscathed in appearance, finally explained. "You may or may not have noticed, Skimnoddle, but when we reached the caves, I discovered that my ingredients had been stolen. So had everyone's. You can see the result." He waved his arm broadly at the dwindled numbers of travellers.

Skimnoddle knew better than the rest that the collection of precious items had been stolen. It was too early to reveal his own news. He must wait for things to play out a bit longer. His experience as a performer served him well.

"And Kyer?" he pressed, masking his knowledge behind sincere anxiety. "Where did she come from?"

The elf fought back emotion as he outlined Kyer's sudden appearance out of virtually nowhere followed by her pitching herself over the edge.

"What about you?" Harley turned to Fredric, who stood silently to one side.

"I didn't steal the stuff, if that's what you mean." The strength of Fredric's voice still gave evidence of his background. "But it's obvious one of my company did." He looked pointedly back at the last one of his retainers. "I care just as much about the lady's survival as these people, so I knew whose side I had to fight for. And will continue to fight for, so if you know anything at all about the theft of Alon's remedy, I suggest you speak up right now."

Harley stood his ground, but surprise showed in his eyes. "Me? On my last breath, I swear I don't know anything about it."

Fredric's gaze sharpened to an acute warning. "You had better hope I never find that out to be false."

Skimnoddle stepped between them, his tiny figure threatening, though one man could easily have attacked the other over his head. "Or what would you do, oh disgraced former captain of the Shael Castle guard? You may take on that tone with this, my friend and comrade, but do not forget that you yourself are under some heavy scrutiny, having many questions to answer on your own behalf." *Not my best effort, but effective nonetheless.* Fredric blanched and backed off. "Now," he went on, "my love lies wounded. I would fain end this injudicious inculpation and elicit all down to the finest minutia of her trauma, so I may adopt a concordant emotional response."

... *my dear, lovely girl, I know all about your mission, and about you. Did I not say I am your Guardian?... Kyer Halidan.... You killed Ronav Malachite in Nennia. What's more, you enjoyed it. One thing more ... a particular magical gift you have.... your Guardian ... white stone.*

... *magical gift ... magical gift*

White stone.

Kayme's voice ... saying ... something. A warning.

Pain.

Kyer screamed. Derry thanked Aidan that she was unconscious. Setting broken limbs was not a straightforward procedure, and Kyer had several.

Harley's voice drifted down to him. "How shall we deal with the dead?" Derry did not shift focus from his work on his patient. "My only concern right now is with the living. The dead can wait." The captain half expected Harley to take exception to his attitude, but the man surprised him.

"Fair enough," he said. "Can I hold her knee so it's easier for you to set the break?"

Derry didn't bother taking the time to register surprise but shifted to make room for his unexpected assistant. Harley knelt next to Kyer's hip and braced her knee while Derry firmly pulled the lower leg down and eased it back into position. Kyer's gut-wrenching moans made Derry sweat. Phennil had produced perfect splints, and Harley helped Derry bind them to Kyer's leg and arm. Harley checked for her pulse on either end of each break, determining there was so far no damage to her blood vessels. Derry adjusted and dressed Kyer's shoulder after applying his salve. Then he sat back on his heels, his hands resting on his knees.

He'd done his best. The muscles would heal in time, though it would be a while before her sword arm was back to the strength she had toiled so long to build. He had to hope for the best with the broken bones and trust to the goddess that Kyer wouldn't end up with a permanent limp.

Harley had already moved on to Fredric, cleaning the wound in his chest. His work was exceptionally thorough, Derry noted.

"Do you have the tools for stitching?" Harley asked. "This looks to need three or four. And a grade two healing potion, if you have any."

Derry checked over the wound and glanced at Harley. "That's right."

Then he hesitated. "Can you—? Are you able—?"

Harley smiled. "I can administer a healing potion, but I'm afraid my skills don't go far enough to do stitches."

"All right, then, can you take care of Jesqellan?"

Harley nodded and went to work on the mage. Janak and Phennil ate a bite or two, and once Derry had the physicking under control, they hurried with Harley and Skimnoddle up the mountain to care for the dead before nightfall.

And at last, at long last, Derry the physicker-adept, who would have died by nontactile strangulation if not for the woman who lay moaning near him, finally sat down to rest. To rest, to eat, and to wonder many things: Who had stolen the ingredients from each of them? What was the purpose of the white rose? How had Kyer gotten into the caves when he had the rune pattern?

Derry felt for the young man, Harley. Apart from his leader, he was the only remaining member of his travelling party. How did he feel about that? Derry wouldn't have blamed him if he feared his own throat would be cut. It was impossible not to notice, though, that Skimnoddle and he appeared to have taken a shine to each other while the rest of the group had been up the mountain. And he clearly had some background in physicking.

Thick, scattered clouds darkened the sky, and the flicker from Derry's small fire seemed to be sucked into the night only a couple of feet above the ground. The captain had thought he was not sleepy, but he must have dozed off, for now he was roused by the sound of footsteps. He fumbled half-heartedly for his weapon. The clouds had parted to welcome the light of the waxing moon. His patients rested on the outskirts of the firelight.

"Job's done, Captain," Janak said.

Derry sat up, blinking, and nodded. "Where?"

"We found this handy cave with big doors, so we opened them and tossed the bodies in," Harley said cheerily.

Skimnoddle snorted and though Derry was slumped practically double with exhaustion, he chuckled quietly.

"No, seriously," Harley said, "we found a spot in the woods to the left of the doorway."

The three gravediggers settled in nearby. Harley stood awkwardly, the flames lighting him from below. Skimnoddle answered the unvoiced question.

"Harley, my good man, I do believe you are indeed one of us now. No sense your sleeping in a separate camp." And he waved him to fetch his bedroll and belongings.

Derry awakened immediately, taking advantage of the distance. "Did he give you any clue about who might have taken our goods?"

"No," Janak replied.

"Janak and I were thinking that with the other group dead, mostly anyway, we're free and clear to search through their stuff and find it," Phennil said.

"Exactly what I thought," Derry said.

"I have a hard time believing it was him, though." Phennil nodded in Harley's direction, though they could barely see his outline in the moonlight.

"I suspect everyone until—" Derry stopped himself as Harley approached.

"I've been thinking." Harley dumped his pile on the ground and slumped next to it. "The only way to prove I didn't take your stuff, and to find out who did, is to search through all the dead folks' things. Whoever took it had to put it somewhere."

Skimnoddle raised a hand dramatically. "Enough. I can keep you in suspense no longer. I know unerringly who has the medicinal elements we have worked so hard to obtain."

"You do?" Derry said.

"Who has them?" Phennil leaned forward toward the halfling.

Skimnoddle smirked. "I have." And when his companions stared at him, speechless, he added, "Never foreseeing the fate of the culprit, fully anticipating the individual's return, I took the liberty of stealing them back this afternoon."

Phennil whooped with joy and leapt to his feet, scooping the halfling up with him and swinging him around.

"Where was it?" he cried.

"Who had it?" Janak said at the same time.

Derry just sighed deeply.

Fredric and Jesqellan stirred. The mage rolled over, the dose of pain-relieving tea holding him to sleep, but Fredric raised himself onto an elbow to find out what the excitement was about.

When Phennil placed him on solid ground again, the halfling straightened his tunic and belt in a dignified manner, crossed his ankles, and lowered himself to a seated position.

"So, where was the stuff? Out with it, man." Phennil leaned down to slap him on the shoulder.

"Firstly, I shall tell you that my own supply of items was not taken, yet by the means of certain tricks I know and will not share with you, the attempt upon my person did not go undetected. This led me to believe that the rest of you would have suffered the same fate and likely did not possess the skills to avoid such a violation. Applying my skills at speculation and deduction, I was able to conjecture the identity of the guilty party. My suspicion was confirmed when I performed the search and found the goods."

"That's all wonderful, but who was it?" Phennil said.

"I'm sure you will not be surprised. It was Misty."

Many comments and reactions followed. Derry found himself looking over at Fredric, who stared blankly into the air in front of his face. When his eyes met Derry's, the captain said, "What do you suppose Kyer knew about that?"

Fredric's brows contracted. "I believe they were in on it together, and somehow Misty and Juggler went against the plan."

"And just what do you know about it yourself?" Janak said.

Fredric straightened slowly as the accusation sank in. "What are you saying? That *I* was a party to all this?"

"It isn't unreasonable," Phennil said. "Misty and Juggler were under your command."

Fredric shook his head, his hand spread out in his defence. "You don't understand about those two," he quietly pleaded. "They worked for themselves alone. They followed along with the rest of us because it suited them at the time and for no other reason."

"I have just one question," Harley said, clearly relieved to be out from under the veil of suspicion. "How, by the Hammer God, did you steal the stuff when I was sitting here the whole time?"

Skimnoddle smiled as if to say, "I'm afraid you'll never know."

The excitement ebbed and the group fell silent again. Janak made an apologetic grunting noise. "Bringing us 'round to reality, there hardly seems a point in having the rest of the ingredients if we don't have the dust from up there." He jerked his thumb up the mountainside. "I had a look at those doors, and even with the rune pattern, there's no way of knowing how to get in there."

"Does our sly little magician have any ideas?" Phennil nudged Skimnoddle, who shrugged.

"It won't be necessary," Derry said softly and rose, his boots hardly making a sound on the dirt ground as he moved over to Kyer. He knelt next to her agonized body and felt an ache in his chest as he observed the lines of pain on her forehead, despite his heaviest dose of tea. He tried to brush away those lines with the palm of his hand, but she merely spouted a small gasp of breath in response. The lines remained. He carefully slipped his hand inside her armour where he'd left the sack and drew it out.

Only when he turned around did he become aware that all his friends had been watching him the whole time. Assuming his usual businesslike air, he returned to the fire, cradling the sack in one hand.

"There." He held it out. "Kyer joined us from inside the caves. She had already been successful, though at enormous cost." He stopped talking, for fear of tears spilling over.

Twenty-Five

Only Time Would Tell If He Was Right

Gilvray estimated they would arrive at the Indyn Caves by late tomorrow afternoon. They'd left around suppertime the day before, heading south at first. Major Carlo Chadha had capable command of the outpost while Gilvray was off on his errand "to ensure that the raiders had not returned to the Black Mountains." Chadha had objected at first. Anyone else could have taken the errand. Gilvray insisted it had been his responsibility last winter and, therefore, his to follow up. Chadha appeared to believe him. They slept when the moon was high and altered their direction to due west in the morning.

Lieutenant Marcus Flemming had agreed to come along. He was the only other one who knew about the key and the real purpose of the errand. It was Flemming's suggestion that had prompted Gilvray to come on the journey. *Only fair to include him.* They'd brought a few other riders with them, who had sworn not to reveal the true location of the major's errand.

Gilvray patted the pouch at his side. He didn't know how the key worked, but he was sure that between him and Flemming, they'd figure it out. *And then . . .* He smiled. Such a gift he would have for his lady! She would be so happy with it, and so happy to see him. He would forget his minor indiscretion as he bathed in the light of her joy.

They had two weeks until Colonel Greenburg was due back. Plenty of time.

Crabgrass blades scratched the mage's legs, and grasshoppers jumped free of his bare feet. He plodded alongside Kyer's travois, which had been adjusted so Trig could pull it, and studied the lines on her face. She seemed to feel no relief in spite of Derry's efforts.

Jesqellan had reported his wellness that morning and they'd made ready to head south at once. From the six horses left by Fredric's dead companions, the company took what supplies they could use, then Jesqellan spoke to the animals, directing them north to Seaview, where they would find good stabling. He felt better after one night. Kyer, on the other hand . . . The magical aura still emanated from her like ripples in a lake. Part of him wanted to demand that the horses be stopped so he could search through her belongings, her clothes, her pouches and pockets, to find the sources of magic that felt like heat from a fire. Jesqellan could not sort through all the confusion of thoughts and doubts. He rubbed a palm on his bald head and clutched his staff. *I need to meditate.*

Why, if Kyer wanted to ensure her plot to kill Alon Maer was carried out, did she go to such lengths to acquire the rune pattern? Why, if Kyer *wanted* Alon to die, did she enter the caves and find the dust?

Alternatively, why, if she had nothing to do with Alon's illness, did she know about the snake necklace?

If Kyer could Gate, as Fredric had said—and all evidence pointed to the truth of that—why had she not told them? *Because it is evidence of her culpability.*

Jesqellan bristled. How could Kyer, a farm girl from northern Heath, possess such a skill?

The question of *how* Kyer had managed to enter the caves was one that

Jesqellan chose to block out. There were simply too many mysteries surrounding the girl.

The mage had doubts about Fredric in light of recent events. But his doubts about Kyer were stubborn and would be less easily washed away.

Jesqellan stepped quickly ahead, so he would not have to walk next to her.

Gilvray's estimation of travel time was only a little off. Being away from his command duties at the outpost brought on the joy of freedom, and he hadn't pushed his men. Home leave beckoned, wherein true freedom would be his. Why not celebrate and get into the spirit early? So when they stopped to rest, and one of his men pulled out a jug of spirits, they had partaken.

Nightfall saw the company arrive at the foot of the Indyn Hills. It was a little later than he'd hoped but no matter. They would ascend the path in the morning.

They'd padded the travois with her blankets to make it as comfortable as possible. There was not much else they could do. She was strapped in with her own belt and sash to keep her from being flung out, or sliding off the end. Their journey would take them at least another three weeks at this rate, probably closer to a month, and Derry was worried. In spite of his efforts in setting Kyer's broken bones, he was certain there would be some permanent damage, which was the reason he had decided against solidifying them with a healing potion at this time. Jesqellan was still too unwell after his own injuries to try taking some of her pain through his Transference spell. The mage argued that even if he performed the spell it would have so little an effect on the injured woman it was not worth the time it would then take Jesqellan to recover enough to travel. The company had debated returning to Seaview for help, but the need to acquire the final ingredient, and to get the cure to Alon Maer was too great, and they decided to press on.

Too many difficult decisions! the captain thought ruefully. Then scolded himself. *You wanted this. This is what a knight does.*

A day and a half south across the grassland they entered a scrubby pine forest that filtered the light but not the dusty heat. The pass through the mountains was at least another full day away. There was still so great a distance to the houses of healing at Bartheylen Castle!

They had tried to force feed Kyer broth but it had made her ill, and she let out a groan as they tipped her on her left side. Derry hated to increase her pain, but they could not risk her choking on her own vomit. She actually opened her eyes just then, and Derry smiled at her encouragingly, though he couldn't be sure she saw him. It seemed that in these more wakeful moments, the pain was too much and she slid back into the painless bliss of unconsciousness. She was able to keep the tea down better than the broth, so he'd stick to that. It did little to ease her discomfort but it kept her sleeping, and was better than nothing.

Derry frowned and stowed the waterskin with the remaining tea on Kyer's horse.

"I've been thinking, Captain."

Phennil's elven footfalls made not the slightest whisper on the dry pinecones and needles that crunched beneath Derry's feet. The voice drew Derry out of his worry.

"What about?" he said, with no curiosity.

"About the last ingredient. The sap from the Tree of Life. You have to take it so slowly with Kyer. Why don't I head southeast and collect the sap? Then I'll meet up with you further down the road."

Derry agreed that it was a good idea, and presented it to the group.

"I'll go with you," said Fredric.

"And so will I." Janak eyed Fredric with poorly disguised suspicion.

Derry had to admit he shared the dwarf's sentiment.

"All right," Derry did some quick calculations of distance and geography in his head. The mountain range to the south of where they now stood was a V shape, one side of which extended northwest all the way to Burns' Gulf. The other extension culminated in the very place where the party had become ill so many days ago. In the crux of the V lay the Tree of Life, protected on three sides by mountains. "But you'll have to backtrack all the way to the pass. Is there much point?"

Slyness crinkled the corners of Phennil's mouth. "You do remember I am a product of the Guarded Realm, don't you, Captain? And my parents *are* lady and lord of the province next door."

"Ah," Derry nodded in understanding. "All right. We will continue directly southward. Once you have the sap, meet us . . . where?"

"How about the eastern tip of the Bolivar Chasm? Do you know it?"

"Good. If we reach it and you're not there, we'll leave a mark. When you arrive, you'll know we've passed it and you can catch us up. If there's no mark, wait for us there."

"Excellent," Phennil agreed. "Leave the double-dagger symbol, and we'll know it's your mark."

"Captain."

Derry turned to Harley as he nudged his horse over to Phennil's.

"With your leave, I'd like to join them." Harley cast a quick but pointed glance at Fredric before returning his attention to the captain.

Derry managed to hold a neutral expression while doubt played dice with his instincts. Was the young man daring him? The captain did some more calculations, this time on what he knew of each individual's skills. Could he, Jesqellan and Skimnoddle adequately defend themselves from possible brigands without Harley? Balance that with Phennil's situation.

Could the elf and Janak stand up to Fredric on their own? Further to that, if Harley proved to still be in Fredric's camp, could the elf and dwarf hang on to the upper hand? Derry saw something in Harley's intense gaze. Was it a dare? Or was it pleading? A look over at Skimnoddle decided it.

The halfling gave the impression that he was paying no attention, but had pulled out a coin. As Derry watched, he tucked it into one fist and blew through it. When he opened the hand, the coin was gone. Then he leaned over and drew the coin out of his pony's ear. Then he began the process again. *Illusions are everywhere. The truth can be hidden, right before your eyes.*

Derry breathed in the hot parched air. *I have to follow my instinct.* "Yes. Join them."

Harley bowed his head.

The trees thinned and the party emerged from the sparse woods, and the envoys prepared to separate. After checking their supplies, and making sure they had an extra waterskin to carry the sap, they waved farewell and veered off to the southeast to find the Tree of Life, the sun still high but leaning casually toward the west.

Perhaps after we link up with them, I'll send them on to Bartheylen Castle, Derry thought. He and a couple of others could continue the plodding journey with Kyer, but the main objective must still be to get the ingredients to Alon Maer as swiftly as possible. Oh, such a great distance still lay between them and their destination!

"How long do you suppose it will take them?" Jesqellan asked.

"I'd say about three days to get there." Derry stared in the direction of their destination. "Phennil seems to know another way out. Another three, maybe, to get to the chasm? But we haven't even considered the other protections surrounding the Tree."

"Magical?"

"Some of them, yes," Derry said. "Admittedly I don't even know for sure. The Tree is the very subject the Realm Guards are watching over, and I don't believe for a moment they would leave it wide open."

"Mayhap I ought to have gone with them." Jesqellan watched their departing comrades, who had already galloped into the distance, well out of earshot. "They could conceivably need my assistance."

"There is soundness in what you say," Derry replied from atop Donnagill's high back. "However speed is of the essence, and I needn't point out that your footsteps more closely match the speed of the travois than their horses. Besides, we will certainly need your assistance."

Jesqellan looked up at him from the ground his bare feet trod. The mage smiled and shrugged. It was hard for his friend to admit weakness, and Derry admired his acceptance of it this time. The situation was too grave to toy with.

"Speaking of which," Jesqellan said, "Skimnoddle has been guiding Trig and his cargo for quite some time. I ought to fall back and take his place."

At the head of the group, Derry was left alone with his thoughts—an internal struggle he'd been avoiding. Derry twisted in the saddle to see Skimnoddle's bow to the mage as the latter took hold of Trig's reins. The halfling trotted back and mounted his pony with the swiftness born of experience. Derry smiled to himself, remembering the trouble he'd had at the start of the trip. He recalled Kyer's disparaging look as the halfling wound up backwards in the saddle. It struck him suddenly how long this negative sentiment had been growing. Had he been carrying this ill feeling toward his friend since way back then? He glanced down at Donnagill's black mane, matted from lack of care. The day they left, he'd stood combing it through his fingers, soothing the beast's fretting. He had been angry at Kyer since before they'd left Shael.

They'd all been emotional when they returned from the previous mission. It had been a difficult time for them all. And on top of it, they'd learned of Alon Maer's illness. Kyer had surprised him by being the first to volunteer for this mission; he had never understood it, frankly, and she hadn't exactly been forthcoming. For his own part, he'd opened up to her: he'd confided in her his disappointment in not being awarded his knighthood, and what did she do? She brushed him off and snapped at him.

Wait. No she hadn't.

Derry watched a hawk circle off to the west, pinpointing its prey far below. Derry understood what the graceful bird must feel like; his mind circled his troubles in the same way.

He was wrong. Kyer had not snapped at him for confiding in her. Just the opposite. He remembered her kind, reassuring tone as she told him he *had* impressed Val, that the duke simply had not had time . . . He pictured again the scene in the stairwell at Shael Castle. The opposite. He had snapped at her. Worse, in fact.

Val hadn't given him a knighthood, and he had blamed Kyer for it. Why? Because he hadn't forgiven her for killing Ronav. More than that, it had offended his sensibilities that she had challenged his leadership by disobeying an order. His confidence had quaked. She always seemed to know her own mind; Derry was ever second-guessing himself, and he envied her.

Gradually, continually, the gap created in those short days at Shael Castle had widened. He recalled asking Jesqellan to be his second on this mission, the smug tone with which he had asked, knowing Kyer was within earshot. Derry had grown so distant from Kyer that he was no longer able to see her clearly. The blame for the distance lay with him alone. He had taught her not to trust him. And he had been all too happy for the excuse to not trust her. *She cannot be the enemy.*

Donnagill plodded between the bushes and torchweed, with their tall candle-like red flowers. Tiny black flies perched like sentries at their tops, then disappeared down among the greenery, protecting their homes from the parade of travellers. Kyer lay on the travois behind Trig, but Derry didn't need to see her. Her face was etched in his mind.

Her ardent determination as she volunteered for the mission. Her kind smile as she assured him he deserved a knighthood. Her near hysteria when they found her the morning after she'd followed Fredric. The taunting smile as she'd stood on the porch in Seaview, just before going off with young Tod. The profound hurt and anger as he'd accused her outside the army encampment. And now, agony and helplessness.

Each image of his friend flitted through Derry's thoughts, and scraped out his heart. So many facets to her passions, and how easy to misread them. In the short time he'd known her, she'd become the best friend he had besides Valrayker. They'd been through more than most friends experienced in a lifetime. And yet lately, anger and mistrust had replaced the respect and affection they'd built. How solid was the foundation of such a short acquaintance? Would he ever be able to undo the damage he had done and stitch the rent in their friendship? What if she didn't survive this terrible journey?

Derry felt sick at the thought. He needed to ask her forgiveness. If he couldn't do that, he wouldn't be able to live with himself. *I must get her safely to Bartheylen Castle so she can be healed so—I can speak to her again.*

Leagues upon leagues remained in the journey. The pass would not be easy, then on to the chasm. Beyond that was at least a six-day ride to the border from the Guarded Realm into West Equart, and that was for a healthy rider. With Kyer on the travois, it would take longer. And after that . . . Derry didn't even want to think about it. As he absently steered Donnagill around a series of rocks and boulders, he heaved a sigh. *It's just too far!*

He choked back a sob and thought of the other thing that had been on his mind.

The white rose.

She'd promised Kayme she'd keep it close to her heart. And yet, since it was in her possession, she'd been trapped underground in an earthquake and hit in the back with an arrow. She was accosted by Fredric. She'd become moody and preoccupied, as if some dilemma were gnawing at her. She'd even fallen off her horse. And now this terrible fall. Was the rose the source of Kyer's troubles?

At first light, Ryerson Gilvray's mind was set on climbing the path. But as they prepared breakfast, one of his men alerted him. In the darkness of their arrival, they had not seen the remains of someone else's campfire. It was cold but only a day or two old. Anxiety pressed its fingers across his shoulders.

Gilvray posted two men at the foot of the hills, sending them to patrol the base of the mountain to the north and south. Marcus Flemming accompanied him, of course, along with two others.

They plodded up the path in the close morning heat. Excitement built in Gilvray's gut with each step closer to his goal. When he reached the top of the switchback path, he paused. The plant that crossed in front of them normally opened for them to pass. This time it blocked their way. Gilvray had never visited the doors without the colonel and did not know the trick to get rid of the plant.

There was a feeling of pressure on the side of his head, and his thoughts were penetrated by the *voice* of the treyurne. He nearly cried out in surprise. At its request, Gilvray pulled out the key, and after what was apparently a moment of puzzled thought, the plant pulled back its thorny tendrils. He walked forward.

The air was motionless, soundless. As if a glass dome had been placed overtop of the clearing, it had the appearance of being outdoors but without the rustle of a leaf or a sigh of wind. Something wasn't right. The dirt ground was dotted with tufts of grass, with tree roots, and rocks jutting through. It was hard packed in places, untouched since the last rain, yet loosened in others, as if it had been stirred. It looked so . . . tidy. The men fanned out within the area. *Not stirred, raked.* The same effect as when someone cleaned up after . . . Gilvray crouched and toyed his finger in the dry dirt. *Aha.* Droplets of blood, clumsily covered over, as if in haste. It wasn't long before more signs were found, including a shriveled aspen tree and crushed bushes where it looked like someone had fallen over the edge. *Who?*

Gilvray shook his head. He was mystified and more than a little concerned. Who had been here? And where had they gone? Gilvray wiped his palms on his trousers as he scouted around the clearing. How did they get past that treyurne? No one was authorized to be here, not even himself, in truth. This did not look good. *The doors.* He headed toward them. "Flemming, you two, check over the rest of the clearing."

"Sir."

Gilvray stepped hesitantly through the gap between the two pillars. The dusty, sandy dirt felt as though there were solid rock beneath it, like a front porch for the doors. He gazed up at the excruciatingly complex design of runes on the door. They seemed to crawl around the stone, even as he stared at them, like ants around their nest. Pulling out the key, Gilvray held it up and compared its design to the multitude of etchings on the door. Finding a match was utterly hopeless. He leaned against the pillar and stared at the ground, thinking.

He stared at the ground. His eyes came into focus. He stared at the ground, and a crease formed in his forehead. What he saw puzzled him. He replaced the precious key in its pouch and slowly knelt on the chalky dust ground of the threshold. Reaching out his hand, he traced with his finger in the air above . . . a footprint?

Several. One set. Coming and going. *Into and out of the Indyn Caves.* As well as what could be the prints of one horse's shoes. A second, larger set of prints on the north side of the door.

"Major!" It was Flemming calling from the other end of the clearing. Gilvray didn't look. "Yes?" *Someone got in . . .*

"What do you make of this?"

"What is it?" *Who could have—?*

The Lieutenant hesitated. "Uh, I think we just missed some company, sir."

Head spinning with confusion, Ryerson Gilvray joined Flemming at the far end of the clearing. They looked into the woods. "A *grave?*"

"Only a couple of days old, I'd say."

Gilvray pressed his lips together, his heart racing, his guts churning with mounting anger.

Someone had trespassed here. They didn't have the key, yet they'd made it past the treyurne. They'd fought and several had died. But what disturbed him most was that someone had breached the cave doors. Without the key.

"Sir, is this anything?" One of the younger soldiers crouching on his haunches at the edge of the clearing peered at an object on the ground. "It looks like leather."

Gilvray joined him. The thing had been stepped on, pressed into the loose dirt. Gilvray picked it up between his thumb and index finger to examine it. It looked like an ordinary leather belt pouch. It felt empty, but he checked. Then he turned it over.

Neatly engraved in the leather was a perfect reproduction of the rune pattern on the key to the Indyn Caves. His mind whirled. *Who—?* But he knew the answer before he finished the question. His mouth went dry. Racing back over to the cave doors, Gilvray knelt down and examined the footprints, mentally bringing up a picture of a certain pair of boots that had been passionately flung to one side a few nights ago.

Gilvray would have wagered his home leave that the person responsible had penetrating green eyes. Those dark eyes that dared him. *Alternate circumstances.* He'd been sure she couldn't be there just to see him. This was confirmation that his instinct was correct. *Whore.* She'd violated him and he wanted to scrub himself clean.

He forgot his own desire to attempt entry to the caves in his deep-seated fury that someone else had already done it. If Greenburg heard about a breach to the cave doors, that posting north of the Sea of Khûn would become a horrible reality. He stormed back onto the switchback path.

With his men reassembled, Gilvray sent out two scouts to find which way the intruders had gone. Upon their return, he barked out orders. He sent a couple of men back to the outpost with strict instructions not to report to Major Chadha. They would gather supplies and head south to reunite with Gilvray. The rest would go with him. Ryerson Gilvray was on the hunt.

Jesqellan took hold of Trig's bridle. "Ho there, beastie." Trig *chuffed* at him, which Jesqellan interpreted as a welcome. The mage reached a hand up for the horse to sniff, and because Trig didn't snap at him, he stroked the animal's soft auburn neck. Eyes front again, Jesqellan peered around the warhorse that blocked much of his view and could just barely make out the thin blue line that was the mountains to the south. They would assuredly reach the pass by nightfall. That would make it nearly four days since they'd left the foot of the Indyn Hills. *We're behind schedule*, he remarked to himself and wished he could think of a way to speed up their passage. But then, there was no point in going any faster than the party who had gone to find the Tree. Jesqellan frowned.

Days ago, when they were all angry and frustrated at Kyer's odd behaviour and lack of communication, it was easy to believe that she was not entirely trustworthy. But now, with her continued suffering from the consequences of killing Misty—the one who had stolen the ingredients from them—Jesqellan had the feeling that certain guesses he had made were not quite accurate. Fredric's story had rung true at the time, but was that only because Jesqellan was open to negative thoughts about his comrade? A terrible leaden feeling grew in the pit of Jesqellan's belly.

Phennil didn't like this. Not one bit. *Fredric Heyland wants glory; that's what this is about.* The former captain wanted Kien's faith in him restored. Was his intention to share in the party's success? Or steal it? Phennil had confided his concerns to Derry before they had parted.

"It is a valid worry," Derry agreed. "The other side of it, is that he needs you more than he needs us at this point. I believe he is sincere about saving Alon's life, so if you are the keeper of the sap, he will be motivated to protect you." The captain glanced over at Kyer. "I believe we in our small party have more to fear from him than you."

Phennil couldn't argue with that. Still, he vowed to keep a wary eye on that fellow.

They had curved around the northern spur of the mountain range. Phennil intended to hug the hills as closely as possible, following them southeast to the narrow gap that formed a natural gate to the home of the Tree of Life. The aromatic scent of pines and balsams wafted along the wind that descended the hill alongside a trickle of a stream. Leoht splashed through the cool water. Phennil's blond hair whipped him in the face as he glanced behind him where Harley rode alongside Fredric. They didn't speak to one another, but Phennil had the sense that Harley was watching Fredric. *I'm still not sure about him*, Phennil thought. But his instinct was to trust Harley over Fredric. Only time would tell if he was right.

The sun was suspended in a cloudy haze about an inch above the hills to the riders' right, showing a few more hours' riding were still available today.

They should reach the entrance to the valley where the Tree of Life grew by late on the day after tomorrow.

Gilvray watched the approach of his men and supplies with the warmth of the thinly veiled sun on his cheek. Relief sighed through him, and he breathed the scent of the pine forest in which they'd made camp. With the arrival of the rest of his men, they could resume the chase, and soon now, very soon, he would punish Kyer for her betrayal and for stealing whatever it was she stole from inside the caves. The only thought that settled his nerves was that this mess would be cleared up before the colonel returned. He would have Kyer and the other intruders in custody, and they would have to explain themselves to the colonel. Gilvray would more than likely be rewarded for his handling of a delicate situation. He hoped. On the other hand, the colonel might be furious that the emissaries had been permitted to leave in the first place.

The soldiers rode up, saluting as they dismounted. "Sir," the spokesman said, "we have news as well as supplies."

"Oh yes?"

"Sir. Major Chadha had a messenger from the colonel."

Warning bells clanged in Gilvray's head. "Go on."

"They will conclude their business early. He returns in one week."

He had heard that temperatures north of the Sea of Khûn *occasionally* rose above freezing.

. . . my dear, lovely girl, I know all about your mission and about you. Did I not say I was your Guardian? You are looking for the cure for Alon Maer.

You killed Ronav Malachite in Nennia. What's more, you enjoyed it. One thing more . . . a particular magical gift you have. . . .

His touch sends shimmers down my body. Eyes, deeper than a midnight sky.

. . . white stone. Keep this with you, and I'll always be able to find you.

. . . gift? What the hell did he mean by 'gift'?

. . . Kayme. You don't need that.

. . . others needed my assistance more than you . . . Now you need it more than anyone else.

. . . You owe me nothing.

. . . white stone. I'll always be able to find you.

. . . You owe me nothing. White stone. Rumbling . . . bouncing . . . aching.

That face. Who is . . . Skim . . . Skim something. Lips moving, can't hear. . . . Always be able to find you.

White stone.

Skimnoddle looked eagerly into Kyer's open eyes. "Good morning, dearest love." He rested a hand on his heart. "Fear not. You are under the expert care of our physicker adept. We enter the pass today. You will be fine. Be brave, my love."

She reached up her right hand to fumble with the pocket in her trousers, fighting the pain in her shoulder. She looked worried. "It's all right, Kyer," he said with genuine earnestness. "Whatever troubles you will cease." Her clenched hand dropped to the side of the carrier on which she lay.

Skimnoddle moved to take his place leading Trig.

Jesqellan came around to walk behind the travois and make sure Kyer didn't tumble out as they headed up the slope into the pass. He stepped on something nestled in the pine needle floor as he passed Kyer. It was a small, white stone. He sensed the presence of magic in the air, as he always did when he stood next to Kyer. He shuddered and glanced down at her closed eyes, troubled by the pained expression. What was she thinking about right now? He kicked the stone aside and took up his place just as the travois jolted ahead, pulled by Kyer's four-legged companion. He tossed a Tracking Confusion spell onto the trail behind him. As they moved forward, Kyer's pain seemed to dissipate; the tightness around her mouth and eyes ebbed away.

It must be that the rocking of the carrier soothes her, he decided.

Fredric sat straight and tall in the saddle, imagining—or recapturing—the grandeur of his former days. Determination flowed through his veins. Or was it desperation? He felt as if he were back in the army, riding toward his first battle, a young soldier, eager to prove himself to his commanding officer. Only this time the object of his focus was a scatterbrained elf. He gritted his teeth and choked down his resentment. *If I'm going to get what I want out of this, I have to be successful with him.*

The plan to defame Kyer was on rocky ground. At the start, Fredric was pretty confident that he'd won Jesqellan and Derry over, maybe even Janak and the halfling. The elf was problematic, but Fredric had felt that even he could be convinced with the right words. But then Kyer had killed Misty. That was a bold move, and one that looked to be in her favour. Still, he had not yet given up. Fredric adjusted his grip on the reins. No, all was not lost. Derry and his party were teetering on the brink of believing in Kyer's treachery; they could still go either way. Some things still looked bad for Kyer, and in spite of her saving Derry's life, Fredric was sure that he'd be able to draw up a picture that would convince them Kyer and Misty had been working together. Explanations could be created for everything. No, the shadow of doubt over Kyer was not yet lifted. Maybe there remained some way for him to ensure it never was.

In the meantime, Fredric's other goal had not changed. It was vital that his service on this mission be remembered. Surely Lord Kien would recognize him for his renewed commitment in spite of his past indiscretions! And if he succeeded in regaining Lord Kien's faith and trust, he would be in an even better position.

Destroying Kyer Halidan would be much easier then.

Valrayker folded the letter and tucked it away in a drawer. He left the study, candle in hand, and made his way up the long, dark staircase. Very few people travelled this stairway, and even they used it infrequently. He had forgotten the utter stillness that billowed around him as he climbed. It was like climbing up into dense fog. The sounds of hustle and bustle of the castle remained below, insulated by the cloud. His candle flickered in a breath of air, indicating the pinnacle was near. He protected the flame with a hand.

At the top of the castle spire, he knocked softly on the slightly open door.

"Come in," a voice said. "I heard you approaching, so I opened the door."

"Hello, Piper." Val stepped inside the tiny room where the wizard spent most hours of her week. The duke's gaze bypassed the massive crystals and talismans that Piper employed in her craft and went straight to the point.

"I need you to Gate me to Bartheylen Castle. My presence is requested."

Piper nodded slowly. "Fine. I need to meditate on it and prepare. Return in an hour."

Valrayker thanked her and made his way back downstairs to take his leave of Governor Lyndon. They put finishing touches on the governor's list of responsibilities during the dukes' absences: brief the new mayor about the improvements to the Airdrie trade route; hear the evidence against the livestock thieves who had been apprehended four days ago; settle the argument over property lines between the quarrelling residents of Dock Street; head up the committee to choose a winner of the art show. Then Val found Acadia and bid her farewell. She passed on her best wishes for Alon's good health. Val gathered his belongings and returned at the appointed time to the spire room.

"Ah, just in time," Piper whispered, waving the dark elf in. "I am ready to open it for you."

"Thank you, Piper. I'll see you next time."

"My best wishes to my Lord Kien." Piper placed her hands upon the jagged crystal on the blue velvet–covered table and breathed out. Moments later, an archway appeared, as tall and as wide as any doorway. It sparkled like iridescent air and was as tangible as a rainbow.

Beyond it, Val saw his destination. He stepped through and the Gate vanished.

He walked through the courtyard of Kien's largest castle and asked the steward where he could find his friend.

"He's been expecting you," Moira said. "He's in my lady's chamber."

Val nodded and made his way there. He knocked and entered. "I'm here."

Twenty-Six
How He Felt about Her

Why don't you come and meet her?
Dear heart, your real mother. Come and meet her.
They won't miss you . . . they've carried on without you.
Swimming through darkness . . . hazy brightness far away.
. . . meet your true mother, learn everything about yourself?
Swim! Must get through.
A shimmering archway in the air before them.
Pushing darkness aside . . .
. . . tall woman . . . dark curls . . . Misha.

Derry looked up as a movement caught his attention. He rushed over to
where Kyer lay, eyes wide open, seeing something or someone that wasn't
there. He passed a hand over her face, and she did not blink.

"Kyer," he whispered.

It's me. Misha.
From his lordship, my lady.
The serpent is a symbol of undying love.
It is done.
I see myself in the glass. I am Misha.

... tall woman ... dark curls ... hand outstretched—
Derry.

Derry stroked Kyer's fiery forehead. "Jesqellan, pour the tea. Quickly." Kyer's arms strained against the bindings that held her to the travois. She struggled against some force that frightened her. Her eyes widened in panic.

That woman was killing Alon Maer.
That woman was killing Derry.

"Misha!" Kyer screamed.

"It's all right. Kyer, it's all right." Derry held her head steady with both hands. "Hear me. It's me, Derry."

Jesqellan rushed over, cradling a steaming cup in both hands. Skimnoddle stood aside, thumbs crooked through his beltloops, watching with concern.

"Derry." Kyer looked through him.

"Yes." He pleaded silently. "Who," he began cautiously, "who is Misha?"

"Misha," she repeated, and to his surprise, a tear leaked out of her eye and trickled down her cheek. Derry bent and rested his head next to hers, careful not to touch her right shoulder where the muscle had not yet healed.

Whatever ghost plagued her, it had moved on, and Kyer's urgent breathing slowed to normal. Her limbs relaxed. As Derry lifted his head, the mild breeze cooled his face, and he realized his own eyes had leaked a little too.

Jesqellan held Kyer's head while Derry spoon-fed her another dose of the tea that kept her asleep—*mercifully, yet cruelly*, Derry thought with a grim sigh. He didn't like to think how she would react upon fully waking and learning that so many days of her life had passed without her knowledge. Neither did he like to imagine how she would suffer through the jolting and jouncing of the travois if he allowed her to feel every vibration and jerk as it shuddered through each and every bone. It would cause him equal pain, he was sure, just to watch her.

"Nearly ready to go, Captain," Skimnoddle said with uncharacteristic brevity. Whatever game he played when he spoke with his usual grandeur was tiresome even for him in these tense days.

They had slept on a rocky path, cliff with overhanging pines on one side, drop of about twenty-five feet, covered with more pines, on the other. Throughout the whole day of dragging the travois through the stony, up-and-down terrain, Derry wished he hadn't sent Harley along with Phennil. They could have used an extra hand here. It would have been much easier to carry her. In places, the path was so narrow and winding that not only did someone have to guide Trig, but another body was needed behind the carrier to guide it around the corners and to prevent Kyer from rolling off.

There had been no rain, for which Derry thanked whatever god might have been listening. He worried that it was coming though, for in spite of the approaching summer, the haze of clouds felt moist and faintly oppressive. What little breeze there was smelled damp through the pines. The heaviness of the air added to Derry's growing mood of despair. He put the cup back in his saddlebag and tightened a couple of Donnagill's straps. "Thanks, old fellow." Derry patted the great animal on his flank before climbing on board.

"The men are asking if we stop to camp soon, Major."

Gilvray shook himself out of his concentrated reverie. "Yes, in about an hour."

"We've pushed the horses hard, sir."

Gilvray frowned. "I am aware of that, Lieutenant. I intend to get within two hours' distance to the pass before we halt tonight. That way we'll make it halfway through the pass tomorrow."

"Sir." Marcus turned back to tell the men.

Gilvray surmised that they would not know they were being pursued, so they would not hurry. They should catch up in a couple of days. *Unless . . .*

There was a possibility that Kyer and her friends were in a hurry. To save a life. He hadn't believed them at the time, but maybe it was true.

I've got to give the colonel a culprit. He had less than a week to apprehend her.

"*Do you know what this is, Misha?*"

Of course. I made it. "*No, m'lady.*"

"*The serpent is a symbol of undying love,*" *she tells me. She puts it on and centres the circular snake on her chest. It is done.*

"*Please get my looking glass off that table, Misha. I want to see what it looks like.*"

I go back later to help her undress. She still wears the serpent. Good. As I'm leaving, I see the looking glass on the dressing table. I walk over. I will put out the candles. My back is to her as she climbs into bed. I slip the mirror into my apron pocket. I need it more than she does now.

Kyer whimpered and Jesqellan flinched on her behalf as the travois bumped over an exposed root in the path. "Sorry, Kyer," Jesqellan said.

It was the third day since they'd separated from Phennil and the others. Derry stared hopefully off into the trees, southeastward, as if by staring intently enough, he might see their progress. Had they reached the Tree yet? Derry forced himself to turn away. There was no use in fretting about the others.

He and his party were nearing the end of the pass and would be through the southern tip of the mountain range by midday tomorrow at the latest. *Thank Aidan.* The going would be much easier once they were out of the mountains. They camped under a rocky ledge, sparsely sheltered in front by a grove of elm trees. After a bite of supper, Jesqellan lowered himself into his meditative position off to one side.

"I'll watch, Skimnoddle," Derry said. "I don't feel drowsy."

Skimnoddle shrugged and settled down under an elm on the far side of the fire. The travois nestled under an overhang of rock for the night. Derry checked Kyer's pulse all around her broken bones. He tucked blankets around her and laid a hand on her forehead. Satisfied that Kyer's breathing and heartbeat were regular, Derry pulled the rose out of his saddlebag, where he'd hidden it.

"Jesqellan, I need your expert opinion."

The mage nodded, always prepared to express his expert opinion.

"I am not certain, of course," Derry continued in a low voice. "You see, I have been wondering about whether there was a cause of Kyer's accident."

Jesqellan raised his eyebrows. "Go on."

Derry sat next to him at the fireside. "Kyer asked me not to say anything, but I am quite concerned, and I am sure she would not mind under the circumstances—"

"Fair enough. What is it?" Jesqellan said.

"Kayme gave Kyer a parting gift. A white rose." He pulled it out and held it up so Jesqellan could look at it without touching until he'd drawn some conclusions as to its safety. "Kayme asked her to 'keep it close to her heart,' which Kyer has done. I know you've been saying you sensed magic on her; this is one of the items I think is causing that feeling."

Jesqellan held out a palm toward the rose. He whistled low, nodding.

"Several times since receiving this, Kyer has suffered some sort of trouble," Derry went on, "usually isolated to herself." He outlined Kyer's mishaps from the earthquake to her terrible fall. "I have a concern that it is the rose that has caused Kyer so much misfortune."

Jesqellan chewed on his lip and thought. "Why do you suppose Kayme would wish to do Kyer any harm? I thought he was quite taken with her."

Derry thrust aside the feeling that comment produced in his stomach. "Yes, and you know what else he kept saying. 'Everything has its price.' Do you remember that? Perhaps he gave Kyer the information we needed, and he's making her pay the price."

Jesqellan looked doubtful. "Why then fill our saddlebags with food and supplies? Besides, I thought the price she paid was the evening she spent with him."

Derry shook his head. "I know, it's just . . ." Derry wasn't sure how to bring this up. Kyer had shared this in confidence. "I worry that she may have offended him in some way. He had to keep his promise, but perhaps he is making her pay the price for . . . something else."

Jesqellan's expression was quizzical. "You are not making any sense."

Derry got to his feet. "I'm not sure why Kayme would wish her ill. But you know how she is. She could have said some typically impertinent thing and insulted him, the way she did with Phennil's father. She can be too glib. Who knows what kind of comment would offend the most powerful wizard in Rydris? Jesqellan," he stopped and knew he had to tell the mage, to make his point clear. "Jesqellan, Kayme asked Kyer to stay with him."

The mage's eyes were like two full moons at midnight. He pressed his fingertips together. "Stay? With him? There?"

Derry nodded. "And she refused him."

Jesqellan said nothing.

"So you see—"

"He may have been offended by that," Jesqellan suggested, as if it were his idea.

"Yes," Derry agreed.

"You had better let me take a look at that."

Derry handed him the rose, still fresh as if it had been cut from its root only moments ago, its petals still firm and silky. It was not closed tightly as a bud, but it had not opened any more than when Kyer had first shown it to him.

The Moabi held it carefully and turned it gently in his fingertips, studying it from all angles. His face was pensive.

"A white rose. A gift from Kayme," he murmured. "How appropriate." He paused reflectively. "It is indeed magic," he went on, "and undoubtedly possesses a powerful spell. I believe I can study it and learn what kind of spell it is. Since it came from Kayme, I shall have to concentrate very hard, and it may take quite some time. I will need absolute silence for the rest of the evening, and I will require extra hours of rest to regain my strength afterward."

"I thought as much. We have no reason to fear for our safety here, I believe. You can take all the time you need." He said the words, but hoped Jesqellan would not need very much time. Even stopping to sleep felt like an indulgence.

Jesqellan sat cross-legged with his back to the fire, the rose held in the tips of his delicate fingers, almost is if he were not touching it at all. He stared at it intently, trying to read what was stored inside it. Derry glanced over to where Skimnoddle slept a little distance beyond the fire and settled himself down a few feet from Kyer. One ear open for approaching danger, he stared upward through the darkness of the elms to the cloud-studded sky. Stars peeked out and were hidden again as the wind pressed the cloudy coverlets toward the west.

If that damned rose caused Kyer these injuries from which she'd likely never fully recover, he'd—well, he didn't know what he'd do. He shifted his gaze from the stars to the travois on which she lay relatively peacefully. Suddenly he was struck with another desire; one he had not felt in a long time. Getting up slowly, to avoid disturbing Jesqellan, he moved to his saddlebag and withdrew a loosely bound book. Leafing through its many occupied pages, memories returned to him of people and places he had not seen in many months. Their faces looked up from where he had captured them and spoke to him of other days. He fished out his charcoal pencil from a pocket of the bag and sat down again. When he found the next vacant page, he allowed his eyes to move over to Kyer again and placed his pencil on the paper.

Derry jumped and nearly dropped the book. He had fallen into a doze and had dreamed he was walking along the ramparts of Equart Castle and tripped on an uneven place in the brick. The full moon was overhead now, and there were several fewer blank pages in Derry's sketchbook. He'd tried his hand at drawing Jesqellan while meditating, but the mage's back was to him, and his memory couldn't provide him with a clear enough image. He'd had more success drawing Kyer with that impish expression she'd worn during her introduction to Kien. He picked up his pencil where it had slipped to the ground and got up to check on her. Jesqellan had not moved, and the captain admired, even envied, the mage's ability to remain motionless for so long. *It must be so restful.*

Beads of sweat had formed again on Kyer's forehead, and her body twitched occasionally. Derry bathed her face and soaked a clean rag in the tea that eased her pain. He held it up to her lips and squeezed some drops into her mouth. She accepted them with a sleepy tongue.

A sound across the fire startled Derry, and he turned around, hand on his hilt. But it was Jesqellan. The mage was inhaling deeply and breathing out through pursed lips. It was the hiss of the intake that had caught Derry's attention after so long a silence. Jesqellan stood up slowly, straightening his legs and rolling his spine up, vertebra by vertebra, and finally raising his head. He stretched and shook himself to stir the blood that had slowed to the pace of cool molasses during his meditations. He handed Derry the rose, and the captain offered him a drink of water, which he accepted.

"I have learnt what the rose's power is," Jesqellan announced proudly, though his voice hinted at his weariness. Derry waited patiently while he paused for effect. "You were right, in that the rose made considerable contribution to Kyer's mishaps of the last few weeks."

Derry braced himself.

"Not at all in the way you suspected, my friend." The mage's dark eyes shadowed with gravity. "The rose holds an extremely strong spell of protection, Derry. It is my belief now that without it, Kyer would very likely have been killed by that fall, if not a long time ago. It might also explain why she did not fall ill when the rest of us did. Our friend must have made an even greater impression on Kayme than we thought. He has shown by this gift that he desires very much for Kyer to stay alive."

Derry's eyes were wide, and his jaw had dropped. He picked it up again.

"But . . . why?" he wondered out loud after a moment. "It seems so unlike Kayme to show preference for anyone."

"I agree," Jesqellan said. "He keeps to himself, lives only for himself, and certainly does not owe anything to anyone. I find it odd that he would put himself out in this way."

Derry exhaled deeply.

Jesqellan required several hours to regain his strength and circulate energy from himself into his staff and back, to restore them both. He resumed his meditative position on the far side of the fire.

Derry picked up the rose from where he'd left it on the rock and twirled it in his fingers, avoiding the thorns. Instead of returning it to his own saddlebag, he slipped it back within her leather cuirass, where he had found it, and it could do the most good. He brushed her hair off her forehead, willing the lines of pain to smooth over. Pulling himself away he picked up the waterskin of tea and sat next to Kyer's belongings. He opened her saddlebag and as he tucked the waterskin inside he noticed a flat, oblong object wrapped in black cloth. Curiously, he drew it out, glancing over at Kyer as if she might suddenly awaken.

Derry unwound the cloth and gazed in wonder at the object. It was a small hand mirror, framed in gold, with pearls inlaid in the handle. He turned it over and traced the etchings on the back, watching the way the firelight danced on the shiny surface. Then his heart stopped in horror.

Just at the top of the handle, above a diamond-shaped design of pearls, were engraved the initials *AMB*.

Alon Maer Bartheylen.

Derry flung the cloth around the mirror again and practically tossed it back into the saddlebag. He retreated away from it as though it might explode like a fireball. *Madness!* His hands were slippery with sweat, and he wiped them on his trousers. *How did she—?* But he knew the answer. And he knew what it meant.

He'd asked for solid evidence.

Derry didn't bother waking Skimnoddle to replace him on watch. He paced around, ate a little, and checked Kyer again. Kneeling next to her, he brushed the untidy hair away from her face. *How could you, Kyer? Why?* He looked over at the saddlebag, imagining the black-wrapped package within. *I could take it out right now. I could fling it down the hillside, and no one would ever have to know.*

Derry jumped to his feet and pressed the heels of his hands into his eyes.

What was he thinking? Had he lost his mind? He would never be able to look Dunvehran or Kien in the eye if he buried this knowledge. But if he didn't, would he ever be able to look Kyer in the eye?

He sat down again. Hard. Despair flooded through him. What did it matter? He'd already destroyed their friendship. Reparation was now an unattainable goal. If she was guilty, he would simply get over the loss.

Captain Moraunt stared at Kyer's sleeping form for a long time. Finally, he picked up his sketch book and tried to capture the lines of pain around Kyer's eyes as they were eerily shadowed in the firelight. He focussed on her lips, which were parted slightly, her breath passing shallowly between them. Through his mind and his hand, the pencil was an extension of his vision. The charcoal replicated her untended hair, unwilling or unable to smooth it. Though still tied back, it was loose and unkempt, and wisps of it formed a delicate frame around the face that, for the first time ever, looked helpless.

When his hand stopped moving, Derry looked at his drawing. He stared at it, seeing how accurately he had duplicated the image of the unconscious woman. His brow furrowed, out of concern for her, out of anger for what she had done, out of frustration at his inability to help her, and because of the claw that twisted his heart as he gazed at her and began to understand how he felt about her.

The sun was rising as he returned the sketch book to his saddlebag with a trembling hand.

Gilvray sensed dawn's approach just before the soft glow of light awoke on the mountaintops to the east. He roused his men, allowing them only a moment to eat and prepare to travel. They would enter Pineridge Pass by midmorning. *And we must be through by tomorrow night.* It would be tough going, but they must make haste if they were to close the gap.

Colonel Greenburg would return to the outpost in only a few days. What would Chadha tell him? He thought of the Sea of Khûn.

He pushed Kyer Halidan's face aside and thought of his lovely young wife, wondering how soon he'd see her again.

They had made excellent time. By early afternoon, Phennil led his small party around the last wall of rock and tree to reveal the entrance. He felt certain they'd been watched for at least that whole day. All manner of beings guarded the Tree of Life and all the paths to it, on the cliffs next to them as well as across the gap to the eastern range. Every bird, every squirrel, even some of the bees Phennil suspected of being guardians.

"If my geography is correct," he announced to Janak and the others as they reined in next to him, "my homeland is a mere three days' flight east of where we stand."

Janak looked puzzled. "We've come full circle, then?"

"Very nearly." Phennil pointed to the southeast. "You see that arm of the mountain? Beyond that is the southwestern tip of the Donnan Forest. And if you flew eastward, within the forest, Plicatha would appear below you."

"Well, I'll be skewered," the dwarf said. "You figure your da can smell us from there?"

Phennil laughed. "Maybe if Kyer were with us, he could."

Janak's eyes narrowed. "Whaddya think? Has he recovered from her yet?"

"Maybe not but my mother was quite taken with her." Phennil smiled and nudged Leoht forward.

A handful of elven guards was scattered across from cliff face to cliff face, the entrance to the valley of the Tree of Life. Ten standards of the Guarded Realm made a colourful gateway. As Phennil and his companions approached, a guard stepped forward, her hand held out in front to halt the travellers. Phennil dismounted and walked the last few paces, recognizing her as a companion from his own earlier days as a Realm Guard. *I think her name is Gwereth?*

"State your name and business," the guard said.

Phennil smiled awkwardly. Why had she used the Rydrish tongue when he was clearly a wood elf like herself?

"Gladly," he said in insistent Elvish. "As I think you know, I am Phennil Fyrhen, son of the Lady and Lord of the Donnan Forest." Did Gwereth's eyes widen at the mention of Phennil's name? *Naturally she's heard of my mother and father.* "My companions are Janak, son of Flicka, daughter of Jerra; and—" he hesitated, having forgotten to think of how he ought to refer to the others. "Uh, Hunter and Harley of the Guarded Realm."

"Business?" The guard spoke a little more curtly than necessary, Phennil thought.

"We are on an official errand for Lords Kien Bartheylen and Valrayker of Equart, both, as I'm sure you are aware, of the Southern Alliance. We come to collect the final ingredient in what we hope will be the cure for a deadly illness that has affected Lady Alon Maer."

"And the Tree of Life is needed for this cure?" Gwereth asked redundantly, continuing in Rydrish.

Why did the guard sound disdainful? "Yes, Gwereth," Phennil explained patiently. The guard flinched only slightly at the use of her name. "We need her sap."

The guard cried an order, and the rest of the guards snapped to attention. Her voice rang loud and clear between the arms of the valley. "Hear me, Phennil Fyrhen of the Donnan Forest. You and your companions are forbidden entrance to the valley of the Tree of Life. Please turn around and go back the way you came."

Stunned, Phennil couldn't disguise his confusion and concern. He looked about him at his friends, who stared back, equally dumbfounded. "But ... but *why?*" he stammered in Rydrish, aware of how childish it sounded. "By whose decree?" Even as he asked, he knew what the answer would be, and his elven heart dropped.

"By order of your father."

Twenty-Seven
I Have a Bad Feeling about This

With head held high, Phennil jammed his foot in the stirrup and flung his other leg over Leoht's back, turning him around. He did not glance back as he led his little party back the way they had come.

Fredric came up alongside Phennil with a frantic look in his eye. "What, that's it?"

Harley was still, watching the elf, waiting for a response.

"Have you taken leave of your senses?" Janak growled from behind. "We can't give up now."

"Silence," Phennil barked.

They obeyed.

Phennil waited until they had rounded the spur of the mountains and were out of sight of the guards. Then he steered Leoht toward the tree-covered hills and stopped only when they were surrounded by balsam firs. The late-afternoon sun was not visible from the north side of the mountain, and the milky cloud cover added to the feeling of twilight among the trees. Phennil dismounted and felt like smashing something with his fist. Instead, he paced back and forth a few times, shaking out his hands and smelling the coolness of the air. Instinctively he noted that rain was threatening. He muttered under his breath and whipped out his bastard sword.

"*Scorrik!*" he yelled, slashing at the branch of a mountain ash. Only the leaves were sliced off.

Harley raised his eyebrows at Janak.

"I don't know what it means, but it didn't sound polite," the dwarf said.

Phennil sheathed his sword, and having erupted some of his rage, he turned to his men. "We are most certainly *not* giving up."

Janak glowered. "Was it because of Kyer that he won't allow us through?"

Phennil sighed. Apparently his words about Dregor's evil penetrating Donnan's complacent peace had affected his father very deeply indeed. He chuckled humourlessly. "No, Janak, it was not because of Kyer, but because of me."

"What are we going to do?" Fredric said. "I cannot imagine they would let us through now, even without you."

"I have not lived most of my life in the Guarded Realm for nothing. Now listen up."

The old Phennil would have given up and returned to the main group empty-handed. This Phennil had stood up to his father.

This Phennil was now prepared to defy him.

There it is. Derry heaved a sigh of relief, though only the first stage of this dreadful journey was over.

That morning, Derry had felt a rush of freedom as he burst out beyond the natural gateway of the pass and into the open air. The opening was flanked by stands of aspens, trembling and fluttering in the west wind that scurried along the southern edge of the mountain range. He'd darted back up to help Jesqellan, who struggled with an anxious Trig, as Skimnoddle guided the Kyer-laden carrier. The halfling's pony whinnied his aversion to fending for himself as he brought up the rear. That was a couple of hours before midday, according to the approximate position of the obscured sun.

They'd journeyed all that day toward the gaping cleft that ancient water had carved in the earth.

Now the enormous ravine, known as Bolivar Chasm, stretched out before them and extended into the distance on either side. Somehow Derry felt that everything would be fine now that they'd triumphed over the pass. Evening was upon them.

"Shall we camp here?" Derry consulted his companions.

Jesqellan nodded. "I do not want to follow the edge of the gorge at night and get too close."

"Besides," Skimnoddle agreed, "Kyer seems restless."

It had been so long since Kyer had spoken a word that they'd fallen into the habit of speaking of her as if she couldn't hear. Derry felt a little self-conscious about it, moreso because that morning he'd refused to give her any pain-relieving tea, which may have contributed to her restlessness. Derry'd explained to the others that she should be sufficiently healed for her pain to have abated on its own. But in his soul, he was punishing her for his discovery of last night, a discovery he intended to keep to himself.

"It has been four days since we separated from Phennil," the mage remarked as they made camp. "How much longer would you estimate it will take them to reach the chasm?"

Derry shrugged. "Phennil hinted at knowing a direct path, but I don't know where it might be. I guess it's a full day from the mountain to the chasm."

A thousand years ago, a river had flowed southeast out of Burns' Gulf far to the northwest beyond the mountain range the company had just descended. Now it was dry but had left in its wake a long and wide ravine full of twisting trails carved out by the streams. The rivulets had converged on a deep lake before exiting the canyon through a narrow chasm that flowed southeast. As the valley once united with plainlands, it widened and became a shallower river. So many ages had passed since the river had ceased to exist that the farther extensions of the dry riverbed were barely recognizable as such. A traveller with little tracking skill might cross the grassy lowland area without knowing that a river had passed across the land. Where the river once egressed at the far end of the ravine made a decent landmark for the company to reunite and regroup.

Skimnoddle whipped up a paltry meal with the bits and pieces from their saddlebags, combining them with a jackrabbit who was in the wrong place at the wrong time. The three friends ate, and Derry spoon-fed some of the broth to Kyer, who, much to his gratification, not only swallowed it, but kept it down. A few spoonfuls were all she required, but it was the most she had ingested since her fall nearly a week ago.

Later, Skimnoddle went for a twilight walk, "to organize my thoughts, thrusting aside the fretful ones while profiting from and filing away the constructive, optimistic ones."

Jesqellan meditated. And Derry brewed Kyer's tea.

While it steeped, he knelt at her side and checked her pulse and temperature. At one point she opened her eyes.

"Kyer," he said gently, brushing strands of hair away from her face. In the firelight he could not tell if her eyes were clear or clouded. One word answered his query.

"Misha," she said breathlessly.

He shook his head sadly. "No, it's Derry. Who's Misha?"

The muscles in her eyelids contracted ever so slightly. Had she understood? "Derry," she murmured.

"Yes." He gave her an encouraging smile.

To his dismay, this did not have the effect he'd hoped for. Her eyes brimmed with tears the way a tidal pool fills with water. Then her brow furrowed anxiously, and she whispered words that sounded like, "Matching . . . gift," but he couldn't be sure.

He patted her hand. "Yes, we're bringing Alon a gift." He didn't know about the matching part.

Was she shaking her head? He couldn't tell if it were sadness, confusion, or frustration. "Gift," she said again.

The physicker fed her some tea, and soon her body reacted to the medicine and drew her away into sleep.

Skimnoddle returned soon after. Before Derry had a chance to speak, the halfling jumped in.

"If you were to ask whether I found my walk successful, I would have to supplicate for clarification: Were you perhaps making a reference to whether I feel in good health physically, having stretched my short legs to their greatest extent in a rapid, alternating fashion? Or, as I suspect is more likely the case, were you alluding to my exiting comment, as per my thoughts, specifically the 'profiting from' clause. Having elucidated your purpose, you would likely elicit that not only my thoughts, but the evidence before me, have driven me to a proposal."

Derry hesitated before speaking, just in case the diatribe had not concluded. *Apparently the lower altitude has loosened his tongue.* "What proposal?"

"Just this, dear Captain. My submission would be that we increase the distance between ourselves and the pass from which we descended this morning." He lowered his voice. "I suggest we make this relocation at the earliest possible convenience. Perhaps now."

Derry's quizzical expression did not carry to Skimnoddle in the flickering light. *"What?"* His impatience betrayed his loss of hope. "I don't understand what you're saying."

Skimnoddle, in a display of uncharacteristic sensitivity, knelt next to the captain and put a hand on his arm. "I am sorry to trouble you, Derry, but while I walked, I smelled smoke. Now, I know you'll say that it was from our fire, so I will forestall your suggestion by pointing out that I walked west.

The wind is from the north this evening."

Derry stared at him dumbly. He knew the words ought to make sense, but he couldn't piece them together.

"From the mountains," Skimnoddle went on. "My point, Captain is that it was someone else's fire. Someone who is well below the apex of the pass tonight. On this side. It could be a friend. But then, it could be a foe. I don't know of any friends who would be following us. So I recommend we move."

Finally Derry understood. *But I'm so tired.*

They disturbed Jesqellan's meditation to include him in the discussion. How far along the chasm's edge could they travel at night? More important, how long would it take the people on the pass to catch up to them? Anyone on horseback could travel swifter than they could with Kyer's travois.

Skimnoddle voiced the suggestion Derry had been hoping to avoid. "What if we were to enter the ravine?"

There was indeed a downward path not far from where they sat that would lead them into the heart of the chasm. Once, many years ago, Derry had followed his leader down within the trails that circled around hills and spires of rock, pits that were once waterfalls or had been gouged out by swirling undercurrents. Derry wouldn't choose to go down there if there were any other option.

If the party on the pass were indifferent to them, they would be out of sight, out of mind, for no one would enter the chasm unless they had to. If they were being pursued, which Derry did not like to imagine, at least they would have a head start. *Which we'll need.* He looked dolefully at Kyer.

"All right," the captain conceded. "Would you be willing to take a watch? For a little while? If I could just have some rest, then we could head down into the ravine at moonrise."

Skimnoddle nodded.

Derry fell into a surprisingly deep sleep.

Phennil held his breath as he neared the corner. His companions assured him that the invisibility hat did work, even better now at sunset. The first time he tried Valrayker's gift, in broad daylight, Phennil had looked like an outline of himself. Now only sudden movements drew attention, the way a mosquito catches the corner of the eye. Phennil felt sure that once the sun was down altogether, he'd be reliably invisible. And the fragrant feather, contrary to having a strong scent that masked his own, absorbed the odours around it, eliminating all but the expected smells of local nature. His noiseless footfalls were imperceptible, even to elven guards. They should be completely unaware of his passing. Still, his heart thudded like a rug beater. He wished he had a magical item to cover that sound.

He paused behind a fir, the last obstacle between him and the entrance. Placing his hand on the trunk, he murmured to it for reassurance. *Fear not*, it said, *the woodland creatures know you are of pure heart.*

Thank you, my friend. Good. So it was just the elves he had to worry about.

Good? His own people?

With a deep breath, Phennil plunged out into the open. Though the darkness was gathering, he paced himself carefully. It was like a dream of walking down a long corridor, the doorway at the end seeming to stay just as distant, no matter how many steps he took toward it. He was definitely in easy arrow range now. Any minute, one of the guards would look up, see him coming, and cry the alarm . . .

Somewhere up the mountainside, Janak was leading Harley and Fredric along the ridge through the trees. They'd meet him at the other end, so he could approach the Tree from the front; she might not trust him if he snuck up from behind. With any luck, the trees were communicating well today and allowing the passage of the two-legged beings although there was no wood elf there to translate for them.

Focus! Phennil scolded himself. *Don't worry about them.*

He was close enough now that if he weren't invisible, the guards would be able to throw stones at him. *Okay, veer to the right.* Nice big gap between those two. They could almost spit on him now.

Phennil stopped short. A guard had lifted her head and was looking right at him. He raised his hands, about to tell her not to shoot.

"It took you long enough," the guard said in Elvish.

Phennil shut his mouth and glanced over his shoulder. He ducked just in time for a medium-sized dryad to swoop through where his head just had been. Her butterfly-like wings were an unnatural-looking striped pattern, as though she'd had them painted. He knew dryads did that sort of thing, but he'd never seen anything like this one. As he followed her with his gaze, he was pretty sure she turned and winked at him. He breathed a sigh and adjusted the invisibility hat.

"It's only that the sylvan sprites returned with a report . . ." the dryad began, but then she flew too far away for her tiny voice to carry back to Phennil's ears. It didn't matter what she said; the result was more important. The three guards at the western end of the entrance followed her over to speak with the commanding officer, leaving an enormous gap for Phennil to slip through. Biting his lower lip, he focussed his gaze straight ahead and walked. *If I can just make it past the guards . . .*

"What's going on?" A guard nearly collided with Phennil on his way out of the woods. Phennil danced a few polka steps to avoid him, heart banging in his throat.

He was through.

He walked about fifty paces beyond the entrance and the stretch of guards who protected it. Then he broke into a run.

Janak cursed and swore inside his head but dutifully kept his hand off the handle of his axe. Losing his temper with a bunch of trees at this point would serve no purpose. The damned things apparently had just a terrific bloody sense of humour, but whatever it was they were laughing at, the dwarf didn't get the joke. They were green and leafy—*all right, needly too, then,* he corrected himself as a pine branch swiped him across the face—and they were much taller than he. That's all he knew. He hesitated to add that trees also made marvellous fuel.

Fredric and Harley followed along, and each man led a horse, with Leoht tied behind Harley's. Travelling along the side of the mountain was tougher than walking the bare ground, but whatever Phennil had said to the trees had been effective.

Phennil said the trees were on their side. *So don't do anything to rile them or you'll blow the whole thing.* Janak didn't know where this confident, take-charge elf had come from, but this new fellow certainly seemed to have everything under control. And he had not one, not two, but *three* other men following his orders. Janak couldn't help but be pleased for the young fellow.

The trees, for their part, showed the trio the path by shifting aside. They never did it so Janak could see the boles move, but the direction they were to head was plain as the hair on his face. *Whack!* A massive pinecone dropped and clonked him on the head. The dwarf looked up to raise a fist at the perpetrator and promptly received another one right in the eye. "Dang it, I only have the one good one," he moaned as they rubbed their branches together in self-congratulation.

How much longer till we reach the Tree? he grumbled.

Phennil kept his eyes and ears open for more elven or human guards who may be posted along the trail. The path itself was wide enough for half a dozen soldiers to walk abreast. How much farther did he have to go? The slow incline of the path wasn't nearly as steep as the walls on either side that formed a V. Still, it would get to him after a while. He'd been running for at least an hour, and his breath had shortened. Finally he gave in and slowed to a walk. He had been a child when last he was here, and he'd been on horseback that time, so his memory provided him no answers. Looking around, he saw no landmarks that meant anything to him either.

A bat swooped around his head and carried on. Moments later, a raccoon scurried across his path and melted into the darkness. Phennil wished he'd thought to eat something before starting on this crazy venture. Was that the last corner just ahead?

"Hsst!"

He stopped and looked wildly about, an arrow instantly ready to fly.

"No, no, up here," the voice said. "You must get out of sight."

Phennil searched upwards and saw a screech owl sitting on a particularly long branch, almost as if it had been posted there on watch. Phennil could just make out its ear tufts silhouetted against the sky.

"Quickly," it insisted and flew down to encourage Phennil with its wings up the steep wall into the trees.

"Why?" Phennil held his bow close so it wouldn't crack against a fir and realized, with some embarrassment, that he wouldn't have used it anyway. *I could never release an arrow against another elf.*

"Sh." The owl flitted back up to its branch, leaving Phennil concealed behind the thick foliage.

A moment later, Phennil appreciated the owl.

"Evening, Claire," a male Elvish voice said.

"Carris."

Phennil craned his neck to see through the trees, but all he could see were shadows. A patrol of night guards headed away from the Tree. Phennil couldn't see how many there were, but these were wood elves. They needed no lanterns to see at night, and they walked just as silently as he. Hat or no hat, he'd have walked right into them. He tightened his stomach so it wouldn't growl.

"Any news?"

"Sylvan sprites reported more enchanted animals heading into the mountains from Donnan Forest," the owl replied, punctuating with little hooting noises.

"You did not hear it from me, but I wish Lord Fyrhen would look into that."

Phennil caught his breath. Claire squawked.

"Anyway, looks like rain. Good night, Claire." And Carris and his patrol continued down the hill.

Claire floated noiselessly down to peer at him from another branch.

"Thanks," Phennil said.

"No sweat." The owl bobbed her head. "It should be clear sailing from here."

"I appreciate your assistance. Is there any word of my friends, who are trying to reach the Tree through the forest?"

"I'll go have a look." And with that, Claire whooshed upward and away. Phennil heard her screech as he stepped back out onto the trail. *That sound freezes the blood in high summer.*

At last the ground levelled off, and Phennil knew the Tree was near. He peered around the last bend to be sure an ambush wasn't waiting for him. *Don't be silly; these creatures are trying to help you.* The path opened to reveal a glade, in the centre of which was his destination. He hastened toward the Tree of Life.

It dwelt in a pool of luminescence, defying the nature of which it was a part by merging the characteristics of several trees. Its arms were an angular mass of reaching and criss-crossing branches, resembling a larch, yet it was not a conifer. The dense, beechlike foliage with waxy, sparsely toothed leaves gave the Tree a sculptured appearance. The ferns and wildflowers gathered at its feet fed off its nutrients, and life flowed through them so they glowed, casting an eerie radiance upward from below. A spring bubbled up from under the Tree, forming a tiny pond before the water trailed off into the trees on the far side. Cattails outlined the water, and the surface was dotted with the brightest water lilies Phennil had ever seen. Their shiny petals shone like lanterns in the night.

Phennil wended his way through the ferns and cattails to the stepping-stones that would take him right up to the Tree. This was such a magical moment! He wished Kyer could be here. *She would appreciate this.* Reverently, the elf tiptoed across the rocks and knelt at the base of the Tree. In spite of himself, he felt jittery. *I've got to hurry.* The waterskin was slung across his chest, and he ducked under its strap. He laid it on the ground next to him and placed both his palms on the bole of the Tree of Life.

I would not presume to disturb your splendour if it weren't for a dire need, he said to her. To his surprise, vibrations tingled through her skin and into his hands. He looked up into her branches, and her magnificence rained on him. It was like music filling the air, filling his body, filling his soul. A symphony of . . . well, life. A glorious grin split his face.

You are welcome here, the Tree of Life told Phennil Fyrhen.

Phennil did not want to leave, but he had to hurry. At some point, another patrol would arrive, and he had to be hidden in the trees by then. He kissed the Tree's skin and held the lip of the waterskin up to the little wooden trough that waited there. He pulled out the small stopper and released the liquid, letting the lifeblood of the Tree drip into the travelling vessel.

Phennil was surprised by its consistency. He'd expected it to be thick, like the sap from a cedar or a pine. But it was more like water. Still, it would take a while to fill the waterskin. After five minutes, it was about a quarter full. A few minutes later, a third.

Suddenly his blood froze. It was the piercing cry of a screech owl. Was Claire returning to tell him his friends were on their way? *Oh, please hurry!*

As if she'd heard him, the sap ran more quickly. There was a *whoosh* overhead, and Phennil glanced up from his task to see Claire alighting in the branch directly above.

"Oh, hello." He turned back to make sure he hadn't wasted any of the precious liquid. "Did you find them?"

"Sure."

The tone of Claire's voice alarmed him, and he looked up.

A night patrol of ten elves stood just inside the circle of light emanating from the Tree. Could they see him? *Damn, I'll have to be satisfied with half a waterskin of sap.* Slowly, slowly he replaced the stopper in the bark of the Tree, thinking that it must be visible, even if his hat concealed him.

"Thank you, Claire." Phennil recognized the voice of the same patrolman, and his heart sank.

It had been too easy; he ought to have been better prepared. Now they'd caught him in the act. "So you decided to lead them back to me, hunh?" he asked Claire as he replaced the cap of the waterskin and slung it over his shoulder next to his bow.

Claire daintily shrugged her screech-owl shoulders. "Carris gives me voles."

"I can't compete with that."

"Now, Phennil Fyrhen, I may not be able to see you, but Claire can, and she is sitting directly above you. Unless you can fly, she will continue to be above you, so I know exactly where to aim."

"You would shoot another elf?" Phennil asked, disgusted.

"Ah, so you still have elvish ethics. Then neither will you shoot me. Come away from the Tree."

"Look, Carris." Phennil rose, and glanced up at the traitorous owl. "I don't know what you people have heard from my father—"

"I don't ask the whys and wherefores; an order is an order. You're not welcome here."

"That's not what the Tree told me." Phennil darted out from underneath Claire. Before she was aware, he'd dashed across the stepping-stones and was following the stream toward the trees. Claire shrieked and went after him. He couldn't do anything about the movement of the plants through which he crashed. Carris let an arrow fly, and by sheer luck it only caught him in his right calf. Down he tumbled with a cry, and his hat flipped off. He tried to scramble to his feet but failed, overcome by pain and shock that Carris had shot him. Claire dived down at him, and he batted her away as he crawled frantically through the dark purple monkshood and orange columbine. Carris and his men were coming, arrows aimed, though they did not release them.

A whistle sounded from somewhere, and Phennil fell to the earth among the plants and hid his head as a cloud of light erupted from the base of the Tree, in a flurry and flapping of wings. Craning his neck to see, Phennil stared in wonder. Much of the light that bathed the Tree of Life was not radiance, but nymphs; thousands of them, tiny creatures with the swiftness of hummingbirds that glowed like a hand-shielded candleflame.

Claire shrieked again and fell to the ground, a tiny pinkish arrow sticking out of her chest. Phennil heard Carris's voice. "Nelferch! What are you—" and the elven captain dropped like a sack of bricks, as if dead. Within half a moment, the entire patrol was down. Phennil's body drooped, and he allowed himself to moan in pain. He didn't know which was the greater wound: the arrow in his leg or that he'd been shot by one of his own kind. *Everyone has gone mad.*

A nymph alighted on a stout stem next to Phennil, and he gazed at her in awe. He'd never seen one before. She stood no taller than a squirrel on its haunches. "I'm Nelferch." She tossed her glimmering hair out of her pale eyes as she glanced about at the carnage and grinned. "I don't know how we're going to explain this one to them, but . . ." She shrugged. "Oh well." She reached into her—Phennil could only think of it as clothing, though the term didn't suit the way the garments fluttered like aspen leaves in pale, luminous colours. "Quickly. Drink this." She held out a little vial that could not have contained more than a few millilitres of liquid. He took it but looked a question at her. "It's a healing potion," she said as if he were an idiot. "You think you're going to make it through the pass on *that*?" She pointed to where two nymphs worked on removing the arrow from Phennil's leg.

"Are they—?" Phennil waved a hand around the clearing.

She giggled. "No, they're not dead. Our arrows only put people to sleep. We've bought you an hour or so. Heh, except Claire," and Nelferch giggled again. "She took the same hit as the elves, and she's a mite smaller than they. She'll be asleep till tomorrow night." Her tittering was joined by the others', and the little clearing was filled with music.

Phennil drank the sweet liquid and shook his head in amazement at how quickly it began to work. The nymphs had used their small hands to work the arrow out, and with the potion, the wound started healing over. After about five minutes the bleeding had stopped and the lesion looked a couple of days old. The pain was lessened considerably, so it felt like a bad cramp rather than a nasty arrow wound.

"Thank you for . . . this," he finished lamely.

She feigned embarrassment. "Oh, 'twere nothing. The Tree welcomed you; I don't know where these nits figure they're of higher consequence than she is."

"I can't believe they fired at me." An overwhelming sense of betrayal enfolded him like a fog. A wood elf had shot him. His father had ordered that he be turned away.

"Sorry, Phennil Fyrhen. I know the Lord of Donnan is your father, but things have been rather odd lately. Anyway," and she gave her pretty little shrug again, "only the Tree makes the rules around here." She sighed. "The elves won't speak to us for weeks."

Phennil couldn't help himself. He laughed softly. "I don't suppose you'll miss much." The other nymphs twittered and flitted about, and a strange, contrary happiness began to flush out his melancholy. "The Tree . . . may I go thank her properly?"

"Sure, go ahead if you like. It's not as if she doesn't already know. You can waste your hour however you like, but when these fellows wake up, they're not going to be in high spirits."

Phennil speedily went and thanked the Tree and returned. "I have to wait for my friends anyway."

The nymph slapped her hand against her forehead. "Silly me!" she cried. "I forgot to tell you that we sent them on. You should be able to catch up with them quickly, though. Just follow the Spring Stream through there, and the trees will show you the way. You know that much. Oh, and listen to directions from chipmunks, but not the squirrels; they're nothing but nuisances." She gestured to two other nymphs who flitted over. "These two will accompany you to light your path."

Phennil thanked Nelferch and her friends and, snatching up his invisibility hat, limped through the trees.

As she watched him run off, Nelferch looked about her at the sleeping elves. "Oh, what harm can it do?" She fired another arrow into each of them.

Gilvray stood with his back to the camp and breathed the smoke-scented pine forest surrounding him. With hands clasped behind his back, he faced tomorrow's journey. It would all be downhill, literally. The major sensed he was gaining on his quarry, and consequently his nerves rattled with anticipatory triumph. They were making such excellent time, better, even, than he'd expected. And if he pushed them to be up before dawn again . . . *Out of the pass in the early morning and nothing between us and them but grass.*

And then what? Information first and foremost. But then Gilvray would have to apprehend Kyer because she was the one who not only stole the rune pattern, but actually breached the cave doors, trespassing on ancient, protected ground. *Her friends aren't going to let her go without a fight.* Maybe he'd apprehend them all.

His twelve men against Kyer's half dozen? A cinch. Nevertheless, Ryerson Gilvray steeled himself.

"I have to stop," Phennil moaned. "Just for a little." Nelferch's arrows would have kept Carris and his patrol asleep for a while, but they were likely hot on Phennil's trail by now. And they'd be able to negotiate this path with greater agility than his own little party. *But I've been hobbling along all night.* Phennil lowered himself onto a salal-covered deadfall, leaving Leoht waiting patiently next to the stream that was the runoff from the spring by the Tree of Life. It was also their path. Phennil lay down on his back, lifting his wounded right leg onto the log, and shut his eyes.

Harley checked the elf's wound to ensure he hadn't damaged it further. "It looks pretty good. That was quite a potion she gave you."

"Can you imagine if she'd given me a standard-sized dose?" Phennil agreed.

"Still, I'm sure your nymph friend did not intend for you to run nonstop on it." Harley pulled Phennil's trouser leg down again. "A few minutes, then, and we must go."

Fredric shifted his weight from one foot to another and held on to his and Harley's horses. The walk was challenging for the animals, in spite of not carrying their riders. They had tried riding but decided it would be easier for all concerned if they led the animals. It wasn't so much a path as it was the bank of the stream, and the slippery rocks were many. The moon, just past full, still gave only piecemeal light through the clouds and branches.

Janak stood a few paces upstream, watching back toward the coming dawn and listening for any sounds of approaching elves. Phennil didn't bother telling him there was not much point. Elves could travel noiselessly, even when they hurried. *They'll be upon us before we hear them breathe.* This thought served only to frustrate him. He'd caught up with his friends after about an hour of limping after the flying torches. The two nymphs had left him to return to the Tree once he'd found his friends. They would have served not only to light the way, but as signal beacons for the patrol of wood elves that would surely catch up with them soon. The Tree might make the rules, but the elves were certainly not listening.

"I think we should go now, Phennil," Fredric said in a low voice. "I have a bad feeling about this."

"I agree." Phennil reluctantly rose, wincing, and picked up Leoht's reins. "It's too quiet."

Twenty-Eight

Here in the Middle

P hennil resented the meagre predawn light. It played tricks on the eyes, letting him think the night sky was growing paler, but doing so at such a gradual rate, he couldn't rely on it. And what was the point of light that didn't adequately illuminate their journey down the switchback on the west side of the mountain? All night Phennil had led his companions along the dim wooded trail. The wider path to which the trees had guided them was easier, though the pain in his leg nagged him to rest. They could still hear the stream rushing down the steep hillside at each southern elbow of the trail. Phennil's little party stumbled with exhaustion, coupled with a growing sense of unease; Carris and his men ought to have caught up by now. Had he simply gone back for more men? Or did he know something Phennil did not about these blasted hills? Or maybe the trees were slowing them down?

There was naught to do but press on. A stone, kicked off the edge of the path by a horse's foot, tumbled and rolled down the precipitous slope. When some squirrels encouraged them into an opening at the north end of the switchback, Phennil heeded Nelferch's advice. "No, thanks very much, all the same." He looked about hopefully for a chipmunk. Seeing none, he accepted the directions given by a nuthatch.

"Can you trust them?" Janak growled with impatience bred of too much walking, not enough sleep, and no food.

"I don't know," Phennil snapped, his own patience at a low ebb. "Do you have any better ideas?"

A stubborn tree with the appearance of a small sycamore refused to shift aside, in spite of Phennil's polite request. Its mottled trunk looked puffed out as it stood in the centre of the path, and its branches extended the full breadth of the narrow way. *Please, we need your help*, Phennil repeated. He peered uncomfortably over the brink.

The sycamore did not so much as quiver.

Fredric reached for his sword. "We'll just cut the damn thing down, then."

Phennil stayed his hand, an unpleasant thought having occurred to him. "No, don't," he ordered. Slowly, slowly, Phennil backed away, amid protestations from Leoht.

Almost imperceptibly, the tree had grown taller, stiffening. And without further warning, the branches lashed out. Phennil, at the front of the party, was hit square in the stomach and tossed backwards into Fredric. The wood elf hit his head on Fredric's chin and both yelped. The backwards motion set all four travellers off balance, and they tumbled over the edge into the ferns and brush.

Phennil slid ungracefully down the steep hillside, bruising his limbs against deadfalls and rocks that were hidden beneath the greenery. Leoht, too, was sliding and frantically struggled to regain his footing. He screamed the way only a horse can scream. "Don't fight it, boy!" Phennil cried. He heard the muffled yells of his companions as they tumbled along with him, and he was reminded perversely of a childhood nursery rhyme. *Over and over and over, they tumbled and bumbled and stumbled.* Of course, this little slide had not been caused by the ground *rumbling and crumbling*.

Suddenly he stopped rolling and sliding. A body slammed into him, knocking his breath out with a *hooph*!

"What in the seven hells was that?" Fredric had halted, back to back with Phennil.

Phennil breathed with short gasps. "That, my friend," and he used the term loosely, "was a maul tree."

Fredric leapt up and helped Phennil to his feet. A frantic scramble succeeded in righting Janak and Harley. The horses stood at the bottom of the slide, staring at their two-legged companions as if wondering what the fuss was about. All except Harley's animal.

A quick arrow to the beast's head abruptly ended his suffering from a broken leg.

"Damn nuthatches," Phennil muttered and looked about for his bearings as Harley transferred his few belongings onto Leoht. To his delight, the stream flowed close to horizontally just off to the left, and the trees were much thinner. If they just ploughed on westward, they should emerge—

"Shit!" Harley looked up the way they'd come. "They're here!"

Wood elves had appeared far above them on the highest layer of the switchback.

The time for mucking about had passed. Phennil leapt up onto Leoht, dragging Harley behind him. Dwarf and man followed suit, and they urged their horses to follow the stream. *Please block them*, Phennil implored.

The question was, in a race between wood elf and wood elf, whose side were the trees on?

Arrows rained down on them from the top of the switchback trail. Phennil clung to Leoht's mane, pain both in his wounded leg and in his heart. *They're firing at us*, he repeated over and over in disbelief and bewilderment. *Elves firing at elf, dwarf, and human.* They did not hit anyone. On purpose?

Phennil looked back and up the steep hillside. Through the trees, he could not count their foes. Some ran down the back-and-forth trail, and a few trotted straight down the side. They were gaining, and Phennil urged Leoht forward. An arrow whizzed past his head, thudding into an aspen as

Phennil circled round it.

Enough. He reined in and came to a halt, dismounting in a sea of sword ferns. Bow at the ready, he took aim.

"Phennil, what are you doing!" screamed Janak.

Another arrow darted toward the elf and he ducked. He hesitated.

I can't do it. Sweat beaded on his forehead. *I can't shoot an elf.*

"Hold!" Carris called to his troop. The elven captain's arrow was nocked and ready. He stepped cautiously forward. Continuing in Elvish, he called to Phennil from sixty paces away. "I don't want to shoot you."

"Then lower your bow." Phennil's aim was steady.

"Come. You know you won't shoot. Just drop what you stole from the Tree of Life, and no harm will come to you. Or to your friends."

"Back off, Carris," Phennil yelled. Carris discontinued his approach. "I won't give it up. We need it. And the Tree gave it to me freely," he added pointedly, his arrow fixed on Carris's head. Sweat trickled down his cheek.

"The Tree is naïve," Carris said. "And so are you. Times have changed, Phennil Fyrhen. Old alliances cannot be counted upon. Even our brothers betray us." He paused then added, "And our sons."

My father has gone mad. Everyone has gone mad! The absurdity of the past weeks flooded Phennil's thoughts. Wildcats in the Donnan Forest. His father's refusal to act. Accusations and bad feeling. Kyer lying on a travois, maybe dying, all because her friends had lost faith in her. *The Tree knows the truth better than my own kin.*

A bird swooped down at Carris. He let fly his arrow and Phennil reacted.

Phennil's bow *twanged* even as Carris's arrow hissed overhead. Carris had only an instant to register shock before the arrow penetrated his skull. Phennil screamed in agony.

He had killed an elf.

Harley yelled to him from atop Leoht's back. Phennil felt himself hoisted up behind his friend. The trees, as if sensing his turmoil, stood aside for the riders to bolt through. They, at least, were minding the rules. The other elves would surely lay the responsibilty for his death at Phennil's feet. Harley rode as if they were in pursuit already, but Phennil heard nothing. Like when he was a child, the time he was under water for far too long. No sound but water in his ears and his own inner screaming. He felt nothing but Leoht's lithe body undulating beneath him. His own heartbeat eluded him.

The trees thrust the riders out into the open, and they flew across the rolling plains in the colourless dawn light. They rode for an hour before stopping to rest the shattered horses and themselves. Phennil flopped onto a spread of buttercups. Harley took care of Leoht.

"Thanks," Phennil said.

Harley shrugged. "You'd've done the same."

"I'm sorry about your horse."

Harley shrugged again. "These things happen."

Derry and his little party awakened in their new camp. Skimnoddle had allowed Derry a couple of hours' rest before rousing him and Jesqellan. They had descended the winding trail by the light of buck moon, just past the full as it rose above the mountains where Phennil and the others must be. It was a tricky descent, but they made it, then allowed themselves a few more hours' sleep. Daylight would facilitate their journey through the warren of paths.

A good rest had eased Derry's troubled mind. He had convinced himself that the smoke Skimnoddle had smelled had come from the halfling's imaginative head. They would be through the gorge in a matter of hours, and Derry had every confidence that Phennil and the others would be waiting for them, and there would be no further delays.

"Are you sure you know your way through here?" Jesqellan sounded uncharacteristically apprehensive.

"I've been here once before," Derry replied with as much confidence as he could while still being honest. "If we keep going east, we'll reach the Lakewood, and the upward path is just beyond it."

They trudged eastward, hugged up against the wall of the ravine. About an eighty-foot wall towered over them; not a sheer precipice, but impassable except by the pathway they'd descended in the night. Scrub trees jutted out of the sandy incline, their roots poking out as if reaching for water in the air. Sage and other grasses dotted the walls too, their fragrance dry and tingly mixed with the smell of sand. On the riders' right was a museum of sheer, buttelike formations. Lichens and liverworts coated their north sides in a green fur. A traveller could saunter in and around them, and though they might suffer a few setbacks in the form of trails that came to dead ends or culminated at unfathomably deep sinkholes, so long as they kept in roughly the same direction, all the twisting, turning, up- and downhill pathways would ultimately lead them to the Lakewood, a sparse forest which had sprung up at the far end of the gorge within the spoon shape that had once been called a "bottomless" lake.

Derry guessed that in an hour or so, he would lead the party around the far end of the buttes, doubling back on himself, into the counter-clockwise path that arced around the Hill of the Dead.

The travois drew smoothly along the dry, even terrain. Kyer's face was pinched, in spite of the lack of usual jouncing, and Derry worried that she dreamt again. *Perhaps we should stop for a moment.* But before he could call a halt, the sound of whinnying horses reached them. It came from above and was amplified by the reverberations in the curves of the rock that surrounded them.

Derry's gaze flew skyward. A familiar blue uniform stood high above. Several more uniforms flanked him, with bows drawn and pointing down at the little party in the chasm. *This would explain Skimnoddle's smoke.*

"Halt!" came the call. The voice was remarkably clear.

"We have." Derry's apprehension added an impatient tone to his reply.

"I am Major Gilvray of the Realm Guard. If you recall."

"I do, sir." Derry's mind worked quickly to anticipate what this might be about and how to skirt around it. "You're a little south of your jurisdiction, aren't you?"

"True. However, my jurisdiction extends as far as necessary when there has been a disturbance at the Indyn Caves."

Damn it. If Jesqellan had not been injured himself, he would have remembered to obliterate the signs of their presence there. "And why do you bring this to our attention?"

"We tracked you from the caves to this place." The major's tone suggested that Derry ought not to deny the connection. "I would find it easier to discuss the matter without yelling."

Derry patted the neck of an anxious Donnagill. "What is to discuss?" he called. The sound carried so effectively, he did not have to strain his voice to be heard.

The major altered his stance and did not answer right away.

"We found evidence of a breach of the cave entrance."

The captain met the nervous gazes of his companions before tilting his head upward again. "We know nothing of a breach. Perhaps you are mistaken."

"Not likely, Captain Moraunt." Gilvray's sarcasm carried clearly down the cliffside.

"You can make no accusation to us," Jesqellan announced coolly. "When we met, you claimed not to know the caves existed." Derry glanced at him. *Good point.*

"Immaterial." Gilvray lifted his hand. "You left this behind at the caves." Derry paled. *Kyer's pouch.* He'd dropped it and forgotten it.

"Wait there," Gilvray ordered, mounting his horse. "I prefer to speak face-to-face."

Bows lowered and men mounted and rode west to the head of the trail.

"Quickly now," Derry said. "We ride."

"He said to wait," Skimnoddle said.

"I am not under orders from the Realm Guard," Derry said. "We ride. Now."

The urgency was lost on none of them.

From so far below, Derry could not count the number of soldiers Gilvray had with him. The odds were unlikely to be in Derry's favour. He was deeply concerned. Gilvray knew Kyer had stolen the key. What would the Realm Guards' retribution be for such an act? If they didn't hurry, they might find out.

Derry calculated rapidly, glancing to the rear every few seconds. *We have about a forty-minute head start.* But he looked anxiously at Kyer's travois, at Trig, fighting to break loose from Jesqellan's hold so he could run. Jesqellan, who would not ride a horse, trotted along, his legs straining to pick up speed.

Derry felt like screaming with agonized frustration and despair. Even if they left Gilvray behind in the chasm, the major would eventually catch up once they were out of it at the other end. *And what if Phennil isn't there?* Would they have to leave the others behind? Oh, it was utter foolishness to think they'd be able to shake Gilvray!

Derry clung to one thought: How familiar was Gilvray with this ravine?

Fredric was glad for the rest, though the urgency never left the little party. Propriety would insist that the elves bury their dead captain right away before continuing the pursuit. But the same propriety *should* have prevented the exchange of arrows. No word was spoken until Janak suggested they carry on. They rode another few hours, closing the gap between themselves and the chasm, before stopping again to rest. It was only midmorning.

Fredric was stunned that Phennil had killed the elven captain. Even though Carris had fired first, it looked as if he'd been startled by the bird. When Phennil finally spoke, it was to agree with Fredric's unvoiced thought.

"It was a mistake," the elf insisted. "He didn't mean to." He was having trouble eating.

"And neither did you," Janak argued with his mouth full of bread. "The fact remains: he fired first. You did what any self-respecting warrior does."

"Fire at his own kin?" Phennil said in disgust.

"Pah," Janak said, crumbs scattering. "You just don't want to believe that another elf fired at you."

Phennil glared at the space in front of him then looked away.

Something else was on Fredric's mind, and maybe a change of subject was in order. "Listen, Phennil. I've been thinking."

He felt the dwarf's distrustful glare but ignored it. Phennil turned to him, hurt still glimmering in his azure blue eyes.

"We can't see the elves following us yet," Fredric said. "But that's because we're on horseback and they're on foot. They may still be pursuing us."

"Your point?"

He had to word this carefully. "If we all go to the meeting place, we'll lead the elves there too. Do we really want a host of enemies on our trail all the way to Bartheylen Castle? How will we outrun them with an injured person on a travois?"

Janak growled at him. "What's your suggestion?"

Fredric looked around at them all as if requesting their indulgence. He didn't want to come across as if he were trying to take over. "Why don't I take the sap on to Bartheylen Castle, and the rest of you can head—"

Phennil was instantly on his feet, sword in hand, the tip within a foot of Fredric's face. Too close for comfort. *An elf who has killed another elf clearly does not possess the same scruples as he used to.* Fredric already knew that Phennil suspected his every move, and now he also realized that this Phennil was ruthless. He would not think twice about killing Fredric. *Thank the gods Harley's here.* His own man would stand up for him.

Phennil's voice was soft yet fierce. "Oh, you'd like that, wouldn't you? Fredric Heyland gets to be the hero."

Fredric's tongue played with his teeth, and he hoped the truth didn't show on his face. *I hate him.* Time to be the diplomat again. "Whatever you may have suspected me of in the past, right now I'm concerned about getting back to Bartheylen Castle and saving the life of my lady. If that means involving some heroics, then so be it. You know as well as I that we will be held up by Kyer."

"No thanks to you."

Fredric's sword crossed Phennil's. "I did not push Kyer over that brink."

"You didn't have to. It's your poisoned words that have turned our whole party against her. She's been doomed since we left Seaview. Before that, even."

"You know nothing," Fredric said. "I speak only what I know to be true. If your little lady friend is guilty of treachery, she did it to herself."

"Take that back." The elf bent his knees and elbows in battle-ready position.

"I don't want to kill you!" Fredric roared. "I want to get that sap back to the others without drawing the enemy with us."

"I won't give it to you. I trust you as much as that maul tree."

With a growl of rage, Fredric flung his sword arm back and swung his weapon around. It clanged against—

Harley's. Astonished, Fredric met the cool gaze of the only one of his men who hadn't been lost in the battle at the caves.

"Put your sword away, Hunter. You are not the chief here."

Apparently I've lost all *my men.* Fredric held his sword against Harley's with some pressure, just to show he was not giving up willingly. Eye to eye, the two humans held another sort of showdown. "Fine." At last Hunter withdrew his weapon.

Shit, Hunter kept saying to himself. *They're not going to remember my support on this fool's errand; they're going to remember* that.

Phennil curled up in his cloak on the grass. Harley sat bolt upright next to him, hand on his sword.

Roman needed absolute silence in the chamber. Kien knelt next to the bed, holding Alon's hand, damp with perspiration, stroking it. Roman's strange little cone-shaped cup was pressed against Alon's distended belly with the other end of it held just inside her ear. Occasionally the healer shifted the cup and listened again, and Jorri, the apprentice, waited with the bellows poised to puff should her mentor signal her. Val sat in an armchair near the end of the bed and could tell nothing from the prime healer's expression. He wished the procedure would end so Roman could ease Kien's anxiety, not to mention his own. At last she raised her head and looked to her lord directly.

"It is fainter than it was last week, my lord," the prime healer said gently, a worry line visible between her eyes despite her calming voice. "At twenty-two weeks, he has plenty of room to shift; it could easily be that he has turned 'round."

Kien's voice was hoarse. "But it could also be that he is . . . succumbing." Val knew how much pain it cost Kien to admit any sort of frailty, even in his unborn child.

Roman tilted her head toward one shoulder in acknowledgement. "But it is too soon to tell. Take heart, my lord. The wee one's a fighter like yourself. And the lady."

Kien pressed Alon's hand to his cheek, a gesture Val had become familiar with since his arrival a few days before. "Thank you for your kind words," Kien said stiffly.

Val heard the resentment even if the healer did not. He had known Kien for several hundred years, so even the slightest variation in timbre of the high elf's voice was recognizable. He also knew that his friend was searching for something, or someone, to blame for making his wife and his child look weak. That impression could easily be extended to himself, and appearances were everything to Kien Bartheylen.

The strongest man in Rydris must not look weak.

Skimnoddle watched the warhorse about fifteen paces ahead of him. He turned back to check for signs of Gilvray and his men, so he could warn the captain.

Still no sign of their pursuers. He saw Jesqellan again perform the spell that would hide their trail.

When he glanced down for his periodic check of the invalid, he did a double take.

Kyer's eyes were wide open.

He could not tell if she saw and registered their surroundings. She had, over the past few days, opened her eyes, yet she hadn't reached complete consciousness. From atop his pony, he was too far away to see whether her eyes held that same glassy stare. But her face looked squeezed with pain, and her body held tension, as if she were trying to prevent herself from tumbling out of the carrier.

What goes on in her beleaguered mind?

One thing more ... a thing you possibly don't even know yourself. I know about a particular magical gift you have. Jolting ... aching ...

... a particular magical gift you have.

You don't need that.

A shimmering archway. Stabbing pains ... pull out of the clouds!

... a gift ... a thing you possibly don't even know yourself. Climb out! ... hurts ...

You don't need that.

A shimmering archway. Step through it to a new place. Out of the earthquake.

You don't need that.

An archway. Like a gate.

A Gate.

"Damn it!" Gilvray cried, reining in. He was sure this was the spot. He looked up. Yes, that was the bit of rock jutting out that he'd seen from above.

I shouldn't be surprised they didn't wait. Why was there no trace of where they'd gone? The tracker was off his horse, scrutinizing the ground for any sign.

"Do they have a mage, sir? This is magical obliteration; it has to be. It's too thorough."

Gilvray's memory went back to Kyer's little group. That small, black man with no hair. In the robes. *Damnation.*

"Is anyone of you familiar with this valley, this ... chasm?" He cursed his lack of geographical knowledge of the terrain south of the Pineridge Pass. *Shouldn't have spent so much time drinking whisky in Trosh.*

"Sir." It was a relative newcomer. He'd been with the outfit only about six weeks.

"Barton?"

The young fellow urged his horse forward. "I have not been here myself, sir, but my father has. What he told me about this place is that its paths are treacherously winding and some of them come to dead ends. But with persistence, one can find the river valley's exit at the east end. Will we continue the pursuit, sir?"

"Of course we're going to continue the pursuit," Gilvray snapped. "We have every reason to believe that those people breached the seal of the caves. They were trespassing, and they may very well have pilfered from it."

Barton bowed. "Then we must stick to this wall until we come to the end of a stand of rock towers then turn to the right."

"Okay, then. You will ride at the front with me, so we may get out of this Guerrin-bereft abyss." He nudged his horse forward.

Janak jerked awake at the pounding in the earth. The sun was high. Past midday. He cursed himself for dozing off and roused the others in a hurry.

"We slept too long!" he cried. "They're coming."

Phennil scrambled to his feet. "By the Goddess, they're coming fast."

They vaulted onto their animals, Harley riding with Phennil again, and flew in the direction of the chasm with the enemy at their heels.

Derry slowed down to navigate around the acute angle to the right without spilling Kyer. The Hill of the Dead loomed over them on the left, blocking out the diffused sun with its stark, dark greyness.

Derry stopped to make sure the others got around the corner safely.

"The Hill of the Dead, my friends." He indicated it with an uneasy glance. "They say it was created by the hands of the gods. They held a battle for supremacy with the creatures of this world. Men, dwarves, centaurs, you name it. They were all involved. Except, of course, the elves." He stood in the stirrups and sat again. "We must go."

"None of the elves were involved? Not even the high elves?" Jesqellan asked.

Derry smiled as he chirruped to Donnagill. If any elven faction were to battle with other beings for supremacy, it would be the high elves. "No, so far as I know, not even they. It is said that when the gods won, which naturally they did, they heaped the cadavers of the slain here in what was still a river at that time. The dead numbered so many that the sheer weight of them compressing upon each other eventually turned them into stone. If you look closely, you can see them."

Derry had been inside this ravine only once before, and at that time, he was not the leader. He had taken the time then to gaze searchingly up the rock face. Though age and weather had smoothed the stone, the young man had imagined he saw quite defined outlines of ribs, of knees, of faces.

This time, though, Captain Moraunt shuddered and did not raise his eyes. He quickened the pace as much as he dared. The trail climbed a low-grade slant then curved to the left. Derry had to duck to allow himself and Donnagill to pass beneath a water-carved archway of stone. The others, riding their smaller animals, had more clearance.

As they came to the south side of the Hill of the Dead, the trail forked three ways. Derry stopped abruptly, a frenzy of memories flipping through his head. *Which way? Oh, why didn't I pay more attention?* They could ill afford to make the wrong choice. If the trail came to an end and they had to turn back, they'd likely run right into their pursuers.

Derry leafed among the memories and his common sense. The path to the right obviously came from upstream. The one straight ahead appeared to go steeply downhill up ahead, and the captain had no recollection of steep trails on his previous journey. *Fine, then.* Eastward lay their destination. He led the party to the left.

"The second we get out of sight of this fork, obliterate," Derry ordered Jesqellan, who didn't have to be told twice.

It may have been mere coincidence, but Derry soon knew he'd taken the correct trail. They faced east for a time, then due south, passing another trail off to the right, which the captain ignored without hesitation. The trail took an abrupt curve to the left. The rock was rounded out and smooth, and Derry pictured water crashing and swirling before being tossed eastward in a splashing and foaming torrent. The sound of hooves fit into his imaginings all too readily. He stopped, raising his hand to alert the others to silence. Was it just a trick of amplification? Or were Gilvray and his men not far behind?

Jesqellan threw his obliteration spell again, but Derry knew it may not be enough. If he could hear Gilvray, then chances were Gilvray could hear them. And they were not burdened with an injured friend. *Come on, we're nearly there. I can feel it.* He hastened forward, veering to the right of a rocky cliff that had once been a fifteen-foot waterfall, choosing instead the pebbly higher ground, with weeds and small shrubs. A shadow passed overhead, and Derry looked up to see a raptor disappear into its home in the cliff face, its talons full of dinner.

The path began a slow descent, following the water's bizarre pattern. Derry glanced back to see that Jesqellan was managing Trig and received a signal from Skimnoddle that Kyer was safe.

The rumble of horses behind them grew louder. Derry also heard a cry of some command being given.

"They must have someone with them who knows the paths," Jesqellan said.

The next fork came into view. The trail to the right went straight and looked to be the correct choice. But Derry paused a moment. Sheer walls surrounded them, nearly touching the clouds with their coloured layers of rock and soil. The captain chose the trail that swerved left.

He sighed with relief. The pathway went north for only a few paces then bent sharply to the right, and soon the cavernous chasm opened before them in a breathtaking scene.

An alpine meadow, stolen by the gods from the mountains and concealed down here in the dry river valley. A greensward, confettied with wildflowers of all varieties, shades, colours, fragrances, blooming against all natural laws imposed on the above-ground world. Bees and birds buzzed, flitted, and twittered, and a light sprinkling of dew dazzled in the hazed-over sunlight.

Beyond the meadow of flowers, about the same distance as the gatehouse at Shael Castle across the ward to the door of the keep: the Lakewood.

They raced as fast as they could, without spilling Kyer, through the flowers, crushing them mercilessly with their passing. Beyond the wood lay their destination. At least they'd have a fighting chance once they had their full party together again.

The trees drew nearer and nearer. What type or sort of trees they were, Derry did not know or care. He looked back. Still no visible sign of Gilvray. *Trees, here we come.*

Donnagill ducked into the relative darkness, and only when he'd gone far enough to make room for his companions did Derry pause. A call reached his ears before he could turn around.

Gilvray's blue uniform belched forward out of the cliff-lined paths. He did not slow the pursuit. The flight was useless.

Derry gritted his teeth in despair and threw despondent glances at his companions. A quick look at the pain etched on Kyer's face reminded him that he hadn't given her any tea, and he worried that she might regain consciousness, here in the middle of all this. *There's nothing for it.* He hollered the others to hustle, kicked Donnagill, and together they fled through the forest.

Twenty-Nine

It Is All Very Complicated

I n the early afternoon, Roman sent Kien out for some fresh air, and Jorri went to fetch more herbs from the gardens. Roman placed her amplification device on Alon's belly again.

Val waited until she was through. "If you need me for any reason," he said, "I'm going to go see if I can be of assistance to Governor Plushek while Kien is, more or less, out of commission."

He was a few paces from the door when Roman stopped him.

"My lord."

He turned back to see atypical distress on the prime healer's face.

"I wouldn't trouble you, sir, only with Jorri and Lord Kien not here, I thought it was a good opportunity."

Val returned to the bedside. "I've always been a proponent of taking advantage of opportunities," he encouraged her and sat in Kien's chair.

"It's just that—" Her expression had resumed its usual placidity, but she lowered her voice and spoke quickly. "I've not been . . . *dishonest* with Lord Kien, but I have omitted certain details. Perhaps it is foolish of me, but I keep hoping your company will arrive with the medicine. I have assumed that since there has been no word in all this time, they at least have learned *something*, or else they would have arrived long ago." She waved her hands. "Never mind.

"The fact is, Lord Valrayker, the baby's heartbeat has grown steadily fainter and fainter over the last couple of weeks. I don't know what to tell him. Just now, sir, I could not hear it at all." Roman sank onto the bed and sobbed into her hands.

Valrayker crossed his legs and stroked his chin. He set his mind to stringing the right words together to tell his best friend that their efforts had failed.

Shimmering archway. A gate.
Too much jolting. Pain . . . throbbing pain.
I must wake up. Wake up. Something's wrong. They need my help.
Who're you kidding? You can't do anything. Broken.
We have to get to Bartheylen Castle.

Phennil was filled with an ever-increasing sense of foreboding. The chasm was dead ahead, and Derry and the others were nowhere in sight. Behind them, the hooves of the elves pounded nearer and nearer.

Down in the chasm is our only chance.

Jesqellan let go of Trig's bridle and leapt aside. "Carry on!" he cried to Skimnoddle. "Don't wait."

Skimnoddle sped past him.

Jesqellan gripped his staff before him and crossed his arms as though embracing a child. He closed his eyes and delved into the recesses of his body to his depth of understanding, all his training. He concentrated and the words puffed out from between his tight lips.

It isn't much, but it will help.

He turned and, in spite of the aching in his short legs, ran full out to catch up.

Gilvray was in the lead, his guide by his side. Together they dashed across the meadow, the other riders close behind. But before they were halfway across the field, something odd happened.

Gilvray felt as though he'd been sucked into some gelatinous substance. He could still breathe; he could still feel the pounding of his heart. He could hear the squeal of his horse. He tried to look around, but his every movement had been slowed, sluggish, as if he were wading through mud. Panic rose in his throat, and he felt a cry of anguish build, but when he went to let it out, his teeth and lips struggled to part even slightly.

What is happening?

When he finally burst out of it, whatever it was, it was like being shoved from behind. He fell off his horse, who, in the aftermath of its panic, bolted. The rest of the men erupted out in a similar fashion. Some lost horses as Gilvray had, and everyone, to a man, needed a moment to recover. They had travelled only about half the width of the meadow, and Gilvray could not tell how long it had taken. It was as if time had stopped.

"Light!" Derry shouted and felt like crying. *Through the exit to . . .*

Derry slowed down, sensing that something was not right. *Oh no.* About ten paces from the edge of the wood, he stopped and dismounted.

Skimnoddle pulled up alongside, followed by Jesqellan.

Jesqellan looked a question at Derry, and the captain held a finger to his lips. Skimnoddle remained with Kyer while they stepped cautiously toward the edge to peek out beyond the wood. Another meadow, just like the one on the western side, though narrower. The sandy face of the ravine bordered the meadow on the far side, and the V-shaped pathway where the water used to escape the confines of the lake was close by.

A cloud of dust filled the downward trail from the upland, accompanied by more pounding hooves. The dust descended the hill, resolving as it neared, into riders. *They can't have sent men around, can they?* Derry crouched back behind a thick-barked tree.

"It's Phennil!" Jesqellan cried as their friends reached the bottom of the trail and raced across the meadow toward them. Aching legs notwithstanding, the mage jumped out of the cover of trees and waved his arms wildly. Derry joined them, relief flooding through him.

"Success?" he called. The four horsemen reined in but didn't dismount.

Phennil nodded wearily. "Thank goodness you're here. How quickly can you move?"

"We have wood elves on our tail," Janak said.

"We have Gilvray and his men on ours," Derry said. "We've got to go now."

Exhaustion and despondency were manifest.

"I hope you know another way out of here," Derry said, and Phennil nodded again, eyes scouting the ravine wall's south edge.

Jesqellan hurried to Skimnoddle, who had been stroking Kyer's forehead.

"We have to give her—"

The mage grabbed Trig's bridle, saying, "There's no time. I've only held Gilvray off for a few minutes, and Phennil's brought his own company."

"But Kyer is—"

"Move!"

They dragged their shattered forms into the light. Behind them, horses and men crashed through the woods. Above them, wood elves stood primed with arrows nocked.

They were trapped.

Bartheylen Castle. We have to get there.

Kyer's eyes opened.

Bartheylen Castle, she told herself and the space before her.

A shimmering archway, like ripples in the air, formed next to her, about five paces away. The archway was hers. Effortless. She had made it. She could unmake it if she wanted to. It felt so natural.

Through that archway, she could see a sort of town. Plains spread out around it. In the centre of the town rose a gigantic structure. She had never seen it before. But she knew it.

Bartheylen Castle.

"Gate," she said, in a weak laryngitic whisper. She became aware of others around her. "Gate," she said louder. It was important that they hear her. She swallowed.

"Gate!" she croaked.

Jesqellan stood poised, staff in hand, in a quandary over which way to look. Some of the elves remained at the top, while the rest had begun a swift descent. They'd be here in moments. More dangerous was Gilvray, whom the mage could hear getting closer and closer. The Moabi wanted desperately to slow them down again. *But I'm so tired.*

He scolded himself. *You're a battlemage. A shaman!* Mere depletion should not prevent him from success in battle. He drew his staff in and bowed his head.

A strange sound permeated his brief attempt at concentration. He looked up, seeking its source. He heard it again, and this time recognized it for what it was.

He scurried over to Kyer, whose eyes were open and flashing with desperation to get someone's attention. She met his alarmed gaze and immediately flipped her head to one side. Dumbstruck, he realized what she'd said: Gate.

Jesqellan gasped and thanked his gods he was the one who had heard her. He was the only one who would understand the significance of this. He saw what lay on the other side of the Gate, and in the crux of the moment, the fact that she could do what he could not did not matter.

"Can you hold it open for us all?" he asked breathlessly.

She nodded.

The mage jumped up. "Everyone. This way." Nobody moved. They were too bewildered. "The Gate. Go!" He pointed at it with his staff. "There's no time to lose!"

Phennil looked at him fearfully but seemed to know that if there was a time to trust his comrade, it was now. The elf, with Harley behind him, raced through the Gate.

Gilvray urged his horse on as if he were the one being pursued. He could see his quarry through the last few trees. He drew his sword and cried out.

The sun blinded him as he broke out of the wood, and he lifted his arm to shade his eyes. The sight that met them caused him to catch his breath. Derry Moraunt kicked his heels into the flanks of his warhorse and galloped through—what was it? A doorway. Made of nothing.

Jesqellan the Moabi mage was the only one left. He and . . . Kyer Halidan, fastened down on a travois being drawn by her horse. What trauma had befallen the fascinating girl who had so captivated him? Then betrayed him. As Jesqellan led the animal through the doorway, she lifted her head just a little.

She smiled at him. And was gone.

The doorway evaporated into nothingness, like a candle flame, leaving no trail of smoke to show it had been there at all.

He leapt off his horse and looked frantically for the door. His flailing arms felt nothing. He searched the grass for a clue. Hooves, footprints, the trails of Kyer's travois being dragged, all of them came to an abrupt end. They had vanished.

He looked around at his men; their jaws were open in astonishment equal to his own. A company of wood elves rushed up, their pace slowing substantially, their faces pale as they looked around, baffled.

Still panting from the chase, Major Ryerson Gilvray cleared his throat. He glanced down at his drawn sword and sheathed it, feeling utterly foolish.

"Well, men." He couldn't keep the frustration from his voice. He'd been foiled; there were no two ways about it. "It seems they have eluded us. We will just have to head up that pathway, there. We should be home in about a week."

"What do we tell the colonel?" Marcus Flemming asked.

Perhaps there was no need to tell Colonel Greenburg about the cave breach.

Gilvray sighed and thought of Kyer with a scowl. Then he thought of his wife and his heart ached.

There's always the truth.

Derry sat on Donnagill's back, breathing hard, staring at the sight before him. After the sounds of the chase, the pounding hooves and cries, the sudden silence was like awakening from a frantic nightmare. The breeze ruffled his hair. The journey they had just taken defied reason. He had heard of Gates before, but he'd heard it was a tremendously powerful spell. He also knew that a Gate could only be created to a destination the caster could either *see* at that moment or *had been to*. Kyer claimed she had never been to Bartheylen Castle, so *how could she have opened a Gate to it?* Thoughts flashed through the captain's mind as he waited in the field of brome and bluegrass. The dots of red and white clover and the bright yellow of buttercups were a wash of colour to his unfocussed eyes. His heart sank deeper.

Kyer lay with closed eyes. Creating and maintaining the Gate had worn her out.

The Gate is proof that she's been here before. To deliver a blue serpent necklace?

Derry finally absorbed the silence around him. Dazed, he regarded his companions, who sat or stood expectantly, too stunned themselves to speak. The captain took charge again. He cleared his throat.

"Let's go." He nudged Donnagill forward then paused. "I think it would be best if *I* tell Valrayker about this."

The others nodded wordlessly.

"Who comes?" The sentry held his spear horizontally across the entrance.

"Captain Derry Moraunt, to see Lord Valrayker, if he's here." Derry hastily added, "And Lord Kien."

"On what business?"

Derry began to formulate a diplomatic answer but caught himself. "By the gods, man, we have the medicine for Lady Alon Maer."

The guard started visibly at that and ordered his men to stand aside. Derry and the others flew past and into the courtyard. They dismounted by the stables, and hostlers rushed out to meet the riders.

"Harley, you stay with Kyer, please. I will make sure someone is sent down to take her to the house of healing." Derry ordered as he took out his portion of the ingredients. "You," he said to Fredric, "had better stay out of sight. Kien is not likely in the frame of mind to deal with your issues just now." The captain added Kyer's sack of red cave dust to his collection. He passed close by the exiled former captain and surprised himself. "For my part," he said, low, "I'm willing to put in a good word."

Fredric's face blanked in equal surprise.

Derry, flanked by Janak and Jesqellan, followed by Phennil and Skimnoddle, walked up the curved, stone hill to the main doors. The steward, Moira, happened to be heading toward the door from the gardens and immediately recognized the significance of the group's arrival. She opened the doors for them.

"Moira, where is Lord Kien? And is Lord Val here yet?"

She bobbed her head. "Yes, sir, Lord Val only arrived about three days ago. You'll find them together in my lady's chamber. Shall I escort you?"

"Yes, thank you, that would probably be a good idea."

Derry's long stride easily kept pace with her through the foyer and up the stairs. Their boots' plodding was muted by the straw mats on the floor in the corridor, and Derry was charmed by the baskets of fresh flowers along the walls. *When someone is ill, it's important to keep everyone's spirits up.* The candelabra flashed past his sight as they hastened, and finally Moira's steps took a curve and she stopped outside a door.

"I must warn you to prepare yourselves. The lady is . . . quite altered, you know." Moira knocked. A voice answered, and she opened the door.

"Captain Derry and company, my lords."

Derry hurried in to where Kien and Val both had leapt to their feet, unable to mask their hopeful and expectant expressions. Derry was relieved to see the healer there as well. He wouldn't have to repeat himself.

"My lords, we have been successful." He held out his hands and the items they carried. Val emptied the tea tray of its usual burdens and brought it over. Each one laid his share of the items on the tray, which Val placed on the tea trolley. Skimnoddle placed his little clay bottle proudly next to the other items. The healer rushed over and began peeking inside pouches and sacks. Phennil, blue eyes unusually lacklustre, clutched the waterskin of sap to his chest, unwilling to give it up after all he went through to get it, *which*, Derry suddenly realized, *I don't know anything about*. The reunion with their friends and the abrupt decision to walk through a magical Gate had all happened so quickly.

"Tahleema," Derry said to Roman, pointing out the bottle. "The lichen is called falander, and there's this." He opened the sack of dust and offered it to her to peer into. "Phennil has sap from the Tree of Life too." Derry sighed and his shoulders sagged. The journey was over. The mission was complete. The other four travellers sank into chairs or leaned against furniture. Derry finally noticed Kien, who stood just as tall and proud as ever, leaning against the headboard of the bed. "We went end to end of the Guarded Realm for this stuff, Val, you have no idea—"

"What do I do with it?" Roman asked.

Derry turned to her. "What do you mean? I thought you'd know."

Roman shook her head. "I've never seen *this* before." She indicated the lichen. "I've used tahleema, but as a massage oil, not for medicine, and this . . ." She played with the string on the sack. "This is . . . *dirt*. What am I supposed to do with *dirt*?" Her voice rose in near panic. "And there has to be a spell or an incantation . . ."

"It's something about the dry ingredients and an extract from the flower. Kayme didn't tell us anything else, he only told us the ingredients." Derry's fatigue and frustration were mounting.

"If you'll excuse me, Captain," came Skimnoddle's best orator's voice. "Kayme has not told *us* anything. He has only shared information with Kyer."

"Kyer." Val straightened, darting a glance around. "Where's Kyer?"

"Wounded." Derry pulled himself back together. "She took a bad fall outside the Indyn Caves." Val's eyebrows shot upward. "Getting the ingredients here was priority, so we left her down in the courtyard. We need to get her to the healing rooms."

"Will she know how I am to prepare these things?" Roman asked.

Derry shrugged. "She may. If Kayme has told her yet. If she's conscious."

Roman looked confused but brushed it off, speaking impatiently. "By the goddess, it sounds like treating her wounds may be of equal importance."

Derry tried not to feel scolded for his lack of foresight. He started to follow the prime healer out the door but stopped, a dark thought having skipped back into his memory. *Harley can tell her about Kyer*, he decided. Turning back to Val and Kien, unable to make himself glance over at the lady, he thrust quavering words to his lips. "Does—" he began, swallowed, began again. "Does Alon Maer wear a necklace? Shaped like a serpent?" He dreaded the answer and felt his comrades stiffen to attention.

"Yes," Kien replied with just a hint of surprise, either that the question should be asked or that Derry should know about the necklace.

Derry felt the way he had when he was told his parents had died in the pestilence.

Jesqellan's voice came softly from the corner by the door. "Please remove the necklace, my lord. We have reason to believe it is the cause of the lady's illness."

Kien and Val reacted as if a fireball had just blasted through the window.

They rushed over to Alon Maer, who went into a frenzy as the two elves tried to remove the serpent. Jesqellan rushed over to help.

"Let me, my lords." They restrained Alon while the mage, with a handkerchief around his hands, unclasped the deadly trinket and wrapped it in the cloth.

"I will take this upstairs to Cweivan for examination." He hastened from the room.

Kien's face had turned grey like his hair. The workings of internal rage showed in the lines on his forehead and the pulsing tension in his jaw. Derry knew that the high elf would quickly need to lay blame somewhere and carry out that rage on someone. He wanted out of the room badly.

"How do you know this?" The fuming duke's voice was ironically calm.

Derry cleared his throat. If it hadn't been necessary to remove the necklace to save the life of Alon Maer, he would have wished he hadn't brought it up. He caught Phennil's eye, and the blond wood elf's gaze warned him to watch his words. "It is a theory we have developed over the last few weeks, begun by some information we received."

"How did you know about the necklace?" Valrayker asked.

"We were told by . . . by someone connected . . . that it was a possibility. We don't know that individual's sources. That's why I had to ask if the necklace was real, but now that I know it is, I—"

"I want to know all about this," Kien said through clenched teeth.

Derry held up his hands. "My lord, I'm not prepared to—"

"That is my *wife* lying there," Kien yelled, pointing at the wasted form on the bed. "She is *dying*, and so is my *child*. If someone has murdered my wife and child, I want to know who did it." His fury was a wave on the sandy shore, carrying him across the room, nearer and nearer to Derry.

The captain stood his ground. "Lord Kien, I don't think this is the—"

"I don't care what you think."

Derry knew it was emotion speaking through Kien, but the words slapped him.

Val put a restraining hand on his friend's elbow. Kien flung him off but moved his focus from Derry to Val. "Go out, Kien," the dark elf said in a low, insistent tone. "Speak to no one. Go down the back way to the armoury and cut a practice dummy to ribbons. I will speak to my people and report to you later." There was no arguing when Valrayker spoke in that manner. Not even Kien Bartheylen dared counter him. The high elf spared no glance for anyone in the room but swished out of the chamber.

Jorri, the healer apprentice, returned just then, rushing over to the bed. "Where is her necklace?" she cried.

"We have removed it," Valrayker said.

Jorri sighed in relief. "She mentioned the serpent necklace, that we should take it off the lady, so Roman sent me up here. Your friend is now in the healing rooms."

"Has Kyer told the healer about Kayme's instructions?" Phennil asked.

"No, not yet. She's asking for the captain, here."

A jumble of confusion and surprise welled up inside Derry. Val nodded to him, so he excused himself.

Left upstairs, the remaining three members of the little party waited in silence. Phennil watched the door close behind the captain. He used a hand to push his weight away from the bureau he'd been leaning on and breathed deeply. His eyes met Val's.

"You've had quite a journey, hunh?" Val said.

Phennil was too weary to nod. "Yup."

Val glanced at Alon's limp form and turned back to the wood elf. "Why don't we go down to the study, and I'll call for some refreshment? You can start your story."

"I . . . don't know how much we should say without Derry," Phennil said.

"Fair enough but I'm sure Derry will be back soon." Valrayker led them down the hall to Kien's study, where they were soon joined by Jesqellan, who told them that the castle wizard had begun work on the necklace. Val asked the servant in the hall to bring some extra chairs from the library prior to fetching some food for the travellers.

He poured them each a cup of wine and made them sit. He took Kien's chair behind the oak desk. "Can you at least tell me how Kyer was injured?"

The friends looked around at each other. Jesqellan opened his mouth to speak then seemed to have trouble finding the words.

"I understand the accident occurred at the Indyn Caves?" Val prompted.

"Yes. You see, hmm, you must understand that it is all very complicated," Jesqellan said.

"The accident?"

"No, the accident itself was quite simple. The circumstances surrounding it are more complex." Jesqellan struggled with the story.

Janak plunged ahead. "She fell over the side of a precipice while in the action of impaling another woman with her sword. They went over together." Then, "The other woman died," he added, to clarify the contrast between the two women's outcomes.

"Who was she?"

"We met up with . . . another party along the way. She was a member of that group." Jesqellan's choice of words reminded the others not to say too much about it.

By this time Phennil had worked out a summary. "You see, we met with Kayme, who took a liking to Kyer. He and she spent the evening together, and then he gave her the information about the cure, but she sort of heard it in her mind from time to time. As if he were only telling her what she needed to know at any given moment. We found the lichen in the Cold Fells and she and I were stuck underground after the earthquake—"

Janak interrupted. "Then we were fired at by—"

"Never *mind* that just now," Jesqellan warned him. "We—Skimnoddle —located the tahleema in a town called Seaview, and then we headed to the Indyn Caves for the dust."

Valrayker leaned forward. "I am curious about this part, I confess. It has been many years since I was in the caves. I wonder how much they have changed?"

"You've been to the Indyn Caves?" Phennil's eyes widened.

Val smiled. "You're so surprised. The Indyn Caves are a dark elvish centre. I am a dark elf, after all."

Phennil gaped. "*Dark* elvish? I guessed they were elvish, but— How did we miss that?"

"We missed it because Kyer did not tell us," Jesqellan muttered. "Just like she did not tell us a lot of things."

"Maybe she did not *know*." Janak glared at the mage as Phennil stood up suddenly, wine sloshing on his tunic.

"How dare you bring that up right after warning us not to say anything about—"

Valrayker's voice halted their heated words. "Never mind. Tell me nothing that you do not wish to share without Derry." He waited for the two to compose themselves before saying, "Just tell me about going into the caves."

Phennil sat and dropped his chin onto his hand. Jesqellan sighed. "We don't know. You see, we were . . . separated from Kyer, and she made her own way there. We didn't even know she was there until she came rushing out, stabbed the woman, and fell over the brink. We haven't shared more than two words with Kyer in over a week."

A knock sounded on the door and Derry entered. Harley was with him.

The captain maintained his stoic countenance long enough to introduce the newcomer.

"It's an honour to meet you, sir." Harley bowed.

Val glanced around at his spent group of warriors and smiled. "I'm sure at some point I will learn how you came to fit into this mix. I understand much of the story is difficult to tell." He invited Harley to sit and gave him some wine. "First, my Captain, tell us what just transpired."

Derry sank into a chair. "Kyer told us how to make the cure. Roman has already begun preparing the medicine and readying the incantation. It will be ready in four hours."

Thirty
He Must Find Some Way

Kyer hauled her eyelids upward as if they were sacks of flour. Blinking a few times, she tried to place herself. The last thing she remembered was eyes. Deep, dark, inviting eyes, gazing down at her. They wanted her to do something. *No, that's not it.* Her vague recollections moved further ahead in time. An open area before the pillars of stone. A dark-haired woman, strangling Derry. Dashing forward with her sword straight in front of her, the blade gliding easily through the bitch's body. The force of the move pulling her over . . . no more footing, nothing to grab on to. Nothing.

Kyer gasped and tried to sit up, couldn't, and panic rose like bile in her throat. She frantically looked at the things around her in hopes that new images would block out the one she did not wish to revive. Everything came back to her. The journey, the evening with Kayme, the earthquake, Soren, Gilvray. Derry.

She had vague memories of some bizarre dreams too. Her eyes were wide open now.

She lay in a bed in a room about three times the size of her little chamber at Shael Castle. The whitewashed stone walls might have looked stark but for the tapestries in warm, autumnal shades. Wall sconces with bright candles flickered between them. The door on the opposite wall was closed, and above her head, a small window let no light steal around the shutters and curtains, so Kyer assumed it was night. Another bed next to hers was neatly made up with a brightly coloured woven spread. To the left of where she lay, a fire crackled in a white stone fireplace, and next to that, a small white-robed woman with long, greying hair that had once been dark hovered over a small metal bowl on a table. A dark green silk scarf partially covered her head.

"What is this place?" Kyer's voice cracked from lack of use over goodness knew what period of time.

The woman looked around. "Ah, you've come back, have you?" She smiled kindly but did not stop what she was doing. "You've been away a good long while, you know."

"How long? Where am I? Where's Derry?" Apprehension bubbled within her. "Why can't I move?" She found her right leg was moveable, though stiff, but her other had been bound tightly and felt leaden. Her left arm below the elbow had been immobilized with plaster, and her right arm was strapped across her chest, tied tightly to a splint. "What did I do to three quarters of my body?"

The woman set the bowl on the hob and came over to Kyer, putting a hand on her forehead and three fingers of the other on her wrist. "You're in the house of healing at Bartheylen Castle. You've been here since the day before yesterday, and I believe a week passed prior to that since your accident. You'll have to clarify that with your friends. They're likely asleep right now; it is the middle of the night, after all."

"That long?" Kyer tried to piece her vague memories together. "I remember falling. What the hell happened? How did we get here so fast?"

"That you will also have to ask one of your friends. I was not there, you see. I only entered your life when they brought you here. My name is Imogen, and I am your chief healer, though you will meet others. It appears you were very lucky."

She did not elaborate. Kyer pressed her, but Imogen just smiled patiently. Sharp, stabbing pains shot down her back, and a dull ache throbbed in her left leg. The old woman gave Kyer a warm, evil-tasting drink, and soon a burning numbness crept through her limbs. The strange sensation took her mind off the pain for the short time it took to dull it. But at the same time, her mind faded and she fell asleep again.

The next time she awoke, Phennil sat next to her on a chair. He was reading a thick, dusty book. He looked up as she winced and tried to shift.

"Ah, there you are," he said, as if she had just entered the room. "Imogen told me you woke up last night, so I thought I would come and wait for you." He put a ribbon between the leaves of the volume to mark his place and closed it, putting it on the floor. He then folded his hands on his lap, ready for a conversation.

"We're very glad you're still with us," he said matter-of-factly.

"Are you going to tell me what happened, or are you going to be as useless at providing information as Imogen?" Kyer said with mock irritation.

"Oh, it's good to have you back, sarcasm and all," the elf responded lightly. "What do you want to know?"

"Well, what happened? How did we get here? Did we find the rest of the ingredients?" she added earnestly, the thought having just come to her.

Phennil calmed her with a hand. "Slow down. Yes, we did. We are all anxious to learn how you got into the caves and found the dust. I and . . . some others went along to the Tree of Life." His voice caught and she waited for him to elaborate, but all he said was, "and we got the sap."

With nothing further forthcoming Kyer encouraged him. "And Alon Maer?" Her heart thudded.

"Is improving. The prime healer followed your instructions—"

"What?"

"Yes, from Kayme, I suppose, but you told her and Derry how much of the dry stuff to soak in how much of the sap with whatever kind of crystal for four hours. They've been administering it to her, along with an incantation, three times a day since the night before last, and though it's still early, it seems to be helping."

Kyer breathed deeply of the scented oils that drifted through the room from the brazier at the end of her bed. Profound relief and calm washed over her like a warm wave. She fought back tears.

"That's good, then." Her voice was hoarse with emotion. "It was all worth it."

"As for you," the jovial elf went on, "broken leg, broken arm, lots of repair work done on the muscle of your right shoulder. All in all, you were pretty lucky."

Kyer steeled herself. "I guess it could have been worse. But my weapon arm . . ."

Phennil nodded, unsmiling. "Imogen says you will certainly walk again soon, though I should warn you that you will probably have a limp, maybe for the rest of your life. Your left arm will heal fine. Derry did excellent work there. You've had two low-grade healing potions to speed up the process on the right side, but not so much that the muscle won't heal itself naturally, which will prevent the weaker fibres that sometimes come of hastened tissue regrowth. You'll have to work on that muscle to regain your strength and dexterity in that arm. She says with time and exercise, you'll be back to swinging that sword of yours."

She tried to process the thought of fighting with a limp, but she shelved the information for later. "Where *is* Derry? I expected him to be here."

A shadow fell over Phennil's bright features. "He's . . . well. A lot has gone on in the last couple of weeks. There are . . . things to deal with."

"My, aren't you the cryptic one."

Phennil shrugged and spoke with a hint of what Kyer could only define as bitterness. "It isn't going to be easy to explain a lot of this stuff. You left at the beginning of it, and we didn't see you again until you were . . . over the edge."

"What stuff? You mean all that about the runes? That's why I need to talk to Derry." She saw by the dimness of his eyes that there was a lot on his mind.

"Well, yes, that. And more. You see, that incident was a bit of a catalyst for a whole lot of other things to come out. Stuff . . . that isn't going to be easy to explain." Phennil slowed down, as though reluctant to speak. "Your account is needed too, and Val wants to wait until the healers are sure you are ready for it."

"Val's here?" Then she clued in to his other words. "What do you mean 'my account'?"

"I am under strict instructions not to bring it up." Phennil held up his hands defensively. "I will give you one 'for instance' because I can't stand it." He leaned forward and spoke ever so softly. "Did you open the Gate?"

Kyer felt the colour drain from her face. *That really happened?*

A magical gift. *The Guardian was right.*

"There are so many things I need to discuss with you, my lord." Derry added Val's title to indicate the serious nature of the conversation. As a group, they had filled him in on the major events of the journey, and even about some of the frustrations and suspicions that had arisen from Kyer's odd behaviour. But Derry had asked the others to let him tell Dunvehran on his own about a few of the more intricate details. "But I have struggled to find a way to bring them up. They are . . ." He thought a moment. "Touchy. And I didn't want everyone around because I don't want it to become a free-for-all of finger pointing."

Val held up a hand. "It's all right. If you're ready to begin now, do so."

"Before I do, I have a question."

"Ask away."

"What was Cweivan's report about the blue serpent necklace?" He held his breath and waited.

Val's fingertips touched and he rested his hands on his chest. His contemplative expression made Derry's heart skip. But Val finally answered, "Cweivan found that the serpent necklace held a considerably powerful magical spell. He confirmed the suspicion that it was the cause of Alon's illness."

"Oh," the captain sighed deeply as disappointment sagged his shoulders.

"Aren't you pleased to learn the cause? It will be easier to help her."

Derry nodded. "Yes, of course. It's not that. It's just ... If he was right about that, doesn't it follow that he was right about the other parts of the story?"

"Who?"

Derry braced himself for the more controversial part of the discussion. "We talked already about some of our frustrations with Kyer."

Val nodded.

"And we told you about Fredric. The fact is, Fredric told us about a connection, linking Kyer with the blue serpent necklace." He forced himself to meet his lord's eyes. This would not be easy for the duke. "The evidence is fairly strong. Some in our party believe the report that Kyer is the one who delivered the necklace to Alon."

"Do you trust Fredric?" No judgement was in Val's tone.

Derry sighed. "I don't know. But the evidence points to it."

Valrayker tapped one finger on the desktop. "What sort of evidence?"

"The fact that she brought it up one day, for one thing. We were chatting and someone mentioned snakes and Kyer piped up that the snake is a symbol of undying love. That's exactly what Fredric told Jesqellan."

Valrayker's brows contracted. "Anything else?"

Derry hesitated, frowning. *If I could avoid mentioning the mirror . . .* "I wasn't convinced just by that. It was a strange coincidence, if anything."

"But you believe Fredric might be right about Kyer?"

Derry watched how the skin of his knuckles stretched and contracted as he flexed his fingers. "I don't want to, of course. I am trying to put my friendship with Kyer aside and look at the facts. She obviously knows about the necklace because she brought it up. And you see, we now know she had the means of doing it." He paused to try reading Val's blank expression. "She claims she's never been here, but—sir, she Gated us here all the way from Bolivar Chasm."

Valrayker's eyebrows lifted.

Derry flattened his palms on the arms of his chair. "First of all, how is it that Kyer Halidan, supposed farm girl from Hreth, can *Gate* when Jesqellan hasn't even begun to attempt that spell? And secondly, everyone knows you can't Gate to some place you have never been before unless you can see it in the distance. How did she open a *Gate* to Bartheylen Castle unless she's been here?"

Valrayker's expression remained impassive. Derry had to convince him.

"Kyer has undergone a change of character, Val. She's been dishonest about so many things from the start of this journey."

"And has contributed help in so many other ways," Val pointed out.

Derry tried not to hear him. "I think she Gated herself and Phennil out of the cavern in the Cold Fells. She told us some cocked-up tale, and I didn't believe it at the time. And you remember her story about escaping from Ronav's headquarters when we were on our way to Nennia."

Again Val nodded. "I do recall. I also recall her puzzlement."

"*Supposed* puzzlement, anyway," Derry suggested.

Val shrugged, as if admitting the possibility.

Derry stopped. "This isn't easy for me, you know, Valrayker." The duke drew back as if Derry had splashed a cup of water at him. Derry flushed, aware he was overstepping himself, but pushed on. "You don't like hearing these things about her; she's kind of like your prodigy, but I have to tell you about it." He felt himself pouting and unclenched his fist. Would Val have defended his captain so vehemently if the tables were turned?

"And another thing too: Kayme gave Kyer a rose," Derry went on, purging himself of all that had troubled him. *Nearly all.* "It's magical and for a long time, I was concerned that it was precipitating a lot of Kyer's troubles on the journey. Jesqellan told me it was just the opposite. It has a powerful protection spell. Can you think why Kayme, the greatest wizard in Rydris, would feel it important to protect Kyer Halidan to that degree?" His voice had risen as his incredulity burst forth, and he finally caught himself. He leaned back in his chair.

Dunvehran rested his palms on the desk. "I will give it some thought." The duke mirrored Derry's posture. "I have one question for you."

"All right."

"When did you start seeing eye to eye with Fredric Heyland?"

It was all extraordinarily interesting, Valrayker decided, leaning back and putting his booted feet up on Kien's desk. Derry was right about one thing: he did not like hearing the evidence against Kyer.

On the other hand, Valrayker had his own suspicions about Kyer. He counted them out on his fingers, weighing them against what he had heard in the reports from his company. Entering the Indyn Caves, wine, Gating, magic swords, roses, Gating...

Valrayker tapped his fingertips together and gazed at the clouds through the window. *It might be time for a chat.*

"Do you realize how many days I have been lying down?" Kyer was unable to mask her irritability. Phennil's visit the day before had been the only one of its kind. Not one of her other friends had come around since she had awakened.

"It's better for you to keep low," Imogen said with excruciating reason.

"No, it isn't," Kyer contradicted petulantly, raising her voice. "Look, I'm bored, lonely, and unhappy. If the well-being of the patient has any effect on her healing, then sitting up would be the best thing for her right now."

Imogen stood over her, the picture of eternal fortitude. Hands clasped in front, she shook her head at Kyer, almost sadly.

"Oh, very well," she sighed. "For a little while."

"That's perfect," said a familiar voice. "I wish to talk to her for 'a little while.' What a coincidence."

"Val," Kyer said as if all her prayers had been answered.

Imogen and Valrayker helped Kyer up to a sitting position, the healer fussily adjusting pillows behind her. "*Thank* you," the warrior said in all sincerity.

"Now, my lord, you are not to wear her out," Imogen warned, though she did not specify the consequences.

Val grinned at her back as she left; then he turned to Kyer. "It's in healers' contracts to say shit like that."

Kyer burst into laughter that sent shooting pains through her entire body but was the best feeling she'd had for nearly two weeks. "Oh, Val, I've missed you. Where is everyone? Do they think I'm contagious?"

Val sat in the same chair Phennil had occupied. He spread his hands out on the edge of the bed. "I *am* sorry. Your friends are concerned about you, naturally. But I am afraid some barriers have been drawn up, and they are feeling somewhat distant."

Kyer's hackles rose. Something was wrong with all this.

Val went on. "Besides, I wanted to talk to you first. I have some questions, and I didn't want the others coming in here and raising your ire."

Kyer smiled because he winked at her. How did he know she had already leapt to the defensive? He was soothing her indignation before he'd ignited it. Then a thought occurred to her.

"Before you say anything, I need to know if— Did Derry tell you about our argument?" Kyer's stomach churned at the memory of all the accusations that had flown that night. Her own guilt was a ghostly creature that hovered around her, clinging mercilessly to her memory.

Val smiled his gentle smile. "He told me about it, yes. He also explained some of the frustrations that built up to it."

Kyer closed her eyes, frowning. "Well, if you want to know my side, he was right about a lot of what he said. I thought at the time he was out of line, but the more I thought about it, the more I became conscious that I ought to have shared more with him. I had been stubborn and . . . childish, really. That's why I went back to the caves. I'd decided to leave—" She broke off, realizing what she had just admitted, and another ghost rushed in to join the first as she remembered that she never had the chance to confess that she'd killed Ronav in cold blood. She turned away from the dark elf's grey eyes that seemed to know so much. "You should never have taken me on in the first place."

His hushed voice matched hers. "Ah, but you see, if I hadn't, who would Kayme have been so taken with? Skimnoddle, perhaps?"

He wanted her to laugh, but she couldn't just now.

"With whom would he have shared all the facts about the cure? I gather that in spite of all these accusations, these dreadful things you are supposed to have done, you played a key role in the discovery of just about every item on that list of ingredients. Maybe you did walk away. Twice, so I hear." She stiffened at that. "And at some juncture, I'd be happy to listen if you'd like to tell me more about that. But you came back. You completed the task.

Another individual might not have done so. And in some cases, nobody else *could* have done so."

Kyer gazed at him with strange reluctance. "What?"

Valrayker's demeanour altered slightly. "How did you manage to open the Indyn Cave doors?"

"I had the key." The surprised curiosity on his face confirmed her suspicion that he had not heard this important detail. "I can't tell you how I learned about it. You'll have to be okay with that. I found out that the key—I assume you know what I'm talking about?"

Val nodded.

"The key was in the possession of Colonel Greenburg of the Realm Guard." She told him about their arrival at the outpost and Gilvray's refusal to admit he had the rune pattern. "Had the colonel been there, I'd have offered to deliver the key to you."

"Did you happen to learn . . . how the colonel came by it?"

Kyer had to reply with caution. Her vow of secrecy was sacrosanct. "The key was delivered to the colonel with the idea of getting it to you. The one who originally possessed it is believed to be dead but passed it to another for safekeeping, who gave it to the colonel."

"Dead." Val fell into a deeply thoughtful silence. Kyer could almost hear the thoughts swirling in his head as he tried to piece the story together. She hoped he wouldn't press her for more information, or she'd have trouble keeping her promise. She was relieved when finally he spoke. "So the colonel still has the key?"

Kyer nodded. "The colonel himself wasn't there when we were, but his second, a Major Gilvray, was guarding it."

"I'll send someone to get it. Or I'll go myself. Wait, if the colonel still has it, how did you—?"

Kyer smiled sheepishly. "Well, I sort of . . . stole the rune pattern from Gilvray. I copied it. That's what I was doing when Derry thought I was—

well, I *was*, but not for the reason—never mind." She chose to ignore the amusement twinkling in the dark elf's eyes. "So I stole the runes, and after I rode off, after our argument, it occurred to me that even though I'd left the drawing of the pattern with Derry, I was the only one with a red jewel. To my knowledge anyhow." In spite of herself, excitement coursed through her as she told the story. "I rode to the caves, got past the treyurne plant, and went to the cave doors. It took me a long time to find the matching pattern on the door, but I finally did. I let torchlight shine through the pommel of my sword and . . ." She shrugged her good shoulder. "The door opened."

Val said nothing for a moment but stared at her thoughtfully, not allowing any expression to give her a clue to his contemplations. Sunlight streamed through the window and fell across his knees like a lap dog. "So what happened once you were inside?"

Kyer gave him as much detail as she could about her experience with the sentries of the caves, how she'd found the dust, and how she'd finally escaped. "They didn't like my sword at all."

"Where is this new weapon of yours?" He followed her indication and rose to fetch it. He sat back down and examined its sheath. Though his voice remained matter-of-fact, she thought she detected a strained quality to it. "Derry and Jesqellan told me about your little diversion. May I?" She nodded and he drew it out of its sheath.

As with every time she'd removed it, the blade caught her breath with wonder. The simple beauty of it, its stunning sheen, its absolute perfection.

"So, the sentinels, they didn't like this, hunh?" He murmured quietly as if to himself. "No, I should say not." He sheathed it abruptly.

"Why?"

"Because it's a dark elvish sword, of course."

Her jaw dropped. But before she could ask him to elaborate, he said, "Now, what can you tell me about a blue serpent?"

The words arrowed into her. *First Jesqellan and now him.*

"I had a dream where I was a maid here at Bartheylen Castle." She tried to recall how many times she'd dreamt it and when they had begun. She told him how it became more detailed with each recurrence. She told him about delivering the serpent necklace. "Alon explained that the serpent is a symbol of undying love; I suppose because when it bites its tail, it creates a complete circle, unbroken."

Her throat had gone dry, and Val helped her to a sip of water.

"Anyway, Alon put the necklace on, and as soon as she did, I—whoever I was in the dream—felt I had succeeded in some task. When I woke up, I had a horrible feeling that the necklace was the cause of Alon's sickness." Kyer looked at Val hopefully. *Please explain it.* He gave no reaction. "I remember thinking, after I woke up once, that when I was a maid in the dream, I knew I wasn't really a maid." She glanced up at him again to see if he comprehended. He met her gaze quizzically. "I mean, the slippers didn't feel right, and the dress was uncomfortable, as if I wasn't used to wearing one like it."

Val cocked his head. "What did it look like?"

Kyer shrugged and her face warmed as she realized what he wanted to know. "It—was a simple shift. Blue. With a darker blue apron."

Val was silent. He picked at a hangnail on his left forefinger. "Funny," he said finally. "That is exactly what the maidservants wear over in the keep."

Something in his tone prevented her exclamation of disbelief. Her brows rose.

"And curiously enough," he went on, "Alon Maer *was* wearing a necklace exactly fitting the description you just gave me."

Kyer wanted to shrink away from his unwavering gaze. "You're not serious."

Val went on as if he hadn't heard. "When Cweivan, Kien's wizard, examined it, he discovered—can you guess?"

Kyer nodded.

Val leaned forward ever so slightly. "It's odd that you should have such an accurate dream."

"What are you trying to say?" she croaked.

"There are some who believe that you would be unable to swear upon your life that you have never been to Bartheylen Castle before." His eyes were frosty.

Blood seeped out of her cheeks. Her gut feelings had always told her to trust Valrayker. That faith was wavering as the insinuation stuck her side like a rapier.

She pleaded. "I do swear it! *You* don't believe that, do you?"

"Some wonder how you could Gate here without having been here before."

"I don't know!" she yelled. "How in seven hells *should* I know?"

"Others wonder how you can Gate at all and why you didn't tell them before."

Perspiration beaded up on her neck. She shook her head, and her voice pushed out barely above a whisper. "I don't know." Why was he attacking her this way?

"Which one don't you know?"

She strangled a burst of emotion. "I don't know how I can Gate. I didn't tell them because I didn't know I could do it."

"How did you come to know?" he pressed.

Kyer shook her head, imploring. "I—don't know. I—think you'd better go now."

"Very well." He stood up. *"Vayam seonel hætsol bourdrin praiesse,"* he said in Dark Elvish. *We will learn what it all means soon.*

Kyer jumped out of her skin, automatically replying, *"Vy lohs ain."* I *hope so.* Instantly she regretted it. He stared at her, expressionless.

He'd caught her unprepared. She was too riled up, too shocked to pretend she did not understand what he'd said. The words proving her comprehension slipped out beyond her control. The heat of an intense blush was as if she'd pulled the blanket over her head. Val was still watching her, and she was stuck. The truth was out.

She tore herself away from his heavy gaze. With her good leg, she dragged her body down until she was flat. When she looked again, the dark elf was gone.

That made two things he now knew that he had heretofore only guessed. But rather than answer all his questions, it made more. The obvious questions were: Who are you? How—no, *why* are you here? He had a suspicion, but . . . He shook his head. It didn't make any sense. He would almost stake his life that it was impossible. Almost.

He was certain Kyer herself wouldn't know any of those answers. And he felt confident that revealing anything to Kyer would be a very bad choice. No, there was one person to whom he absolutely needed to speak, who would be able to shed light on the subject. Too bad there simply wasn't time right now.

The dwarf rested a tray of food on the low wooden wall that separated Fredric's stall from the next one. Fredric leapt on the food as if he were a starved street urchin. He took it in one hand and fed himself a strip of beef with his fingers as he sat down in the hay. It smelled great, even mixed with the smell of hay and horseshit. "What took you so long?" he asked with his mouth full. "Bad enough I'm stuck out here without being nutrition deprived on top of it." He sopped up gravy with his bread.

Janak didn't respond right away but grunted.

Typical inarticulate dwarf.

The dwarf illustrated quite the opposite. "Don't get querulous with me, big fella. Your popularity is under question, remember. All it would take is a badly timed slip of my tongue to Kien, and you'd be hunted down and slaughtered."

Fredric bit his cheek and cursed. He spared the dwarf a glance without looking up.

"Be grateful I found a way to excuse myself early from dinner to put some food together for you at all." Janak picked at something on his arm.

"Wha—" Fredric swallowed his mouthful. "What's being discussed? When do I go speak to Kien?" Gods, he'd missed food from Kien's kitchen.

"Not sure." The dwarf rested his elbows on the edge of the stall. "Derry's treating it all really careful. Kien knows Alon was magicked sick; they took the necklace from her right away. There's no speculation about who did it. Not yet.

"We've told Val lots about the whole trip, and I think Val knows your part in it. Derry wants to be cautious about how he words things to Kien so he doesn't set him off."

Fredric shrugged. "I guess that's fair, but I need to speak to him soon."

"Damn right it's fair. Derry's putting himself on the line for you. You know that, don't you?" Janak went on. *He must love the sound of his own voice.* "Val won't want any finger-pointing without solid evidence. And it's going to be hard to convince him about Kyer. He's pretty keen on her. It'd be bad news if the blame were thrown at Kyer without proof."

What other proof do we need besides the Gate? "Why not let me talk to him? I'm the one who knows what really happened."

"Who knows how Kien would react if Kyer were blamed too soon? Derry wants it to be fair."

Fredric stopped mid-chew. "Too soon? For the truth?" He pointed his knife at Janak. "If Derry wants it to be 'fair,' then I should be involved." He swallowed and took a big gulp of milk. "She has all the advantage here, with all her friends to speak on her behalf. It's *my* story that has all the evidence against her. What about me? Who else is going to speak from my side?" he demanded, getting to his feet and slipping on the straw. "I don't want to get to see Kien only after they've already decided that their precious Kyer had nothing to do with it." He kicked the straw for emphasis, strewing it across his dinner tray. He leaned on his arm against the other wall. "I need to see Kien before—" *Before Alon recovers. Before Kien finds out too much. Before someone somehow proves Kyer didn't do it.*

Fredric hardly heard Janak say, "I'll talk to him, but I don't know." The dwarf left.

The threads of his plan were unravelling! The whole point was that he would humble himself before his lord and tell his story. Kien would be ready to blame someone, and Fredric would provide him with a target. Kien would be forced to reinstate him. *It's my reward for turning in the killer!* Fredric knew Kien: There was not a chance that the duke would ever hear him out if Kyer were already in too positive a light. His only hope was to get to Kien before the others did. He must find some way to tie up the end of his plan; seal Kyer's fate while repairing his own.

Thirty-One
a Family Called Halidan

Derry sat hunched in the library just down the hall from Kien's study and Alon's chamber. He had tried three chairs and could find comfort in none of them. A book sat supported by his flexed fingers, morning sunlight striping across it from the window, but he could not have described its contents. Its pages smelled musty and faintly like pipe smoke. Its cover bore the title *Home Fires: Tales of the Fall of Equart* from which he had hoped to glean some insight, or at least perspective, about his current situation. Or maybe a glimpse of home. The handwritten words swam before his sleep-deprived eyes, and after twenty minutes, he had absorbed none of them.

"Aha," said a gruff voice, and Derry, too tired to be startled, glanced up to see Janak in the doorway. "Haven't seen you at the last few meals."

Derry shrugged. "I've not been very hungry. Just grabbed a bite to eat in my room."

"I met with our beleaguered renegade last night. He's getting impatient to have his say."

Derry rolled his eyes and uttered a small growl. "He's just going to have to wait."

"That's what I told him."

The captain didn't respond but tipped his head back and stared at the ceiling.

Janak's bewhiskered jaw jutted forward. He sighed, and shunted his form toward Derry and lowered himself into the chair opposite. "You know, you two had been inseparable."

Derry didn't pretend he didn't know what the dwarf was talking about. He looked out the window, across the tops of the low buildings on the other side of the courtyard, out to where they'd emerged from Kyer's Gate. "Some things have happened, Janak. I'm not sure where I'm at right now."

Janak shifted as if he didn't care for that chair any more than Derry had. "I don't say too much, Captain, but I do know one thing: You're not going to sort any of this out by sitting around ruminating." He leaned forward and softened his tone. "By the gods, man, she saved your life. You have a problem with Kyer? Go talk to Kyer."

As if I hadn't thought of that, Derry thought crossly. But he checked his temper. "I intend to but I don't know what to say to her. I haven't decided yet how I feel about all this." *And there's that damned mirror.*

"You're more likely to figure it out if you leave your indecision in your stuffy little room and face her." Janak rose. "That's all I have to say."

Derry slapped the table next to him. "I'll speak to her when I'm good and ready and not before."

"Have it your way."

Derry watched Janak walk out. His eyes smarted.

Fredric had slept on it. And his sleeping mind had puzzled over his dilemma. As he'd slowly awakened in his warm, aromatic accommodation, his unconscious mind had shared its findings. As soon as he could that morning, he'd taken steps to put it into operation.

It felt like a cheap course of action. It galled him a little. But Fredric was desperate. Even though Derry had said he'd speak on his behalf, Fredric had to be realistic: Val's insipid, green captain had never been one of those who'd admired Captain Fredric Heyland. In spite of his good intentions, Derry Moraunt would want to defend Kyer. It would come much more naturally to him. So Fredric had chosen a desperate method of getting Kien's attention.

He slipped unseen out of the kitchens. *Now it's all about timing.* All he had to do was wait long enough for Kien to receive the information. Then the stage would be set for Fredric's entrance: he would enter and tell his story. By that time, Kien would be ready to listen.

Val's voice answered Derry's knock. The captain swallowed hard and entered.

"My lord, I must tell you this." He closed the door.

Val raised his eyebrows at him.

Keep going; don't spare him. Derry didn't sit down.

"Sir, there's something I didn't tell you yesterday." *Because it will hurt you.* "My heart tells me I must. In the name of justice." *Because I promised Fredric. And because I can't stand your blind defence of her.* "You need to know the truth."

"Of course, Derry." Valrayker's eyes were steady; his voice, sober.

"I wanted more evidence before I'd believe Kyer capable of such a crime. I wanted something more substantial." He hesitated.

"You got it and you wish you hadn't?" Val said.

Derry stared at the air before him. "Anyway, I guess I'd better show you this." He placed on the desk before Val the bundle of black cloth he had confiscated from Kyer's belongings. The dark elf lifted aside the corners of cloth, and his grey eyes enlarged when he saw the gold mirror.

"It's Alon's," Valrayker said matter-of-factly. "I've seen it before."

Derry looked away. "If Kyer was never in Alon's room, I can't imagine how she got hold of that."

Valrayker turned the thing over and over in his scarred hands, his eyes narrow, lips pursed. Derry thought he looked just as grave as when he'd told them about the lady's illness. "How did you happen by it?" Val asked.

"I was putting . . . something away and found it in her saddlebag."

"It is damning evidence, to be sure." Val exhaled heavily.

And you don't like it at all, Derry thought.

Both men jumped as the door opened. Horror flashed upon Val's face but disappeared as quick as lightning.

"Have you ever heard of knocking?" Val asked casually with a smile.

Kien moved closer. "It's my study; I didn't see that I had to knock." Then the duke's gaze fell on the item on the desk. "Where did you get that?"

Val didn't want to tell him. Derry knew by the dark elf's nonchalant expression. And for some reason it irked him.

Kien picked up on the hesitation. "Where did you get that?" he demanded. "It's been missing for weeks."

"Kien, there's a logical explanation, I'm sure . . ."

Derry couldn't believe it. *He doesn't want Kien to think ill of Kyer.*

"I found it," Derry blurted.

Valrayker's eyes closed.

"Where was it?" Kien asked.

Val pleaded wordlessly with Derry. Captain Derry Moraunt would not lie. "It was in Kyer's saddlebag."

Derry had no idea Kien's face could be any paler, but what little colour there was, drained. "How did it get there?" the high elf demanded, dismissing Val's protestations.

Derry hated what he was doing to Val, but it had to be done. "Kien, I'm afraid we have some reason to believe that Kyer has been here before."

Kyer felt sick and miserable. Imogen insisted she eat her oatmeal, and no amount of griping would change that good woman's way of thinking. Kyer forced the muck down her throat. But she did not feel better.

Even after Val's horrible little visit last night, still nobody came to see her. She was somehow in trouble, and her imagination ran rampant. Derry and the others didn't know about her dreams. Jesqellan had been upset when she mentioned the symbolism of the serpent, yet she didn't know why. In one instant, Val commended her on her contribution to the mission, and in the next, he, of all people, had all but called her a liar. She was so perplexed her head swam, her eyes stung with the hurt from his remarks, and she was sick to death of lying down.

Valrayker had tricked her. Brendow had told her to never reveal her knowledge of the Dark Elvish language under any circumstances. What would Valrayker do? Would she be punished? But then it struck her to ask, *Why did he speak to me in Dark Elvish at all? Unless . . .* Had he suspected all along that she knew it? He'd tested her and she failed. Kyer wanted to slam her fist on the bed, but her injuries forbade it. Her frustration and fear gave more power to her thoughts and more intensity to her loneliness.

What did her friends think she had done? *Why did I even come on this mission?*

There was one person who could remind her.

"Imogen, please," she begged. "I have seen way too much of these walls. Isn't there *some* way you can help me to get out of here?"

The healer did not like it, but she finally agreed. She tied Kyer's right arm against her chest in a sling and provided her with a crutch for underneath her left arm.

"Now, young miss, you take things slowly, rest frequently, and come back within twenty minutes."

Kyer nodded, agreeable to any conditions, so long as she could see the light of day. Grasping the crutch was tricky with the fingertips that stuck out beneath her plastered left arm, so anything other than "taking things slowly" was impossible. She was slightly light-headed too, this being the first time she'd been fully vertical in two weeks. Miraculously she managed to hobble out of the house of healing.

She found herself at the edge of a courtyard dotted with trees, framed with flowerbeds, and surrounded by low buildings. All except the keep on the opposite side. A cobblestone pathway curved down a hill off to her left, and the smell of horses told her what lay at its foot. *So this is Bartheylen Castle.* If she hadn't had to concentrate so heavily on walking, she might have been more awed by the structure, the asymmetrical design, the angles and towers and buttresses. She took this in superficially, staying mostly focussed on the bright, cream-coloured stone that paved the courtyard. It was so smooth, she didn't have to worry about tripping.

The fresh air smelled good and felt better. The sunshine warmed her blood. She could almost feel it thickening and coursing vigour through her where there had been none. She shuffled along, seeing no one but the odd pair of guards.

A stone bench under a beech tree provided a spot to catch her breath, with mock orange and honeysuckle on the breeze. Then she continued her journey, limping up the path to the door of the keep.

A few paces away from the front steps, Kyer glanced up from her feet to see a figure hurtle out of the door. Whoever it was dashed down the steps, and in its haste, nearly collided with Kyer.

"Look out!" she cried, trying to sidestep and nearly toppling over. Years of *wæpnian* training served her as they should, and even on a crutch, her light-footed steps saved her. Having regained her balance, she recognized the hooded face of Fredric Heyland. He looked at her as though she were a ghost.

"What in Guerrin's name are *you* doing here?" she sneered. "Got another message for me?"

Fredric glanced back toward the door, as if expecting to see someone. Whatever his reason for haste, he apparently decided to take the risk of talking to Kyer. But a dagger was in his hand before he spoke. "I should have killed you when I had the chance."

"Why didn't you?" she asked rhetorically; they both knew the answer. His eyes flamed under the shadows of his hood. She met his gaze levelly. "Put that thing away, Fredric. You won't kill me now either."

"If you tell a soul you saw me here, I *will* kill you. You have my word on that."

Kyer's eyebrows arched. "Tell me again what your word is worth, exactly?"

"Cocky bitch," he said through tight lips. Then they curled into a sneer. "Soon I'll be more welcome around here than you are. I can't wait to see you try to get out of this one."

Stuffing the dagger away, he resumed his hurried pace along the path and turned the corner with a swagger in his shoulders.

His words, Kyer was sure, related somehow to Valrayker's. Foreboding gnawed at her, but she was determined to reach her destination. She watched him until he was out of sight; then she braced herself to climb the steps.

Once inside the castle, she had to wait for her eyes to adjust, after the brightness of the sunlight's reflection off the stones. But once her pupils had dilated and she could see clearly in the dimness, she stared around the small foyer. She blinked a few times to see if the image would alter. Her head whirled and she inhaled deeply to steady it. Kyer had been here before. The image in her mind's eye was identical to the room before her. Her skin prickled with the eeriness of its familiarity.

The wood floor was polished as smooth as glass. A great circle, the centre of which formed the belly of a star, whose six arms extended to the white stone walls, reflected the light. Made of strips of dark wood, the inside star contrasted with the arms that reached out from behind, as if over the original star's shoulder. An even lighter shade of wood, more pine coloured, had been used for still more arms behind the second, all against a background of some pure white wood. Polished and shiny in spite of hundreds of years of footsteps treading over it, the parquet foyer was as if assembled yesterday. Kyer felt like a ghost, an ethereal visitor in this reality. She stepped forward.

Every detail of the sconces on the stone walls, the wall hangings, the wooden beams that peaked in a circle above, the curve of the walls, every aspect of this foyer was familiar. She longed to kneel and run her fingers along the smooth wood, but crutch and sling were insurmountable obstacles.

Her gaze locked on a door at the northwest point of the star. Her dream-self had opened that door. Behind it, Kyer knew, was the staircase that led up to where the Lady Alon Maer had received her "gift." Was she up there, the woman in the portrait who had compelled Kyer to come on this mission? If she could just see for herself the flesh-and-blood Alon, maybe Kyer would be able to feel that she had done some good after all.

Then, she decided, as soon as she could ride again, she'd leave.

A door over at roughly the northeast position opened and closed softly. Kyer, gaze fixed to the door that was her goal, paid no attention. But when the footsteps stopped, the suddenness of the silence snapped her out of her thoughts. She turned to the figure and flinched with surprise.

It was Derry.

How long had it been since they had spoken those horrible words to each other? Kyer had been only semiconscious for so long, she'd lost track. To her, it seemed like a very short time. The warmth of a flush crept up her neck and spread over her face. What must he think of her? He must have found the designs she'd etched into the leather pouch, but had it been enough to earn his forgiveness for the terrible words she'd uttered? Did he wish she were able bodied enough to wield a sword, to defend herself against his defence of his honour? *I ought to . . . apologize . . . or something.*

She came to the realization that neither had spoken, though several heartbeats could have been counted. She swallowed, wishing she could draw sound through her lips.

"You're . . ." he began, "upright."

As ever, she could read nothing in his face. Anger? Contempt? Remorse? Relief? All or none of the above? Or perhaps only half.

"Such as it is." She looked around at the floor, the wall. *Say something*, she told herself. Had she broken the best friendship she'd ever had with foolish behaviour and even more foolish words? Why wouldn't he give her a clue? "I've been waiting for you to come visit me."

He looked away, as if a fly had buzzed past his head and begged his notice. What did that mean? Shame, embarrassment, total lack of interest?

"I've been busy."

If that isn't a noncommittal, lame excuse, I never heard one before. Dismay and regret fed off each other and quickly bred anger. Kyer felt her old self slinking back in. "That's just fine. I'm going out of my mind with pain and boredom and the only two of my so-called friends to come and see me are Phennil and a certain dark elf I don't know where I stand with anymore."

The captain's eyes flickered at the mention of Val's visit. Kyer hobbled a few steps closer to him.

"We haven't spoken in two weeks, or whatever it is, and apparently I nearly died in that time. You've supposedly got questions for me. What is going on?" Kyer heard the plaintive note in her voice echo back to her off the flat surfaces in the room. Derry still did not look at her. His head had lowered, and the muscle in his jaw swelled and contracted the way it did when he was angry. Kyer's head thrummed with the pulse of her blood.

Derry thrust words out, holding others back. His right hand pressed the air in her direction, commanding her to stop. "I cannot talk to you right now. It's too—there's still far too much—" He finally met her desperate gaze. The anguish in his eyes matched the seething in her heart. "I'm not ready yet," he said. "I haven't decided."

He seemed to be asking her to understand something that was hopelessly beyond her, as if she'd walked in on the tail end of a discussion and was expected to comment on the issue. She opened her mouth to speak, closed it again. Her head felt just a little woozy. *I need to sit down.*

"I have to see Alon Maer." Reverting to her initial plan, she achieved a sense of outward calm. She gave him a slight nod, like one she'd have given to someone she had just met. Hopping to turn herself in the desired direction, she limped toward the northwesterly door. With the fingertips that protruded pathetically out of the plaster on her left arm, Kyer fumbled with the latch. Her vision swayed. The door open, she directed herself through it.

Derry's voice stopped her.

So did the sound of his footsteps pounding toward her. "*There's* a question I have for you."

She involuntarily cringed against his forefinger wagging at her as he lunged her way.

"*How do you know that's the way to Alon's chamber?*" The bridge of his nose crinkled with disbelief. "You've never been here before, so you said, and yet there you go as if you've done it a hundred times." He gestured wildly at the door, his stance wide. "By the *gods*, Kyer, how do you know these things?" He squeezed his forehead between his palms as though suffering with a terrible headache. "The layout of the castle, the blue serpent, damn it, the bloody *rune pattern*? How did you know he had it? How did you know about it at all? What did that gods-take-him *Fredric* say to you?" The volume of his voice had intensified, and he drew it back down again.

"*And how—by the blood of all gods—did you Gate us here?*" His left hand clenched the door and his right held the doorjamb. He towered over her as if he had doubled in height, the potency of his emotion overwhelming.

The questions hit Kyer like darts. Her head spun. At that moment, it occurred to her that being vertical for so long after having been horizontal for much longer was perhaps not prudent. A wind filled her ears, Derry's voice faded, and her vision hazed over. She wilted.

Derry swooped down to catch her, and checked her pulse. *Damn you*, he thought at her. *Damn me.* He scooped her up and, enlisting the aid of a young lad who'd just emerged from the great hall, Derry carried her up the stairs. The lad carried her crutch and opened doors for the captain and his burden.

"Where to, Captain?"

"Lord Kien's study," Derry answered without thinking. *I guess I'm ready after all.*

Kien cursed his fingers. This was a particularly difficult passage, a winding sequence of sixteenth notes, and his fingers simply would not heed his commands. Too often, recent events had proven he could not have everything the way he wanted by giving orders. The scheduled meeting was hours away. Val meant well by telling him to find healthy ways of dispelling his frustrations while he waited, hence his return to his room, but this was only making things worse. Kien frowned, licked his lips, and placed them again against the mouthpiece of the flute. A deep breath in, and 1-e-&-a—tri-pl-et—3--e-a—*yes, that's it*—1-e-&-a, 2-e-&-a—

A tap on the door of his chamber threw his concentration. "What now?" he barked.

The door opened tentatively, and a young maid appeared with a tray. Her face was flushed with guilt and instantly after establishing eye contact with him, she lowered her gaze to the floor.

"Your lunch, my lord. You wanted it brought here."

"Yes, yes," he gestured impatiently. "Bring it." Kien laid the flute on his lap.

She hustled over and set the tray on the table beside him, though she did not look at him again. *Everybody's cowering*, he thought with annoyance. She took the lid off the wine decanter and set it on the tray.

"Will that be all, my lord?" she murmured.

Kien arrested a snarky rebuke. "Yes, Glyn, you may go now."

Glyn curtsied. The duke watched her go and ground his teeth. For weeks now, his staff had been walking on eggshells whenever he was near. His rational side understood that they loved him, that they loved Alon Maer, and that they did not want to make the mistake of bestirring his temper. But he was tired of keeping his rational side at the surface. He hated being treated like a delicate piece of glass. *Nobody wants to be the one to cause me to shatter.*

Bullshit.

The duke of three duchies would not shatter. The strongest man in Rydris would not crack like some mere human.

Kien picked up the flute again. Breathe, 1-e-&-a—trip-l—*shit*. Rage shivered along his skin and he raised the flute to smash it onto the music stand. It hung in the air, gripped by Kien's rigid right hand. His cheek muscles twitching, Kien lowered the instrument and rested it on the stand gently, like a delicate piece of glass.

With shaking hands, he poured a cup of wine and took a steady sip.

I can't take much more of this.

He lifted the cloth napkin by the corner, and gravity unfolded it. He laid it on his lap. Lifting the lid off the plate, he noticed a corner of white underneath it. He pulled it out. It was a folded piece of paper.

Opening it, he glanced at the short, handwritten note. He closed it and put it back on the tray. A picture came to his mind of a conversation that had taken place not all that long ago.

Last spring. In his meeting chamber at Shael Castle. He recalled the eagerness in Valrayker's voice as he drew her forward.

"This is the only one you haven't met yet. She joined us just a week ago and has already forced us all to keep on our toes," Val had said. *"From your own home duchy, Kien, this is Kyer Halidan."*

Kien remembered the dark eyes that had unflinchingly met his, the handshake that did not tremble. He remembered his immediate impression of her beauty and her character, the lack of intimidation in her voice. How dare she not be afraid of him?

"Where are you from in Heath, Kyer?"

"Hreth."

"So far north!" he'd exclaimed. *"What brought you southeast to join up with this lot?"*

The thoughtful pause, the cheeky smile as she replied, *"My horse, actually."*

His surprise, the chuckle he'd had to suppress before answering, *"Ah yes. I have one of those, also."*

Kien picked up the note again.

It pains me to tell you that the necklace was delivered by Kyer Halidan. Ask her about the symbolism of the serpent. Ask her if she can Gate. Out of fear of repercussion, I will only identify myself as

One who loves you

Stuffing the note inside his jerkin, Kien rose to his seven-foot height. *I could also ask how she obtained Alon's mirror.* His fingers vibrated, the only outward sign of his rage, the only crack in his control. He wrestled them into stillness and took steady steps over to where his greatsword leaned, sheathed, against the wall by his bed.

Two lives: Alon and my child. He strapped the weapon on his back. *Two lives for each life.*

Kien Bartheylen was tired of keeping his rational side at the surface. In that instant, he buried it.

She owes me four.

An icy calm settled over him. *Taking action at last.* He stalked out of the room.

Valrayker selected two varieties of doughnut and an apple, and after depositing the latter in his pocket, he sampled a bite of each plump, cakey treat. They were still warm from the fryer, and glaze crinkled on their surfaces as they cooled. His mouth watered. The maple walnut one was particularly tasty, so he took two bites in a row from it. Then, so as not to make the chocolate one jealous, he took two bites in a row of it too. Glyn came into the kitchen as Valrayker steered toward the door, licking a crumb off the heel of his hand.

"What's the matter?" he asked when he saw the girl's expression.

She put her hands on the counter. "I think I made him angry."

"Lord Kien?"

She nodded. "I don't know how—I guess I interrupted him, but he did ask for his lunch at this time and I didn't want to make him cross by being late, but it seems I—"

Val hushed her gently. "Never mind. I'm sure he's more cross with everything else than he is with you, Glyn. Don't worry, he'll come 'round before long."

She smiled. "You're right, sir. Thank you, my lord."

"No problem. Anyway, I'm on my way up to see him. Shall I double-check his mood for you?"

Her smile broadened. "Yes, my lord. He's in his own chamber."

When Val reached the third floor, he popped the last bite of doughnut in his mouth before finding Kien's chamber empty. Kien's lunch was untouched; not difficult to understand a diminished appetite under the circumstances. But nor had he cleaned his flute and put it away—unheard of from his meticulous friend. Val looked about the room for a clue to his whereabouts. It didn't take long for him to notice what was missing.

He stepped out of the room to see a servant lad closing the door of Kien's study just down the corridor. Val assumed Derry or Phennil was using the room, which reminded him he needed to speak to his captain.

Later, though. I'll go find Kien in the practice field. Val was glad his friend was getting some exercise these days.

Kien felt the sunshine on his face as he stepped out the main doors of the keep, felt its warmth, its energy, and for the first time in weeks, it felt good. He nodded to each of the guards positioned there and recognized with pride the way they hefted themselves to an even straighter pose to have their lord standing near. He stood a moment on the step, hands clasped behind his back, soaking in the light, breathing the invigorating floral scents, and relishing the feeling of well-being that had come over him.

"My lord," said a voice with a hint of surprise, and Kien looked down upon the dark green and grey uniformed figures of Captain Senad with Corporal Gorder approaching the steps. "What a pleasure to see you out of doors."

"Thank you, Vivika, Rondo. It's a pleasure to be seen," he agreed and hopped down the two steps to ground level. Even at the same level, he towered over them. A thought struck him. How timely that the clerk should appear just now.

"May I borrow Rondo for a few moments, Vivika?" The captain clapped her heels together and bowed. "Follow me, Corporal. I believe I have an assignment for you." He walked and she followed.

"Unofficial, my lord?" Even with her shorter strides, she kept up with him.

Kien nodded affirmation and headed straight across the courtyard to the infirmary. He was conscious of the stares of his people as they went on about their business, though, to be sure, their steps had more lightness upon seeing him. He brushed a hand through his steel-grey hair and planned his move. He'd had visions of bursting in, but the reality was that the infirmary doorway stood a little low. He could not burst effectively while stooping, so he settled on entering rapidly. Followed by Rondo, Kien strode down the hallway until he found the right room. He all but filled the entrance. Rondo waited outside. One hand he placed on the wall near his head, ready to draw once he'd found his target. But the only person in the room was a healer.

"Your Lordship, how good to see you, and how kind of you to come and visit my charge." Imogen sketched a bow.

"Hm, yes." Kien lowered his arm. "Where is she?"

"She went for a walk, and to be honest, I expected her back by now. Perhaps I ought to accompany you to the keep to find her."

"No matter, Imogen; I will find her myself. No doubt she will need some assistance to return."

He enjoyed the puzzled look on Imogen's face. "Very well, my lord. Thank you."

Kien stepped out and gestured for Rondo to follow him again. Once outside, he led her over to the centre of the courtyard where no one was nearby.

"Here is your assignment: You are to go to Cweivan and have him prepare a Gate. You are going to a place called Hreth."

"Northwest Heath?"

"Correct. Tell Cweivan he must reopen the Gate after one hour, so that you may return. Once you are there, you will ask around until you find a family called Halidan."

"Yes, sir. Halidan. What is the message?"

"No message."

"No message?"

"You kill them."

Thirty-Two
If Only She Would Recover

Valrayker was perplexed when he did not find Kien on the practice field. He asked after him in the armoury, but no one there had seen him. Val sauntered back through the service door on the cellar level and wound his way along corridors and up the stairs to the hall behind the kitchens. He peeked in to see Glyn chatting away with some other young people as they ate their lunch. No Kien, though. *Where else would he go with his sword?* A side door in front of him opened, one that connected this hallway with the foyer, via a narrow passage, and Corporal Gorder joined him in the back hall.

"Corporal." Val trotted a couple of steps to reach her. She stopped.

"My lord."

"Have you seen Kien?"

"Yes." She waved backward over her shoulder. "I've just come from speaking to him. Now I must hurry on my errand." She bowed and started toward the door that led to, among other odd chambers, Cweivan's rooms.

"Did he mention where he was going?" Val pressed.

"Yes." Rondo did not stop this time. "He was going to find the one they call Kyer. Business with her, I understand. Good day, my lord."

Business? With Kyer? Val stared at the door as she shut it behind herself. *And he needs his sword?* Val's finger tapped against his thigh, his thoughts racing. Turning abruptly, he went out the way the woman had come in. He charged up the main staircase.

Harsh words were being flung at her and she winced. Then she realized the voice was in her head. It was actually quiet around her now, and Kyer's fingertips felt a soft texture, like yarn or fur, though whatever was beneath it was firm. She heard rustling and urged her eyelids open.

A blurry Derry knelt over her, holding an object before her still-bleary eyes.

"Have you seen this before?"

Kyer blinked several times, coaxing her eyes into focus. She lay on her back, with something jammed underneath her, forcing her head into an awkward tilt. The object was gold in colour, she could tell that much. Round on one end, tapering down to a narrow handle, by which Derry held it. When the fuzzy edges of the item hardened and she could see it clearly, she was struck by its familiarity. She said nothing but flipped through the files of her memory, searching for a match.

All of a sudden, the memory clicked into place: Alon's mirror.

"Yes, I have seen it before."

Derry's face, which by now was as clear as the object he held, froze. His colour drained and the air around her smelled hot and electric. She didn't understand the significance of the mirror. Why was it here in—Kyer glanced around and surmised their location—Kien's study? Alon's chamber was just down the corridor.

"Why do you have it, Derry? What does it mean?"

He raised his arm with the swift motion of a swordsman, and she cringed, thinking he would hit her with it. A growling sound emitted from deep inside him, and he all but leapt to his feet. "*Why* do I have it?" he snapped. "What does it mean?" He stormed across the floor, the mirror still clutched in one hand. She watched him, an awkward thing to do with her head tilted back. He was on the return path now.

"How about *where* did I get it, Kyer?" he fumed, quieter, pointing the thing at her like a sword. "How about why did I find it in *your* saddlebag? How about why don't I call Kien in here right now to let him know that the suspicions are true?" His breaths came in short gasps, and he dropped into a nearby armchair. Kyer was too stunned and confused to produce any sound. "Why, Kyer? How could you do it? And make such fools of us all? It'll break Phennil's heart. He defended you unfailingly."

He gazed at the ceiling of the chamber, and from her vantage point, Kyer could see only the underside of his chin. But she was fairly certain a sob had escaped his throat.

"Derry, I—" Her heart thudded against her ribcage. "I don't know what to say."

"How about you start by being honest with me? Please, if it's for the first time in our short history, will you tell me something truthful?"

Stung, she clamped her mouth shut and thanked the gods he was looking away and couldn't see her biting her lip to dam up tears.

"Well, first, can we get this damn cushion or whatever it is out from under my back? It's bloody uncomfortable."

He looked down at her then. "I put it there to raise your heart above your head. Because you fainted." The physicker in him could not be stifled.

"I'm awake now."

He hesitated, staring at her, but reached a decision. He exhaled deeply and pushed himself off the chair to kneel next to her. Kyer found that her eyes wanted to retract away from his. She let them. His hand was as gentle as ever beneath her back as he slid the cushion out. He then lifted her head the same way and slipped the cushion under, so when he lowered her head, it rested on the softness.

Kyer felt a *twang* in her heart. She didn't know why, but he was angrier with her than he had ever been, even after she killed Ronav. Yet he still took care to make her comfortable. *Derry Moraunt, you're the most gentlemanly man I—* She swallowed hard. All she'd said to hurt him the night they parted was nothing compared to whatever was on his mind at this moment. His friendship was now so distant as to be beyond her sight. He sat back in the armchair.

"Derry." She forced sound out of her tight throat. "Alon's mirror . . . I don't know what you're talking about."

His glare pierced straight into her heart. His voice was frost. "Try again."

Frustration, self-loathing, self-rebuking bubbled within her and crawled along her skin. "What do you want to hear?"

He slapped his hand on the arm of the chair. "Just say it, Kyer. The mirror was in your saddlebag. I don't like it, but there it is. I asked for evidence, and you had it with your belongings all the time—"

"I don't know what you're talking about!" Kyer screamed at him through gritted teeth. He looked like he'd been stung by a wasp. "Evidence of what?"

Derry stared at her from his chair as if they were circling in a duel. "That you tried to kill Alon Maer."

Kyer's supine form turned to ice. "*What?* No, that was a chambermaid."

Derry continued. "Nice try. How would you know that even if it were true? You gave her the necklace. Everyone knows it; we've just been waiting for more evidence. And I found it in your saddlebag: Alon's mirror. Which you could not have unless you had stolen it from her chamber when you gave her the serpent. It explains why it was so important for you to come on this mission, though you pretended not to know her. We know you've been here before, in spite of your claims to the contrary, because you Gated us here, and every wizard in Rydris knows you cannot Gate to an unknown location. There. Is that clear enough for you?"

It was Kyer's turn to stare at the ceiling. The patterns hammered into the tin would have fascinated her on any other day. Thoughts, images, memories of conversations, with Derry, with Phennil, with Val, all tumbled through her mind like rocks on a cliffside. They rolled, bounced, cascaded, and each one pelted her. They dragged her with them, spinning, jouncing, so she couldn't see them clearly. They were a jumbled mass, and when Kyer and her thoughts landed at the bottom, she rolled onto her left side and, sweat beading with pain, pushed herself up with her immobilized left hand. Feeling dizzy and dusty, her chest heaving with breaths, she sat slumped on the rug in Kien Bartheylen's study and poked about for the thought that would tell her what to say.

"And when am I supposed to have done this? I've been with *you* for weeks—"

"I have no idea where you were before we met in Wanaka," he said coldly.

"What can I do?" She panted after her effort. "Give me something I can swear on that will make you believe me." She met his gaze with imploring eyes. "I swear on—on—anything. I won't say 'my honour' because clearly you don't think much of that right now. On my sword, on my *life*, on anything you want. *I didn't give Alon Maer that necklace.*" She knew it was a chambermaid called Misha, but why would he believe that?

Derry's expression did not alter. She had not impressed him.

"What, then?" She shrugged helplessly. "What can I say to make you believe me?"

Who was Misha? She wracked her brain, feeling certain she ought to know. Until she answered that question she would never convince him.

He drummed his fingers on the chair's arms and pouted. "You can start by giving me some explanations."

"How? How can I give explanations for things I don't understand myself?" She ran the tips of her fingers through the soft, dark green and gold pile of the rug. "I don't know anything about Gating. I don't know what the rules are. If I can Gate, it's as much of a surprise to me as it is to you. Maybe it has to do with my medallion. I can't explain it any better than that. You want me to tell you how I got Phennil and me out of the cavern? Well, I guess I Gated us out. Naturally, not understanding what the hell had just happened, I was a little reluctant to 'explain myself' at the time.

"I think you also asked about the rune pattern. That's simple enough. When I went back into the camp to get some food, I overheard a conversation between Gilvray and someone else. He told the fellow all about the rune pattern, and I actually saw where he kept it. I wanted to tell you when I got back to camp, but you said something that pissed me off, so I didn't feel like it. I devised my own plan and figured you wouldn't let me do it if I shared it with you anyway, so I just went and did it."

Kyer's voice had grown hoarse throughout her story. Some of her words sounded stupid to her ears. She still didn't look at Derry. "It was childish of me. I—I didn't realize that until later . . . after we'd argued and I was left to my own thoughts for a while. I was childish about a lot of things." Her head felt as heavy as a saddlebag full of potatoes, but she forced it up so she could finally meet the eyes of her captain. Her lower lip trembled. "I'm sorry, Derry. I don't know how things went so wrong. I should have—" She shook her head and struggled to hold back sobs, her lip trembling. "I should have at least told you that there were . . . things . . . going on that I couldn't explain. I shouldn't have just brushed you off all the time. I'm sorry, Derry."

His blue eyes were ringed with pink, but they met hers for a moment before he rubbed them with his fingers. "Some of the things you said that night were like daggers in my chest." Kyer's heart sank even lower. She had known she'd hurt him. "I had to admit, after I'd had some time to think, you were right about a few things. I said some awful words to you too. And for that, I, too, am sorry. I also recognize—" His fingers moved absently to his throat, "—she would have killed me if not for you."

In their brief glance, Kyer felt a flutter of warmth. Had they narrowed the gap even a tiny bit?

"I would still like an explanation for the mirror, not to mention for the fact that you know the layout of this castle like someone who has spent a good deal of time here." The hard edge had slipped back into his tone.

Kyer scrunched her eyes shut. When she opened them again, he was still waiting. "Not the whole castle, Derry, just the way to Alon's chamber. I don't know where the kitchens are or the guest quarters." She'd surprised herself. She hadn't thought before about the limitations of her knowledge. All she knew, she had learned in a dream. "I have one question for you."

He gestured to indicate she should pose it.

"Do you *want* to believe that I tried to kill Alon?"

He looked taken aback and hesitated before answering. A tiny crease opened between his brows. He slowly shook his head and whispered, "No."

"Then don't."

A clamour in the corridor broke their connection and both heads snapped toward the door as it was flung open.

Rondo waited patiently while Cweivan finished preparing the spell. To create a Gate was tricky enough; to create another one after an hour and hold it open so a nonwizard could pass back through it must be quite a feat.

"All right." Cweivan pressed his hands together and exhaled fully.

"Is it ready?" Rondo asked.

"I can only send you to the edge of the village," the mage said. "I cannot create a Gate to within it but I can get you as close as I have been. You will have a bit of a walk."

Rondo watched Jesqellan nod in understanding. Valrayker's mage had been speaking with Cweivan when Rondo arrived with Lord Kien's order, and he had asked to stay and watch. "I'm very interested in the Gating spell just now," he'd said.

Now, he rose to join hands with Cweivan, offering as much of his own energy as he could spare for the spell. "So it's true that a Gate cannot be opened to a place the wizard has never been?"

"It's true." Cweivan placed his spell scroll on the table before him. "As castle mage one of my duties was to travel the length and breadth of Heath. I did not cover the entire map, but certainly came within a useful vicinity of most places, in an effort to widen my travel options. Took me two years, but there's no point in being able to open a Gate if you can only go between two or three locations!

"There is one exception, and that is if the wizard has created a Locator. Any object can be made into a Locator, and a Gate can be opened to within a certain radius of it, no matter where it has been taken." He raised his hands above his head, slowly lowered them, and pressed his palms together, eyes closed. Corporal Gorder recognized a relaxation and focussing exercise when she saw one.

"I will reopen it in one hour and hold it for ten minutes if you aren't there. You will have no more than that, Rondo," Cweivan warned. "I would not be able to do it at all without Jesqellan's help. Hurry with your errand and return. If you do not arrive before we must close the Gate . . . I'm afraid you will have to find your own way home."

"I hope you have money for a horse." Jesqellan smiled.

Corporal Gorder shrugged, adjusted her sword at her hip, and nodded to Cweivan.

A moment later, an archway of quivering air opened before her. Beyond it lay a picturesque valley by a stream in the foothills of a mountain. Stretches of grasses and farmland aligned the stream. A dirt road led down a hill out of the Gate, at the far end of which she could see a little bridge, and a cluster of low buildings. The road was dotted with puddles and rivulets, and a splash of water *tocked* on Rondo's boot.

She drew her hood up and stepped through the Gate into the rain of Hreth.

Halidan, she repeated to herself for the umpteenth time. *You will earn me my knighthood.* She hurried along the road.

Kien slowly pushed open the door to Alon's chamber. Alon lay still, and a tiny spark of anger flickered in his belly. As Kien approached, he could hear that the raspiness of her breathing had eased. Roman sensed his need and rose from her work, gliding away to tend to something on the other side of the room.

Sitting on the edge of the bed, he placed his warm right hand on Alon's cool brow. Her closed lids hid her warm dark eyes from him, and the spark of anger flared into glowing fury. He caressed her long hair. He kissed her soft lips, the taste of lip balm sweet on his tongue as his jaw tightened. With his shaking left hand, he drew a gentle line down the side of her neck where a glittering gold chain had lain. He traced a small, loving circle in the spot below her throat where the blue serpent had been allowed for months to secrete its spell. Kien's brow contracted.

Step one had been taken. His hand ran down Alon's body to her abdomen, still tenaciously swollen with—*it had better be another life*. Kien felt the invigorating surge of rage warm his blood.

I will avenge you both, he vowed.

Kien stormed to the door.

"My lord—" Kien heard Roman's alarmed voice, but nothing was so urgent as his next task. The door flew open beneath his hand.

He charged down the corridor, half blind, and careened into another body.

"Where is she?" he roared.

"That depends," said Val, his hands on Kien's chest. "Why do you want her?"

Kien's face burned and he glared at Valrayker. "Get out of my way. Your little *prodigy* is finished." He pushed by, peering into the library as he passed. Nobody.

Aha! He saw the next closed door on the left and knew where he'd find her.

The door slammed into the wall, and the door handle shattered, bits of glass tinkling to the stone floor.

Kien Bartheylen, a quivering giant, took an instant to locate her in the room. Kyer's eyes locked with his and he smiled. She gasped, cringing in spite of herself. She felt as if she were trapped in the cavern again, nearly drowning in the hot pool. The huge elf's sword appeared in his hand from overhead. It was pointed at her as he stepped forward.

"Kien!" Valrayker's voice cried as he flew in from the corridor.

Kien didn't flinch. "Two lives for each life. Yours is last. Pray now."

Suddenly Derry's body blocked her view. Not quite a foot shorter than Kien, he made a decent shield.

"If you think you can strike her down without a struggle, you are mistaken," Captain Moraunt said, quiet as falling snow. Kyer struggled to her unsteady foot and swayed until she could place her hand on the wall. Kien's sword followed her movement.

"You killed my wife and child."

Kyer's head swam. "No! I didn't. I just finished—"

"Captain Moraunt, step aside if you have any honour in you."

Derry didn't budge. "You accuse her falsely; you'll have to go through me."

Kien snorted. "Fine. That will make three out of the four she owes."

Fear for her life was a powerful motivator, but it also twisted her thoughts into an inaccessible mass. Kyer's life depended on the answer she could not think of.

Valrayker did not touch Kien's sword but pillared himself next to it. "Kien," he growled. "There will be no lives forfeited just yet."

"Too late," Kien snarled. "My lands. My justice."

"On what grounds?" Derry demanded.

Kyer tried to control her juddering breaths.

Kien reached into his jerkin and whipped out a folded piece of paper.

Val took it and glanced over it. Kyer watched the light in his eyes dim then brighten again with a cold glow. "This is an anonymous letter," he said. "You would take her life for an anonymous letter?"

Kyer desperately tried to find the thread within the mass of memory. There was a connection. Somewhere. A chambermaid called Misha and . . . *Who?*

"And why not?" Kien snapped. "She took two lives for just as little reason." He took another step forward, and Derry stepped to the side to block him.

"Prove it," Kyer blurted and fervently hoped she wouldn't regret it.

"I don't need proof, hellwhore. I asked for a name, and I've got one."

Kyer wondered perversely how Kien could hold that greatsword so steadily for so long with one hand. Kien glared at Derry and looked about ready to slice his head off. She flipped through her mind and grasped some details. Someone who was a powerful enough mage to make a *Malison*. Someone who could pass herself off as a chambermaid. Kyer saw again the face in the mirror. Someone who might have *accidentally* shared her memories with Kyer through physical contact.

"Wait!" she yelled. "I know who did it!"

Derry turned to her, astonished.

Kien took that moment to swing. Derry ducked and pulled Kyer down with him. She screamed with pain. The clang of steel deafened them in the tiny chamber, and Valrayker stood there, feet apart, two hands gripping his sword, which had blocked Kien's and held it horizontal.

"Alon," Val said loudly, "*is not dead*!"

Kyer lay on the floor trembling, Derry's arm across her, and watched the truth dawn in Kien's eyes.

Kyer's gaze met Derry's, and they spoke at the same time.

"Misha."

Sendra Flack shook out her dust rag over the railing of the shop's front porch. The rain was the first Hreth had seen in three weeks, and it was welcome. She could not tell the hour, but she was certain the sun was well over to the west of centre, and her heart quickened. It had been ten days since the last visit, just the same number as had passed between it and the one before. It wasn't too much wishful thinking to expect a visit this afternoon. Sendra took an involuntary glance down the road. *As if I can see anyone coming from here!* she teased herself. The main road from Fri was two blocks away. *You're as bad as a schoolgirl.*

Stepping back through the front door, open to allow admittance to the fresh northwesterly breeze, she gazed around her store with pride. Not even the most scrutinizing eye could have found a speck of dust on those shelves. And the echo of hollowness was not nearly so musical. Tell, the dispatch rider from Drakenmoor, had been true to his word. Folks from that city, as well as Fri and several other towns and nearby villages, had been generous in their help.

A barrel of pickles here, a crate full of clothing, both adult and children's sizes, there. Crackers. Thread. Tools. Even the sugar Jessica had been after for weeks. Still not as fully stocked as she used to be, at least Sendra could provide Hreth's people with the basics. And many of the goods Sendra didn't even bother charging for; they'd been donated, and it wouldn't have been right for her to profit by it. Her shop had become somewhat of a gathering place, to sort the items and make sure they were distributed evenly, according to need.

Bianca's—*Magistrate Ardra's*—plans were coming together. Tell proved to be an invaluable ally, for who would question a dispatch rider travelling frequently from town to town? And if he carried small quantities of a green gem and sold them to any one of the many buyers in Drakenmoor or Heatha, the largest city in Rydris, who would pay attention? Hreth had started purchasing more building materials, and restoring its devastated farming industry.

Sendra hung the rag up in the cupboard and wiped her smooth hands on her apron. Not all that long ago—a few weeks—she'd bemoaned her lack of salve. But her homemade one worked just as well. And she was glad too because Tell loved the feel of her soft hands on his body. His supervisor had given over the northwest route entirely to Tell, so he could visit Sendra's little village regularly. Even Tarqan had commented on the change in his mother's happiness since Tell had entered her life. Sendra smiled to herself, picked up her little prybar, and knelt next to a crate.

With a groan and a squeak, the lid lifted off. The contents practically exploded out of it, and Sendra laughed aloud. Wool. Bundle upon bundle of wool, directly from the sheep. It wasn't yet washed, or carded or dyed. *Della Halidan will love this.* Sendra breathed in the lanolin smell, extra heavy after being boxed up for so many days.

I'll go and tell her it's here, Sendra decided.

She rose and headed around the counter, gasping when a shadow appeared on the floor in front of her. A woman stood in the doorway. Short dark hair, light brown skin, wearing the dark green and grey uniform of Bartheylen Castle. The sword at her hip was concealed, but it was long enough for the tip of its sheath to show out the bottom of the cloak. Sendra recovered herself.

"Good day. You gave me a turn! How can I help you?"

"I am Corporal Rondo Gorder from Bartheylen Castle," replied the soldier. "I'm looking for the Halidan family."

Sendra's hand moved to her middle. Her heart had sped up again. "What—is there a problem? It's Kyer, isn't it?"

The corporal nodded. "I am not privileged with all the information, but I have a message for the Halidans directly from Lord Kien."

Sendra forced herself to breathe. "I was just headed over to see them, myself. I'll take you." She fetched her cloak and swung it over her shoulders.

The corporal stood aside to let Sendra lead the way. Sendra shuddered involuntarily as she passed the swordswoman. *I don't like the sound of this at all.* Slowly and deliberately, Sendra closed the shop door and locked it. Then she led the corporal down the road to the Halidans' farm.

Corporal Gorder kept her eyes to the front. She was here on business, not a sight-seeing tour. She couldn't fail to notice, as her companion led her north on the puddle-dotted dirt road, that virtually all the buildings in this village had either been rebuilt recently or were under reconstruction. The boards had not even had time to weather. And there were patches of burn-stained ground on the road, piles of burnt timber. Two men were hunting for bits they could salvage from a pile of broken and scorched pieces of tools, hunks of iron that used to be someone's stove, and half-melted pieces of tin in odd shapes that might have been a lamp sconce or a wash basin. She saw similar heaps of rubbish elsewhere. The rain made *tinging* sounds on the metal, and the petrichor still carried the faint smell of burnt wood.

"Were our troopers helpful when they were here?" She finally recollected the service they had been asked to provide.

"Oh yes, sir," answered the shopkeeper. "Most families still wouldn't have roofs over their heads if your soldiers hadn't come."

Rondo nodded. "I'll see to it that more are sent when I get back to Bartheylen Castle."

The shopkeeper, who was not short by human standards, had to look up at Rondo as she walked. "I half-hoped that's why you were here," the woman said. "To oversee what they had done and to determine what else we need."

Rondo felt the hint of a pang inside. "I'm not here to spend time checking over their work today." But then, to say something hopeful, she added, "I've seen enough to recommend that we send more aid."

"Thank you, Corporal."

Rondo said nothing. *A good deed to make up for what I'm about to do.* She couldn't simply walk up to these Halidans and behead them. What if they weren't together? She'd have to send the shopkeeper away before carrying out her orders.

"These Halidans." She stepped nimbly over a deep-looking puddle. "They all right folks?"

"Indeed, yes," the woman said. "Good people. Hard workers. Responsible members of the community." She sounded as if she were pleading their case without knowing their fate had already been decided. "Young Kyer is their adopted daughter, you know. They always did right by her, even if the other townsfolk didn't care much for her. She's—she's not in trouble, is she?"

Rondo sensed, rather than saw, the sidelong glance.

"I am not at liberty to share any information with anyone but the Halidans."

"Yes, of course, it's only that, you see, I was always rather fond of the girl. Not many were. My son and she . . . well, it wasn't to be."

The shopkeeper stopped walking and gestured with her arm.

"There's their farm. They raise corn and sheep and hens. I was coming to tell Della about the shipment of wool. She's the best in the village at transforming raw wool into a useful product."

Corporal Gorder gaped at the flat, desolate remains of a farm. She felt utterly perplexed. *What is Lord Kien thinking?* The farm had been razed to the ground. A new house was being erected next to the charred remains of the original, but it was not yet complete. A few stubborn stalks of corn had uncurled themselves out of the wreckage, but they'd been flattened so early in the growing season that even to a soldier's eye, their productivity was questionable. They'd never grow in time to sprout ears.

"Dregor's devils destroyed everything they had, save those few animals there," the woman went on, hands in her apron pockets. A crude fence penned a dozen or so sheep and a few hens, most of whom were huddled under a shelter at one end. "The Halidans took the brunt of the attack, really."

She stepped forward, calling, "Della, Gareth!" The place felt deserted. "I'm sure you're in a hurry, so I apologize for taking your time, but I thought they might still be here. Building, I mean. I should have known, what with the rain. They aren't living here yet," she explained, turning around and leading Rondo back the way they'd come. "After the attack, they went to stay with friends down in Clinton for a spell. They didn't get started rebuilding as soon as everyone else, and people seem rather . . . reluctant to help them, I'm afraid."

What is the matter with these people? Rondo thought, staring down the road before her. *Why wouldn't they help them?*

"I suppose," carried on the shopkeeper, as if reading her mind, "they're worried that Dregor will return, and if they help the Halidans, Dregor might lump them all together. I don't know."

"Where are they living at the moment?"

"With a friend in town, just up the road from my store. I am sorry, I ought to have tried there first, I guess."

Rondo held up a hand. "This is no trouble," she said politely, though she glanced upward and cursed that the heavy cloud cover prevented an accurate assessment of the time. She guessed that she'd used about twenty of her precious sixty minutes in walking from the Gate to the village and up and down the north-south road. Besides, the storekeeper was clearly a kindly woman who was fond of the Halidans. She need not witness the upcoming event. "If you could just direct me to the house where they are staying, I will attend them myself. You need not accompany me."

"All right. I should get back to the store, anyhow. My message to Della can wait." She directed the corporal west on the road that ran along the front of her store. "Up here to that corner, turn left, then right at the stand of cottonwoods. Brendow's cottage is on the left. You can't miss it."

Corporal Gorder thanked her and swiftly employed her long, soldier's stride to carry her to her destination. The deed must be done quickly if she were to get back to the Gate in time. Lord Kien would be hard pressed to offer her a knighthood if she didn't return for a week. It took her only a few moments to reach the trees in question. She went along the road only a few paces before stopping. She scratched her head and looked up and down the road.

There was no cottage. Tall grasses and wildflowers bent and swayed with the lightening rainfall and breeze, their soft scents fresh in Rondo's nose, the only evidence that she was still alive and had not lost her mind. *You can't miss it*, that woman said. She seemed to have her wits about her. Did she suspect ill intent and was purposefully preventing Rondo from undertaking her orders?

Rondo whirled around and stormed back to the general store. *I do not have time for this!*

Another ten minutes had passed by the time she arrived back at the store. *I'm going to be stuck here*, she grumbled. *Not* carrying out Kien's orders in favour of getting home was not an option.

Kien Bartheylen was never fazed by the jolt of a solid block, but this time the vibrations shinnied up his arm like a tenacious child climbing a cherry tree. For some reason, this was different. The shock of making contact with another weapon, not with his target, and that weapon belonging to Valrayker . . . Kien stared at his friend.

Alon is not dead. The words echoed in Kien's head, reverberating with the clang of Valrayker's sword. And suddenly Kien picked up on tiny details that had somehow eluded him.

Alon's forehead, when he'd rested his palm on it, was cool, not feverish. Her lips, when he'd kissed them, were soft. Not supple, not yet, but neither were they cracked and bleeding with the dryness of illness. Her sleep was restful, the creases of strain and suffering had smoothed over. Her breaths were quiet, easy, evenly spaced.

Alon was not dead.

Kien nearly collided in the doorway with Phennil.

"My lord, she's asking for you."

Fredric dipped his hands in the trough and rubbed his face. Then he used the dampness to smooth down his hair as best he could without a looking glass. He tucked the long sides behind his ears and straightened the waistcoat he'd borrowed from the groom. He felt grubby as hell, his attire hardly appropriate for the conference he was about to hold, but maybe it would buy him some sympathy.

He felt sure of his timing. By now Kien would have found his note. With Alon still incapacitated, Kien would still be in quite a state. The duke's fury would now be properly focussed on Kyer, so Fredric's story would be well received.

Fredric allowed himself an anticipatory smile. *Back to my old life!* And it was Kyer Halidan who'd get a taste of banishment and disgrace.

Heart leaping, he headed up the path toward the keep.

"That woman." Kyer finally connected the two faces. "She was killing you." Kyer blinked rapidly. Tears would be decidedly inappropriate right now.

"That's Misha?" Derry asked.

Kyer nodded. "*She's* the one, Derry. Not me."

Derry sat up and helped Kyer out of the position he'd knocked her into to avoid Kien's blade. "But I don't understand. How do you know?"

Kyer shook her head. The woman had been with Fredric when she met with him by the lake. The jolt she felt when the woman touched her forehead, *that*, Kyer was sure, was when the dreams had begun. "I saw her in my dreams. I kept dreaming about the corridor and the box with the necklace in it and giving it to Alon. I don't know why, so don't ask me. That night when I slept in the Indyn Caves, I had one more dream. I picked up Alon's mirror and looked in it. It wasn't my face, Derry; it was hers. *That's* where I'd seen the mirror, and *that's* why I know she tried to kill Alon Maer.

"And when I saw her strangling you, she looked only vaguely familiar. Wrong clothes, no hat, wrong place. So I couldn't turn them into the same person right away."

Derry's eyes were wide with wonder, or disbelief. "If only Alon would recover, we could ask her if she recognizes you."

"You don't believe me."

He raised a hand. "No, quite the contrary. But if she doesn't recognize you," he shrugged, "then you didn't do it."

Kyer smiled, relief and gratitude flooding through her. "If only she would recover."

She looked up. Their conversation had been so intense that Kyer and Derry had blocked out the activity in the room.

Val and Kien were gone.

Thirty-Three
Her Very Soul Seeping

Sendra poured steaming water from the kettle into the teapot to steep while Tell hung his soaked riding cloak by the stove. The door that connected her back kitchen to the shop remained open so she could be aware of customers.

"I got the impression it isn't good news she has for them," Sendra said.

"But she didn't give you any clue?" Tell asked.

Sendra shook her head. "I did try to explain Gareth and Della's position. I guess I was hoping to gain her sympathy, and then maybe she'd give me a— gods' breath!"

The door to the shop banged open. Sendra flew through the connecting door to see Corporal Gorder fuming in the doorway.

"What are you playing at?" the corporal demanded.

Tell snapped to attention and saluted, but the corporal ignored him. "*'You can't miss it,'* you said." Her eyes narrowed with rage. "There is no cottage down that road."

No cottage? Sendra gripped the counter and felt the blood drain from her face. Instantly she recalled the one and only other time anyone had gone looking for Brendow's cottage and hadn't been able to find it.

The messenger lowered her voice to an intimidating hiss. "I am in a terrific hurry, and I strongly urge you to take me to the Halidans, or I shall have to bring you back with me to see Lord Bartheylen."

Sendra nodded, trembling, and threw on her cloak. She hurried to the door, hoping Tell would follow.

The corporal hustled alongside her as she trotted up the road and turned left. When they rounded the corner by the trees, Sendra glanced up the lane anxiously. She stopped.

"There, you see?" She waved her arm. "It's right there." Tell smiled at her. As solid as ever, Brendow's cottage stood on the south side of the lane, its cross-hatched windows bedecked with planter boxes loaded with early summer blooms that quivered with the light raindrops. How could the corporal have overlooked it?

The messenger's jaw pulsed. Her eyes flaming, she gestured with her head for Sendra to take her all the way to the door. Sendra supposed she might be afraid the cottage would disappear again. *And maybe it ought to.* The people who had been unable to locate Brendow's cottage had intended to do him harm. What was this corporal's message?

Sendra went ahead of her up to the front door. She raised her arm with trepidation. *What trouble am I causing?* Her hand shook and an anxious lump formed in her throat.

"Hurry up. I am nearly out of time," Corporal Gorder ordered.

Sendra knocked and after a few seconds, Brendow opened the door.

"Hello, Sendra. What a pleasure."

"Brendow, this is Corporal Gorder," Sendra said, a tremor in her voice.

"I have a message for the Halidans," the corporal announced. "From Lord Kien Bartheylen."

A tiny muscle beneath Brendow's right eye tightened. Sendra wondered what he had guessed.

Derry scrambled to his feet, hauling Kyer up after him, and together they exited into the corridor. Kyer hobbled along on her crutch and cursed her condition.

Phennil peered out the door as they approached. He was grinning broadly.

"I'm so glad you're here, Kyer. We did it. *You* did it."

Kyer slowed her already halting pace, uncertainty making her hesitate. *I'm about to meet Alon Maer.* These were not the ideal circumstances in which to meet one's hero.

Phennil's smile changed, as if he could read her thoughts. He laid his hand on her left shoulder and squeezed it. She felt his affection for her, and it gave her courage. The elf was the only one to whom she had confided her passion for undertaking the mission. He hadn't forgotten. He knew what this meant to her.

Kyer gave Phennil a nod and stepped past him into the chamber.

It was startlingly familiar; exactly as she had dreamed, although the bed was nearer the window and, in her dream, it had been night. There was the bureau, the little table, the wing-backed armchair, in which Janak sat, out of place with her memories. Kyer could not see Jesqellan, but Skimnoddle and Harley, of all people, flanked the fireplace. Val and Kien stood by the bed, Val with a restraining hand on the high elf's arm. Kien's hand still twitched on the hilt of his sword, and his cold grey eyes regarded her with suspicion.

A healer hovered behind the bed, in case her charge required her attentions. The Lady Alon Maer was sitting up in the bed, propped with pillows. She held a mug of something hot, cradling it in both hands. Her face was thinner than Kyer remembered, the hair tousled and tumbling over her shoulders like a blanket, the skin paler and looking dry like parchment. And of course, she was in a nightdress, not a leather cuirass. But even without an introduction, Kyer knew her for the woman in the portrait at Shael Castle.

Emotions careered through Kyer. The love and admiration she'd felt for this woman, sight unseen. Desperate relief that their efforts had paid off. Yet the weight of Derry's—Kien's—accusation pressed down on her still. Would Alon recognize her? What would Kyer do if she did?

The silence of the room finally filtered through Kyer's busy thoughts. She looked at Val, his face impassive as he watched her. She wanted to step forward, but her feet had frozen in place. Then she felt the comforting warmth of Derry's presence beside her, and she knew he wouldn't let anything go wrong. Phennil nudged her from behind, and she hobbled forward.

The Lady Alon Maer's gaze passed to her. Kyer's eyes fastened on the lady's face, searching for signs of recognition. For lack of a better idea, she bowed.

"I understand," said the lady in a warm, smooth contralto, "that you played a large part in this."

Great, thought Kyer. *Can't get much more ambiguous than that.*

Phennil appeared next to her. "Kyer was the one who spoke to Kayme and relayed all the instructions for the cure, my lady. He refused to speak to anyone else."

"Indeed?" Alon Maer said. "That's noteworthy."

Derry cleared his throat. "Kyer was the one who found the way to enter the Indyn Caves and found the final ingredient as well."

"I knew it!" a voice cried from behind them. Fredric Heyland strode forward, looking as if he'd been stuck with a branding iron.

Fredric didn't know whether to feel heart-wrenching dismay or rage. He'd hustled up the stairs and down the corridor, expecting Kien to be in his study. The door was open, and glass was scattered on the floor. He'd hastened toward Kien's chamber but had stopped at the open door to Alon's room. No one had seen him arrive, and glad as he was to see Alon awake, as soon as he burst in he knew he'd somehow made a terrible blunder. "Derry," he said plaintively, "you said you'd speak on my behalf. When were you going to do that?"

Out of the corner of his eye, Fredric noticed his lord's imposing figure and Val's hand preventing him from rushing into anything. But Fredric kept his eyes on Derry.

"Things . . . have sort of . . . changed, Fredric," Derry fumbled.

Fredric darted a glance around the room, frantically seeking his one known ally, but Jesqellan wasn't there to back him up. "Did you say anything about my side?"

"What. Is this man doing. In my wife's room?" Kien said hoarsely.

This could be Fredric's only chance. He stepped forward and dropped to his knees before his lord. "I am sorry if my appearance distresses you, my lord. I want only to prove my devotion to you! In spite of everything that happened in the past, I want to redeem myself. When I heard my lady was ill, I was overcome with grief. And when I learned she'd been given a *Malison* . . . I assure you, I made it my one and only task to seek out the culprit and bring her to justice." He found Alon Maer's eyes and led her gaze around to rest on Kyer. Phennil let out a short hiss.

"What do you mean?" Alon said.

To Fredric's surprise, Derry moved toward him. "You're right, Fredric. I did say I would speak on your behalf." He directed his comments to Kien. "Whatever the outcome may be, this man did join with us. He helped defeat our enemies and aided in getting the last ingredient. I believe his effort to have been sincere."

"What?" Kyer swayed on her unsteady feet and looked as if she'd been punched.

Fredric nodded his thanks for Derry's words. The young captain even gave him a hand to rise. Were he to protest the captain's brevity, he'd risk looking ungrateful in front of Kien. At least Kyer's suffering pleased him. He indicated her. "My lady, surely you recognize this woman as the one who gave you the blue serpent necklace?"

Alon Maer squinted at Kyer. "I—I don't know."

"This is too much for my lady, too soon," Roman's authoritative voice said.

"So you're the one who wrote the note." Kien ignored the healer. Fredric couldn't define his lord's mood. But he did have his eye on Alon's reactions.

"I did. Sir, these men are all Kyer's friends. I can only imagine how difficult it must be for them to think ill of her. I want only that my lady's attacker be brought to justice. My lord, I—I wasn't sure you'd listen to me if I didn't get your attention first." *Alon's with me, so Kien can't be far behind.* He bowed his head.

"Kien, you can't possibly—" It was that damned elf again.

"What do you know about the mirror in Kyer's saddlebag?" Kien interrupted.

Fredric stopped mid-breath. *Mirror?* "I know nothing about a mirror, my lord."

"Derry found Alon Maer's hand mirror in Kyer's saddlebag."

Fredric glanced at Kyer, who was obviously ready to collapse. He glared accusingly at Derry, who had kept that damning secret from him. "I know nothing of it, my lord. But it sounds to me like even more proof that Kyer was here before." His chest swelled with triumph. "She gave my lady the necklace, stole the mirror as a souvenir, and then *Gated* back to join her friends."

Alon gasped. Clearly, nobody had thought to mention Kyer's ability to Gate.

"Yes, my lady." Fredric gestured toward Kyer. "Let her deny that she Gated the whole group of us from Bolivar Chasm to here. Let her repeat her claim that she's never been here before! She can't prove it, but her Gating proves she was here."

Roman said, "I must insist—"

Phennil jumped up, pointing an outraged finger at Fredric. "You'd do anything to try to clear your own name. You'd do anything to get revenge on Kyer! Deny *that*!"

The whole room erupted in cries and flying accusations. Alon covered her ears.

"Wait!" Derry cried. The hubbub stilled. "I can prove Kyer didn't do it."

Fredric stared, his blood roiling. *So much for speaking on my behalf, you bastard.* He watched intently as Derry took up a piece of paper and a pencil. Curiosity gnawed at him, but Harley's hand stayed his desire to move toward the other man. No one said a word as Derry began to draw. A log on the fire *chuffed* as it fell. Had the tension in the air been smoke, Fredric would not have been able to see Kyer, even as she stood so close. Derry's pencil swished and scritched along the paper.

"There." He dropped the pencil on the table. He snatched up the paper and held it up in front of Alon. "Is that the woman who gave you the necklace?"

Alon leaned closer to the drawing. She peered at it, studying it. She lay back on her pillows and closed her eyes. "Yes," she said. "That's the maid who was here for a short time. I think her name . . . was Misha."

Fredric was stunned. Derry showed the page to Kyer, who nodded gratefully. Then he let Fredric see it.

Derry had sketched an amazingly accurate likeness of that dark-haired bitch, Misty.

Kyer had not done it. The sketch was irrefutable proof.

Fredric had no words. He stared at Derry, at Alon, and did not know what to do.

━━━━━

Kyer felt the heat of Kien's rage from where she stood three steps away from him. It emanated from him like a bad odour.

The duke stepped forward, and the room was quelled beneath his formidable determination.

Kyer's knees quaked and she stumbled. She had been upright for far too long in her weakened state. Derry reached out his hand to steady her.

"Where," Kien rasped, "is this *Misha*?"

Kyer glowered up at him. The duke steadfastly avoided eye contact with her.

"Misha is dead, my lord," Phennil said. "Kyer killed her to save Derry. That's how she got injured herself."

Lord Bartheylen's jaw trembled. In his steely eyes, Kyer read his vitriolic resentment at being cheated out of vengeance.

Vengeance! Kyer's memory clicked. Something about lives being forfeited. "Kien, what did you mean when you said it was too late?" Her voice was as unsteady as her footing. "Something about Derry being three out of four?"

Kien's lips pressed together. The only sound in the chamber was Roman, rubbing her hands together as she crushed herbs into the brazier. The heady scent floated through the air, any designs on soothing the mood lost on the gathering. Kien's milky white skin blanched to a sickly hue. He stared intently at a spot on the wall. "It would be a good idea if I went to see Cweivan right now." Pointing at Fredric, he growled, "You will putrefy in the Seventh Hell for your part in this."

Fredric quailed. but stood firm.

Valrayker's black-clad form rushed toward them. "Kien, what have you done?"

"I must hurry." Kien fled to the door. "The Halidans of Hreth might already be dead."

Kyer froze with terror and stared, unseeing, at the wall.

Rondo Gorder worked as Captain Senad's clerk to conceal her true position in Kien's personal army. Even the captain did not know the depth of Rondo's skills. In her career, Rondo had experienced all sorts of odd occurrences, but the reappearance of a missing cottage full of people was the first of its kind. She'd questioned her sanity only briefly. There was still time to achieve her purpose and return to the Gate, though she did not like being in a rush for such a task. She assessed the situation as swiftly as only a highly skilled assassin can. Damn it, she did not like an audience, either, but an order was an order. She would take out the Halidans expeditiously, then she may have to contend with the bewhiskered dispatcher—dispatchers were rigorously trained—but she was Kien Bartheylen's special messenger for good reason. The old man and the shopkeeper were inconsequential.

The old man stepped back and allowed her to enter the large front room of the cottage. Her quick eye saw wall-to-wall bookshelves; a thick, braided rug on the floor; a dining table in the corner; a much higher ceiling than was usual for such a place. Two people had risen from armchairs near the window.

"You are the Halidans?" she demanded.

"Do you have news of our daughter?" the man asked, which was answer enough.

With a shake of her arms Rondo had a knife in each hand and thrust.

Kyer collected herself after an instant and raced after Kien, crutch and all. Fed up with the sling holding her right arm, she snaked her hand out of it. The shoulder didn't hurt as badly as she expected it to. *Glad something's going well.* "Stop!" she called after her duke. He did not look back.

"There isn't time." He flung open the door to the stairway.

Screw protocol. "Stop *now*!" Kyer yelled.

To her surprise, Kien halted. He stared at her as if she were the first person in Rydris to ever give him an order. Val pulled up beside her and grabbed Kien's arm. "You ordered them *killed*?"

Kien pointed crazily at Kyer with his free arm. "I thought she'd killed my wife and child. Two lives for each life." To him it was an incontrovertible right.

"You got some crummy *note*, and you ordered my parents *murdered*, you bastard! And you think I'm not going to be upset about it?" She didn't try to keep the growl out of her voice.

"My wife was *dying*," Kien said with terrifying intensity.

"And where do you think you're going now?" she demanded.

Kien spread his arms wide. "I'm going to stop it. Cweivan has a Gate open this minute. If you want me to stop it, you'll not interfere."

"There isn't time for that." Kyer inhaled deeply, not even sure she could do this deliberately. Instinctively, she pressed her hand to her medallion through her tunic and concentrated. She felt energy draw through her body, though the metal remained cool. Her head quivered just a little. She was as astounded as the two dukes when an iridescent archway appeared before them, right in the centre of the corridor. Amazed at how easy it was, she nearly lost it but narrowed her eyes and held on. She'd guessed who she needed to speak to first. The Gate had opened directly in front of Brendow's back door.

"Try going this way," she said.

Valrayker pushed Kien through the Gate. As Kyer started to follow, he raised his hand, pushing her back. "No, Kyer," he said sternly. "You cannot come."

"You're mad." Rage flared. "My parents are being assassinated!"

"Exactly. You will stay here," Val ordered. "You will reopen this Gate in one hour to bring us back. For now, it will close."

He went through.

Shaken, Kyer obediently closed the Gate and hated Valrayker with the fierceness of a subjugated dragon. She couldn't feel her feet. Her whole body was numb, and she felt as though she were floating several inches above the stone floor. In the deafening silence of the corridor, she saw only red as she blinked at the spot where the Gate had been.

Fredric saw his hatred mirrored in Derry's eyes. Neither spoke. They didn't have to; Fredric knew what he was thinking. Every person in the room was thinking the same thing: Fredric Heyland had tried to bring Kyer Halidan down. He was the one responsible for Kien's action against her parents. If they died, guess who would be blamed?

I am not sticking around here for Kien to come back and slice my body into bite-sized pieces. He had to move, and the time was now.

Derry shook his head. "Don't think you're running off."

The detestable captain could warn him all he liked, but a quick dart of a glance confirmed Fredric's suspicion: their safety more or less assured inside the keep, the others were all unarmed. Fredric, on the other hand . . .

He drew his sword. Extending it before him, he described a semicircle, making eye contact with each of his foes. Harley stood nearest, his face unreadable, but his attitude too relaxed to be trusted. Janak's fingers twitched, his stump of a body poised to strike. The stupid halfling was frantically thinking of a way to stop him. Phennil just looked dazed, and Derry—well, Fredric had to admit that the young captain seemed to have matured . . . or something.

"Really, I must ask you all to leave," the healer insisted. Her stern voice made everyone jump, and Fredric saw his chance. He whirled around to race for the door, but Harley had anticipated his move and was quicker. Snatching up the tea tray off the cart that stood next to him, Harley tossed it in Fredric's face. The teapot smacked his eye, and the cream pitcher emptied down his neck. Hot tea soaked his borrowed waistcoat. Harley used the diversion to leap over and shut the door. Fredric crushed a porcelain cup with his boot as he ploughed through the mess. Derry's breath was all too close behind him, but Harley was the only one between Fredric and escape. His former mate reached for a chair to block his exit. In doing so, Harley'd opened himself up. Fredric slashed him across the gut, and the stench of blood oozed into the room as he bounded over Harley's body.

"Turncoat!" Fredric hissed at the gasping man below him. Skimnoddle threw himself down at Harley's side, effectively obstructing Janak's attempt to stop Fredric. Derry grabbed his right arm as Fredric reached for the door. Fredric slammed the pommel of his sword into Derry's head, and the captain went down. Fredric flung the door open and sped through.

He wasn't alone. Phennil was right behind him.

He made to dash toward the stairs but crashed into a still figure. It was Kyer. She slammed into the wall, not even making a sound. But she'd given Fredric an idea. Before she could complete her slide to the floor, Fredric hauled her up. Both arms around her, he held his sword to her neck. She was so wasted, she had nothing left to fight him with. Phennil halted his pursuit mid-stride, stricken with fear.

"Don't—don't do anything stupid, Fredric," the elf pleaded.

Kyer sagged against him and moaned.

Fredric smiled. *This couldn't be working out better.* "Out of all of them," he said quietly, "you were the one who wasn't convinced. I got through to the others, mostly, but you . . . You were never going to join my team, were you? Smartass. And now you're going to let me go because you know as sure as you're a pretty boy elf that I hate her. And I will kill her if you so much as raise a hair to stop me leaving."

Phennil clutched his arms to his sides. Fredric clenched Kyer tighter and tested the edge of his blade on that slight stickiness of sweat on her throat. He longed to draw it further and feel the scrape as her flesh opened beneath his blade, but she was no good to him dead. Not yet.

"Stop it." Phennil whimpered.

Fredric nodded toward the staircase. "Walk ahead of us. Make sure nobody makes a move on me, or Kyer's going to hang out with the gods. You got that?"

Roman dashed across the room, uttering heartfelt expletives in a foreign tongue. Derry's head throbbed but he'd be all right. Janak aided him to a sitting position.

Skimnoddle was kneeling by Harley's side, holding his hand and rocking to and fro. Derry had much to learn about the halfling, who one moment had all the boisterous confidence of an actor, and in the next was as vulnerable as a child. Roman demanded cloths and water and a myriad of other items which Janak fetched for her from the supply by Alon's bed.

Alon lay still and alone. Warrior that she was, she told them she was fine, and insisted Derry help those with more urgent need. Roman sent Skimnoddle to find Jorri, her apprentice. Derry had to trust that Roman would get Harley's bleeding under control. The captain wished his new man well, but he had to find Fredric.

As he hastened out the door, he collided with Jesqellan.

"Good God, what has happened?" the mage cried at the sight of Harley, the blood, the broken tea things, and a lot of missing people.

"No time. Where's Fredric?" Derry rushed by, and Jesqellan didn't respond. There was no sign of Fredric, nor Phennil in the corridor. Kyer's sling was tossed aside, and her crutch lay on the floor against the wall. A closer examination revealed flecks of fresh blood between the stones. Dread constricting his throat, he raced down the stairs, Jesqellan's bare feet rushing along after.

Kyer was thinking as hard as she could, which wasn't very hard at all. She searched numbly through all the little pockets in her mind where she kept her thoughts and memories. There were so many to sift through, yet nowhere could she find a memory of a day quite as bad as this.

Sure, there was the day she was attacked on her way home by eight young men, but she'd won that fight, so did it count? Then there was the day her boyfriend was cross with her for deciding to leave Hreth and accused her of betraying the whole village. Practically every day she'd gone to school was up there on the list of crummy days. Oh, and there was the day she killed Simon Diduck in Wanaka. But that was also the day she met Valrayker, so it couldn't have been so bad. There was even the day she'd been taken by Ronav, beaten almost senseless, and nearly mutilated by his men. Yup, that was a fairly bad day. But even that didn't hold a candle to this day.

Fredric tightened his arm around her middle and something wet from his clothing soaked through her back, but at least he had taken his sword away from her throat. It wasn't that he was a gentleman. It was that he needed that hand for balance as he dragged her down the steps. She wasn't much help, with her injured leg, and the bastard had let her crutch fall to the stone upstairs.

Pain shot through her from all angles, and she struggled for breaths, yet at the same time, she felt virtually nothing at all. She continued her list. On top of her present predicament, she'd passed out in the foyer, been accused by her best friend of trying to kill Alon Maer, and narrowly escaped decapitation by Kien Bartheylen. After finally being exonerated, she'd found out her parents might very well be dead at the hands of Kien's assassin. She'd opened a Gate purposefully and consciously for the first time, which had exhausted her more than she'd have figured, and she'd been ordered to stay behind.

Because all that wasn't quite enough to prove her mettle to whomever wanted to know about it, she'd been bashed into a stone wall and was now a hostage for the cur, Fredric Heyland, enjoying the rare luxury of being hauled unceremoniously through Bartheylen Castle, down the front steps and across the flagstone courtyard she'd admired earlier. She noted that it was still nice and flat.

She also noted that her shirt front was sticky with blood from her own neck.

And that damn mirror. Her name had been cleared, but the question still stood: How in seven hells had Alon Maer's mirror arrived in her saddlebag?

Fredric's grasp slipped and she nearly blacked out from excruciating pain as she stumbled. Fredric cursed at her. She hopped on her right leg as he heaved her along.

Under normal circumstances, Kyer would have come up with some beautiful cutting remarks with which to torment her captor. Today she had nothing. *Exhausted* didn't cover it. *Faint* was only part of it. *Shattered* was starting to come close. Ah, she recognized that smell. *Stable.* Oh, thank goodness for the dimness of the indoors. *Hi, Trig, if you can see me.*

Fredric shoved aside a dispatch rider about to mount his horse. The fellow protested but stopped when Fredric's sword tip aimed at his eyes. Fredric leaned her against the horse's flank and growled at her to climb on. He helped her with this—*What a gentleman!*—and got himself seated behind her. He'd put his sword away, but she felt the sharp point of a dagger at her side.

As they rode out of the stable, the afternoon sun made her cringe again. She wasn't sure, but she almost thought she'd seen Phennil standing there. *Odd*. That might have been his voice, too, crying, "Let them by! Let them by!" as she and Fredric and the horse passed through the castle gates and ran hard toward the sun.

Gates. She'd made a Gate to Brendow's house. To save Gareth and Della. She was aching and weak with hunger and exhaustion, and her parents might be dead. A sob choked out of her. *What a lousy day!*

"So we've beat the smugness out of you, and at last we see the real Kyer under that supercilious act." Fredric spit off the side of the horse. "You're no better than me."

He sheathed the dagger, and they galloped westward across the grasslands. Fredric looked back where they'd come, and swore. He urged the animal onward, more swiftly. Something whizzed near them and stuck in the ground, startling the horse: an arrow. Fredric wrestled the animal under control. Apparently they were being pursued.

Fredric realized his time was up. He slowed the horse.

He punched her, hard, in the ribs. So hard she deflated with a ragged, gutteral moan. He then tipped her sideways and shoved her off the horse. She landed on her right side, and her plastered left elbow caught against an object, a thing embedded in her side, neatly between her ribs. Kyer gasped for air between jolts of pain and tried to clasp the dagger. She couldn't reach with her unbending left arm. With a groan of agony that sounded like scraping stone, she rolled onto her back. But her wounded right shoulder did not permit her right hand to reach over for the knife. *I guess he thinks I deserve this.* Fredric leaned onto the pommel of his saddle and smiled down at her.

"Well, darling," he said matter-of-factly, "I know you thought the sex was great. I'd screw you one last time before I go, but I don't have time, and besides, I'm not into doing it with corpses."

He kicked the horse's sides.

"So long!" he called and raced off.

Kyer writhed among the buttercups, her mouth grasping at the air. She felt her very soul seeping, dripping, trickling out of her along the blade of a knife.

She stared unseeing into the azure sky. She watched Derry, whirling and smiling on the dance floor.

Thirty-Four
To Call You My Friend

Several *clanks* of metal and a thud met Val's ears as he and Kien burst into Brendow's front room.

"What do you mean by interfering with Bartheylen orders, old man?" a woman's voice demanded.

"Your orders have changed, Corporal," said Kien Bartheylen, filling the space with his formidable bulk.

The room was crowded, and Val couldn't see whose weapons had clashed together. He stepped up next to Kien and saw a middle-aged woman holding a cup, wearing an indescribable expression, with two swords crossed in front of her. One of the swords was the assassin's. The other was Brendow's. Two large knives lay on the carpet nearby.

"Bren d'Athlan," said Kien.

"Kien. Dunvehran," replied Brendow. "It's old home week."

"Rondo, stand down," Kien ordered, a reassuring hand extended. "It was a mistake."

Rondo paled and seemed to search for words.

Val noted Kien's generosity at admitting a mistake, though he also observed that his friend had neglected to say it was *his own* mistake. "Long story, all this," Valrayker said, and turned to the woman with the cup. "Do you have any more of that tea? You must be Kyer's mother."

✦

Jesqellan's rich voice chased Derry down the stairs. "I'll follow; you tell me everything."

"Kyer is innocent." Derry called upward as he hastened down. "I drew a sketch of Misty, and Alon Maer identified her as the one who delivered the necklace. It's just as Phennil said all along," he concluded as Jesqellan reached him at the bottom. "Fredric's story was a fabrication, intended to defame Kyer and buy Kien's forgiveness." Derry flew through the door. His guilt gnashed his insides, for being too ready to favour Fredric's words before his faith in his friend. Jesqellan would surely feel it all the more.

When Derry caught up with Phennil, the elf was leaning against the massive hinge of the castle gate. A small cloud of dust was about fifty yards away, galloping westward. He started to yell for a horse, but Phennil put out a hand. Tears streamed down the pale cheeks as he said, "Don't. You can't do anything, or he'll kill her." He coughed. "I let him go. I could have stopped him, but he'd already cut her neck. He hates her, Derry, he told me. He's going to kill her. It's my fault. I'm sorry." Phennil buried his face in his arm and sobbed. Jesqellan came up behind them, his face wooden with shock.

Derry clenched and unclenched his hands. "Phennil, this is not your fault. You're the one we should have been listening to all along. The rest of us were too busy wanting him to be right. I am the one who owes you an apology." The elf raised his tear-streaked face. "I've been unkind and unfair. I have not treated you with the respect you deserve." The ball of dust edged farther and farther away, and Derry reached a decision. "Another thing you're right about: He hates her. He'll kill her whether we follow or not."

"I'll get horses." Phennil dashed off to the stable.

"What about Valrayker?" Jesqellan asked quietly. He hadn't intruded his own penitence between theirs, and Derry had forgotten he was there.

Derry's heart sank. "Damn. I forgot the dukes went to see Cweivan."

"No, they didn't," Jesqellan said. "I was with Cweivan the last two hours. Why did they want to see him?"

"Did Cweivan open a Gate to Kyer's home village?" Derry asked urgently. When the mage confirmed this, the captain sent his brain into action. They must have known there wasn't time and made Kyer open a Gate. Why she hadn't gone with them was anybody's guess, but it didn't matter now. "Jesqellan, you've got to go back to Cweivan and tell him to reopen the Gate. You must go through and find Val and Kien. They went to try to stop the Halidans' being assassinated."

"But we already opened it to let Corporal Gorder back through," Jesqellan protested, though he appeared startled at the woman's occupation. "She wasn't there, so we had to close it. We can't open another one for several hours."

"Get up there and be prepared to do it as soon as you're able, then," Derry ordered. "Or Val and Kien won't get back."

Jesqellan hurried off, back up to the tower.

Phennil trotted up, leading two horses, and within moments, they were off. It didn't take long to see they were gaining on their prey. Derry felt sick at the thought of what Fredric might do when he knew he couldn't get away.

"Head groom loaned me this." Phennil grinned and held up a longbow.

"Are you sure that's a good idea?" Derry spoke loudly above the rumble of the horses' hooves.

"He's shielding Kyer in front. I figure I'll shoot him in the back before I hit her."

"Agreed. Phennil, I'm glad you didn't leave."

Phennil nodded his thanks. "I get nervous sometimes. But you have to admit that when people find fault with me, it's usually because of the way I smell, not because I'm not good at what I do." He smiled shyly as he assessed his target. He fired an arrow, which narrowly missed but spooked Fredric's horse.

Derry nearly choked on his heart as he saw Fredric, about eighty paces ahead of them, slow, then shove Kyer off his horse. The former knight paused momentarily then galloped off. Kyer was lost among the grasses in the distance. She did not get up.

Phennil cried out. They urged their mounts faster, afraid of what they would find.

Jesqellan pounded up the stairs, back the way he'd come. He stopped abruptly, just prior to slamming into the owner of the feet that appeared on the steps before him. He looked up, warily, into Janak's unreadable countenance. Eyes peered down at him through slits among the hair. Jesqellan shuddered.

"I—I've got to go find Valrayker and Kien," Jesqellan said to Janak's belly. He moved to pass on the railing side of the winding staircase. Janak shifted his bulk. Jesqellan was blocked.

"She was innocent," Janak said. "All along."

Jesqellan tried to stammer, produced nothing, and simply nodded.

"I believed," said Janak. "Not because I wanted to or it felt right." The slits widened and blinked. "I believed," the dwarf said, "because it was you." He added one further thought. "She saved your life too, that day."

He pushed by, flattening Jesqellan against the inside wall. The mage's feet were dangerously close to losing purchase on the narrow end of the step. He stared down after his dearest friend and tried furiously to think where he had gone wrong.

Skimnoddle helped Roman and Jorri get Harley onto a stretcher. Roman had done some things—Skimnoddle hadn't paid attention—to stay the bleeding, and now it was prudent to remove the injured man from the lady's room. He found himself strangely squeamish and followed a few steps behind so he wouldn't have to look. He'd seen open wounds before without reaction, but this one bothered him. In an unoccupied chamber down the corridor, they lay their burden on a sofa, and Roman and Jorri proceeded with what they did best.

Skimnoddle stayed out of the way of the healers' hustle and bustle but hovered nearby. When Roman had finished with liquid cures and stitching, she moved on to her Healing Hands remedies. Harley's breath was still too ragged for Skimnoddle's liking. He moved closer.

As if he knew the halfling was near, Harley opened his eyes. Skimnoddle saw the smile there. He lifted Harley's chilly hand and held it in both his smaller ones.

"Bastard got me a good one," Harley whispered.

"You're going to be fine," Skimnoddle said. "These are pre-eminent healers."

Harley's eyebrows shrugged. Skimnoddle knew when he was being humoured. He attempted reassurance. "You didn't lose much—well, the wound wasn't—I mean, Roman was in the same room when it happened, so she took immediate action."

Harley gazed around him, seeing only Skimnoddle, the healer's head and shoulder, and the sofa back. "Really, you know." His voice rasped like a dagger on a grinding stone. "Dying wouldn't be such a bad thing. What have *I* got to lose?"

Skimnoddle squeezed the hand that was only slightly warmer for his holding it. "Perhaps you have nothing," he said with quiet steadfastness, "but *I* have."

—†—

Brendow made introductions all around in that calm manner of his that soothed everyone's rattled nerves. Valrayker was delighted to meet some of the characters he'd heard of in Kyer's personal history. He was pleased that they seemed excited to meet him. He was especially glad to see Brendow again. Twenty-five years was a long time to go without seeing good friends, even to a dark elf.

It was only right that someone should provide an explanation, so as their host refilled the kettle and set it on the hob, Val briefed them. Naturally he left out the part about Kien more or less losing his reason, since the duke wouldn't thank Val for demeaning him in front of his subjects.

The high elf towered above them, his head brushing the ceiling. "You will understand," Kien told them in his most intimidating tone, "that I was fraught with fear at the prospect of losing my wife and child. It was this distress that led me to give the order. But we stopped it in time, so no harm done."

Was that supposed to make the Halidans feel better? Val wondered.

"Candidly, I'm glad we were here with Brendow," said Della Halidan. "*He's* the one whose sword knocked two knives aside."

The assassin shied back into a corner, sheathing the sword she had drawn to defend herself against Brendow.

Val smiled, admiring Della's pluck. Not many had the nerve to speak so boldly to Kien Bartheylen. *Another place Kyer gets it from!* He signalled to Kien not to take it any further. "My friend feels profound remorse at his action," Val said warmly. "He is still in the midst of great shock himself and will punish himself severely over this incident once it all sinks in." He nodded soothingly to Kien, whose annoyed look was concealed from the others. "But if you would care to list all the village's needs to get back on your feet, Lord Bartheylen will be overjoyed to carry out your wishes. Right,

Kien?"

Kien glared at Val and bowed to the gathering, who then bustled amongst themselves to create the list.

"Where is Kyer?" Gareth said. "Why didn't she come with you?"

"Kyer is not at her best today," Val said. "She had sustained some injuries in weeks past and was feeling unwell this afternoon. She sends her regards." He briefly outlined the role she had played in both the missions she had undertaken for him. Her parents beamed.

The shopkeeper and her dispatch rider friend poured the tea, and Brendow brought some over to Valrayker.

"She doesn't know about the attack, does she?" said Brendow. "That's why you didn't bring her."

Val nodded. "The story of her injuries was true, however you are perceptive, old friend. I will receive some sharp words for excluding her when next I see her." Val glanced over at the rest of the party and hesitated.

Brendow caught his glance and lowered his voice. "But will you tell her?"

"That depends." Valrayker recognized that this would be his only chance to get some answers. "Brendow, what do you know about her? Where did she come from? I don't think she even knows, herself."

Brendow kept his voice low but switched to Dark Elvish to be sure.

"No, she does not know," Brendow agreed. "Nor do the Halidans. Her sudden appearance in their cornfield brought her no end of trouble during her childhood."

"But how did she get there?"

"I cannot guess! She couldn't have done it herself; she was naught but a tyke."

"You don't know?" Val's stomach lurched with surprise and disappointment. He rubbed the back of his neck. "I thought for sure you would know."

Brendow shook his head. "I was away from you all for too long. I confess I was hoping you would be able to explain it to me."

Valrayker let out a growl. "I have the tiniest of suspicions of who she might be, but . . . No, it just doesn't make any sense!" He described the recent discovery of Kyer's ability to Gate, which deepened the furrow between Brendow's eyes.

Brendow shrugged helplessly. "The only guess I have is that she was somehow left behind."

Val leaned his hand against the bookcase. "How can that have happened? Surely someone would have got word to . . . *someone*."

"Not without breaking the vow."

Valrayker conceded the point. "It has not yet been twenty-five years. Furthermore, how did she get to you? How would she have known to find you?"

"That must simply be coincidence." Brendow's face took on an uncharacteristic uncertainty. "Val, did I do right? Was I right to teach her your language?"

"Yes, old friend; your instinct was correct. How did she manage to find me?"

"She wanted to travel. To search for the very answers you and I are discussing. My thought was that she would be best served by finding you. I didn't know where you were, so I sent her to the only place I knew you'd wind up sooner or later."

"And now she is in my protection. For what *that's* worth." Val rubbed his moustache and scowled. "I was hoping to have something to tell her. The question now is: What, if anything, do I tell her when I know virtually nothing?" He looked over to where Della and the shopkeeper were creating a list, with Gareth looking over Della's shoulder. The dispatch rider stood firmly as if guarding them, while Rondo had been persuaded to have a cup of tea. Kien held a little cake in his fingers and looked uncomfortable.

Brendow sighed. "The more we tell Kyer, the more the enemy could find out."

Valrayker nodded. "And how powerful a tool would one such as she be in the hands of the enemy? If we are wrong, then things would not go well for her." Valrayker eyed the volumes on the floor-to-ceiling shelving. "I have no reason to believe the enemy is aware of her. If I did, I would tell her my suspicions immediately."

"It's hard to know for sure what is the right choice." The *Wæmniar* frowned. "However, I think you're right. There is no point in sharing conjecture. We must learn more. She will be safer, at least for now."

"She won't be happy with me, but I believe it would be best to hold off until it's absolutely necessary. To keep her safe."

"I must defer to you in this, as she is in your care."

Valrayker thought the man was looking as healthy and robust as ever. He switched back to Rydrish.

"You would be proud of her, Bren d'Athlan. And she speaks often of you."

The old man nodded. "I'm glad. And to know that she found you brings peace to my heart and soul."

Val raised his voice. "And now Kien, Rondo, we must be ready to go." The villagers seemed curious about their rapid mode of transportation, but none of them ventured to ask, to Val's relief.

The three of them stood outside Brendow's back door, gazing over the newly sprouting fields of barley. The weighty clouds hugged the mountain, sagging so close overhead, Val thought he might be able to touch them if he stood on Kien's shoulders. The light dimmed as evening fell into the valley. Finally Valrayker exhaled fully. "Kyer is not opening the Gate."

Kien fumed. He paced back and forth a few times, folded his arms and leaned against the house. When he spoke it was like the words puffed out unbidden, so low Val couldn't be sure he'd heard anything. ". . . own personal Cymrion."

Val turned his head sharply. "What did you say?"

Kien shook his head and looked out across the river. "Nothing. A joke someone made."

"Who?" Val was appalled.

"Someone I used to know," he said dismissively. "Shall we go back inside? How long do you suppose we'll have to wait?"

Jesqellan had been sitting for two hours on the black stone floor outside Cweivan's tower room, his knees tucked up under his robes. His spirit could not have been lower if he had been buried a hundred feet underground.

Clarity. He'd prided himself on his ability to see to the heart of a person's troubles and move past them. Fredric had praised his objectivity. *What objectivity?* Ridiculous.

No, Jesqellan had replayed that fateful conversation over and over. Fredric was a shrewd man. He'd known exactly how to get to Jesqellan. He'd inflated Jesqellan's ego then preyed on his pride by piercing it with the one piece of information that could plant the seed of jealousy. The notion that Kyer was capable of a spell he had not even begun to prepare for was like mould, the way it took root and spread, poisoning his confidence, his self-possession, and his judgement.

Jesqellan did not know if Kyer were alive or dead. If she lived, how would he make it up to her? And Janak . . . How would he regain the trust and loyalty of a dear friend who no longer believed in him?

The mage pictured a figure seated before him, a face that tipped upward, the eyes revealing sadness and disappointment. Jesqellan's heart ached with sorrow. Then he felt a hand on his cheek, the soft, loving touch of the one who had understood him better than any. He knew what he had to do.

The door opened. "I am ready," Cweivan said. "But you will not have much time. I have not regenerated for long enough after the previous spells and am nearly spent."

Jesqellan got quickly to his feet and entered the chamber.

"I was able to fix a location closer to the village," Cweivan went on, "because I observed it through the last Gate. But I beg of you to hurry." He looked down at Jesqellan out of tired hazel eyes.

Jesqellan nodded and offered Cweivan his hands to boost the energy for creating the Gate. Both closed their eyes for concentration and hummed as they drew energy from within.

The Gate opened. Jesqellan withdrew his hands and passed through it.

Kyer slowly lifted her heavy eyelids. Blinking a few times, she tried to place herself. *Why do I have a feeling I've done this before?*

This time when she tried to sit up, she had pains in different places from last time. But she succeeded and propped herself with a pillow. Then she finally noticed the other dissimilar detail that set this morning off from the other one: Derry was sitting in the chair next to the bed, his head lolling on the chair back as he dozed.

"Hi."

Derry awakened with a start. "Oh, hey." He rubbed his face. "You look like you've been dragged by a horse."

"Thanks." She smirked. "You look pretty shitty yourself."

He smiled wryly and worked the back of his neck with his hand. "It's been a rather tough couple of days. How do you feel?"

"Like I've been dragged by a horse."

"You might as well have been. That knife barely missed vital organs. When Phennil and I found you, I thought—well, we really weren't sure." He peered at her, almost shyly. "It hadn't been long since Hunter dumped you. If we'd been further behind, I hate to think—"

"Do I have Imogen to thank again?"

Derry nodded. "Yes, and Roman herself. Now that Alon is stable, Kien was prepared to give up his prime healer. I suppose you might take that as an apology."

Kyer had forgotten all about Valrayker's expectation that she'd open a Gate for them to return. "They got back, did they?" She chuckled quietly. "Even if I hadn't been carted off and stabbed, I wouldn't have been in a hurry to fetch them. I figure they deserve to be stuck in a remote village for a while."

Derry shrugged. "I guessed they had gone to Hreth, so I sent Jesqellan back upstairs to Cweivan. He was too tired to open another Gate right away, so he had to rest awhile. Jesqellan eventually went through and located Val and Kien. But don't worry; they were stuck there for several hours."

Kyer felt like grumbling. "I guess even a few hours in Hreth would be like a punishment to Kien, for all that he's the duke and he's never visited there my whole life."

Derry leaned back in the chair. "While you're feeling good and resentful, he wants us to keep the whole assassin thing under wraps. Bad for his reputation. Plus, it'd blow the assassin's cover."

Kyer just looked at him blankly. She felt in no shape whatsoever to process *that*. Instead, she studied the tapestry on the wall and blew a long breath out of puffed cheeks.

"Kyer." He didn't go on right away. When he finally spoke, it was with quiet earnestness. "I had this whole speech planned, but it just feels stupid. So please let me say it. I regret my treatment of you. My behaviour on the journey was—well, let's just say that you were right about a lot of what you said that night. Your words hurt so much because they were true. I had not behaved as a good captain should. Whatever happens now, I need you to know how glad I am that you're around for me to say that. You're a worthy warrior, Kyer. I owe you my life. And I'm proud to . . . not only to serve with you, but to call you my friend. If I may."

Kyer's lip trembled for all her effort to hold it steady, and her eyes welled. She quickly averted her face, for fear the tears would spill over. There was a tremor in her voice. "I don't know what I'd do if you didn't."

The silence that followed was comfortable, companionable. The awkwardness that had stemmed from the buildup of frustration and mistrust had dissipated entirely. They chatted amiably as they used to, each filling in gaps of the story that the other had not heard. She told him how she'd opened the cave doors, and he told her about the harrowing journey south to the chasm. He also told her about Jesqellan determining the white rose's power. Her jaw slackened in surprise.

"Honestly, I thought Kayme gave it to me as a token to remember him by. I thought its only magic was that it stayed fresh." A shadow passed across her mind. "I suppose a lot of trouble would have been avoided if I had shown it to Jesqellan the night he asked about magic on me."

"Who can say? I was no help there," the captain insisted, jumping to her defence. "I knew about the rose and didn't mention it either. I did nothing to talk him out of his suspicions. Anyway, that's behind us now," he said firmly. "I didn't mean to upset you. I only thought you should know."

"What about the mirror?" she asked.

Derry frowned, looking as if he'd broken a family heirloom. "I wish I'd never seen the damn thing."

"But where did it come from? How did it get into my saddlebag? You believe I didn't—"

"Yes!" Derry insisted with vehemence enough to make up for not believing her before. "I don't know how, but it must have been Fredric. At some point, he must have had access to Trig." He shook his head and shrugged. "There can't be anyone else."

"No. I can't think of—" She stopped, and suddenly felt like something was lodged in her throat. Oh yes, there was *one*. One person who could have done it. And her heart wrenched with shame and plunged to the bottom of the deepest abyss. What had she done? Her mind raced. Who knew? Was it too late?

"What is it?" Derry said.

She shook her head. No. She was not prepared to discuss this with Derry. She could still make amends. Instead she yanked herself up to level ground and in a hoarse voice said, "Or Misty herself, maybe." Then she changed the subject. "Maybe we'll never know, but all this"—she indicated her injuries and the infirmary room—"has eclipsed the main event. We ought to be celebrating." She picked up the mug of milk from her breakfast tray and said, "To Alon Maer."

She drank and passed the cup to Derry, who agreed, "To Alon Maer."

"Do you suppose," Kyer said thoughtfully, lying back on her pillows, "that Fredric truly still cares so much for Kien? Or was it all just for show?"

The captain rested his palms on the arms of the chair. "I think he got his priorities crossed. There's no disputing that he blames you for his change of lifestyle, so he was out to get you. But," and Derry clasped his hands on his belly, "I believe he truly did wish to be forgiven by Kien, and even to work with him again." He rose and wandered to the window. "You devote your life to someone, like that, from boyhood. All your life lessons have been learned with his guidance; he's more like a father than an employer. To be knighted is the grandest honour, when you consider how effortless it was to serve." He paused briefly, reflecting. "Yes, I have no doubt that Fredric could not shake that."

She watched her friend's face for a hint of his own feelings. "What about you?"

"Me?" He gave her an understanding half smile. "I couldn't shake it either."

Not long after, Derry departed leaving Kyer alone to delve deeper into the fleeting thought that had unsettled her. A certain figure who had featured prominently in her pain-induced dreams. Who often during their journey had appeared out of nowhere. Who would always be able to find her, so long as she carried a white stone she had, at last, chosen to discard along the path.

Who claimed to have her best interests at heart but, she only in this moment allowed herself to admit, could so easily have deceived her.

Kyer stared blindly at the ceiling as an ember of fury whispered to life within her.

An impromptu debriefing took place in Kien's study that evening, with wine all around. The invalids were absent, and Derry insisted on a toast to their good health. Val listened to each anecdote of what had transpired after he and Kien had left and had the sensitivity to look abashed over Fredric's escape with Kyer as hostage. Kien, Derry observed, remained as aloof as ever, not even a glimmer of recognition that his actions were at the heart of the troubling events of the day. For the first time, Derry questioned what his lord saw in the high elf.

"What I still don't understand is why?" Phennil frowned. "Why did Misty and Juggler want to kill Alon Maer?"

Derry agreed. "Who were they to you, Kien? To Alon? Had you met them?"

Kien waved a hand dismissively. "I meet so many people I can't possibly remember them all. I imagine they had some grievance, some ill-informed perception that I had," he rolled his steely eyes, "*wronged* them in some way."

"And why not just slit her throat?" Janak caught himself, and gave Kien an apologetic nod. "Sorry, your Lordship, but if Misty had the opportunity to be alone in the room with the Lady, why this ghastly, protracted process?"

"They wanted him to suffer." Val shrugged. "We will never know their real motive, but I think we can infer that they believed Kien deserved to be punished for some reason."

"Kien?" Phennil scowled. "Why does it have to be about Kien? Sorry, your lordship, but it was Alon who suffered most and would have died."

Valrayker's mouth formed an O of surprise. "Phennil, you're right. I don't know why I thought— But why would Misty and Juggler have wanted to punish Alon?"

"Perhaps they did not," Skimnoddle said, and heads turned. "Whoever hired them did."

Derry was moved. Both Phennil and the halfling were able to see things from a perspective the others had forgotten. *I must keep learning.*

Around him the talk had gone back around to what happened after Fredric left Kyer for dead.

Jesqellan told of Derry's instructions to have Cweivan Gate him back to Hreth to find the dukes. "It was a terribly difficult spell," he said off-handedly. "Cweivan is probably still sleeping to recover from yesterday."

Derry picked up on Jesqellan's tone. Only Janak grasped its meaning.

"That's it, isn't it?" Janak leaned around Phennil to eye Jesqellan. "It annoys you that Kyer can do a spell that you can't. And she's not a mage." He looked as if he'd never laid eyes on the Moabi before.

Jesqellan stared ahead of him, shame-faced. "It just doesn't make sense."

"You would have ruined her!" Janak's volume increased. "You'd have seen Kien draw and quarter her and hang her pieces like gargoyles on every corner of this castle. She'd have served as a vivid reminder of why nobody crosses Kien Bartheylen. All over jealousy about a spell?"

All eyes were on Jesqellan, although Derry noted that Kien did not deny Janak's assessment of his character. The mage shook his head wordlessly. *Gathering courage?* He spoke finally, softly, and with more humility than

Derry had ever witnessed from the mage. "They say arrogance is a form of blindness. I have been sightless these many weeks. I thought my Moabi Shaman training brought me a step closer to the gods. Greater self-possession, greater understanding. Greater clarity. It appears I am a mortal, after all. Capable of overconfidence and fallibility. And yes, Janak my friend, indulging in fancy. I have been humbled. I do not know how I am going to prove to all of you, and especially to Kyer, that I have learned, but I beg of you to do me the honour of not doubting that I will try."

The stillness lasted for several breaths before Derry broke it. "You have my support, Jesqellan. I myself have been culpable. In fact, Phennil is the sole person who stood by Kyer all along."

Phennil blushed and as if to dismiss the attention, said, "But, Val, let's face it, Jesqellan isn't the only one who is curious about Kyer's ability to Gate. She has said many times that she doesn't deal with magic, yet it's clearly an advanced spell."

Jesqellan nodded. "If I may be so bold, sirs, Cweivan has explained in detail the limitations of such a spell, and my own experience yesterday has proven to me that the spell is utterly impossible for a lay person to perform. So tell me, my lords: *How*, not to mention *why, can she do it?*"

Derry watched the two dukes exchange uneasy glances. Kien gave Val a subtle nod. Valrayker *ahemed* and sat up straighter.

"I must ask for your absolute discretion in this. All I am prepared to say, at this point, is that there is one circumstance wherein a person is able to open Gates without the same limitations imposed on you or I. One. And in that circumstance, no spell is involved.

"You will all have to be satisfied with that."

Derry didn't know what Valrayker meant, but he could not tell from Jesqellan's open-mouthed stare whether he knew any more.

After another night of deep, restful sleep, Kyer's left hand was stiff but no longer required immobilization. Although Fredric's stab wound still stung on the surface and ached when she moved, bandages and salve had done wonders for it. And though her right shoulder needed a good deal of stretching and exercise before she'd wield her sword properly, she could at least move it without sharp pains slicing across her chest and down her arm. All 'round, she felt better than she had in weeks. Her leg still needed the splints for a few more days. Last night Imogen had decided that the bones had melded back together well enough to speed up the process with a higher-grade healing potion. "And if you're going to go traipsing about without my leave like you did the other day," the good healer had scolded, "I had better heal you before you break every bone in that obstinate body of yours."

Kyer grinned and stretched. "To be fair, much of that 'traipsing around' was not my choice."

There was a shuffle in the corridor, and Derry stood in the doorway. The curtains and shutters were open to let in the bright morning light. Kyer shifted her half-empty breakfast tray over to the bedside table and sat up. It was much easier to do now.

"What is it?" Kyer smiled up at him. Derry looked at her with a new sort of energy. He was . . . luminous. He stepped into the room. She gestured for him to sit down, but he shook his head.

The blond fringes of his hair softly curled above his blue eyes. Kyer had never seen his hair long enough to know that it curled. *It looks . . . well, nice.* But it was his eyes that astonished her. They glistened.

"Kyer." His chest lifted with each breath more noticeably than if he'd been relaxed. "It has happened."

The glistening eyes shone, and Kyer knew exactly what Derry was talking about. A smile spread across her face, and she had a feeling her eyes were glistening too.

"I told you so," she said.

Derry's face lit up, filling the room with sunshine. He plunked down in the chair; he could, now that he'd told her the news.

"It's what I've always wanted, what I've worked for since I was *seven years old*!"

"I know."

"*Sir Derry*. Don't you think that sounds . . . like . . . ?"

She laughed. "It sounds damn good."

"Do you know what Dunvehran said to me?" Derry sobered and looked to Kyer more like the Derry she first met. "He told me the reason it took him so long." His voice sounded like his throat was lined in cotton wool. "He said it wasn't enough for me to *behave* as a knight in order to *be* one. He said I had to believe in myself. I guess I always thought I'd be better at believing in myself if he knighted me. But he said no, it doesn't work that way."

"He always believed in you," Kyer said. "He was just waiting patiently for you to come around to his way of thinking."

Derry perked up again. "The ceremony is tomorrow afternoon. Everyone in the castle is invited to the great hall. Alon might even attend for a while if she's feeling well enough. The tailor is making me dress garments in Equart colours. There will be a feast and dancing . . ."

His eager voice carried on, and Kyer smiled to herself. *Dancing. I never did get around to asking him.* This side of Derry was entirely new to Kyer. She had initially met his formal, proud self, who took things so seriously that he hardly ever cracked a smile. He'd unwound like fishing line over the weeks that she'd gotten to know him, before winding up tighter than a crannequin in the past month.

His face went sombre. "I know what you've said in the past about not wanting a knighthood, to be tied down to one person; I don't mean to offend, but . . . I do wish it were both of us. You deserve it as much as I, if not more."

Kyer knew what he meant, and smiled.

He brightened again. "You'll be well enough to come, won't you? I wouldn't feel right, somehow, without you there."

She tossed a pillow at him. "Nobody has enough money to pay me to stay away."

Thirty-Five
I Don't Need Glory

They had provided Kyer with a chair, just in case she was unable to stand for the entire ceremony. It was nice of them, but at the moment, she felt better than she had in many weeks. Physically, at any rate. She nodded to Harley, sitting stiff and pale next to Skimnoddle across the aisle. Having heard his story of his defection from Fredric's ranks, his aid and defence of Phennil in the journey to and from the Tree of Life, as well as his friendship with Skimnoddle, Kyer was equally appalled as the others by Fredric's assault on old "Average Height Guy" and was pleased to see him recovered enough to attend the ceremony.

Derry stood solemnly before the dais at the top of the room. He caught her eye, and she smiled encouragingly at him. He hadn't seen a barber yet, but his blond hair was neatly combed and wisps of curl hung around his ears. He looked magnificent in his Equart garments in black with a dark blue jerkin, highlighted by a few preferred pieces of polished plate armour. Kyer had often described him as proud, but in the past, his pride was akin to haughtiness. This was different; today he was proud of his achievement, and it was well deserved. Excitement danced in his eyes and seemed to shoot out the tips of his fingers and toes.

She stood just to the right of the dais with Phennil to her left. She held her crutch loosely in her left hand, though she no longer depended on it for support. Her sword hung at her hip just for the occasion, its weight on her shoulder and across her chest. She caressed its jewelled pommel absently, and dreamed about a time that she'd be able to swing it again.

The great hall hummed with the low murmurs of a hundred people anticipating an exciting and rare event. Afternoon sunshine streaked through the high windows and dazzled on the armour worn by many of those present. Kyer couldn't suppress her self-satisfaction at seeing the Lady Alon Maer seated on the dais next to Kien. She still looked peaked and weary, but her smile was warm, and every back in the room was a little straighter upon observing it, every chin a touch uplifted. Kyer nodded inwardly, remembering the night she sat on the foyer staircase in Shael Castle with Phennil, gazing at the lady's portrait. Such a long time ago.

By contrast, Kyer allowed herself a glance at Valrayker. The sight of him sent a stormy-grey cast over her soul, despite the sunny occasion. She hated not knowing where she stood with him, and was left feeling a hollowness she didn't know how to fill. Val sat next to Kien, making idle comments she could not hear while he waited to begin the ceremony. Resplendent in his black dress garb with dark blue trim, and his gleaming breastplate enamelled with the tree and flower of Equart, he smiled and nodded to the others of his company, but he didn't meet her eye. Kyer wished she weren't mad as hell at the man she used to call her hero.

She was disturbed by his lack of response to her breach of the Indyn Caves and her ability to speak Dark Elvish. Worse, that he had trapped her into showing it. It was downright deceitful.

Worse, though, was his stiffness and rejection. Every word of his gloomy visit to her room rankled: the conversation that had started in a friendly manner but finished with accusations, trickery, and hints of mistrust. Whereas everyone else knew she'd been proved innocent and had at least behaved as if they wished to make it up to her, Valrayker had barely given her as much as a nod or a glance since he had returned from Hreth, the minimum to acknowledge her presence. He had neither explained nor apologized for excluding her from the visit to her home and had answered her query with a laconic, "Your folks are well." He'd taken her Gating for granted, failing to recognize that the ability was haunting her like a stalker. Surely he ought to offer, if not elucidation, at least some compassion.

None of it, though, was enough to snuff out the healthy fury that smouldered over an uncommonly tall, pale man who carried the scent of wildflowers wherever he went.

Finally Kien and Dunvehran rose, the dark elf looking every bit worthy of his formal name as his black hair tumbled across his shoulders and his grey eyes shone from beneath his brow. His moustache and beard were trimmed and framed an easy smile meant for everyone but Kyer. She frowned and bile bubbled in her gut. Then she cursed herself for being so angry on Derry's special day. *It's Valrayker's fault*, she thought petulantly then added, *It's also someone else's.*

"My friends." Kien's voice rang out, gladness and welcome reverberating around the room. "I, Kien Bartheylen of Heath, Koral, and Shae, and my comrade Dunvehran, Valrayker of Equart, are proud to be Lords of Rydris. We stand here with you, beneath the light of a sun that shines upon all our lands. We share this light with all who daily defend those lands from the yoke of tyranny. Our purpose today is a glad one."

Kyer hardly heard a word of the ceremony. Kien and the dark elf were outlining the story of Alon's sickness and the journey of those who aimed to eradicate it. There was applause at each of the high points of the tale. Kyer studied the wooden arches that held up the ceiling of the hall.

Special thanks were being given to the members of the party. More applause for each name. Kyer observed the statues situated on pillars about the hall. *I'll have to go have a look at who they are.* Her own name was mentioned, but she just stared ahead of her and fidgeted.

"Now," said Kien's voice, "we are come to the point in this ceremony which gives us the most pleasure."

Kyer made herself perk up. This was for Derry and she resolved to disallow her own vexations to detract from Derry's long-awaited moment. To her surprise, Valrayker stretched out his hand, and Skimnoddle stepped forward, wearing a bright yellow tunic and deep red, billowy trousers. With his hands behind his back, he stood with head held high, and his voice rang through the stillness of the hall.

O heroes bold, your journey now is ended.
Your faces meet our joy 'pon your return.
Our thanks and admiration you have befriended.
Our love and faith undying you have earned.
Come you now to hear our gladsome voices soar
'Til loyal hearts are drawn unto adventure more.

Kyer heard a chickadee's cheerful chatter out in the courtyard. She drew her attention away from the halfling's heartfelt song to see Valrayker of Equart staring at her, his eyes unreadable. Startled, she frowned and flipped her gaze hastily to Derry. Skimnoddle's singing had made her chest swell with pride and her chin tilt upward with joy in spite of herself. She corrected those positions and scowled. *Can we please just get this over with?*

Val stepped forward.

"Today is a solemn occasion. The valour that has been shown by this warrior before me is of the highest order. Today we honour the valiant conduct shown by him in defence of his lord, his lands, and his fellows.

"Derry Moraunt, in recognition of said valour, I offer you knighthood to me, Dunvehran of Equart, and humbly request your devotion and service."

Derry knelt before his lord.

"Are you resolved to accept this position and uphold the spirit and fealty that it represents?" the duke went on.

"I am," came Derry's voice, clear and confident.

"Give me your sword."

Derry drew his weapon and laid it across his palms to present to his duke. Dunvehran gripped it in his right hand and held it high.

"See here!" he cried. "This is the sword of a knight of my banner. I give it my blessing. May it serve me and its bearer unerringly." Then he tapped Derry on his right shoulder with the sword before returning it, pommel first, to his hand. "I present to you Sir Derry Moraunt!" The crowd erupted in vigorous applause, and a tingle went up Kyer's back.

Derry rose and Kyer grinned to see his beaming face. The dark elf embraced him, and the new knight approached his friends. Kyer shook his hand heartily.

"Congratulations, Sir Derry," she said warmly. His overabundance of emotions was too much for even the most stoic of captains, and his laugh erupted in spite of himself.

"The ceremony is not yet concluded," Kien said, and the crowd noise subsided. "There is one more whose selfless conduct is worthy of recognition." Kyer glanced sidelong at Phennil, and he shrugged down at her. Kien couldn't mean him, Phennil's devotion was to the Guarded Realm. Jesqellan perhaps?

"Kyer Halidan," said the Duke of Heath. "Please come forward."

She stared at him and didn't move. Derry squeezed her arm. *So this is how ice feels when spring hits.* She was shaking and she didn't know why. *Move your foot. Just pick up one foot, the other will follow.*

Somehow she arrived at the front of the dais and stood before the enormous high elf. He spoke above her head, and she observed that Alon's shoes were red.

"This young woman made no small contribution to myself and my lady. She faced a good many dangerous situations, largely on her own, including being the liaison with the great wizard Kayme. She is to be thanked for all her efforts to save the life of my lovely Alon Maer." He said it as if it were an instruction.

Huge applause. Kyer's face was on fire. *I am "to be thanked,"* she thought wryly, *but I note he didn't say thanks himself.* Alon rose and nodded to her people.

"I would like," Kien went on, "to show my appreciation in the way I know best."

Ah, yes, because trying to have my parents killed was such an impressive display of gratitude.

"Kyer Halidan, in recognition of your valour, I offer you knighthood to me, Kien Bartheylen of Heath, and humbly request your devotion and service."

The crowd gasped and murmured, but Kyer's breath stuck like a dagger in her throat. She felt, rather than saw, Derry's look of horror, and it didn't take a Perceptor to know he was thinking, *How's she going to handle this one?* Out of the corner of her eye, she saw Phennil's uncertain smile. Only he knew why she'd come on the journey.

Kyer forced her eyes up, to meet Kien's cold stare head-on, just like the first time they met. He looked hopeful and her resolve wavered. A smile began to take shape on her lip. Then she saw the smugness in the duke's grey eye. And the answer came automatically.

"Lord Kien, I humbly thank you for the offer, and admittedly, the opportunity to serve my lady—" She bowed toward the woman in question. "—is an honour. But I'm afraid I cannot accept." And with that, Kyer bowed and returned to her place.

The hall was so still, it might have been empty. Heat swirled up Kyer's neck and face like a wave at high tide, and she fervently wished someone would take control of the situation. It was Alon Maer who came to her rescue.

"We accept and respect Kyer's response, however disappointing it may be to be bereft of her exclusive employ. All the same, I thank you, Kyer, for all you have done."

Relief swept over the audience, and they applauded enthusiastically to make up for the awkward pause.

At last Kyer found herself outside. The crowd milled about, enjoying refreshments while servants switched the great hall from ceremony setup to grand feast layout. Sir Derry was surrounded by well-wishers, and admirers of a myriad of shapes and sizes swarmed around Kyer's male counterparts, hoping to catch an eye, touch a sleeve, or garner even the briefest of attentions. A word or two would be a brush with greatness.

Kyer stood apart from them. No one seemed to have the courage, or the aspiration, to approach the woman who'd refused a most honourable offer from the duke. Suddenly, though, the duke himself took her by the arm and led her, stumbling, away around a corner. He was smiling but it was for the benefit of the crowd, not for her.

Detached from the throng, he whirled her around to face him, which she did, undaunted by the way he towered over her. "What is the meaning of this? Do you think it is every day that I give knighthoods? Can you possibly imagine that I simply toss knighthoods around the courtyard for men to peck at and pick up like chickens?"

Kyer rolled her eyes. "Spare me the histrionics, Kien. You offered me a knighthood out of a sense of moral obligation, nothing more. You think that's going to make up for you ordering my parents murdered?"

Kien scoffed. "Is *that* what this is about?" He made it sound as if it were as trivial as someone missing a lunch date. "Your parents are alive and well —"

"No thanks to you. From what I heard, it was the freakishly fast reflexes of an old man that saved them."

Kien stretched his arms out wide. "You humiliated me before that entire crowd."

"No, Kien, you humiliated me. At least you tried to. You thought that if you offered me a knighthood out of the blue, in public circumstances, that I would be too embarrassed to refuse. You'd have 'done right by me' and would consider the matter history. Well, that might work with someone else, but not with me. Just because you're the duke of three duchies does not give you leave to manipulate me." Kyer gave him her back and walked away.

Kien took some time to collect himself before rejoining the revellers. The head server from the great hall approached soon after to inform the duke that the hall would be ready for the guests in about fifteen minutes. Kien thanked her and went to find Alon.

He found his wife inside the keep, seated on a sofa with several well-wishers paying her tribute. His heart swelled with pride that she was his beloved, her beauty and strength intact. He longed for their daily life to return to normal. He seated himself next to her and placed a hand on her knee. She covered it with hers.

Moira, the castle steward, excused herself for interrupting. "My lady, my lord, Imogen has given Kyer Halidan leave to remove herself from the House of Healing to a chamber in the keep."

Kien raised his eyebrows. Since when had this been his concern?

"I wouldn't trouble you, my lady, but she has requested a special room: an upgrade to a suite. To make up for 'certain recent experiences' she said. I don't claim to know what she means by that—"

Kien opened his mouth to order her to tell Kyer to go sleep in the stable if she didn't like the visitors' chambers in his castle, but Alon beat him to it.

"Of course she can have a suite, Moira. Give her the Trefeln Room."

Alon's deep brown eyes met Kien's. "It's the least we can do, don't you agree, my love?"

He studied her briefly, and understood. Kien could pretend he felt charitable for the sake of his wife. "Certainly," he reluctantly agreed. "The least."

The path Bianca climbed was more established with her frequent passing. She no longer had to hack and slash through the bushes, though the warm weather throughout the summer had encouraged their growth. Bianca didn't mind, as it kept the trail somewhat obscured. She breathed in the fresh scent of the forest and allowed it to calm the constant tension associated with the responsibilities of a village magistrate, especially a village in regrowth, like Hreth.

Bianca felt a great deal of satisfaction that with their new resource, those nearby towns who had donated goods were now being repaid through the purchase of lumber, seed, and equipment. The village's new layout, easily adopted since so many buildings had to be recreated from the ground up, would, she was sure, confound any attacker. Today she had begun the morning training session as always, to keep her eye on the progress of Hreth's little army before leaving them in Tarqan's expert hands. However, her pleasure in the way her plans had been embraced by the villagers, and were being brought to fruition so successfully, did not smooth the jagged edges of her responsibility. Her visits up this mountain were the most effective way of gathering her thoughts. Standing on the hilltop and looking down over her village allowed her the perspective to plan better than any map table. *And of course there is my new wingwoman*, Bianca thought with a laugh.

This hike always served as a transition in her mood, bridging the responsibility of the magistrate and all that entailed with the freedom and joy of developing a friendship with a dragon.

She began to sing before she reached the top of the path. By the time she emerged onto the bottom edge of the scree, her friend was waiting for her by the rock outcropping, hopping on one foot and flapping, gently, so as not to disturb the loose pebbles and cause a landslide. The rainbow colours of her skin and scales were bright even in the overcast.

"Good morning, Ellaj!" Bianca sang.

"Good morning, Mamma," the dragon sang joyfully, her blinking silver eyes illustrating her excitement. "I can't wait to show you what I've been practicing!"

Bianca climbed up the steps the two of them had dug into the hillside, until she was uphill of Ellaj and standing in her sizeable shadow. "Have you grown again since last week?" Bianca sang. Ellaj's chuckle was like the gurgle of a creek. She lowered her head so Bianca could stroke her under her soft, leathery chin. The dragon cooed and nuzzled her nose into Bianca's neck.

Singing her gratitude for this friendship, Bianca looked out over her village. The breeze of Ellaj's warm breath on her neck was a balm that soothed, encouraged, loved.

Bianca nodded. "Let them come."

Fredric Heyland—no, Hunter—adjusted the shoulder strap of his pack and nudged the flank of the horse he had stolen from Kien Bartheylen's stables. After dumping Kyer, he'd ridden aimlessly, but aimless riding had eventually become purposeful.

His revenge—ruining her reputation, destroying her life as she had destroyed his—had been thwarted. Golgathaur's "evidence" had proved faulty. He didn't even know for sure if he'd succeeded in murdering her.

Maybe suicide's a more viable option. Golgathaur had set him up. Hunter spat.

I'll kill him. As soon as the words materialized in his mind, he dismissed them and cowered shamefully with fear of the dark man. Why had the lieutenant set him up? What did he stand to gain by it? Golgathaur had suggested that Kyer had the means of delivering Alon's necklace. And that part was true. The idea of framing Kyer had been planted, and Hunter had been only too eager to jump on it. He never dreamed she could be proven innocent by a god-damned *sketch*. He'd been *so close*, but he'd wound up making a fool of himself.

And where did it leave him?

He reined in and the horse stopped, snorting. Slowly, hesitantly, he reached down to the pocket in his trousers. He had to stand in the stirrups to get his hand all the way in. It was deep inside.

When he sat again, he looked down at the white stone in his palm. Rubbing it gently, he spoke the name. "Golgathaur."

Golgathaur was surprised only at how long it took for the summons to come. At Hunter's accusation of a setup, he merely shrugged. "It was a good plan, but can one ever completely account for human behaviour? One does one's best." He showed Hunter where to make his horse comfortable then took him to the hall. Greok seemed unimpressed at the introduction, opening one eye a slit and puffing a little. Lord Dregor, on the other hand, seemed genuinely pleased to meet the new recruit. Especially when Hunter knelt on the black floor before him and presented his sword laid across his hands.

"I offer you my sword and my service, Lord Dregor, Lord of All."

Dregor shrugged his brows at Golgathaur, as if to say, "Why don't *you* speak to me with such reverence?" Golgathaur breathed on his pendant, and polished it on his waistcoat.

"We accept your sword as well as your service," his lordship said.

Soon after, Golgathaur left them to get better acquainted. Besides, he had one more errand.

Golgathaur had listened to Hunter's story of all that had happened at Bartheylen Castle. One question remained in the tall man's mind.

A moment later, a Gate opened at the head of the Pineridge Pass. The lieutenant's eyes widened to see where the Gate had brought him. Not a soul could be seen or heard. Only the north wind in the trees and some crickets chirping. A smattering of little animals scurrying about their preparations for nightfall. A whippoorwill.

He bent at the waist and kicked around the underbrush. There, slightly off the path, as if knocked aside by passing feet. Golgathaur reached down and picked up the white stone.

Kyer Halidan's locator stone. He turned it over in his fingers and stared unseeing down the path.

His mind's eye took him back all those weeks ago to a door, which he unlocked and passed through.

"How are we today?" Golgathaur said to his guest.

"Not as good as we would be if we were allowed to leave." She smiled sardonically.

"Always such a cut-up. You bring a smile to my face, no matter how bleak the world seems to me."

"Then my life is complete."

Golgathaur laughed and poured them each a beverage. They clinked glasses, he with a sense of fun, she with joyless resignation.

"To what shall we toast today?" he asked. His guest waited. This was not the first time he had asked the question, and she was used to not being expected to suggest an answer. "Shall we toast the future?"

"So long as you envision a future where I get to leave here."

"How about we celebrate a thing that is just for you!"

Her face lit up. "I get to leave?"

"You see, we can't all share in the joy of our bloodline carrying on into the future."

She nodded wisely. "When one is stuck in a cell every day it is difficult to form stable relationships."

He *tsked* her. "I keep telling you, this is not a cell."

She shrugged and blinked. "I try to base my opinions on solid evidence."

"Speaking of evidence. As I was saying, you are a fortunate person."

"When were you saying that?"

"I was speaking of bloodlines. Now I have not had the good fortune to connect with a person who has done me the honour of allowing me to share my procreating skills; at least, not to the degree where such partnership has resulted in procreation. You, on the other hand, have had that experience, that good fortune, if I may call it such; at least, I have been given the impression that such a partnership existed between yourself and another at one time." He paused, looking at her significantly.

She did not smile. "I have been in this cell so long I hardly remember anything that came before."

He leaned forward and rested his chin in one hand. He tapped his face with his fingers and scrunched his brow looking quizzical. "That might explain something."

She leaned back in her chair, and raised her eyebrows, her lips pursed.

"In an earlier chat similar to this one I learned—you may recall you were under some . . . strain . . . at the time." He sat up straighter and dropped his hand to the table. He gave her a self-deprecating smile. "I came away from that chat believing I had learned that there was a small-scale version of yourself wandering the paths of Rydris. But strangely, I believed that copy to have been a boy."

Her face was devoid of emotion, except for the tiniest hint of fear in the corner of her eye.

"And this is where I come back to what you said about evidence. Although I have searched Rydris far and wide for twenty years for evidence of this boy-child, I have found none. However, peculiar though it may sound, I *have* recently discovered evidence . . . of a girl."

A tautness in her eyes and the corners of her lips betrayed her, but Golgathaur had to admire her for her bravery and skill.

"Fear not, she is in good hands. She seems to have inherited your skill with the sword, not to mention your temper.

"I continued to pursue the matter because you see, you have never behaved as someone who has nothing to lose." He cocked his head and looked thoughtfully at the ceiling. "I wonder if she feels the same?"

Drops of liquid appeared on the bottom edge of her eyes, and she pushed away from the table. She stood up and walked away, head high. Golgathaur watched her, admiring how her body moved, how it healed. She hardly walked with a limp now.

When she wheeled around again, her hands were clenched in white-knuckled fists, and rage had etched lines and contours on her face. From that side of the room a growl formed and burst out of her like a storm wind.

"Stay away. Keep your loathsome, feculent self away—"

"Or what?" He rose, arms spread out in a dare. "Or you will do what?"

She clung to the mantel and her body convulsed with wrath.

He moved to leave. Hand on the door handle he said, "There isn't much you can do while you're stuck here in this cell."

He closed the door behind him, shot the bolt home and waited.

Only when he heard her muffled sob did he reward himself with a smile and walk down the stairs.

The Guardian stared down the path in the Pineridge Pass. He shrugged, put the white stone in his pocket, and a moment later, vanished.

Kyer set another log on her fire and hobbled back to her armchair. She placed her stockinged feet on the footstool and opened a third bottle of fine elvish wine from Kien's cellars. Her ire had abated to a point where her heart no longer beat the inside of her ribcage like a war drum. She wouldn't quite call it "relaxation," but more like a numbness, wherein at least she had managed to banish Kien's face to the back of her mind. She filled her glass wine goblet, and raised it to begin yet another toast to Derry and Alon Maer.

When the knock came on the door, it didn't startle her. It annoyed the hell out of her.

"I thought I made it clear I didn't want interruptions," she called. She completed the toast with a sizeable sip. A pleasurable tingle finally buzzed within her limbs, but with the unwelcome arrival, the irate trembling of her hands redoubled. She stared at the leaping and crackling flames, determined that they would quiet her wrath. Another swallow of wine washed down the bad taste in her mouth. Her solitude had lasted all of an hour and a half.

A soft, familiar *ahem* echoed in the corridor outside her door. *Damn.* Was she ready to talk to him yet? Moreover, was he ready to hear her? "All right, fine then, come in."

The door opened. Valrayker's silhouetted figure was framed by torchlight from the castle corridor. "Gee, thanks." He closed the door behind himself, and his features clarified with her firelight.

Kyer took a large swallow of wine and glared at him. He waited in her entryway as if he were about to approach a bad-tempered badger. "Don't be sarcastic with me, Valrayker."

"Only a few days ago you complained about being left alone."

"Totally different," Kyer snapped at him. "I was being actively ignored." She swallowed her rising rage with another sip of wine. She hadn't invited him. Why did people assume they would be well-received? "Now I want as little *people* contact as possible." She ought to be in the great hall celebrating the momentous occasion of Derry's hard won and well deserved rise. Instead, because of Kien's little self-serving ploy she had to spare her friends her mood, and the very real possibility that someone might set her off. Her fingertips played with the red jewelled pommel of the sword that leaned against her chair.

Val leaned against the door. He tucked a lock of black hair behind a pointed ear and folded his arms. "Look, I know you're not altogether happy right now, but may I at least sit down?"

Kyer had demanded a switch to a suite instead of a standard bed chamber in the visitor quarters, not because she needed or even wanted such luxuries as comfortable armchairs for entertaining guests. She had demanded it because it was the least Kien could do. The second least thing his lordship could do was provide the cart of bottles of fine Elvish wine. She hadn't yet thought of the third least thing the high elf could do, but when she thought of it, she would demand that too. Kyer nodded at the other chair. She picked up the bottle and topped up her glass. Her recently stabbed ribcage protested the movement, and a grunt escaped her throat.

Val sat. Kyer ignored him. She had no intention of offering him wine or making small talk or playing host in any way. Let it be known that he was not welcome.

"Can we talk?" Val asked.

Kyer drank, annoyed that the interruption should take away from the rich flavour of the wine. "So long as *talking* doesn't involve any further lectures, accusations, or near-death experiences, I suppose that'd be okay."

Val grimaced.

"Forgive me, Val, but you must understand where I'm coming from." Kyer winced again as she shifted her position.

He laced his fingers together on his belly. "Of course I understand.

However, if we're to clear any of this up, we need to talk."

Kyer drank. She thought. She drank some more. She liked elvish wine. It tasted good. And though she never seemed to get tipsy as quickly as others, it usually helped her relax. She sucked air in through her lips and let it mingle with the wine to enhance the flavour. In truth, she wished for nothing more than to clear the air, for things to go back to the way they were before the mission began. But she was not so naïve as to believe that was possible.

"God damn it, Val, all I want right now is to do what I'm doing at this moment. I don't know if I'm ready to talk. Or listen. You have a bit of explaining to do, yourself."

"Then let me explain it! Blood of Guerrin, Kyer," he said with more than a hint of irony, "with your crummy communication skills, it's no wonder you got yourself into such a mess."

"I didn't get myself into a mess. You need to get your facts straight. Haven't you listened to *anything* your captain has been saying?"

"I *have* listened to my captain, and everyone else, and if I'm ever going to get my facts straight, I need to listen to *you*." His dark gaze met hers and held it. She didn't look away. "Which means I need you to talk to me, Kyer. Please. Upon my honour, I will listen."

She scowled. The entreaty in those grey eyes told her he was through with games. The Duke of Equart was humbling himself to her, something a few short months ago she would never have dreamed of. Kyer drained her glass and picked up a new bottle and a glass for Val. "I'll tell you what." She pulled out the cork. "Meet me at the bottom of this bottle, and then I'll see if I'm ready to talk to you."

Valrayker swallowed and lowered his glass; just a mouthful remained in it. Looking over at Kyer, he saw that she still had at least two swallows left in her glass. The bottle was empty. He watched as she stared into the fire and took another sip. She swirled the deep red richness around in her mouth, as she had every sip before this one. She slurped air between slightly parted lips, savouring the enhanced flavour. *She's going to make this last all night.* He would have preferred to celebrate in the hall below, along with the others, but Derry had understood. Suggested it, even, refusing to allow Val to put this chat off until tomorrow. Finally Kyer let the liquid dribble down her throat.

At last, she tipped the glass up so its bottom aimed at the ceiling.

"So what have you—?"

She stopped him with her hand. She wasn't finished yet.

Only when she had parted with the final taste of ambrosia did Kyer speak. It had taken them three quarters of an hour to get through the bottle.

"Did you know Kien was going to offer me a knighthood?" she said.

Valrayker was surprised at her first question, but he was up for it. "I knew. I tried to tell him it was a bad idea."

"Uh hunh. And do you have an equally eloquent answer for why you demanded I open a Gate to Hreth but then didn't allow me through to see my own parents?"

Val's sigh could have extinguished a candle. He'd known this was coming, and he shook his head. "Sadly, no. At least, I have an answer, but not one that is likely to satisfy you. I'm sorry."

She cocked her head but still didn't look at him. "I appreciate your honesty."

"I'll always be honest with you, Kyer. I may not be able to give you the whole truth, at times, but I won't lie to you."

She glared at him then. "All right. So why haven't you spoken to me for the last three days? Why, in the name of every god and goddess, can I perform a spell that got me accused of *murder*, and nearly got me and my family assassinated?" Her voice rose to an intensely restrained shriek. "And while we're having it out completely, did you know all along that I speak Dark Elvish, and what are you going to do about it?"

"Phew, is that all you wanted to know?" His own temperature was rising in spite of himself. But he clenched his teeth, relaxed. "One thing I can tell you is that I suspected you spoke Dark Elvish. Now I know. And I intend to do absolutely *nothing* about it."

He saw her relax, and only then he realized that she'd been on the defensive, awaiting his response to that question.

"Mostly, though, my answers to your other questions have to be the same as before: I cannot tell you now." *For your own protection.*

"Great," she said with feigned cheer, turning to the fire again. "Thanks for coming to see me."

"Kyer—" he began in exasperation. Honestly, she was confirming his suspicions all over the place.

"No, really, Val, it's been terrific to see you after all our weeks away. Another fine, meaningful discussion—"

"Fine! I think you're Cymrion." *Shit.*

Kyer's face froze. He withered beneath the icy shafts of her motionless stare.

"At least part Cymrion. I don't know why or how you're here and not with the rest of them. I don't know!"

Still she stared at him.

"I didn't mean to tell you that. Because I don't actually *know* anything. I haven't told the others; I can't trust that it won't somehow seep out, and I *must not* risk the enemy guessing something like this." There was one thing he longed to attempt, but it would fly in the face of what he had just said.

Her jaw remained slack and she continued to stare.

"Oh for the love of all that is sacred and mysterious, please say *something*. If I have to open another bottle of wine, we'll be here all bloody night."

She blinked. Swallowed.

"Look, I'm sorry these few days have been so horrid. I'm desperately sorry I can't be more forthcoming. There are reasons, that's all I can say, mostly for your protection, and I beg of you to try to understand that. Someday, maybe, but not now."

In an attempt at humour, he added, "What do you want me to do to make it up to you, offer you a knighthood?" He expected a snort.

She sent a startled glance into the flames. "To you?"

"To me. To prove that everything's all right."

"Sounds good."

"R-really?" He scraped his jaw off the floor.

"So long as you don't breathe a word to anyone."

"What's the point, then?"

"I don't need glory; I just need to know you're on my side."

Val paused, not quite over the shock of this sudden turnabout. "And it would please me no end to know you're on mine."

She still studied the fire. Trying to process his revelation? Or thrusting it aside, to be dealt with later. He slowly brought both hands to his throat and unpinned the brooch he'd worn there for half his life. He lightly fingered the tiny tree of Equart engraved into the silver before handing it to her. She looked at him quizzically.

"Derry received public recognition. That brooch is a symbol of our *confidential* agreement. If you wish to end it, you return that to me."

She hesitated only a moment then took it. "Would you change your mind about this," she ran her finger over the tree, "if I told you that I . . . killed Ronav Malachite in cold blood? I sought him out on purpose to kill him, without giving a thought to bringing him before you and Kien. I didn't allow him a noble death. I toyed with him like a cat with a mouse. He was afraid and I laughed at him. I told him what I was doing as I did it. *And it felt good.*" The glance from the corner of her eye was like a dare.

Valrayker was speechless for a moment. "This has been bothering you awhile."

"Since before we went away. I—tried to come and talk to you about it, but you were busy. And then I thought—" She bit her lip. "—that you might not want me on the mission if you knew how ignoble I was." She smiled a little.

"How long did it take you to realize what you had done?"

"No time at all. As soon as I did it, I knew it was wrong."

Val nodded and considered his next words. "Kyer, you are learning. You told me once that you are too impulsive. You can't train yourself out of that overnight. But you *are* learning. I have a feeling that if you had an encounter with Ronav now, after your recent ordeal, you would handle it differently." She nodded. "Now if I refused to employ anyone who had ever killed in anger, I would have a pretty slim roster."

For the first time in days, they exchanged the warmth of a smile. Kyer pinned the brooch inside her tunic.

"Can I borrow that?" Kyer indicated Val's not-quite-empty wineglass. She winked. "So we don't have to open another bottle."

He figured she'd had her fair share, but he handed it to her.

She took a deep breath and closed her eyes. Opening them again, she mouthed a word to herself and dipped the fourth finger of her left hand (the weakest finger on her nondominant hand) into the rich, red wine and ran it slowly around the rim of the glass. Valrayker soon understood, and as he watched her perform the ritual, he also watched a peace pass over her face and move through her body. She took the final sip, and having completed, at last, the Toast to the Dead for Ronav Malachite, Kyer was at ease.

Valrayker smiled at her and hoped she felt his pride.

"Now," he said, "you do recall that there's a party downstairs that's been going on for hours? Shall we join it?"

She got to her feet, which were just as steady as if she hadn't consumed three and a half bottles of elvish wine on her own.

"Someday," she ventured. "Someday, will you explain it all to me?"

He smiled at her. Slowly he nodded. "Someday."

"Will there be wine at this shindig?" she asked.

"You better believe it."

She took his arm. "Let's go."

End of Book Three

Dear Reader: Reviews go a long way to helping authors reach more readers. If you enjoyed *Gatekeeper's Deception II - Deceived*, I would be thrilled if you would leave a friendly review on Goodreads, and/or the site where you purchased it. Thank you so much.

Please visit my website to learn more.
https://kristawallace.com

Turn the page for a sneak peak at my next novel,
Gatekeeper's Revelation

Gatekeeper's Revelation

A few weeks before present day

The war stopped.

When Duchess Tannis Malfi's soldiers awoke in the morning they stepped out of their tents to see steam rising across the fields. In the distance where the enemy tents had been spread, making the landscape look like it was covered in drifts of snow was instead a series of spirals of smoke from pyres. Like candles dotting the foothills of the mountain. It appeared that Dregor's forces packed up what they needed and left in the night. The allied soldiers looked at each other fearfully. What did it mean?

Scouts mounted their fretful horses and rode, scarves over their noses and mouths, through the muck of blood and mud toward the enemy encampment. They feared a trap, and many a body was rippled by a shudder. But the enemy camp was devoid of life signs. Carts, barrels, broken weapons were heaped and burning, anything of use having been taken away. A nearby gully had served as a dumping ground; no dignity for their dead. Dignity was for the civilized, and nobody could argue that Dregor's soldiers had a shred of "civilized" about them.

The entire enemy army had departed during the night. Traces of their passing scattered the land heading northeast, following the ridge of mountains.

The scouts returned to their own camp, to report. The general dismissed the scouts and gave the order to her army to be at ease, but wary. She set a watch for all directions, just in case.

"One has to ask," she said, as she poured liquor for herself and her subordinates, "Why would the enemy simply call the war off? If it's over, what was the point?"

She shrugged and led them in a toast to Tannis Malfi and Valrayker. Then added, "I hope the enemy has found whatever it was he was looking for."

All across the continent soldiers from Ballin, from Shae, from Kel, from Heath, from Equart and the Guarded Realm, stood wary, bracing themselves against the collective chill in their souls.

Present Day

The Great Hall was awash in music and dancing. A long table of food had been picked over, but Kyer stood next to it grazing over the bits and pieces of chicken, cheese, tiny tomatoes, greens, and some crispy bits from the outside of a chunk of roast pig. Amid the crowd her friends caroused and celebrated. There was Kien Bartheylen, Lord Arrogant Prick of this duchy and this castle. Kyer did not see his wife Alon Maer anywhere, and assumed the Lady had gone to bed. Her pregnancy alone would have excused her from staying at the party, but on top of that she was still recovering from her long illness. Kyer poured herself some wine and silently toasted the Lady, her own small celebration of what she and her friends had done to find the cure.

"Wish you could join in?" said a voice. Kyer was pleased to no end to see Harley upright.

"I'm not in the same mood as they are today." The wine was delicious, but her disposition had gone to vinegar. "It's more enjoyable to watch them."

"I don't blame you after the stunt Kien pulled today."

Kyer had to chuckle. "Yeah, he was surprised at my reaction, to say the least."

"So I hear," Harley said.

Kyer raised the wine bottle in offering.

Harley shrugged. "The Healer says I'm not to, but I think a little won't hurt."

Kyer poured him a small cup of the deep red liquid. "What shall we toast?"

Harley sighed. "New beginnings?"

"That works." Their pewter cups *tinged* musically.

"I never got a chance to thank you," her companion said.

Surprised, she said, "You have nothing to thank me for."

"Yes I have. If you had said even one word against me, there is no way Valrayker would have welcomed me. Of all your company you are the one who really knew what I had been involved with."

Kyer shrugged. It was hard to even remember Old Average Height Guy being a part of the enemy camp. She liked Harley. She couldn't help it. Nothing but respect for the way he'd duped her the day they met. Harley had played his part well and had been suitably sheepish for a villain. That he had eventually turned on his Chief and joined them had come as a surprise, but in spite of herself, not an unwelcome one.

He had stood up to his former leader, Fredric Heyland, now known as Hunter, who had then fled, after slashing Harley through the gut. It was a much more serious wound than any of Kyer's had been, and he was still trying to heal. He had been close to death, and his recovery slow. Every action Harley had taken since their paths had converged had been in support of Kyer's mission, as though he had discovered that there was something else out there for him to do.

Derry *whooshed* breathlessly up to them, having released his dance partner with a bow.

"I'm so glad you came down Kyer, it didn't feel right without you."

The man had been enjoying wine all evening, or he'd never have said such a thing to her. It helped also that he was one of the celebrants. She smiled and said, "Harley was telling me how pleased he is to be part of our company."

Derry gave him a slap on the shoulder. "And we're glad to have you on the good side."

"It's an honour, Sir Derry."

Derry blushed at the new title.

"I hope to make up for lost time," Harley said, then tried to downplay his enthusiasm. "Anyway, I appreciate whatever good words you've put in."

"From what I was told you earned it," Kyer assured him, and Derry nodded. "I was out of it for most of the time, but the way you tried to stop Fredric from getting away showed you were done with him." She chose a piece of cheese from the tray.

"With him, with Misty, with all of them." Harley shuddered. "Especially the Spectre."

"The Spectre?" asked Derry.

Harley drained his wine cup. "He's the leader. He's the one who made Fredric Chief after Ronav was killed." He poured himself some ale, the preferred choice of his Healers. "Name's Golgathaur really, but they call him the Spectre because of the way he appears and vanishes. Tall fellow. Pale. Always in black, kind of like Lord Valrayker, only—" He cocked his head thoughtfully. "Tidier? No offense, Sir Derry, but Lord Val is much more relaxed, if you like. Golgathaur's appearance seems to mean a lot to him. All his pleats pressed nice and neat, if you see what I mean. Scares the life out of me. Chills me to the bone, as it were. Always cheerful and smells like flowers all the time, only you don't dare associate that with anything pleasant in his case."

Kyer had stopped chewing. Tall, pale, dressed in black. Smelled like flowers. She knew this man. The food she had eaten churned in her belly like poison.

"Why not?" asked Derry. "Does he have an agenda of some sort?"

"You could say that, Sir. He's Lieutenant to Dregor."

Kyer nearly choked. She felt like she'd been kicked in the gut. It was all she could do to not flee from the room and fling herself out a window. All the music and revelry in the Hall was suddenly muffled as if someone had closed a door on it.

The man who had convinced her he was helping her. Who had since betrayed her and tried to frame her for murder. The Guardian was Golgathaur, Lieutenant to Dregor.

Less than an hour ago Valrayker had told her he did not want to risk the enemy learning that she could Gate. For her protection, he had said. Too late.

The enemy already knew everything. She had told him herself.

To be continued...

Acknowledgements

In my time on this earth, thus far, I have had the good fortune to meet some amazing people. Some of them are fellow writers, and others have other skills and talents, but together they have formed a community to whom I am enormously grateful for gathering around to support me and my work: My wonderful webmaven, Stephanie Kwok. Myst DeVana and Andrea Howe, whose editorial nitpicks have improved the stories immeasurably. Peter Andersen took the serpent photo, and some Photoshop geniuses, Brian Rathbone and Brayden Fengler helped make my covers excellent. Jonathan Lyster is my writing/critique partner and a computer genius without whom I would be years behind where I am. Beth Wagner cheers me on virtually, on a weekly basis. Every writer should be so lucky to have a mentor like Brenda Carre.

This book also received helpful critique from Elizabeth Stricker, Rob Smith, Stuart Hollet, Colleen Condit, and the late John Pitts. I thank you all.

Special thanks to the Original Six (Rob, Dougie, Matt, Brian, Phil and Garnet), and to all my *[totallyfantastictitle]* podcast listeners, especially Paula, John, Teresa, Edwin and Chari.

And to my family: Matt, David & Heather, and Maggie. Truly, you people keep me upright.

Who is Krista Wallace?

Krista started out as a singer, studied Theatre and got her degree in Acting at UVic, then eventually added writing to her creative endeavours. She has sung classical, musical theatre, rock, R&B and jazz. She has been the vocalist for FAT Jazz for something like 427 years, and is half of a jazz duo called The Itty Bitty Big Band. She writes primarily fantasy, but dabbles in other genres, in both short and long fiction. Combining all her artistic exploits, she took on audiobook narration, and producing a podcast, [Totally Fantastic Title], which then branched into the production of her own audiobooks, which she is publishing in paperback and ebook. Krista grew up in the Port Coquitlam vortex, and so was naturally pulled back there after her time away.

To be continued...